D1047904

'Not only engaging and seductive, it is also clever, witty and artfully designed ... Dawson is a fine impressionistic writer – outstanding is a kiss which takes place among Nell's beehives, an erotic, subversive wedding tableau – and this is a novel of scents and savours, of both love and "Lust's remembered smells"' Stephanie Cross, *Times Literary Supplement*

'To contrast with the flighty Brooke, Dawson invents Nell, a brilliant creation – honest, stubborn and grounded ... a seductive book, evocative and well paced, the tale split between Brooke and Nell, the two narrative voices strong, distinctive and consistent ... Written about a poet by a poet, *The Great Lover* in some ways seems to reveal more of what we'd like to think of as the "real" Brooke than various biographers have done to date.' Vanessa Curtis, *Scotland on Sunday*

'To translate this well-known figure into a novel, with all his contradictions, requires capacious knowledge and a gifted imagination. Fiction and fact are here blended with sureness and subtlety' Frances Spalding, *Independent*

'Seamlessly weaving together snippets of Brooke's letters and poems with her own lively prose, Dawson delivers a story that is both entertaining and evocative ... Dawson's novel transcends the historical facts and truly comes to life. In Brooke, her effortless blending of the known details of his life – his fraught love affairs, travels and development as a poet – with a vivid emotional portrait creates a character of real complexity ... More to the point, by endowing him with self-deprecating humour and warmth, Dawson manages to conjure up the legendary charm that seemed to bewitch every woman, and many of the men, Brooke met.' Catherine Heaney, *Irish Times*

'I have read it twice. The first time at speed, for its onrushing vigour and narrative pull; the second, more slowly, allowing proper time to test the sentences, savour the detail of English society in the handful of years preceding the First World War, and most pleasing of all, to enjoy the author's obvious relish of the novel's central, teasingly rendered romance between Rupert Brooke and Nellie Golightly . . . The speed and rhythms of rural life, and the greater sense of the wider world of pre-war turbulence, of suffragettes laying siege to the status quo, and artists' coteries flouting convention – all this is rendered so unfussily, and in writing polished for clarity, not dazzling effect, that the reading becomes an almost physical pleasure.' Tom Adair, *Scotsman*

'Gloriously, it is love rather than death that preoccupies Jill Dawson in her distinctive and deeply imagined portrait of Brooke . . . its heroine, and the woman planted exquisitely at its centre, is Nell Golightly, an orphaned bee-keeper's daughter, who despite being self-avowedly "sensible", becomes inexorably snared by the beautiful young poet . . . The narrative, alternating between the voices of Brooke and Nell, charts a mutual fascination blossoming against a backdrop of Fabian politics, bee-keeping, the Suffrage movement, the intrigues of the Bloomsbury set and the poet's mental collapse . . . Jill Dawson has created a world of huge pathos; a subtle, evocative anti-fairy-tale of doomed youth by one of Britain's most subtle and accomplished writers.' Liz Jensen, *Waterstone's Books Quarterly*

The Great Lover

The Great Lover

A NOVEL

Jill Dawson

HARPER PERENNIAL

NEW YORK • LONDON • TORONTO • SYDNEY • NEW DELHI • AUCKLAND

HARPER ● PERENNIAL

This book was originally published in Great Britain in 2009 by Sceptre, an imprint of Hodder & Stoughton, a Hachette Livre UK company.

P.S.™ is a trademark of HarperCollins Publishers.

HarperCollins books may be purchased for educational, business, or sales promotional use. For information please write: Special Markets Department, HarperCollins Publishers, 10 East 53rd Street, New York, NY 10022.

FIRST U.S. EDITION

Library of Congress Cataloging-in-Publication Data
Dawson, Jill.
  The great lover : a novel / Jill Dawson. — 1st U.S. ed.
      p.   cm.
   ISBN 978-0-06-192436-1
   1. Brooke, Rupert, 1887–1915—Fiction. 2. Poets, English—20th century—Fiction. I. Title.
PR6054.A923G74 2010
823'914—dc22   2009036539

10 11 12 13 14   OFF/RRD 10 9 8 7 6 5 4 3 2 1

'One of the great difficulties, and perils, you see, in ever telling anyone any truth, is the same as in ever loving anyone, but more so. It gives them such a devilish handle over you. I mean, they can *hurt*. If I love a person and say nothing, I'm fairly safe. But if I tell them, I deliver myself bound into their hands.'

Rupert Brooke, letter to Bryn Olivier,
end of September 1912

'It is a joy to be hidden, but a disaster not to be found.'

D. W. Winnicott

le 23 avril 1982

Dear Kind Stranger,

Greetings from Tahiti! My name is Arlice Rapoto. I do not know English, only Tahitian and French so a very lovely charming friend is writing this letter to you in England, in the hope that I might be able to find out some things that I have always wanted to know.

I am sixty-seven years old and before I die I hope to find out some thing about my father. My mother was Taatamata who lived for many years at Maharepa on the island of Moorea, Tahiti.

My mother always told me that my father was a very famous man, very pretty. She called him Pupure. (This means Fair One.) He was a sun god, she said, and a famous poet, very pretty. He came to Tahiti in 1914 and stayed three months with my mother at Papeete and Mataiea. Many things written about him after his death, one by the British Prime Minister, and my mother keep this and show it to me. I never met my father. His name was Rupert Brooke. He died in First World War and as him a young man who never married my mother, she said he never know about me. (In England it would be a bad thing if white people knew about me.) Taatamata did try to send him a letter, all that time ago in 1914, but the letter washed down to the bottom of the sea when a ship went down. Mother told Pupure she grew fat with me. She loved him very much. She said he found his true heart in Tahiti and for the first time he was happy.

I have read two poems by him but I would like to hear his voice. I would like to read his letters but mostly hear his living voice, to know what he smelled like and sounded like. How it felt wrap arms around him. I never married and have no children and now I am old I want to know: who was my father, what was he like, and why did all of England remember him?

I belong to an artist colony here in Tahiti and I also some time write some little thing. I wonder if I have poetry in my blood from my *popaa* father.

If you can help me, or write me, it would make old woman happy. I know from a book that he lived in this house, the Orchard, in Grantchester, Cambridgeshire in England, and so I am sending this letter to you. I hope that somebody kind who knew my father still lives there. I am sending the things I already know about my father, from *Times* newspaper. I know he was very pretty.

Mother many times told me I look just like him. I am tall, have thin face and fair skin and hair like *popaa*, like a Western girl.

The whole of England love my father, but his heart belongs to Tahiti and to my mother, Taatamata. He wrote many poems for her. What can you tell me about him, about Rupert Brooke? I'm old now. I want to know: was he good man?

Yours truly,
Arlice Rapoto

~

Obituary from *The Times*, written by First Lord of the Admiralty, Winston Churchill, 26 April 1915

Rupert Brooke is dead. A telegram from the Admiralty at Lemnos tells us that his life has closed at the moment when it seemed to have reached its springtime. A voice had become audible, a note had been struck, more true, more thrilling, more able to do justice to the nobility of our youth in arms engaged in this present war than any other – more able to express their thoughts of self-surrender, and with a power to carry comfort to those who watch them so intently from afar. The voice has been swiftly stilled. Only the echoes and the memory remain; but they will linger.

During the last months of his life, months of preparation in gallant comradeship and open air, the poet-soldier told with all the simple force of genius the sorrow of youth about to die, and the sure triumphant consolations of a sincere and valiant spirit. He expected to die; he was willing to die for the dear England whose beauty and majesty he knew; and he advanced towards the brink in perfect serenity, with absolute conviction of the rightness of his country's cause, and a heart devoid of hate for fellow-men.

The thoughts to which he gave expression in the very few incomparable war sonnets which he has left behind will be shared by many thousands of young men moving resolutely and blithely forward into this, the hardest, the cruellest, and the least-rewarded of all the wars that men have fought. They are a whole history and revelation of Rupert Brooke himself. Joyous, fearless, versatile, deeply instructed, with classic symmetry of mind and body, ruled by high undoubting purpose, he was all that one would wish England's noblest sons to be in days when no sacrifice but the most precious is acceptable, and the most precious is that which is most freely proffered.

❧

30 April 1982

Dear Miss Arlice Rapoto,

I was very surprised but happy to get your letter. I still live in Grantchester, and know the people who own the Orchard (there is both a house, a beautiful garden with the same lovely orchard trees still in it, and a café by the same name). They passed your letter on to me, remembering that I might perhaps have known your father, as I used to work at the Orchard Tea Gardens as a girl.

I too, am an old lady now. I am ninety years old and a widow. I did indeed know your father, Rupert Brooke, for a while.

I am a writer too. Or, rather, I was. I have had stories published in magazines here in England called *Woman's Realm* and *Woman's Weekly* and, once, had a letter published in a magazine called the *Lady*. After the War I took several courses at Night School and continued the education I'd given up as a girl. I once had different ambitions. I would like to rise to your challenge and do my best to answer your questions. I would especially like, if I am able, to do as you ask and tell you what your father smelled like, what he sounded like, what it felt like to wrap your arms around him. And also: what his living voice was like.

I must say, it was an odd feeling to read that newspaper piece you included. I remember reading it through tears at the time, standing in the scullery of the Orchard with a feeling in the pit of my stomach as if half of me was peeling away. I lost a brother in the war, as well as Rupert, my brother Edmund. It's funny but of the sentiments in that piece, 'ruled by high undoubting purpose' leaped out at me. And when I went to look in my favourite biography of your father (written a long time ago, some twenty years I think, by a Mr Christopher Hassall), oddly enough that line was not included. Which was curious, and got me to thinking about biographies. I'm sending

4

you the one I mentioned as it's very detailed and will give you a lot of information, if you can plough through it. I am also sending you a little gift he gave me (I hope it doesn't fall out of the envelope!) and a book of your father's prose-writing, essays and such-like. (Many English people forget that he wrote prose, knowing only his poetry, but to my mind, it contained the best of him.)

You're right in saying he was very famous here in England. Most people can quote a line or two: 'If I should die, think only this of me . . .'

But when I read that 'high undoubting purpose' again in The Times piece, I had to laugh. 'Undoubting' is not a word that suits Rupert. I think he would have laughed at it, too. He did like to laugh, much of the time. Often this was directed at himself. You can probably tell that by reading his poetry. The other poem that people here are most likely to remember him by is 'The Old Vicarage, Grantchester' (the house is still there, too, next door to the Orchard). He offended quite a few folk round here, at the time – 'Ditton girls are mean and dirty, and there's none in Harston under thirty . . .' that sort of thing. There have been a few more recent biographies of him and I wondered whether to send you one of those. In 1964, thirty-four years after Rupert's mother died (he always called her the Ranee for reasons I've now forgotten), Mr Christopher Hassall felt a little freer to write what he wanted. But there were still things about your father that he wasn't able to print. I knew them well enough and don't see the point in hiding them from you. I'm taking a gamble that, like me, you're too old now to care for anything but the truth.

It makes me sad to think that the Ranee never knew she had a grandchild! She died when you would have been fourteen, if I've got my dates right – you would have been born in early 1915, is that right? (My eldest son was born in April of the year before.) You know, she lost all her sons and her husband in the space of a few years. First Dick, Rupert's older brother, to pneumonia (and to drink, and perhaps he had a sort of tendency to, you know, gloomy moods, though naturally that sort of thing wasn't easy to speak of at the time). Then her husband, Parker Brooke. Then Rupert, of course, who was only twenty-seven, and just a few months later her last boy, Alfred. Whatever the shock and scandal, the existence of a granddaughter ... well, I can't help thinking it might have given her a grain of comfort, whatever the Rupert Brooke Trustees might have thought. And I've suddenly remembered that she lost her only daughter too, as a baby girl of one year old. She was the child before Rupert.

Rumours of you started to circulate here many years ago, when a Mr Dudley Ward, a university friend of your father's who inherited the Old Vicarage, was charged with finding out about you. I was not a friend of Mr Ward's, although I always liked him. He married a German girl and had a little boy, Peter. We moved in different circles. I'm not sure how the rumour reached me but I did hear that a letter from your mother, Taatamata, somehow came to light. I believe your mother wrote: 'I get fat all the time.' Well, any woman would understand the meaning in that sentence. Unfortunately, your father's biographers have all been men.

I'm sad to think that I don't know what your father made of this letter, and if he understood that your mother was expecting. You're right – the letter had lain at the bottom of the ocean, after the ship carrying it sank in 1914. It's funny how people here remember the *Titanic* sinking but not the *Empress of Ireland*, and yet it was only two years later, and nearly as many losses. The *Titanic* was full of toffs, of course, whereas the *Empress* was just ordinary people, people like us, that's what my Tom used to say. I think a fairer explanation was that there was a war on, and we thought of nothing else.

What an astonishing thought that the letter came to light at all ... It seems your mother gave it to a man to post, who was going by boat to Vancouver, and he posted it there and it lay in a sealed box with a lot of others from June to December until divers rescued it, and it arrived in Rupert's hands. In Blandford, I believe he was at the time, waiting to be called up.

I do believe your mother was the love of Rupert's life, the one true happiness he had. I think with her he found something he always searched for. I have read his poems (the ones he wrote for your mother and while in Tahiti) many, many times, and that is the conclusion I've come to. One of Rupert's most famous lovers, Cathleen Nesbitt, an actress, wrote a book about him. Some of his letters to her have been published. They are full of loving sentiments – he was good at that, in writing! – but even so. It is possible to see that she was very much on a pedestal, if you know what that expression means. It's only my personal opinion, of course, and others would disagree. Most seem to concentrate on the love affair he had with Cathleen because she was such a glamorous figure, or with Ka Cox, because there is so much to go on, evidence, you know, in the form of letters. Or just before he died, a Lady Eileen Wellesley, who he met on the boat coming back, and seemed to take up with for a time. She was a plain sort. At least I could see what he saw in the lovely actress Cathleen Nesbitt. Cathleen writes in her book that she didn't feel Rupert would ever have been 'a one-woman man'. In your father's early letters there's a fair bit of showing off. Don't get me wrong – I'm not saying your father was a false man. But he was a clever letter-writer.

I think you are right about the South Seas and how the English prefer to forget this part of his life. Perhaps people find it difficult to square the idea of the golden Apollo, the intellectual gentleman-soldier, finding peace not in an English meadow but on a tropical island far away. And with an unmarried coloured lady, to boot. I hope you don't mind me describing your mother like that? I did one time try to find out about you, and I even went so far as to write to the Hotel Tiare Tahiti, where I believe

7

your father stayed. But I'm told many hotels in Tahiti are called that, the *tiare* being the national flower and all, something like a gardenia, is that right? And that your mother moved to the island of Moorea, which from your letter I see is true.

As for my point above, I'm not a sentimental woman, and I stick to my guns. Those same people would not be able to say with any authority who was the love of *my* life, either, if they were using only evidence, and hard facts. They might assume that it was Tom, since we were married for fifty-two years. (My Tom died in 1965, having had a good innings, as we say – he was seventy-four. He survived being called up in both wars, so I was luckier than most.)

Well now, my wrist soon aches when I write for a long time these days, so I will have to leave you to read the biography I'm sending. A biography is a good way to find out things but to my mind, well. It has its limits. After all, a biography is written by a person and a person does not always understand another as well as they might think. I enjoy a good biography as well as the next person but I do think they set too much store by facts and not enough by feelings. As a girl, I set a lot of store by facts, but I learned that they could be wrong. Then another thing: biographers spend so much time going on about the person's death, and who wants to dwell on that? I mean, in your father's case, the war was only the last eight months of his life, and yet that's what he's remembered for, his war sonnets, especially the one I quoted, 'The Soldier', which they still read out at every war-memorial service, year on year.

My daughter Janet now, she became quite an expert on Literature here in Cambridge (she's retired now). She told me that Rupert's poetry was sentimental and it was unfortunate that he wrote such patriotic nonsense when other poets were about to see for themselves how bad the war was. His reputation did go downhill after that, and there are other war poets who are much better known, like Siegfried Sassoon or Wilfred Owen.

Of course he didn't even die in action, and for some people, septicaemia from a mosquito bite wasn't the right kind of death for a poet-hero. I don't know much about all that. All I know is that, in the way of daughters, my three girls don't think of me as having a life before I had them, and certainly not as being in love with anyone before their father, so I have never told them about that side of my life.

It was Janet who told me there has even been a new memoir donated to the British Library, written by a young woman called Phyllis Gardner, who was a lady artist at the Slade in the days when that was quite unusual. After his death a couple of new loves came to light – Violet Asquith, who had sent him an amulet to wear round his neck, and the plain one I mentioned, Lady Eileen Wellesley – he used to move in some grand circles at that point in his life. But previous biographers knew nothing of Phyllis and didn't include her in any of their books. He was with Phyllis an awful lot during the terrible year after his nervous breakdown. (It tickled my daughters to think I'd known Rupert Brooke, of course.) It was an eye-opener, I can tell you. That Phyllis was crazy about him.

Oh, yes, and he was handsome all right. I didn't always think so. He was famously described by one of our writers, Mr W. B. Yeats, as the 'the handsomest young man in England', and it used to make him cross, to be honest, all the kerfuffle about his looks. I'll send you a postcard photo of him if you haven't seen one before – there aren't any, I see, in the Christopher Hassall book, and you must judge for yourself. That'll be the best way, as people don't agree, do they, on that kind of thing?

There is so much more I would like to ask you – about your mother, and your life in Tahiti and how it was, growing up without knowing your father. In England, we only know of Tahiti through films like *Mutiny on the Bounty*, I'm afraid, and I'm sure that gave a very silly picture – but I'm old now, and though I put this letter down last night and took it up again, my wrist is tired again, and it tires me so. Rupert only ever wrote me one letter, which I've decided I'll include, along with the small gift I mentioned, which I feel should be rightfully yours, so I am returning it. I have kept it all these years. Oh and a poem, one you might already know, as he wrote it while in your country, which he seemed to think contained the best of him.

I hope you are not the easily shocked sort. (Some of the things your father did and described in letters were against the law when he did them.) Janet tells me (Janet, the one who was at Cambridge) that Tahitians have different attitudes to these things from us, that even allowing for exaggeration by Captain Cook and others, your country was far more comfortable than ours with such matters, but I don't know if I believe her. I'm an old lady now, and can still remember how such things were viewed here and, as a young girl, I did find them very shocking.

You asked about your father's living voice and I believe that his letters, along with his poems and the prose writing I'm sending, are the best way to answer you. But he was a difficult man to pin down, and he was in the habit of saying things playfully that he did not mean at all, or were quite the opposite of his meaning, so maybe it's true he was a little more of a slippery fish than some.

I am very sorry that we are both too old to meet. If you ever find your way to England, to Grantchester, do be sure to write to me again, and you are, of course, very welcome to stay with me.

Also to answer your question: was your father a good man?

I suppose I knew Rupert as well as anyone. You must make up your own mind, of course.

I was very surprised but happy to get your letter.

Yours sincerely,
Nell Sanderson (née Golightly)
Grantchester, England

One

July 1909

'We'll live Romance, not talk it. We'll show the grey unbelieving age, we'll teach the whole damn World, that there's a better Heaven than the pale serene Anglican windless harmonium-buzzing Eternity of the Christians, a Heaven in Time, now and for ever, ending for each, staying for all, a Heaven of Laughter and Bodies and Flowers and Love and People and Sun and Wind, in the only place we know or care for, ON EARTH.'

Rupert Brooke, letter to Jacques Raverat, 1909

My name is Nellie Golightly. I'm a good, sensible girl, seventeen years old this August; well brought up and well schooled and blessed with a few more Brains than most. Being the eldest of six and a Mother to them all since my own Mother died when I was eleven years old, I'm accustomed to hard work, no secrets, many loud voices and some small authority. If I have a fault it is that I'm apt to wanting things done my way. Well, truth be told I have many faults: I am feverishly curious, some would say nosy; I have no compunction about reading other people's letters; I'm proud and full of vanity; I've a quick temper although I forgive just as easily; I am not fond of horses and I am wont to be impatient with bees; and, worst of all, I am a girl who is incapable of being romanced because I don't have a sentimental bone in my body. Moons and Junes mean nothing to me, unless it is to signify good conditions for bees.

Now that I have made a list of my defects let me introduce my talents. These chiefly involve bees. I can distinguish a particular swarm from some distance, simply by the sound being made: is it soft and low like a snarling sea, or is it a fierce high note, like an arrow piercing from the sky? I have been stung only once in all my years at Prickwillow helping Father, or these last few weeks at Grantchester helping Mr Neeve with his apiary. I am as tender with the bees as I'm snippy with the children, but I've learned the same rule for both: all creatures are more amiable when they've recently been fed. Let bees gorge themselves on honey and they will be putty – no, beeswax – in my hands.

My strongest trait is one that I've found uncommon in others, and I can't now be sure whether to name it gift or defect: I am able to face, very easily, the ugly facts of things. I can look squarely at them and not look away. I've had this ability since childhood. I've learned to keep it to myself and I've learned that others are not as interested in poking beneath the surface. Mother used to tell me just to 'take things at face value' but I never learned to, so here I am, trapped in my own private musings and conclusions, my dark, bare version of the world, which none seems to share.

Those are my talents, as I can presently think of them.

The worst events of my life took place a few short months ago when Father passed away one day, out in the meadow, dressed in his white veil and gloves, tending his bees. I was carrying the smoker, Betty following at a distance. I saw his white shape slip over like a bottle of milk and I knew before we reached him exactly how much of him had been spilled. All of him. The bees seemed to know it too and were swelling around his head in the shape of a giant fur hood until Betty ran at them, puffing with the bellows to direct them, the soft brown swarm, into the skep. Then we ran for Sam, the eel man from two doors up, to help us lay Father out on the kitchen table.

His funeral was like all funerals in this part of the world. The fen soil shines like black oil when the harvest blade turns it up and is far too soft and rich for any to be buried in it. So Father was carried the nine miles to the surrounding higher land by a large corn wagon, with a team of two horses harnessed to it. My brothers and sisters – Betty, Lily, Stanley, Edmund and Olive – sat around the sides; the younger ones wearing looks of pleased importance, Betty with a face as mine must have been: an expression of flattened shock. We two surely looked – if anyone had cared to examine us – as the land itself does: as if something of huge, terrible weight had just rolled over us. Sam drove the horses and old Mrs Gotobed sat at the back, pouring cups of poppyhead tea from a leather flask to keep everyone quiet.

When the soft, violet-black clods of fen earth fell on Father's coffin, I sipped more tea until my head clouded over and Mrs Gotobed began her nonsense singing of 'The shock head willows, two and two, by rivers gallopading . . .' and on the long, blank route to the sky there was only one white gate, standing out against the black, which, in my poppy-dulled state, I confused with the gate of Heaven. I tried to turn my thoughts to practical matters, such as my plan to present myself to Mr Neeve, the bee-keeper at the Old Vicarage, and whether I might try for a position at the Orchard Tea Gardens (Quiet and Select Up-river Resort on the Banks of the Granta, close to the Mill and offering Breakfasts, Light Luncheons and Teas for large or small Boating or Cycling parties), leaving my younger sister Betty in charge of my brothers and sisters back home. But, as I have indicated, ugly facts are what I dwell on, and ugly facts are what came to me then.

Father had never wanted daughters: he made that plain. Boys can be put to work in the fields, or handle a gun in the punt, put food on the table, he said. That was not a reason but a justification for his feelings, because so could I. I'm better than Stanley and Edmund at all those things. Fact was, girls were more than just an economic burden to him. They were foolish, unimportant, yes, but more than that they were foreign and bewildering, even disturbing. He wished we did not exist to trouble him so. When Mother died he slipped without a word to expecting me to take her place: bring his meals to him, wash the babies, clean the house, help in the corn harvest in season, tend the bees year round, be a new young wife in all ways but one. I never stood next to Father by the skeps, with that soft low drone of bees all around us, without knowing keenly what his estimation of me was. I insisted on going to school, I was fierce and firm, my mother's daughter, and to Sunday School too, at the Primitive Methodist Church here in Prickwillow. I was soon teaching there on Sundays – I reached a degree of learning that Father never did, nor my brothers either. But nothing would shift him, it was just what was. Girls were a waste of breath and nothing on this earth was going to change his mind.

As the last clod fell I thought, Too late, then, to make him proud of me, and I shed brief tears, and that was that.

Or almost. There was one task I still had to do, and it had to be done before the day was over. That was the telling of the bees. So when the red circle of the sun started to slip through the clouds like a coin through a magician's fingers, I took Betty out with me to the skeps, first winding a ribbon of black crêpe around them, and we stood there with our heads bowed, while I murmured the story of Father to the bees. I told them that Alfred had 'passed away' from a long-standing illness common in these parts, the ague, but that they were not to worry, he loved them dearly, and would have stayed if he could. I told them he left them in good hands (mine, and Betty's and Lily's, and the entire Golightly family's); that they need not fear for their future, nor take off and leave us, because they would always be cared for, loved, in fact, and because life goes on, whether we wish it to or not. It is an end we all must come to, I said, though we like to pretend otherwise. When it happens, it shocks us for a day or two, and then the curtain swings back into place and we carry on as before. But the place *behind* the curtain is where we children were right now and we were all frightened by it.

The bees murmured back in low tones to tell me they were listening.

Betty's sniffling stepped up when I said the bit about the bees being loved, and me promising to care for them and that Father would have stayed if he could. I realised that I was saying to the bees all the things I knew Father didn't feel towards us and never said and never would, and that I was making a picture for the bees as if they were my own dear children, of how I would like things to be. If only I had a kind mother or grand-mother who might say those same reassuring words to me! The only care and good sense I've ever known is my own.

One fat drone escaped as I was speaking, then a scout bee took off too, and I knew they had heard enough. I'd done my duty and the bees were sure now to stay. The sky blushed crimson as Betty tucked the end of the last ribbon of black crêpe underneath the skep to stop it flapping and we turned to go back into the house. I remembered then a song that Father used to sing, or was it a poem? 'Stay at home, pretty bees, fly not hence! Mistress Mary is dead and gone!' and I sang it slowly, over and over, in a voice I hoped was something like Father's.

There was something else, too. Pulling off Father's gloves, when Betty and I brought him in from the meadow lying stiff across the wheelbarrow. Gloves that were stained dark and golden with propolis, so that they looked as if they had been burned. The hands beneath were milky white. Soft black hairs on the knuckles. Long, tapering fingers and skin like the downy cheeks of a baby. His daily duties with the honey, the beeswax, the brown clouds of bees and, chiefly, the bathing of his fingers in that sticky, dark brown propolis had smoothed his skin to that of a young man. Like many a daughter, I had forgotten that Father was ever young, and this surprised me. My thoughts went something like: Why, are these the hands of Father, the man I know?

I dreamed of Father that night and, as in life, it was only a glimpse. He was sitting in the chair outside the front door, mending a skep. And as I looked at him, he made as if to get up. That's all. He moved, as if to get up. I could not tell what he intended, whether to move towards me or perhaps . . . leave. Goodbye, I mouthed, in the dream. He looked at me.

Then I was suddenly awake. I had only one desire: the honey stocks. Without lighting a candle I tiptoed to the shelves where they were kept, reached for a comb, a tanner's worth, and bit into it, hard. The sweetness, a lavender and heather mix, spilled over my tongue, slid down my chin and dripped on to my nightdress, clinging to my hair. All around me was the smell of him. Of clover, of grass, of sweat and the filthy brown water, of blood and eels and the smoker; of years and years and years of work, and the smell of his skin, his strong arms lifting me up, over the gate; and his lovely rich singing voice and all that he was to me, despite how little I was to him, was in that blackness, that sweetness. And Father's warm face, sunburned and tired, so tired in his eyes, swam in front of me at last, and then I was crying and digging my nails into the soft chewy cone and spitting out the cappings, and squeezing hard and biting, and sobbing like a baby, and biting.

He will never be proud of me. He will never know the things I'll do, he'll never know my children, never be able to tell me the things I long to know. Father, where are you? I wanted to cry out. Don't go yet! Stay with me, stay with your beloved bees, *please* – don't leave your little Nellie all alone. My mouth was choked with honey. I sounded like an animal. I felt ashamed at last and, sick with the sweetness, I crept back to bed.

Thankfully no child woke to see their sister behaving like a criminal, raiding the stocks. My dreams were full of buzzing and that image again, of Father getting up from his chair, and then – nothing. Nothing more.

My last glimpse of the village as I set off on my journey to Grantchester was of my sister Betty, in her blue bonnet, waving goodbye under the gloaming grey light. She was standing at the Toll House on the river, Blackwing Mill in the background; the huge beam engine beside her, steaming away with a great trundling racket, pumping the water into the dikes. Betty was calling to me to take care, to write often, and promising to do her best with the children. I called back, over my shoulder: 'But, Betty – do your best with the bees!'

And that is how I come to be in Grantchester, presenting myself to the landlady of the Orchard, Mrs Stevenson, recommending myself to her with my talents and keeping mum about my defects.

I have in my bag a book by Mrs Flora Klickmann (*The Flower-Patch Among the Hills, A Book of Cheerfulness: You just smile your way right through*) and drawings of flowers and eels done by Stanley and Olive. The young ones wailed and hollered about why I had to work so far away, further than Ely Cathedral and Cambridge too; but it was on account of Mr Neeve, the bee-keeper, I told them, who had known our Father and was a kind and refined man. Mr Neeve says I might help him when my duties for Mrs Stevenson are done; and for this he will pay me two extra shillings and two jars of honey, so that my poor family (he says), who have been raised on milk and honey, would always live that way, even if our own beehives were hit by the wax moth and failed.

My position as a maid-of-all-work means I live in at the Orchard House and get all my food and lodging free. I can send home almost ten shillings a week, which is not a bad amount for five youngsters, who also have honey to sell. I work from six in the morning until ten p.m. every day except Sundays, when the tea gardens are closed and I have only light duties in the mornings. On Sunday afternoons I will travel the fifteen miles to visit my sisters and brothers in Prickwillow.

Grantchester village is a grand sort of place, after Prickwillow. Its nearness to the university is what makes it grand. It has a huge mill and a fancy church with a gold weathercock, and a famous pool where a famous poet – Lord Byron – once swam. The Manor House is really a farm: Mrs Stevenson tells me it supplies the Fellows at King's College with pigeons from the Great Duffhouse nearby, and vegetables and herbs from the doctor's garden. She started her famous tea gardens over ten years ago, when some students came up the river Cam in punts demanding tea and scones, with honey from the Old Vicarage beehives, asking to take them sitting under the trees in the orchard. She is kept busy now from morning until dusk. In addition to the teas she also lets rooms to a number of lodgers; they, too, need meals and laundry and all the other services that young gentlemen require.

She sees that I am clean and disciplined, and that I read and write well, and she murmurs that she values the good opinion of Mr Neeve. She has one requirement and that is that 'her girls' do not make nuisances of themselves by paying too much attention to the 'goings on' of the young Varsity men and women who frequent her premises, some of whom might have . . . modern ideas.

'I hope you are not a gossip, Nell, nor easily shocked.'

I assure her that I am neither.

I'm shown upstairs to my room. The house smells throughout of apples, a healthy, green, grassy sort of smell: one of the furthest rooms is used to store them. There is also the smell of yeast rising and smoking logs and warm wood and floor-polish. I hear the chatter of girls working in the scullery and the rap of a dog somewhere outside and a constant rattle of china and cutlery. I notice how clean the flagstones are in the kitchen, and the stairs too, hardly a speck on them, which shows me this is a tight ship and Mrs Stevenson, for all her kindness, a strict mistress.

There is no fireplace in the tiny bedroom she shows me. Two small cots and no window greet me; more of a cupboard than a room. The one shelf is empty, except for a carton of Keating's insect powder. I'm told I'm to share with another maid called Kittie. I feel a little pang when Mrs Stevenson shows me this room, which tells me that I was expecting more, and I chide myself for foolishness in thinking that a servant will be a step up in the world from a bee-keeper's daughter.

'I see too much and I hear too well for an old lady,' says Mrs Stevenson, on her way back down the stairs.

Now I'm going to describe something that happens to me often and which I have come to accept as part of me. And yet whenever it happens I am brought up short and reminded all over again of something very strange: how impossible it is to be one person in the world, so different from all others, having these particular experiences at this particular time. And how difficult to explain about one particular experience to another living being, no matter how you might want to. And yet it happened to me right then, on that first visit to the Orchard House.

It's like this: I'm behind Mrs Stevenson on the stair. My hand is on the wooden rail, which is smooth and plain, and like a thousand other hand-rails I have touched, rasping slightly beneath my dry palm. I can see Mrs Stevenson's black skirt, swishing the floor in front of me, and the tie on her apron at the waist, and a wisp of grey hair escaping the pins near her neck, and I believe she is talking, but I cannot hear her. I cannot feel my own tongue in my mouth. The world simply stops. I do not belong. I am separate, outside, looking on.

With the next beat of my heart, the world goes on again. The smell of apples and bread and dusted wooden floors and the chafe of the bib of my new apron against my throat comes back to me; the chatter of cups on saucers floating up from downstairs.

I was much shaken the first time it happened to me, as a girl of six: this feeling that I was separate, outside things, had somehow slipped through some veil of time and slid through to another place, but now I have come to accept it. I have no explanation; it's just how things are with me. When it happens, the world seems more vivid, and things happen more slowly and with all their full colours, scents and sensations. When it stops, life picks up a pace.

Although I fear I *have* left something out in my account of my character. I must add another fault to the list, which I have just remembered and it is this: when I take up a particular idea, I am fixed in it, stuck as fast as the seal that bees make for honey. This seal is the propolis that I mentioned earlier, on Father's hands. It starts off sticky but soon hardens to a form not easily removed. We have to scrape it from the frames with a knife to release the liquid honey underneath but there is always a seal that remains there, that cannot be undone. It has a burned, toffee-brown look. My nature, I fear, is as sealed and capped as propolis. Father would chide me for it, although it was a quality we shared.

I have wandered now in thinking of this, and wonder if a person's character and propolis is a good comparison? But honey has been my life since I was a tiny girl, and I surely can't be blamed if thoughts about honey, or bees, occur to me more often than to other people.

Now, within a week of my moving into the Orchard House there is a small commotion. A young gentleman-poet, having enjoyed a May Ball here a few weeks back, has requested rooms. His name is Rupert Brooke. I have heard of him but that means nothing. Kittie tells me that he will be a very great man and that there is already a space on the school wall in Rugby that he went to (and where his mother still lives) that awaits a plaque for him: he told her this himself. This strikes me as mischievous. It's hard for me to decide if he is teasing, acting the arrogant goat, or truly believes it. Most likely of all, I suppose, is a little of both. In either case, he is certainly guilty of the Sin of Pride and not just about his poetry, either. He is one of those vain men, Kittie says, who has been told so often he is handsome that he is for ever pulling a fresh, boyish stunt, and running elegant fingers through fashionably long, springy hair.

I have not met him yet. Mrs Stevenson has charged me with getting two rooms ready for him. One is to be his bedroom, at the far end, top of the house, and the other, downstairs, is to be his sitting room, for entertaining friends. There's a dirt track running alongside the house that carries the young men and women on bicycles from the university to his rooms, where they can throw stones and call up at the window for him.

After Mrs Stevenson has told me about this Rupert Brooke, and I've listened to Kittie and Mrs Stevenson's daughter Lottie chattering excitedly of him in the kitchen (remembering the May Ball occasion and a separate one when he came with another famous writer to the house: this writer gentleman – an old man, an American, much taken with Mr Brooke – was apparently accidentally clocked on the head with the pole by Mr Brooke when he took him for a punt down the river; and Kittie had to bathe his head and give him brandy), a funny thing happens. I'm quite convinced that, five minutes later, I pass this very same person.

I'm on an errand in Grantchester to fetch milk and a young man passes me on a bicycle, pedalling fast in the direction of the Orchard and Byron's Pool. I feel sure, suddenly, that it *is* him for one reason only and that is one I'll concede: he does have the sort of face that you notice. A face that girls like Kittie would call handsome, or even beautiful. I spent the moments after he'd cycled past me wondering what it was in him that combined to give me this impression. His forehead was high and his hair of a sandy gold colour. He wore it longer than usual, and he wore no tie, either, so that his throat was bare to the sun. I'd only had a second to consider him as he cycled past the church of St Andrew and St Mary, with his long fringe lifting up in the wind like a cock's comb. Cock of the Walk, Father would have said. It would not have been a compliment.

Mrs Stevenson is all 'Snap-snap, chop-chop! On you get by seven o'clock this morning,' and so I set to. The room has been empty for a while. The window is so firm shut that I cannot open it.

Dried leaves, half trapped beneath the frames, flicker to dust when I touch them.

I work hard and don't dawdle. I am sorry that I have no time to poke my head outside to sniff the lilac and the dog-roses in the garden, or breathe in the smell of the fruit trees in the orchard next door. Apple, pear, plum, medlar and quince, and there might be still more varieties. I'm thinking of the bees again and the wild array of honeys that Mr Neeve must make here, with such a source of food for them. Then I think of Father and my heart pinches a little. I picture him with his strong but bony wrist, turning the handle on the honey-spinner, the frames inside rattling, and the table shaking too, with his efforts, making a sound like a ball scattering inside a barrel. In this memory I hear rain too, spattering the roof of our kitchen, and see the fire glowing and the sweat popping on Father's brow, until the first honey appears at the mouth of the tap: fat, like a bulb of amber.

I thought I'd shed my tears for Father two weeks ago. I'm surprised at myself.

These thoughts are not helping get the work done and, with an effort, I turn my attention to an old bitten-looking beam above the bed. Filthy cobwebs hang from it. When I attack them with the duster, shavings fall too, like flakes of chocolate. Of course, no young man from Cambridge will appreciate the labour it is to turn out a bedroom, so I am not expecting any thanks for the fact that I soaked his china candlesticks in soda to remove the grease, nor that I spent an hour and a half with bottle-brush and patience to clean his water bottle. I dither over whether to put on the pillow shams Mrs Stevenson left out for me. Finally I decide that a young poet with such a good head of silky blond hair has no need of frills and might prefer a plainer spot to lay it. Mrs Stevenson favours such things, but Mother used to say that an ornate pillow sham is only 'display', with no place here in England. Such display has come over from the United States.

Mother was always scornful of 'display'. She was full of sweeping condemnations. Her favourite phrase was 'nature needs no ornament' – I remember being told that when I wanted pretty pins to wear in my hair. I always knew the real reason was that we had no money for such things, so I grew to hate the saying, but since Father's passing it has come back to me as a decent one, and serviceable.

'I see too much and I hear too well for an old lady,' Mrs Stevenson said, so I work hard, and with some nervousness for how she will judge me. I sense that the young man is a special favourite of hers and that she is at pains to please him. So I clean the ironwork of the bed with paraffin, rubbing it into every ledge and crevice with the rag and thinking happily of how it will hardly creak now when he rolls over in the night. I wash the tumbler and the soap-dish, carefully using a different cloth from the one for the slop-pail and the chamber, adding a little splash of cold water to the pot before I put it back in the toilet cupboard. I do all this with loving attention, with such a particular satisfaction that I am sitting back on my heels admiring my own thoroughness when Mrs Stevenson bursts into the room with another of her hand-clappings and chop-chops to say that the afore-mentioned will be here in a minute and haven't I got rid of that mouse yet?

That makes my heart skitter in my chest, though whether it is the mouse (which I chase with the broom) or the afore-mentioned it's hard to say. Mrs Stevenson clops downstairs to attend to her scones, which, from the smell wafting upstairs, are in danger of burning. I run behind her.

So it is me who admits him. He appears at the door, tall and sunny, loose-limbed and lanky, with his high forehead and mane of hair that I remember, from my glimpse earlier in the day. I present myself politely, my hands stinging with the efforts of the scrubbing. I hold them tidily behind my back and smile as he grins a glorious grin at me and the sun blazes through the door, warming my face to scarlet. He wears grey flannels and a soft collar with no tie; and his face is rather innocent and babyish and, at the same time, inspired with a fierce life. Perhaps that is the secret of the 'impression' he creates of extraordinary loveliness, the sort of loveliness you'd more often see in a girl than a young man.

He holds a half-bitten apple. 'I say – anyone here mind if I take off my shoes?' he asks. It isn't really a question. He holds the apple between his teeth, bending down to step out of his shoes and socks. Mr Rupert Brooke steps over the threshold and into the kitchen.

His naked toes. I try, of course, not to look. But later, when he asks for tea outside on the lawn at the front of the house, and I bring it to him on a wobbling tray, the milk shaking in the little jug, there they are again. Each toe well formed and strong-looking, like the long white keys on a piano. 'Handsome' and 'shapely' are the two words that present themselves to me, thinking of his feet. And 'wrong' is the next. Or should I perhaps say 'revealing'?

I have mentioned my habit of looking at things too hard, and considering them too assiduously. Like Father's hands and the little shock it caused me to understand that Father was not always old and unlovely. Mr Brooke's toes told me the opposite tale. That he was not only or always a Varsity man, a poet, a person of dust and chalk and King's College, Cambridge, but a human creature who had once been bathed by a mother. How even his toes were, I think, like the feet of – oh, I don't know – an animal, a monkey perhaps, something that can use toes the way an ordinary man cannot. And his ankles, too! The naked ankle bone peeping from his trouser leg so prominent, and angular, so beautifully formed. His ankle could never have been mistaken for the ankle of a young woman. It is undeniably male. Such a curious thought made me shiver.

I have spent long enough in observing toes and weighing my conclusions about them and must surely, I chide myself, have some pressing duties.

Kittie comes to twitter over him. Seeing that I have forgotten the honey for his tea she brings him a pot, and a spoon, and drops a curtsy and pauses until he looks up from the copy of *English Review* lying in front of him on the grass and says: 'Forster's tale: "Other Kingdom". Best story ever written, Nellie. It is Nellie, isn't it?'

'It's Kittie, sir. Nellie's the tall one. The girl with the black hair over there.' She nods towards me and he laughs then and turns in his lazy way to look at me. The garden shudders with a sudden breeze as he does and a purple hairstreak butterfly flickers past my face.

Seconds later I bob a foolish curtsy, just like Kittie, then want to kick myself. Escaping, I realise that even though he is lying on his side on the grass, propping his head on his elbow in an appearance of complete relaxation, he is in fact watching me. He is saying something to me! I hurry close to hear him.

'And hot milk would be good too and eggs, if you have them.'

'Yes, sir.'

'On the lawn here in Arcadia would be admirably suitable.'

I glance down again, at his white feet among the three-leafed clover on the springy lawn. Another of his grins then. A grin that – he must know – is like a taper being lit and would melt any girl's skin to liquid wax. I – luckily for him – am not 'any girl'. He is fortunate that I am the good, practical sort with my head screwed tight and that none of his charms will work on *me*. I pick up my tray at once and hasten to the kitchen, to set to coddling the eggs.

~

I am in the Country in Arcadia; a rustic. It is a village two miles from Cambridge, up the river. You know the place; it is near all picnicing grounds. And here I work at Shakespeare and see few people. Shakespeare's rather nice. *Antony and Cleopatra* is a very good play. In the intervals I wander about bare foot and almost naked, surveying Nature with a calm eye. I do not pretend to understand Nature, but I get on very well with her, in a neighbourly way. I go on with my books, and she goes on with her hens and storms and things, and we're both very tolerant. Occasionally we have tea together. I don't know the names of things (like the tramp in Mr Masefield's poem), but I get on very well by addressing all flowers 'Hello, buttercup!' and all animals 'Puss! Puss!' I live on honey, eggs and milk, prepared for me by an old lady like an apple (especially in face) and sit all day in a rose garden to work. Of a morning Dudley Ward and a shifting crowd come out from Cambridge and bathe with me, have breakfast (out in the garden, as all meals) and depart. Dudley and I have spent the summer in learning to DIVE. I can *generally* do it now: he rarely. He goes in fantastically; quite flat, one leg pathetically waving, his pince-nez generally on. But, O, at 10pm (unless it's too horribly cold) alone, very alone and (though I boast of it next day) greatly frightened, I steal out, down an empty road, across emptier fields, through a wood packed with beings and again into the ominous open, and bathe by night. Have you ever done it? Oh but you have, no doubt. I, never before. I am in deadly terror of the darkness in the wood. I steal through it very silently. Once, I frightened two cows there, and they me. Two dim whitenesses surged up the haunted pathway and horribly charged on me. And once, returning bare foot through the wood, I trod on a large worm, whose dying form clung to the sole of my foot for many minutes.

Yes, marvellous place this. Except that the dear plump weather-beaten kindly old lady gave me a look like a donkey's rump when she saw my bare feet, and one even fouler (if that could be possible) when she caught me making some benign request of the maid. Who is rather pretty with the sort of high cheekbones that give her an almost Oriental look, and eyes of an extraordinary violet colour. I almost had to duck my head closer to take a second look, but that would have been . . . rather obvious.

My bedroom looks as though it hasn't been cleaned since Thomas Hardy was first weaned and the beam above my bed sheds little flakes of rotting wood like a shower of chocolate on the sheets in the morning. As I said, a rustic.

I'm glad to have escaped here, though. The delicious freedom of writing a letter to my darling Noel Olivier while lying face down in bed in a room filled with the scent of dusty lilac – rather than working on Shakespeare or snuffling together in a room of besocked King's men – more than compensates me for the apple lady's opprobrium. Despite the fact that my intention in moving here is to win not one but two prizes and cover myself with glory, I'm not working on either of them – instead I'm lying here daydreaming, writing to Noel, and dreaming up a paper to give to the Carbonari Society next week. The time is right for me to dazzle the Carbonari with fresh thoughts (as I outstandingly failed to do with my poetry a few months ago). So my paper will be called 'From Without' – something about the splendid difference between my life out here among the sun and the dog-roses and the black-haired beauty with the eyes like harebells who brings my breakfast, and *their lives*, with their whirring brains and clever bright eyes, evolving their next joke or two, in the stifling rooms of King's.

I am only two miles away, in Grantchester, but *here* there are so much better things to be concerned about, such as the white bed and the open window with the dark coming in.

The problem is, I'm so certainly and prominently an entertainer of so many various (and possibly not continuously compatible) young people that the likelihood of my paper on Shakespeare and my essay for the Harness Prize and my paper for the Carbonari Society *and* my thousand letters to a thousand friends actually being written is small indeed. I do find it more pressing and a million trillion times more glorious to stand naked at the edge of the black water in perfect silence than sit in stuffy rooms thinking bespectacled thoughts.

Two nights ago I did exactly that. The water shocked me as it came upwards with its icy-cold, life-giving embrace. Then a figure appeared: some local deity or naiad of the stream. In point of fact I know exactly who it was. It was the young maid-of-all-work, the afore-mentioned black beauty: a girl I've discovered is called Nellie Golightly. (Which sounds like something out of a music hall.) The sight of me turned her to stone. I acted as though it was the most normal thing in the world to me to appear naked in front of a beautiful young woman I hardly know. But then she opened her eyes again, picked up a peg that had dropped on to the lawn and marched off without a glance back. Nude young men with stunned erections are obviously *de rigueur* where she comes from.

It's impressive, this refusal of hers to be impressed. I rather like her. I resolve to swim again, tomorrow night and every night. Nell reminds me of a girl I once saw, a working girl with her fellow, standing under a lamp-post on Trinity Street, her face lit up. The intensity with which he kissed her, the freedom, the abandon, all were apparent to me in that glimpse, and then I became horribly aware of myself as proud owner of none of those qualities. Fixed there, staring, like a hungry urchin gazing at a cake in the baker's window. A version of myself that made me shudder, melt back into the soup along with all the other dull, spectacled people from Cambridge. Oh, Grantchester . . . Feeling the grass between my toes, and the river sweep over my head, perhaps at last I might shake off the sensation that my head is not attached to my body, that I am not really here at all.

As for Nell . . . That sumptuous nymph, naiad, the unearthly creature . . . (There is something infinitely good, and gracious, in the dark shadow that forms between her breasts when she leans forward to kneel at the grate or to put something on the table. I find myself dreaming up excuses – 'Could I trouble you for another cup of milk? Yes, just there on the rather low table is fine, thank you . . .' – to allow me to witness it frequently.) I feel sure she is an extraordinarily intelligent girl. Her eyes, now I think of it, are not so much harebells as – the exact shade of violets in a darkening wood. And she smells divine, like honey, of course (for I have discovered that this is what she does, tend the bees, and she has a rare talent for it) and apples and grass and floor-polish. What on earth can such a girl be thinking of as she stands beside the oh-so-refined Mr Neeve with his handkerchief on his head?

Enough about Nell. This kind of distraction will not get the Carbonari paper written.

Last week I arranged, during the visit of one Noel Olivier, that I might be the one to punt her down-river to Cambridge and snatch a few minutes alone with her. Having achieved it, so startled was I by the sudden absence of sisters, friends, parents, tutors and chaperones that I fell devastatingly silent. Noel sat with her chin tucked towards her chest in that way she has, her serious brown head bowed towards the water, dangling one hand over the edge; I stared at the buttons on the shoulder of her grey pinafore and the parting of her mouse-coloured hair, while digging the pole deep into the mud and preparing to do my fresh boyish stunt once more. (Oh, when I was in love with you, then I was clean and brave! And miles around the wonder grew – How well did I behave!)

'You will be delighted to know that I've taken the plunge and signed the pledge – or the Basis, is it? – or whatever the blazes it's called: Mr Rupert Brooke is now a fully signed up member of the Fabian Society,' was my opening gambit.

She looked up, chin still to chest, and her eyes widened in – one can only imagine – joy unmitigated at my marvellous new level of commitment to the socialist cause she holds so dear. Admittedly, she said nothing, but I am sure that these were her emotions; after all, she imbibed socialism and atheism at her mother's breast; her father, Sir Glamorous Dashing Sydney Olivier was practically a founder member, was he not? Still she remained maddeningly silent. Then suddenly her hand trailing the water snatched back towards the boat as she realised she was swirling it in a froth of goose feathers where some poor creature had met an ugly death.

'Such a shame . . .' she murmured. 'If I had a butterfly net I might have caught the feathers – there's a pillowful of goosedown there . . .'

I laughed. 'Ha! Here am I thinking you are lamenting the goose's brief life on earth and about to wish it a better one in Heaven—'

'You know I don't believe in goose Heaven, or any other kind, and neither do you,' she said, frowning slightly, and raising those intense grey eyes to mine.

Here was the part of the trip where the meadows and willows gave way to the rushing sound of the weir and we had to disembark the boat and drag it a few hundred yards over the wooden rollers before launching it again. Noel obliged with admirable zeal, but still, with only the two of us and she in a skirt, it was awkward. I had arranged to drop her with her sister Margery and the others on the sleek, forbidding lawns of King's and as we were now as far as the Mathematical Bridge, I didn't have long to enjoy this conversation. So I paused, pretending to mop my feverish brow, holding the pole still and allowing the boat to drift slowly along the glassy green water. 'Don't I? I'm writing a paper, for the Carbonari, on that very subject . . .'

'Another of your secret societies,' she muttered sarcastically.

I laid the pole the length of the punt and came to sit beside her. She looked up at me expectantly. From the Backs came shouts of students and towards us the thump of wood on water, as a noisy canoe full of revellers approached, scattering ducks.

'But you see, Noel, I was raised on Heaven – things are quite different for you. Dick's funeral was full of heraldic burbling about angels and trumpets . . . and God forbid anyone mentioning – me, for instance – that if life was so glorious, why was Dick in such a dash to be out of it?'

'You think your brother – committed suicide?'

'Oh, nothing as – *considered* as that. I only mean – his drinking, when his health was already poor – his seeming not to care. And sometimes I remember him, you know, so many little memories, over the years. He was six when I was born. I doubt he ever liked me: I was just his horrible pudding-haired younger brother. What he *liked* was to thrash me at cricket, at chess, at rugby. You name it, he excelled in thrashing me at it. But he was there, the backdrop to my childhood, like curtains, like the smell of Watson's Nubolic Disinfectant Soap and now he's – not. I can't quite believe it. Where is he? I ask myself. Dick, where are you? And the answer comes back: nowhere.'

Another boat passed us and the occupants waved loudly and I faintly recognised them – Justin Brooke, and a party, I think – and blushed to be found so still and intent, next to Noel. In my confusion, I hoped that Noel had not recognised the Brooke Bond Tea Boy, Justin, so said nothing, and pretended an insouciant, debonair perkiness, in the face of his leering smiles as his boat slid away from us. If this got back to Margery, I'd suffer. But Noel was tactful. She listened and she nodded and she did not panic, as Mother would have done, at my raising the extraordinary subject of Dick.

'Yes,' she said simply. Then: 'I envy those people who have Firm Beliefs. An afterlife and so forth. It must be very comforting.'

'How few of us realise how little time there is! If only we could grasp this in our imaginations, I mean really grasp it, not just know it intellectually, with our heads, but know it really with our hearts and bodies . . . how long the before and after probably are, and how dark . . .'

I expected Noel to look shocked, then, tell me to 'buck up' and speak of something cheerier. I almost wished she had. Instead she said, 'Yes, isn't that the point of the country, somehow? To remind us, I mean. That there is no 'state beyond the grave'. Last week Bunny and I found a dead mole under the bushes at the bottom of the garden. Bunny thought we should dissect it to see how it all worked—'

Without meaning to, Noel had shifted the mood. I stood up and picked up the pole at once and with one deep push slid us under the Mathematical Bridge and on towards the spires of King's. I also burst out laughing.

'Last week you and Bunny Garnett were skinning a mole? Is that what they teach you at Bedales? How appallingly grisly you Bedalians are. Do tell my dear Bunny that I called him "grisly", won't you? So is he planning to be a veterinary surgeon now? Are you, in fact? I thought it was to be a doctor, last time we spoke . . .'

'Well, I do intend to be a doctor, yes, and I don't see what's funny—'

'Oh, Noel, how glorious you are! How truly, truly magnificent! You are a Prince among Women, a—'

'If you talk to me like a schoolgirl I shall beat you over the head with your own pole.'

'And she would do! I'm sure of it! Oh, what a girl is Noel Olivier . . . she'd throw you in the drink as soon as look at yer . . . !'

And the mood changed, and the memory of Dick was dissolved, and Noel told me not to despair, for in the country you dimly sense, after all, if not an afterlife then a 'wonderful unity . . .' and we agreed on this, and grew peaceful again, after

I had whooped with joy at the damned calming good sense of Noel Olivier.

I'm trying to remember it all for my paper. There is something in the conversations one has on a river, with a beautiful young woman of not quite sixteen, that sound silly spoken to a group of King's men in a hot room.

We must feel and be friends. We must seek in Art and in Life for the end *here and now*.

(How glorious to be In Love with the young Noel Olivier, but why then did I suddenly picture Nellie, with a glossy black curl sneaking loose from her cap, holding out to me my newly polished boots?) We have inherited the world. Why should we go crying beyond it?

The present is amazingly ours.

~

Mr Brooke might be a poet but he is, first, a man and in some aspects he does not differ from any other. A girl charged with cleaning out a gentleman's room knows these things.

So, late that first week I was in the garden, not the orchard; the roses were grey in the twilight but the day's heat still soaked me as I ran about with my last tasks of the evening. I was on my way to the two-holer where it's my job to change the buckets in the hatch. Naturally, it's my least favourite chore and if I could have dispatched it to Kittie, I would. But she has the advantage of her longer time here and greater experience, so I resigned myself and put a peg on my nose. That's why I didn't see him at first. Now, thinking on it, I can't truly believe how it might be possible. But there you have it. A peg was pinching my nose and I did not at first notice that approaching me was the poet who, in the semi-darkness, was quite naked.

My hands flew to my face. I stood there, as if turned to stone, my palms balling my eyes. The peg plopped to the ground. I felt ridiculous, like the child who believes if she covers her face no one can see her, but I honestly couldn't think what else to do. I heard the tread of his bare feet on the mossy grass and I heard that his steps did not falter in the slightest as he approached me. No, there was no hesitation in those steps at all, and I kept thinking: He must have seen me! Why does he not scurry away, or hide, or step back, or run inside the two-holer?

'Glorious evening, Nell—'

I opened my eyes then, thinking he had passed, and his hand flew down towards his private parts and, widening his legs comically, he said: '"Down, little bounder, down!" as Edmund Gosse said to his heart,' and then he laughed, rudely and very loudly. He passed so close that I could smell the scent of the muddy river that wrapped his skin. I continued to wait there, stung with shame and embarrassment, like the most foolish of statues, my face aflame under my palms, until Mr Pudsey Dawson, the bull-terrier from the Old Vicarage, hurled himself out of the shadows barking, and chased after Mr Brooke into the house.

Well, now. I was tired later, but every time the scene formed in my mind, my face would flare again. Undressing for bed, I fancied I heard him – only a landing between us – although likely it was just Kittie snoring and snuffling in her sleep. I closed my eyes, and on the inside of my eyelids I saw him, in all his glory, as Mother would have said, a marbled colour on account of the twilight.

I turned over, turned my face to the wall for shame, and tried to make the picture go away. I sat up in bed, and my heart beat fast with anger. I thought again of Mr Brooke's appearance. I thought again of what he'd said, some clever joke, I knew, from this Mr Gosse I'd never heard of. His laughter, or rather the memory of it, made my face flame again.

Of course a girl like me has seen a man naked before. I've seen Edmund and Stanley and Father – it was my job to lay him out, to bathe his poor stiff body. Sheep's Green and Coe Fen are always pink with boys in the summer, as naked as God made them. We only went there once as children, but it made us smile to see the ladies going for their picnics Up the River and how they hid behind their parasols so as not to see all that pinkness dancing about while the gentlemen had to row like billy-oh but, then, none of those occasions are the same thing. Edmund and Stanley are just boys. Father was an old man. The swimming boys, though, they were not 'horrid', as Kittie says. I always thought them a beautiful sight – thin naked boys dancing about in the sunlight on the bright green grass; the sparkling river; the reckless high dives, when the slim bodies shot through the air like angels coming down from Heaven.

When you lived as we did, four to a bed and in a house as small as the sheds the university men use here for boats, you learn fast. You learn to be like the three wise monkeys and hear, see and say nothing. But now my mind would not leave it alone, and who could I tell? The glory of him: the magnificence, the sheer wicked springing force of it – like a soldier saluting, or like the long fowling gun out in the punt. Oh, to be a man and possess such a toy; small wonder my brothers could not leave theirs alone! I had more sympathy for Father then, these seven long years since Mother's death, thinking how he was just like the sun, rising every morning without fail, and how he struggled to hide it from me.

But it wasn't Father I was thinking of, nor Father who had opened me to these ideas of Nature and of showing a greater sympathy. Every time I tried to close my eyes and sleep I would see it again, and my body would flicker somewhere, like a match being struck. Then at last the anger seeped away and instead I wanted to giggle. How strange to be a gentleman and possess such a thing, and so casually own it that even when a young girl he's scarcely met is accidentally *greeted* by it the gentleman might simply press at it, casually, with the flat of his palm, the way a child might push down a yelping dog; only to have it bounce back up again.

I tried to think hard of Pudsey Dawson, for that snuffed out the flickering-match sensation and dispelled the power of the picture in my mind's eye. Mr Rupert Brooke's splendid maleness compared to a dog! Mr Pudsey Dawson is an ugly bull-terrier, not an attractive beast. He eats frogs. He is too alive, too much of a yapping thing! So springy! It should, of course, be something more glorious, like a great head of strong golden corn, or Pan with his pipes. I smiled, tasting the cool kindliness of the pillow. How offended Mr Brooke would surely be, if only he knew what I was thinking.

~

Oh, the bouncing elasticity and hard heart of Youth! I've just this minute received an appallingly cold letter from the disgraceful young wench with the live hair that is Shining and Free (Noel Olivier, of course), which makes me want to strike her. Instead we plan to visit her again, Dudley and I, to descend on her near the river Eden at Penshurst where Dudley assures me she'll be bathing nude with her sisters (Bryn especially, I hope) or at the very least drinking cream and lying on the grass. There I shall gaze upon her magnificence. Or, rather, Dudley and I shall affect to be passing, hands in pockets. As all those pupils of Bedales are like fish and cannot live long out of water, if we time it well, we should be in luck.

Now, if I can persuade her to bathe nude with me, that might be something. Of course I mean simply innocent, child-like naked swimming. It's always a question of clothes. You become part of it all, and bathe. The only terror left is of plunging head foremost into blackness; a moderate terror. I have always had some lurking suspicion that the river may have run dry, after all, and that there is, as there seems, no water in it. (I knew a man once who never dared to dive because he always feared there might be a corpse floating just below the surface into which he'd go headlong.)

I bathed again tonight in Byron's Pool, and wandered back to the Orchard House, past the tin-roofed lavatory, which that refined working man Mr Neeve calls a 'two-holer'. He says this with a proclamatory cough every time, as if to boast. Perhaps the dear fellow has two arses?

As I passed it, the black-haired beauty appeared again, popping up like a frozen monkey, hands again glued to her eyes while I passed her. I could not help myself from laughing. I thought how like Noel she was, and dreamed a little. Why, their names are practically identical, except for one letter! And yet a girl who lives without parent or chaperone to prevent it must surely experience things that a child like Noel, protected by all those sisters and parents, could not. In point of fact, what could one ever know about such lives as Nell's? About such queer minds, which must remain as mysterious as the minds of water nymphs or coalmen?

I sighed then, and retired to bed to pump ship. After that I wrote to my dear friend and most assiduous correspondent, Master James Strachey – more banter aimed at discouraging and inflaming his crush on me in equal measure. James writes that he's sorry to see that poor Kitty Holloway was arrested, but I cannot for one moment understand his concern for a Suffragette! Has the boy gone mad? And he seriously expects me to help him distribute announcements for Shaw's *Press Cuttings* at the Court Theatre and doesn't at all seem to understand that I am not remotely vexed by questions of Suffrage, in any direction, shape or form. He also said, mysteriously, that poor Cecil Taylor – I can't even remember who he is – has three of something, then enticingly refrains from explaining what he means. 'Three of what?' I wrote back. James jealously believes I'm in love with Apostle no. 244 – Hobhouse (who had an affair with Duncan, according to James). Little does he know the uncomfortable truth of my utter and untarnished virginity. And long may I hide it from him.

Three what? Three *balls* he writes on a postcard, which the Postmaster General graciously conceded to deliver, the following day.

With Hobhouse James is far off the mark. Closer are his questions about Charles Lascelles, who at least has the dignity of being exquisitely handsome and a former love of mine from schooldays. But James writes, 'You needn't think I'm jealous of a ghost,' and I suppose he has a point – Charlie is a boy of yesteryear, with Rugby seeming a hundred years ago now.

All this made for a busy evening of scribbling tonight, after a day of lunches and dinners and teas with the shifting folk of Cambridge, but very little work being done. And, amusing though it may be, my feelings when I'm alone, and all the bright things have departed, are rarely light-hearted, but more often disturbed.

Tonight, as ever, my mind returns to Dick, and the nature of his . . . illness. His drinking. The thing that sticks with me is that horrible ironic letter from Dick's firm. How it arrived – in the midst of the funeral preparations – with its airy news of a better job. Would it have cheered him? Would it have been enough? I never thought so, somehow. His unhappiness seemed deep, constitutional. And that is the fear – that is the dark thought that sometimes nestles up to me, here in this bed. That it might be a familial weakness, this dark, deep despair of Dick's. What paltry gifts do I have to set against it? Only my friends, my many thousands of cheery and airy friends, and my bright thoughts and my Fabian principles (which keep me from the temptations of beer, of course), my writing and my professed desire to live in the here and now and my feeling for art and living – and yes, why, I have persuaded myself: it is true. I am nothing like Dick. No, nothing at all! Nothing like that side of the family.

Thankfully, the unhappy ballooning of these thoughts was splendidly punctured by Nell Golightly, bringing in my milk and apple pie. I watched her set the tray down and stand with her back to my little window so that the light shone through that fine black hair of hers, curling at the bottom of her cap, tinting it red at the edges, as if singed by fire. She has such a way of standing, surveying me and waiting for my instruction, with no hint of subservience or insolence, which I find grand.

I sat upon the bed, cross-legged, and nodded to her, and longed to ask her Important Things – things of which I have no knowledge yet, but I know I would like to ask. Nell reminds me of a young nurse I had once, a girl I thought I had forgotten, who had a manner not dissimilar: straightforward, straight-talking, clean as soap and just as fragrant. And staring at Nell raised the memory of that young nurse bathing me, it must have been when Alfred was newborn, perhaps even before we moved to School Field, because surely once living there Mother never employed a nurse, but was Housemistress to all of us?

What I remember is the feel of friendly fingers rubbing soap over my legs, and splashing water up to my chest. And, looking down, the sight of the water trickling towards my white stomach and my little member perking up like a soldier standing to attention, and saying something to the nurse to this effect, and her smiling – yes, she definitely smiled and did not scold me!, although she ceased her rubbings and her splashings – and then suddenly the Ranee was in the room, casting about us a giant sweeping grey towel of disapproval and worse than that. Worse than disapproval, I knew at once how she felt towards me, all the feelings she swept into the room with her: disgust, horror, dislike, might I even say intense *hatred* for my very childish boyish perkiness. Swirling this mood around me and aiming it finally at such an essential bit of me made me know at once what she felt about all of me.

That nurse – her name suddenly came to me as Dorothy – was soon after dismissed and I was expected to bathe unaided or with my brothers, but not before the girl had muttered to me one day, 'Poor Mrs Brooke, don't be too hard on her, Rupert, for no boy can understand what it is to lose a daughter,' and the two events conflated at once, and I decided in my childish mind that this was why Mother so disliked my male anatomy, and would like to chop it off and make me a girl, like my poor dead sister.

Musing on this only caused the same conflicting feelings to surface and I wished to God I might think of something else. When Nell Golightly had gone, with the soft closing click of the door behind her and the squeak of her tread on the stairs, I turned my mind deliberately, and with an effort, to the group of Young Poets I met that time in London. All of them extremely poor. And how they write – some are good, others bad – as they talk. That is to say, their poems give the fullest value when pronounced as they thought and felt them. They allow for *ow* being *aow*. Their love poems begin (I invent) 'If yew wd come again to me'. That is healthy. That way is life. In them is more hope – and more fulfilment – than in the old-world passion and mellifluous despair of any gentleman's or lady's poetry.

Mightn't Nellie inspire poetry of that sort in me? Mightn't she offer what Noel can't possibly? Because, and Noel's letters make this clear, severing Noel from her family, from her protective sisters who do not allow her to walk alone with a man and were horrified by that simple punt down river, is not a possibility. Whereas Nell is all alone, and has no one here to separate her from me. Only the weight and silence of custom, of my own cowardice, of a million things.

How easy or hard will it be to talk to the maid? There is this strange idea that the lower classes, the people entering into the circle now of the educated, are coarsely devoid of taste, likely to swamp the whole of culture in undistinguished, raucous, stumpy arts that know no tradition. It is only natural that the tastes of the lower classes *should* be at present infinitely worse than ours. The amazing thing is that it is probably rather better. It is true many Trade Unionists do not read Milton. Nor do many university men. But take the best of each. Compare the literary criticism of the *Labour Leader* with that of the *Saturday Review*. It is enormously better, enormously readier to recognise good literature.

Of course, I myself have written for the *Spectator* and do not wish to decry it. But the force of primness that exists in this country, the washy, dull, dead upper-class brains that lurk in the Victorian shadows . . . do I wish to throw in my lot with them? Is it all to be such prettiness, my work, and is that what I'm to be remembered for? Not the short fat man with fair hair who wrote the plays (Shakespeare, idiot!) but the pretty golden one who wrote – what was it again that he wrote? Oh, did he write then, that golden Apollo, so handsome, hardly needed to lift a pen, surely, it was enough for him to flick his hair and bend his arse over some Trinity Fellow's desk, wasn't it? 'Lest man go down into the dark with his best songs unsung . . .'

O, that way madness lies; let me shun that. My head hurts. I have the pink-eye again.

~

Mr Brooke doesn't seem unduly interested in a lady's looks – the lady here yesterday with two other gentlemen was an ill-dressed lump, yet he seemed to like her well enough, laughing and once putting his arm on hers. Her name is Miss Darwin, and she is related to the famous man who claims we are all no better than apes in the forest. She wears a walking skirt with brush braid sewn round the bottom to catch the mud, which is a clever idea, although it looks funny.

They sit outside in the orchard, in deckchairs, and talk about the strangest, most inconsequential things.

'Here, did I tell you that story that a fellow at King's told me? About his cousin who died when she was seventeen, and the poor chap was too deep in his Tripos to really give it his full attention and he rather muffed the grieving part of things. Then one day – oh, yes, thank you, Nell, and cream too, please – he had such a dream. In it he saw the girl standing in front of a mirror, powdering her face. One can imagine how impossible this seemed to him – the child was just seventeen, why would she be painting her face? Then he saw clearly in the glass that she was dead and that's how it struck him at last. She was trying to cover up a ravaged face.'

It's Mr Brooke who tells this tale. He says 'ravaged' in a teasing, theatrical manner, with his eyelashes flickering. But the young Miss Darwin woman doesn't laugh, she continues staring down at a small notebook where she is sketching, and mutters, without looking up, 'A girl of seventeen, painting her face!' To which Mr Brooke replies, 'It was a dream, Gwen. The chap was dreaming. There's a curious obviousness, finality, certainty about it, somehow, when one hears of it, isn't there?'

I remember then that Kittie told me Mr Brooke lost a brother. His older brother, Dick, 'went to the bad,' she said, hinting heavily with meaningful looks. When I pressed her she said that Dick had died of pneumonia, just a couple of years ago, when Rupert first came up to Cambridge, but that it wasn't really the pneumonia that killed him, he'd been a drinker and, worse, other dark things. Kittie tapped her head with one finger to convey her meaning and, annoyed, I swiped at her with the teacloth. I wondered at how Kittie knows so much about Rupert's life. This thought produces a suspicious pang. It is not that I harbour romantic illusions about Mr Brooke – I'm far too honest a girl for that – but only that his loss of a brother makes me feel that he and I, for all our different stations, might *share* something, that we know what it is to reach the end of our childhood and have certainty snatched from us, be reminded what a sad, sorry place the world is. But this is only a fancy, a thought in my own imagination, after all, and not a hard fact of any kind: not real like this tray in front of me and these blue-rimmed teacups and this amber liquid steaming in the pot and the soft molehills on the grass and the sounds of a boatman shouting on the river . . .

Miss Darwin says do I mind if she 'plays Mother', so I set the tray down and leave the rest to them.

My policy on the matter of bumping into Mr Brooke two times now by the two-holer is, of course, to say nothing at all, and to be careful not to catch his eye. But as I'm turning to go back to the kitchen from the orchard he suddenly looks directly at me and says, 'Oh, Nell, have you ever trodden on a worm with your bare left foot, on a moonless night in a Dreadful Wood alone?'

This is the way he talks. I suppose it is thought to be funny, or witty, where he comes from, but I have no reply. The others look up, expectantly. He stares straight at me with his clean blue gaze, and I recognise it for what it is, a challenge. Am I to blush, turn away, stumble? After counting to six (inwardly), I say carefully, 'No, sir. Will that be all?' And it is he who drops his gaze first, and laughs.

Mrs Stevenson is cross when I get back to the kitchen, since I've forgotten to bring the tray. I show her a burn on my hand from the oven yesterday, which is still raw and red in two raised stripes and mention that it is hard for me to carry so much with such an injury. So she fetches the key to the locked cupboard and I'm to help myself to a small pat of butter to rub on the burn. She's very good to us. I cannot think of many maid-of-alls who are treated as well. It is because she has daughters of her own, I'm sure, but that is also the reason she 'hears too much' and I know to be wary of it.

This afternoon there is a further commotion. A painter has arrived at Grantchester Meadows, with no more morals, according to Mr Neeve, 'than the honey bees'. As this man has camped rather too close to the hives, Mr Neeve is exercised over it. The man has two wives with him and a hundred children, all boys (Kittie tells me this, with her customary breathlessness and elaboration) – the children wild and brown and barely dressed, except for tattered yellow and red garments.

Mr Brooke asks me to take a letter to this man, inviting him to tea.

'To tea, sir, here at the Orchard?'

'Be a sensible child, Nell. He looks like a gypsy but I assure you he's the greatest painter.'

As I hesitate I note in the corner of my eye Kittie, with her red hair bobbing beneath her cap, staring at us. She looks for a moment as if she's about to approach us, and so, swiftly, I accept the note. After all, Mr Brooke has entrusted me, not Kittie, to run his errand for him, no doubt already noticing that if one of us were 'Beauty' and one of us 'Brains', I would be the latter.

But I don't mind admitting I'm a little alarmed as I approach the artist's camp, which does indeed look no different from the gypsy camps we see in Prickwillow, full of cheapjacks and tinkers. There's a sky-blue van next to one of canary yellow, about a half-dozen enormous horses quietly grazing and, close by, two tents. And from one emerges an enormous figure – a man –. exactly like a pirate: standing over six feet high, wearing the strangest jersey and check suit, and with a long red beard, just like the beard of Rumpelstiltskin.

As I come closer, I can see that one eye is puffy and shadowed with black, and in the sunlight, gold earrings glitter in his hair. My hand without the sore grips the basket of fruit I'm carrying, the note lying on top. I pick my way between the thistles and flakes of dried cow-pats, coarse as matted hair, remembering how Kittie said a cabman in Cambridge had been too nervous to drive him, this Augustus John, and no wonder!

Now a woman appears from one of the tents and stands staring towards me, shading her eyes against the sun. Her dress is long and a damson colour, her head wound with a scarf. The other wife is nowhere to be seen but the 'hundreds' of boys – more likely six, now I count them – are all in the river, splashing and shouting. One of the horses startles, neighing suddenly – a sound like the drawing of a saw across wood. And so I stop. Far enough, I think.

'I've come from Mr Rupert Brooke, sir. He's sent a message for you.'

I have to shout a little to be heard. I feel foolish for stopping so far, but cannot now make myself shift closer. The gypsy giant strides towards me and takes the basket. The moment he lifts the note from it, with the apples lying underneath, the boys appear, like a swarm of monkeys, their bodies shining wet. They grab at the apples, shouting and splashing me with water. And not a word from the mother to chastise them!

'He'd like you to take tea in the orchard, sir. The pavilion you see there beyond the gate with the tin roof, and the house is just behind it.'

This is all in the note, but the way the artist is staring at it, I'm not certain he can read.

Laughter and uproar from the children mean I must bellow again to be heard. A moorhen joins in with a sudden screechy warning. The lady remains at an observing distance and it is the artist who claps his hands round the children's heads, shouting as he does, 'Splendid! Haven't I always said, Dorelia, how respectable people become indignant at the sight of us, but disreputable ones behave charmingly?'

The wife surely has no means of hearing him at such a distance and over such noise, so makes no comment. The basket now empty, I pick it up, nod my goodbyes and head back towards the gate. I do not like the way this Mr Augustus John stares at me. A girl can always tell such things – if only men realised how clearly their thoughts might be read, they might perhaps try to keep them better locked up.

As I turn, I catch a glimpse of the other wife, a younger version of the first, who might be a sister, or even a daughter. She is drying one of the younger boys with a cloth. This child holds a piece of grass between finger and thumb and whistles, his note piercing the air like a bird call.

Dear oh dear. I can just imagine what Mrs Stevenson will say when this carnival turns up for tea.

≈

Oh, I have written an inarticulate but pleasant enough poem for the *Cambridge Review* at their request. Or, rather, I wrote it last April and yielded it to them now. At least I didn't burn it, although I might grow to wish I had – it's possible. About that blasted child Noel, of course, in the New Forest. 'Oh! Death will find me, long before I tire/Of watching you . . .'

A bitter lie, naturally. I'm tired already. How many years is it since I first clapped eyes on Noel? It was in Ben Keeling's rooms in Trinity, one of those early Fabian Society meetings Ben lured me to. I sat on a window-ledge eating nuts, I remember, and Noel was there all broad-browed and smiling, with her sister Margery and probably some other Newnham girls. I remember Noel dropped a cup, a small green dainty cup of coffee, and the dark brown splash and pieces of crockery flew everywhere, and she was embarrassed. Bending down beside her, gingerly picking up pieces and putting them into a napkin, I remember her deep, shy blush. I was studying her while her eyes were on the cup and the floor. I remember that her skin was not the translucent sort that one sees the veins in, but rather creamy, opaque, thick, even. Was it Nietzsche who said one knows all one needs to about a person in the first fifteen minutes of meeting? What did I know about Noel? That she was shy, yes. That she was passionate, and had genuine socialist convictions. But also something else: that she was somewhat inscrutable, *impenetrable*. Ah, yes. That'll do it every time.

It's a poor sonnet. Considering I don't believe in a 'last land', I wonder why I persist in imagining myself and Noel there in it, her turning and tossing her 'brown delightful head/Amusedly among the ancient Dead . . .'? (But I wrote it three months ago and a lot can happen in three months, including utter abandonment of the concept of immortality.) It's a poem full of 'breezy obviousness', no doubt. Or, as the Master of Magdalene might say, 'conventional in its deliberate modernity, uneven and bizarre'. Must try harder, in fact. The moment it was sent, I wished to snatch it back, but there it is. A longing to be seen and read and known, and yet an even more powerful one not to be; to fabricate and obfuscate and posture and all the rest. It's exhausting. No wonder I have ophthalmia again, no doubt caught from one of Augustus's scallywags – their eyes are as pink as the eyes of albino rabbits. How I passionately long to lock myself wholly up, deny admittance to a soul, soothe my eyes with milk, and read and write only and always (with the regular interval for pumping ship, naturally). And improve, improve, improve! Wasn't that what I came here to do? To escape the distractions of Cambridge life, to patch up my lost scholarly reputation, and not to invite those same distractions to join me here at every turn?

'If he looked like that and was a good poet too, I don't know what I should do.' Henry James's summation. Or, rather, according to Dudley, voiced thus: 'Well, I must say I'm *relieved* to hear his poetry is not good, for with *that* appearance if he had also talent it would be too unfair.'

Oh, one needn't think I don't hear these things. My Prodigious Beauty, incidentally, does not interfere with the proper functioning of my ears.

~

So the whole circus arrives later in the afternoon and, Lord, what a spectacle! There are six boys, it turns out, aged from three to eight and such a tribe they are . . . They even bring their groom, Arthur. The gypsy man says they brought Arthur along for 'washing up' but they still expect him to be fed! It is this Arthur, it turns out, who is the reason for the painter's black eye. It seems he and Mr John are fairly in the habit of disagreeing and like to demonstrate as much to each other with a rain of blows.

My hand is still smarting from the burn, and it's fetch and carry, fetch and carry from three o'clock to six, and I can scarcely hear myself think, what with the racket they make. More scones (we have to keep the oven constantly stoked), more tea, more honey, more butter, more milk, more eggs . . .

The artist is here to paint a Lady Don, at the university, and all the talk is of her. 'A very charming person,' Mr John announces, 'although a puzzle to paint . . .' He says she smokes cigarettes all day and reclines on green drapes for the sitting with a red book on her lap. Somehow I gather that this Lady Don, although of an advanced age, has been harbouring romantic illusions about a friend of Mr Brooke's and Mr Ward's, a man older than them called Francis Cornford. (I think the man has visited. I think he is the tall, older man on a bicycle, with such a mop of curly black hair that it looks like a wig, who is very stiff and shy. Mr Brooke calls him Comus – a part he had in a play they were in. Their habit of nicknames for one another only adds to my confusion but I can't help myself from concentrating hard, from wanting to keep up.) The Lady Don sounds very wretched because she only has her books now, and Mr Brooke blurts out that she should know better 'as she's old enough to be his mother', and they all laugh as if he has said something witty, with Mr Brooke then shouting that hadn't they all taken an oath, during the play, Comus, not to marry within six months of it – and that surely Francis Cornford had broken that oath by making overtures during that time to Miss Darwin's cousin? This last part of the conversation is the hardest to fathom because it seems that Miss Darwin's cousin is called Frances too, and that Frances and Francis Cornford are to marry . . .

During all this talk and kerfuffle the mother does not scold the boys at all for snatching, stuffing food into their faces, tearing at the clover they find in the grass and scattering the leaves all over the linen tablecloth, or leaping from chair to chair or under the tables and so, of course, they do all of these things, all of the time, like a tribe of monkeys let loose in a wood.

When the conversation about the Frances and Francis state of affairs dies down, Mr Brooke and Mr Dudley Ward fire up a curious conversation with the children, chiefly with the eldest one, a boy called Pyramus, who tells Mr Brooke of an imaginary world where the river is milk, the mud honey, the reeds and trees green sugar, the earth cake. (The boys must be starving, to dream up such things. The blades of their brown bare shoulders poke out like little wings. One of them, David, reminds me of my own sweet Stanley, with his long curls, and his fat bottom lip and his habit of lying on his stomach on the grass, gazing at ants and ladybirds.)

'And what would the leaves be?' asks Mr Brooke, his cheeks flushed, one hand brushing back his floppy fringe, persisting with the foolish game long after the children have lost interest.

'The leaves would be ladies' hats!' announces Pyramus, and the party falls to laughing, so that Mr Brooke knocks over the little brown jar of Devonshire cream and another has to be fetched.

Then they carry on to declare that the sky is made from the blue pinafore of the youngest boy, Robin. The sun is a spot of honey on this same blue pinafore. 'What would happen,' asks Mr Dudley Ward, 'if you were all in a tree, and at the bottom a big bear sat and waited so that you couldn't come down?'

'The bear would die after a little,' Pyramus says boldly, with all the adults looking at him as if his views are to be considered, and again the lot of them laugh, as if the boy has said something witty.

This children's game and Mr Brooke's enthusiasm for it makes me cross with him. It's a part of his nature I find irksome. For instance, he has asked several times if he could take tea and 'whales', and it was only this afternoon that he explained that 'whales' was sardines on toast. Seems to me he has spent too long in the classroom with other boys, giving the same boys too great an importance, with their secret games and private names. Our way, where children are not separated and sent to school together but given the duties of adults very soon, produces a more natural child, if you ask me, and more natural adult too, without the two being confused. Mr Brooke and his friends seem not to understand that others might not share their pleasure in childish things. Or, rather, they know full well and delight in shunning all but their school friends.

By the time the meal ends, my poor burned palm is raw and stinging and my neck and shoulders aching. The party breaks up suddenly, on a word of Mr Brooke's, that the Lady Don can't be kept waiting a minute longer, and the children scatter in the direction of the river, so Mrs Stevenson charges her daughter, Lottie, with helping us clear away the tea things. The artist's chief wife Dorelia watches us silently as we do so, shyly pushing a saucer and spoon towards me at one moment, rather than ask me for more strawberries. The younger girl, despite Mr Brooke's calling her a 'second wife', is to my mind merely a sister to the first, and there as a general helpmeet, with no relation to the painter that could be guessed at from the little that passed between them.

Mr Brooke has offered to take the family down-river by boat. As suddenly as the hullabaloo arrived, it disappears. The colourful figures melt through the trees towards the gate and the river, and the cheeky sparrows who had hopped around the table all afternoon now land on it to pluck at the crumbs, joined by a poor straggly robin with naughty black eyes. When I make a move towards him, I'm surprised that he doesn't fly off but guards his little portion of crumbs like an Indian brave. The poor bird must be starving. I name it Pyramus and feel another stab of sorrow for little Stanley and Edmund. No doubt they, too, are out on the river Lark or the mere in this summer heat, but it won't be playing and splashing for them. They will be lying low in the boat, holding the gun for the eel man, Sam, and steadying the recoil in the punt, while Sam shoots wildfowl for Betty to boil up in a pot for his dinner. I pray God he shares some with my brothers, later.

~

And so I punt, and Dudley slumbers and the sweet river slips past us, melancholy and enchanted, and the boys quickly return to their water-naiad forms, while Augustus, with Dorelia lying beside him, sleepily complains of the constraints of patronage. A terrible sprite grips me and persuades me that this should be the occasion for venturing my little speech on that very subject (an essay I have been musing on for the Fabian Society). Trying to sound natural and unrehearsed, I begin: 'Since we all agree that poets and artists matter, and since we know they require periods of development, should it not be the state that provides, you know, bread and cheese and whatever for those who show promise?'

'Huh?' is all Augustus says, so I continue.

'Well . . . the ordinary system of incomplete endowment and jobbery and such things as payment for dedications is a ramshackle affair . . . wouldn't you say . . . ?'

The water plops as a fish jumps, and as we leave the dense trees on the bank behind us and reach Dead Man's Bend, I fall quiet for a moment, the better to concentrate. It's a devil to punt here, if one doesn't know it, as the water is deeper than the length of the punt pole. Augustus is oblivious to the expertise of his chauffeur, however, and continues to drone quietly to Dorelia about the woman who is to sit to him, Jane Harrison, making no attempt to include me in the conversation. My hands sweating, the pole nearly slips through them. I take off my shirt and tie and lay them at my feet. After a cough, I try again, a little more forcefully: 'I mean, it affects the work, doesn't it? You see it in Elizabethan times when most of the best writers lost all their shame (which doesn't much matter) and half their vitality (which does) in cadging and touting.'

Augustus glances slyly at me, interested at last, but unsure, I believe, at this point, whether my remarks are intended to contradict or support his position. His eyes are closed, his arm dangling lazily over the edge of the boat, Dorelia and her sister Edie resting either side of him, and the children bobbing beside us in the water like noisy ducklings. Dudley snoozes stiffly at the other end of the boat (his flimsy weight hardly achieving its task of balancing us), the sun bouncing off his shiny pate.

'I wonder how much more Milton or Marvell might have given us had they had enough to live on? If anything at all, the loss is enormous, surely.'

Now Augustus opens one eye and surveys me thoroughly. Finally, he bestirs himself to speak. 'What about losing half of

Spenser's *The Faerie Queene*? Would have been rather an achievement, in my view.'

'Yes, yes,' I have to agree, flummoxed. 'But it's terrifying, is it not, to think how many artists are living on inherited capital? And if you were to really count the waste of past centuries, one would have to include the artistic potentialities sown here and there in the undistinguished mass of the people, which have perished unconscious in that blindest oblivion – the mute, inglorious Miltons of the village and slum Beethovens—'

Augustus opens both eyes at last and interrupts, with his slow drawl, 'You think poets and artists should compose at the loom, the way William Morris hoped?'

He is calmly smoking a cigarette now. With his curious pale face and his sea-anemone eyes, he might have been a Macedonian king himself, or a Renaissance poet. A stab of envy races through me as Dorelia snuggles up to him and I remember again all I have heard about his prodigious sexual appetites, the many, many conquests. My heartbeat quickens and something akin to fear grows there, when I'm faced with his challenging stare and the feeling that Augustus, after all, is living the life as I am not, and might uncover me as the ridiculous virgin that I am.

'No,' I mutter at once, beginning to wish my little experiment over, adding *sotto voce*, like an insolent schoolboy, 'Although most of Morris's own stuff surely was – probably why the poetry was so dull.'

'What, then?'

'Well, not the idea that the artists of the future will all be those who do common work in the day and have time to compose in the evening – no. And art must always be an individual and unique affair, not "expressing the soul of a community". All I'm suggesting is that the state might endow individuals who show promise with a substantial sum, say, two hundred and fifty pounds a year, in order that they may pursue a life that would otherwise be closed to them.'

Dorelia shifts a little in the boat, crossing one foot over the other so that I am suddenly confronted with her soles: rude and dirty and bare, and this, more than Augustus's hard expression, is what finally silences me.

'I didn't take you for a socialist, Brooke.'

I am pink by now and quite ridiculous. How to extricate myself and prevent him shooting straight to Newnham to make Jane Harrison hoot with laughter about me? 'Well, you knew, of course, that I'm a member of the Cambridge Fabian Society? Although, admittedly, not quite as devout as the Webbs would like me to be, no, nor as interested in economics, it's true, but—'

'He's not a socialist,' Dorelia murmurs in her lazy way. 'He says what he believes will please or provoke you.'

Now my humiliation is complete, and my face flames with a blush of tomato red. Dudley stirs from his drowsy slumber, where he has melted like wax in the sun, unsticks himself from his end of the boat, stands up and offers to take the pole. (I know at once that he has been listening and, in his characteristic, kindly way, hopes to rescue me.) Dudley's moving towards me rocks the boat violently and nearly dunks me in the drink. I'm tempted to leap in anyway, to join Pyramus and David and the others; be free of this scalding torture.

Without waiting for Dudley to take over I drive the pole hard into the water, where it threatens to lodge in the mud and pull me out with it, to dangle, both hands clinging, like a damsel-fly sticking to a reed. We leave the meadows behind and reach the rushing water of the weir at last, which provides a distraction of sorts: Dorelia sits up, pushing her scarf away from her eyes, then calls to the boys once she understands that we must get out, drag the boat over the wooden rollers, and relaunch it to reach the Backs. The boys' splashings and shrieks are temporarily stalled, as they scramble to the water's edge to do our bidding.

So many hands make light work. The boat is dragged over in an instant. Then we are back in the river with a splash, to the accompaniment of many small, excited voices, who remain bobbing in the water.

Now Augustus is explaining to Dorelia and Edie the magical construction of the Mathematical Bridge, and they are readjusting their attitude to the rickety wooden structure and admiring it. I'm tempted to murmur that this is somehow my point. That regardless of age or background, this desire to be an artist surely comes from the same impulse, a very simple one: an overwhelming desire to – *share* or show. 'I saw – I saw,' the artist says, 'a tree against a sky, or a blank wall in the sunlight, and it was so thrilling, so arresting, so particularly itself – that, well, really, I must show you—'

But I say nothing, and hand the pole to Dudley, then stumble across a rocking boat to take up my place in Dudley's vacated section where I hunker down like the bull-terrier Pudsey Dawson after a scolding. Impossible not to be stung by Dorelia's remark. Does she share Henry James's judgement, then, based on nothing more than a glance at my face, that it is possible to deduce I possess no merit in any field of endeavour?

Dudley begins punting in an elegant, smooth rhythm. The boys, tired, suddenly want to clamber into the boat, which they do with much shouting, rocking and tipping, and thoroughly drenching us all.

'I have heard there are some very lovely young women in the Fabian Society,' opines Augustus, when the din dies down. 'I hear H. G. Wells has found it very . . . accommodating.' Closing his eyes again, he settles himself once more among his crowded nest of women and children, while Dudley – with one sympathetic glance at me – guides us skilfully under the next bridge.

I glance up as we slide beneath, to see how the shadows and light on the underside form intricate patterns, like the veins on a leaf.

Naturally enough, I keep this ludicrous, pointless, *poetic* observation to myself.

There is ample work when Mr Brooke and the others leave to go punting. I have to clear the table and, most important, supervise Kittie washing up. Now, although I am the new girl, I have learned something about Kittie. If I don't attend to her she simply makes more work for me later; she has complete want of a system of any sort and you might think she had to pay for water by the pint, so miserly is she with it. Left to herself, she would go on using the same drop – no matter what the colour – to the bitter end. Kittie's mind is on other things. And if her miserly use of water isn't bad enough, her treatment of the teacloths is worse! She doesn't seem to understand that a soiled teacloth is unhealthy and means smeary china. That girl has had no training at all and her home is obviously a poor one.

Yesterday she arrived from an errand at the butcher's in Grantchester with a badge saying *Votes for Women*. A tin badge, with a safety-pin attached. I could scarcely believe it. 'What are you doing with that thing?' I said. 'Take it off this minute and throw it away!' (Kittie does remind me of my sister Betty, with her dreamy ways and her want of good sense.) She looked surprised at my cross tone. In truth, I think she was surprised at how quickly I'd taken charge of things. She carefully took the badge off her coat and slid it into her apron pocket, but she didn't throw it away. 'Where on earth did you get it?' I hissed, as we stood at the basin, wiping the china. 'Surely you'd lose your position here if Mrs Stevenson saw it?'

'I went to Camden Town with my sister Fanny and listened to a woman speaker. Fanny says—'

'Listen, Kittie. Women are destined to *make* voters, rather than be one of them. That's our task in life, not to stand on street corners making a show of ourselves,' I said. This was something Father had told me many times while we stood together by the hives, wiping the bees from the frames with our long sticks of feathers. I thought that Kittie, like Betty, would then fall silent, on account of my greater age and unyielding tone, but to my astonishment she didn't.

'Fanny says we are brave soldiers in the women's army. That the time for talk is over. Action is what we need . . .'

The girl is more stupid than I thought. She pores over the *Daily Mail* every morning, and yesterday she brought in something new, the *Daily Sketch*. She read it all through breakfast, which, given that we are only allowed ten minutes for that meal, seemed to me like a royal waste of time. She read things out to me: women throwing stones and raiding the House of Commons and Mrs Pankhurst smacking a police inspector's face. It made my blood boil. 'Do you seriously think that these grand ladies with their big hats are fighting for the Vote for girls like us?' I asked her. 'Don't you know that, were they ever to win such a thing, it would only be for grand ladies and married ladies and ladies with property? Why should we risk our positions and our good names so that they might vote at every turn against the working man's best interests?'

'Oh, but you're wrong, Nell,' she replied, cool as you like. 'There's many a maid or a girl like us what wants the Vote. Have you not heard of Annie Kenny? Look, here she is, right here, and look how she's lost a finger. That happened in the cotton mills . . .' She pointed at a grubby, blackened picture in the *Daily Sketch*, which I could barely make out.

'Well, that only proves that this Kenny girl is accident prone and hardly to be admired,' I said.

That was yesterday, but it's clear the subject is not forgotten, any more than the badge. I notice that Kittie is fiddling with the place on her apron where the pin was and, to forestall another argument, I say, with a firm tone, 'See that that teacloth is scalded out, Kittie, and do pick another one – otherwise it will never boil clean.'

Mrs Stevenson comes into the scullery; thankfully Kittie falls silent. She hates to be scolded, and within hearing of Mrs Stevenson too. She sets her mouth firm and her brows against me, plunging her hands back into the water with a great splash, practically knocking the bucket off the dresser in her violence.

Our next task is to pickle the day's crop of young walnuts. Kittie is of the opinion that it is now time for a tea-break of our own and a sit-down with our feet up and perhaps to eat up the pieces of abandoned scone, but I soon put her right on that idea. A great basket of walnuts needs doing. I show her how to use only the good vinegar and where to find the jars and muslin. 'And make sure the vinegar completely covers the walnuts . . . and be sure to tie them securely . . . They need a nice dry spot in the larder, up there on the shelf where Lottie won't knock them,' I add.

Kittie complains of a sore throat. She says the smell of vinegar is making her come over queasy. I promise her a piece of flannel soaked in whisky and rubbed with yellow soap to tie round her throat at bedtime, and for a while she accepts this, at last applying herself to her task. Then suddenly, in answer to no remark of mine, she sighs and springs out with 'He's so – he's so fair, isn't he? And so boyish and so – so clever—'

'Who is?'

'Why, Rupert – Mr Brooke – of course!'

I find I can't speak. I am startled by the thump in my chest – my own heart leaping about like a dog when a visitor arrives. What's this about? I ask myself. The Lord knows, you've no interest in the man, Nell Golightly. You're just embarrassed to picture him again, so erect, his arms hugging a bundle of clothes, and that queer, sudden laugh he has, so unexpected but so catching, somehow, like the laugh of a ten-year-old child . . . and as I scold myself, I cannot help remembering the moonlight gleaming on one side of his body, like the shine on polished silver . . .

'Oh!' I sigh, and Kittie glances at me. My hand is stinging and black from the walnut stains. 'I've splashed my scalded palm with vinegar,' I snap, and my eyes prickle with tears. When Kittie turns again to stare nosily at me, I say, 'I find it rather silly that he wanders around barefoot and refuses meat. A boy who is kept by his mother and never did a day's work . . . I wonder if Mother's allowance doesn't run to bacon?'

Kittie shakes her head, reaching for another empty jar. She begins filling it with walnuts, and for the longest time, I believe her angry and refusing to answer me. Then I see with surprise that she is smiling.

'He does have a young face, doesn't he? How old do you think he is? Twenty? Twenty-two?'

'He's here to apply for a fellowship at King's. He's failed his Tripos and that surely makes him—' But I don't know how old that makes him. In truth, I have no idea what this 'Tripos' is, although I've heard Mr Brooke and his friends talk of it. My ignorance must be hidden from Kittie, for it would make her despise me. I know that my authority over her rests on the fact that I am used to shouldering the burdens of a mother. Also that I had two more years' schooling than her.

'Oh, no – not that knife!' I suddenly screech, seeing her about to pick up a steel knife to prise the walnut from its shell. 'The metal gives such a terrible taste – honestly, Kittie, don't you know *anything*?'

Well, that remark does it, and she sets her mouth in a pout and refuses to speak to me for the rest of the afternoon. It is only when Mrs Stevenson's daughter, Lottie, serving another boating party on the lawn, comes running into the kitchen, giggling, that Kittie breaks her sulk.

'He's back! They all are – and on the meadow there was a lady, a lady arrived on a train from Cambridge – another one!

And this one, you wouldn't believe it—' Lottie is saying. She doesn't complete her sentence, ending with a laugh that veers into a shriek. Mrs Stevenson comes into the kitchen then, and Lottie has to wait for her mother to leave before she carries on. 'She's got this hat – enormous! – and she's as tall as a man, but sort of drooping, like a great – like a sort of arum lily, drooping over the field! You can't believe how grand she is. Her nose – like a beak. Like a great parrot!'

'Well, which is it?' I ask. 'An arum lily or a parrot? She can't be both—'

But Lottie ignores my tart tone. 'She lets the children run about her and makes eyes at the painter – she must be another mistress! And the other two wives allow it!'

'Is she coming here for tea?' I ask in alarm, calculating the scones and whether to send Kittie to fetch more milk.

Lottie and Kittie pay no heed to me at all but continue breathlessly. They run about the kitchen muttering and whispering, their voices spilling with excitement.

'She's a lady. A real one. Lady Ottoline, I heard Mr Brooke call her. A lady in fancy dress! Go peep at her, Kittie. Take a look at that great beaky nose! And that long trailing dress in such a lovely shade of green, fanning behind her and soaking up all the mud. It's like a peacock's tail – yes, that's it! She's like a – *peacock*!

'Oh, for goodness' sake, Lottie, how can one person be a flower, a parrot and now a peacock?'

'That hardly matters,' Kittie puts in. 'What I want to know is – why would the artist need a mistress when he already has the lovely wife with the plum-coloured dress and her sister too, for seconds?'

'How many mistresses can one man have?'

Here they put their heads together and wail with laughter. When they set out the tray the cups rattle against their saucers – their bodies shaking with giggles. Lottie can't halt herself.

'And the cart!' she squeaks. 'I heard such a story from Mr Neeve's son. That huge horse they use to drag it slipped and fell down! And the painter – Mr Augustus John – just stares at it, staring and staring at the great brute kicking and struggling, and him just smoking his cigarette, like he hasn't an idea in his head what to do next. Station loafers had to come to the rescue. The man is like – what is he like?'

'A peacock, perhaps? Another kind of bird, or plant?'

But Lottie doesn't hear the sarcasm in my voice. 'He's like one of his own wild boys!' she blurts. 'Honestly, I'm sure he's quite mad. Cyril, Mr Neeve's boy, says the whole of Cambridge is terrified of him.'

And so their twittering continues, and there is nothing I can do to stop them. The surprise of the things they describe keeps hitting my body in waves, and I cannot stop myself wanting to hear more. Can it really be possible that this 'greatest painter', as Mr Brooke described him, has three mistresses? Or even three wives? Why would a grand lady from London want to associate with a raggle-taggle gypsy band in a tent and two caravans? Lottie reports that Lady Ottoline left before tea, finding the meadow sodden and the other wives unfriendly. This makes the pair hoot.

'The other wives unfriendly? *No!*' Kittie howls.

And just at that moment, Mr Brooke steps into the kitchen and murmurs, 'I say – any more whales on toast, girls?' and the two stop dead, curtsy, and then when he is out of the room melt to the floor in a puddle of hysterical laughter.

That decides me. However bad it gets, however often the wicked Mr Brooke wants to parade naked in front of me, I shan't give notice to Mrs Stevenson. Ten shillings a week and a kind mistress is not easily come by. But, most importantly, these two flibbertigibbets need a person of good judgement to knock some sense into them. Lottie might be Mrs Stevenson's daughter but she's worse than Kittie for a lack of good sense. No, it's certain. I'm the only girl to do it.

~

The Fabian Summer School, Wales

This year, Beatrice Webb announces, the university men shall all be put up at Landbedr in the stables and with *several of the horses still in situ*. (There are different rules for the girls.) I am sure she remembers last year when – which of us was it? – Dudley got himself locked out on the balcony with the chamber pot and had to be let in (half naked and the afore-mentioned receptacle all a-slosho with *contents*). She clearly believes the hard floors, natural smells and rudimentary lodgings will upset us delicate Cambridge boys, but little has she reckoned on the Neo-Pagan sensibility I'm encouraging – which positively relishes such privations!

So, that first night we bedded down in our sleeping-bags, tangled our legs in the cotton linings and wormed like caterpillars around in the stables, continuing our usual discussions.

I must confess that it was *not* the absolute urgency of addressing and revising the old Poor Law, dividing it into Health, Old Age and Employment, to demonstrate the different ways that the poor become poor, thus recognising the differing needs of each, no, not quite that.

Rather, James, propping himself up on one elbow, his eyeglasses carefully placed on a shelf next to the horse-feed, opined on the predilections of my own dear brother Alfred, repeating a conversation of two days ago. He said that Podge ('Rupie's darling brother Alfred,' he clarified loudly, for those who might be listening and not know the soubriquet) had plunged into the worm-eaten convention of discussing Sodomy as usual, its uses and abuses. Podge, James claimed, was very sound, and sentimental and, oh, definitely 'Higher', poor chap. But after all – it's surely only in the most special circumstances that copulation is at all tolerable?

We laughed and snuffled inside our bags, like choking insects. So much so that James knocked over the candle and several of us had to prevent a major fire erupting. In the midst of this – us leaping around naked and jumping on sparking bundles of hay – Hugh Daddy Dalton conceived a light lust for James and tried to tickle him gently under the armpits. Poor old James jumped back into his sleeping-bag on the floor but not before Daddy stood over him, waving an immense steaming penis in his face, until James was nearly sick.

This seemed a good moment to turn the conversation to the disgraceful behaviour (Beatrice Webb's opinion) of that 'terrible little Pagan' Amber Reeves. Could it be true that H. G. Wells actually *had* her in her room at Newnham? And, worse still (Dudley, to our left, silently listening, showed by his breathing that he was, of course, actually shocked), that she's now – *carrying his child*? We giggled again, picturing the Marvellous Utopian Scene: Wells sweaty and panting, Amber pert and stranded as an upturned wheelbarrow with its handles stuck in the ground.

Beatrice's interfering in the Wells-Reeves affair, James said, included her spilling the story to Noel Olivier's father, advising him not to let his four handsome daughters run around with Wells. This infuriated me. Gloomily, I stared up at the roof of the stables, at the shifting black shape of a bat. No doubt this would only mean more restrictions for Noel, and my campaign generally thwarted, but I said nothing of this to James, sensing that he was drifting off to sleep.

Sleep was not my mistress that night. Thoughts whirled until dawn slithered her rosy light through the stable windows, and the horses at the other end greeted us with a hot stench of fresh manure. Time already to get up for Swedish drill. I hadn't slept a wink.

The bracing exercises took place on the grass, overlooked by the Welsh sheep-spotted hills, providing us at least with our first glimpse of the dewy Fabian girls. They all looked as if they had slept blissfully without a filthy thought in their heads – even Amber Reeves. (What on earth do the creatures talk about when the lights go out? They actually discuss Fabian ideals, James suggested. Margery Olivier no doubt debates the merits of eugenics in her father's book, how the Germans and Japanese have made such astounding progress in regulating the races. 'Or more likely the exquisite displays of grasses in vases at the house, and the William Morris tiles,' Daddy offered.)

I noticed that the usually at-the-centre-of-things Amber Reeves did not take part in these vigorous jumps but sat instead on the grass, pretending a swollen ankle. Could Daddy Dalton be right, then, about her presumed condition? A sudden image of H. G. Wells twirling his moustache in pride entered my head as I sneaked glances at her, and filled my mouth with a sudden vile taste.

Daddy and some of the other fellows found the alcohol ban intolerable. 'That filthy fake beer, No-Ale, is the only aspect of Fabianism I can't swallow,' he said. Of course, Dudley and I were glad to eschew the whisky our fathers believe makes us manly, and happy to continue the practice wherever we might be, as long as it is not in the presence of those same fathers. Even horribly sober, however, we managed to have a row on that same first night, when Dudders – of course the most devout among us – happened to mention how elucidating he had found the talk that afternoon by the visiting lady, Miss Mary Macarthur, of the Women's Trade Union and Labour League. The one about the appalling conditions of the girl florists in the West End. And then, he added hotly, growing quite pink with the effort, had any of us heard that it was actually Mrs Asquith herself who wanted the florists excluded from the Factory Acts so that they could dress her rooms with flowers until ten o'clock at night?

Well, he had a point, and I found Dudley's earnestness touching.

So I was more than a little angered by James and Hugh Daddy Dalton and the rest for giving him such a ribbing. It was all too familiar – the same dismissive attitude Augustus John had towards *my* socialism. Beatrice Webb has said (apparently) that the egotism of the university men is 'colossal' and we have a long way to go towards proving to her that we might have a serious interest in the subject of Fabianism. But why, I thought, without muttering it out loud to the others, must the two things be mutually exclusive, a sense of humour, or wit, or playfulness, and a genuine socialism. Must we all be cloth sacks and grow our own sandals to be taken seriously?

In the end I was glad to be back in my little room at the Orchard, and to hear my tapioca approaching. Conveyed to me by the lovely Nell, of course. I pretended to be reading – that is, I had Moore's *Principia Ethica* across my lap (the irony would escape her, I think) – so that when she arrived I might nonchalantly ask if she'd read it . . .

She said she had not. I wondered whether to launch into an explanation of its basic tenets, or simply paraphrase Beatrice Webb, who told Dudley a week ago that she thought we 'university men' (she meant us Apostles, I suspect, although she doesn't know there is a distinction) relied upon its dubious morals in a quite childish way.

Still, Nellie showed no interest in learning of Moore's dangerous moral contents, so I accepted the coffee and tapioca she held out to me, taking it from the tray and putting it on the table beside the bed, and amused myself with admiring the way the sunlight fell on a patch of skin at her throat, looking like a spot of lace.

'You've no interest in books, then, Nell? Or – how would the Webbs put it? – in bettering yourself?'

Here she twirled round, and seemed to inspect me for teasing. 'Oh, yes, I do,' she said firmly, after a pause. 'I love books.' And her arm swept around my room at the books tumbling on the floor in piles and on the shelves and propped against the cupboard. Her expression was – what? One of exasperation at all the dusting she has to do? I couldn't read it, but was glad to have detained her.

I took a spoonful of the tapioca from the bowl (considering whether to ask her why she'd brought me the bowl with the chip in the rim, isn't it a little . . . unhygienic?) and *Principia Ethica* slid noisily to the floor and remained simmering there, while Nell opened windows to 'let some fresh air in' and asked if there was anything else I needed.

Bah!

I decided against domestic complaints about the crockery and tried instead to engage her with some talk of the Fabian summer school I'd just been to. Did she know what a Fabian was and how it might differ from a socialist? She did not. Had she been to that part of Wales where the summer school was held? The furthest she'd been was King's Lynn, sir, and to Sheep's Fen, by river. And what about the break-up of the Poor Law of 1834? Did she think it a good idea that the poor should no longer be lumped together and blamed for their ills, but instead, as Beatrice proposes, be divided into separate groups – the sick, the aged, the unemployed – and offered pensions, sanitary care and employment benefits? Indeed, sir, she had never heard of the idea, and had no opinion. I bit my tongue to stop myself enquiring tartly if she didn't feel it might behove her to be better informed, since it was her class that was the most likely to benefit from the efforts of the Fabians.

So I asked if she had even *heard* of Sidney and Beatrice Webb, and it seemed she had, and when I mentioned the novelist Mr H. G. Wells, the recognition flitting across her face made me wonder if she didn't know a little more than she was letting on.

'Does he have a big moustache and – and—'

'A highly disreputable character?'

'I was going to say, did he write *Ann Veronica*?'

'Ah . . . so you have heard of Mr Wells?'

She nodded.

'Of course, dear Beatrice would rather you hadn't read that particular book,' I observed. 'It's entertaining, of course, but he does encourage inaccurate thinking so . . . Mr Wells practises what he preaches, of course. Suggesting that if women were free to act as vilely as some men do, this would magically solve all the problems of the world.'

She gave no reply but glanced pointedly at *Principia Ethica*, the book lying heavily on the floor. If I hadn't known better I might have thought her glance implied a question. Something like: one rule for the boys, is it, and another for the girls?

'I cannot help but agree with Dudley that the devil is in the detail,' I explained hastily. 'That if we really have an eye on progress we should – thrash out the finer points, not just sweep away all that is good and true along with all that is rotten.'

Here I apparently lost her. (The attention span of the British maid is very short.) She shook her head, a dear little movement, and swept at her cheek as if seeking an invisible smut. My tapioca almost finished, the coffee grown cold, I had barely a reason to detain her. I glanced once more at the spot on her throat where the sunlight made a pattern, but a shadow had fallen there. My stock of Subjects to Take Up with the Servant was exhausted.

However, I had not reckoned on the Sex Question coming to my rescue.

'She – she's one of those women who campaign for the Vote, isn't she, this Mrs Webb?' Nellie asked suddenly, as she loaded spoon and bowl back on to the tray.

'Ah . . . you are not a Suffragist, I hope, Nell?'

'No, indeed not!' she returned hotly.

Reading *Ann Veronica* had not corrupted her then. I was immensely relieved.

'I can't think of anything more – *daft*,' she said, 'than throwing stones at the windows of buildings, or stamping things, slogans, on the walls of the House of Commons and getting yourself arrested. I can't see what on earth – I wouldn't take such a risk, sir, myself, if I had a position to think of, or a family waiting for me at home.'

'Indeed. And do you have such a family?'

At last, then, we talked freely, and there was a burst of natural energy in the room as Nellie stood a while longer to describe in the liveliest terms her brothers and sisters, whom she said she missed 'bodily', whatever that meant. It was, though, curiously comforting to be granted this little glimpse, to picture this rural life in the vast flat land of the Fens: the five happy siblings and the bees and flowers and water everywhere, full of fish and fowl caught with a punt-gun – all rather free and fine and marvellous, I couldn't help remarking. She blushed then, and fretted about the time, and said she must return to her duties.

After she'd left I did not at once get up. Talk of Wells (or, rather, thoughts of Wells) breaching those Newnham ramparts (I exaggerate: *walls*, of course) to get at Amber Reeves distracted me, rather. I had a sudden memory of Noel Olivier at Penshurst. Noel Olivier's naked limbs, to be exact. Beatrice's blasted meddling in the Wells-Reeves affair infuriated me afresh when I remembered what Dudley had said about her warning Noel's father not to let his four handsome daughters run around. Damn Beatrice! She's like a bigger, more alarming version of the Ranee, without the Ranee's occasional bouts of charm and financial sustenance.

Still, I did see Noel naked. We bathed by the light of a bicycle lamp propped up in the grass by the edge of the water. Of course we were not alone – although in my mind, we were. A whole bunch of Bedalians – a whole school of them, ha! – was there. And neither could we actually make out one another's naked forms, just white shapes, like the cows at Grantchester Meadows, looming up, ghostly but vivid. We all laughed and dived in the weir. I felt the water-lilies clutching my legs, and that gasping, bracing thrill in my lungs that swimming in cold rivers always produces.

Then when we returned to camp, we sat for a while and I was able to feast on Noel for longer, watching her, again in the bicycle light, near the blazing fire, the river water trickling from her hair down her bare shoulders where her towel had slipped. I stared and stared at those bare shoulders. With such poor light, I couldn't see much: only a few strands of duckweed. The moon rose full and we crawled back into our sleeping-bags and she slept, but I lay awake writing my pathetic little lines, with the vision of her dripping in my mind and she only two tents away.

Wells's emphasis on free love, his conviction that this will be the model for the sexes in future . . . Something about this thought alarms me. The man has said that in order to experiment you must be base. The relationships between men and women are so hemmed in by law that to experiment starts with being damned. Fine sentiment, of course. Intellectually I cannot fault it. But. Is this to be all, then? Are relations between men and women to be reduced to this – to copulation? Will it be the end of love, and of all feelings more holy and beautiful? There is horror for me in that idea and it is this: I don't want my darling Noel to be base. She is a flower in moonlight. She is not childish and befouled like James, full of jokes and phlegm and other disgusting things.

How confusing. It's all very well, but my burdensome virginity remained unlost.

And with this thought another young woman suddenly appeared beneath my window, calling up. Ka Cox. I heard the sound of a bicycle being propped against the wall of the house, and then Ka calling softly, shyly, clearly afraid for others to hear, 'Rupert!'

A stone was thrown before I could push on the window and look out over the hedges. Then I saw her head, wrapped peasant-style in a vivid green scarf, and caught sight of her pince-nez. My mood lifted at once. 'Hello there! I'm still breakfasting – with you in five minutes!'

She beamed up at me, bending to undo some of the tangle in her skirts, which had been tucked into her boots. Thank Heaven! Earnest, dear, horsy Ka, with her matronly bosom, her slightly stooped figure, her serious face and her pince-nez – surely she will work like a charm? My thoughts returned immediately to the Fabian leaflets she was no doubt – in her devoted capacity as Secretary of the Society – delivering. She was more effective than a bracing dip in a cold bath to return a person at once from their lowest to their most elevated thoughts.

'Ka! Such joy to see you!'

The dear thing beamed and beamed.

~

So many books, he has, Mr Brooke. Books sprouting everywhere. I suppose this is how all poets are, or maybe all Varsity men, but it's a wonder. Sometimes I sneak a look at the titles. This makes me sick with ignorance. *A Room with a View* by E. M. Forster. *Montaigne* by somebody called Florio. Piles of copies of the *English Review* magazine. A huge great thing called *The Minority Report of the Poor Law Commission*. How could anyone read such a volume? *Antony and Cleopatra* by William Shakespeare – I recognise that one, of course. The other one I recognise is *The Secret River* by R. Macaulay – this is a brand new book, with flowers down the spine, and in blue ink inside it says, 'To Rupert', so I know this must be the same Miss Macaulay who visited him here at the Orchard. I sneaked a glance inside, but when I read 'the slumberous afternoon was on the slow green river like the burden of a dream' my brain thickened and refused to carry on.

When he asked me, he had no idea how stupid so many books can make a girl feel. I said nothing, knowing how he would laugh – that sudden, high-pitched, girlish blast of laughter he does sometimes – if he knew that the last book I read was *The Book of Cheerfulness* by Flora Klickmann. I was glad – so glad – to have at least read Mr H. G. Wells, although afraid of blushing when I feared he might broach the subject of relations between men and women. I did not venture my opinion of the heroine of that book. That she was a very silly girl indeed to end up in a room alone with a man and not realise what he might think of her.

I wasted a good portion of time in his room and now I have a deal of catching up to do. There's the dusting and the fireplaces, the hateful black-leading to do, then the halls and stairs to be swept, and the boots waiting to be cleaned in the kitchen and, after all that, the lunches for the first guests to start preparing. I can't really understand how I allowed myself to be delayed – after all, he is so *annoying*, and so spoiled, and I always feel he is trying to provoke me somehow, catch me out, make me blush or falter with those questions, put in such a strange way.

After that night, that first night when I saw him naked, returning from his swim in Byron's Pool I have learned that I am a very silly, puritanical girl. He was disappointed, he said, that the lower orders were as bad as the upper ones in this respect. He had thought that a girl raised on bees – birds and bees, he said meaningfully – a girl raised so might be more likely to trade the ' Lilies and Languors of Virtue for the Raptures and Roses of Vice'.

When I did not know how to reply, he said, 'Swinburne, Nell.'

It's this that infuriates me. He speaks in riddles, seeking always to have the advantage. After all, when I told him of my brothers and the eel-hives and the days spent on the mere catching them, I didn't try to trick him with words he didn't know, even though I laughed to myself to hear him describe it as 'such joy and liberation!' and to see from the glow in his face that he was picturing some lazy, playful days of his own rather than the hours of patient work that Edmund and Stanley endure for Sam. I think he is always conscious of the impression he is making, tossing his hair and struggling to hide his real thoughts.

'Life is splendid, Nell, but I wish I could write poetry,' he said, this morning. 'I write very beautiful stories.'

'Do you, sir? Here's your hot milk, and would you like me to bring your slippers?'

'Yes . . . One story I am accomplishing is about a young man who, for various reasons, felt his bookish life vain and wanted to get in touch with Nature. He began by learning to climb trees but, in clambering up an easy fir tree, fell off a low branch six feet above the ground and broke his neck. A short, simple story.'

Then he told me of his recent visit to a place called Penshurst, to surprise some friends of his who were camping there, including one 'very special girl', whose name is Noel Olivier. Her father, he said, is Sir Sydney, as if I should know who that person is. He chatted as I made up the fire in the grate, the morning having a late-summer chill, and so my back was to him, which was a good thing: he couldn't see my expression. He talked of the girl and her three lovely sisters and some strange school called Bedales that the girl attends – *she is a schoolgirl then, younger than me, even!* – a school where, as far as I could understand, nudity and swimming in cold lakes takes the place of book learning.

Well, how am I supposed to reply to that? When the silence between us grew long, and I wondered (with my back to him) if he was awaiting my answer, I decided a safe bet would be to mention that, for myself, I rather like the nice Mr Ward (Kittie calls him Baldy, on account of his bald pate, though we know his Christian name is Dudley) and the sensible Miss Gwen Darwin. I remarked that it would probably be a good thing if he spent more time with a lady like Miss Darwin, for any lady who has the good sense to put a strip of braid around her skirt in order to catch the mud in a place like this is a very resourceful lady indeed. There was a long pause after I said this, then a sudden snuffle of loud laughter. I turned round.

'How on earth did the maid get so familiar?' he said, smiling broadly at me.

I realised at once I had overstepped my place and clapped a hand to my mouth. 'I'm sorry, I— It's in my nature to be quick to judge,' I murmured, and then could think of nothing more to add because the bald truth of this hung in the air between us.

He was still in bed at this point, but he sat up and stared straight at me, with the look of someone about to deliver a speech. 'Parents, now: you kiss them sometimes, and send for them when you're ill, because they're useful and they like it; and you give them mild books to read, just strong enough to make them think they're a little shocked, but not much, so they can think they're keeping up with the times. Oh, you ought to be very kind to them, make little jokes for them, and keep them awake in the evening, if possible. But never, never let them be intimate and confidential because they can't understand, and it only makes them miserable. Perhaps I should apply the same rule to you, Nell.'

'Oh, I truly am sorry, sir, if I spoke out of turn.'

'I'm joking Nellie. I like your . . . spirit. It reminds me of home. Ha! Can you imagine that? You remind me of Mother. Calmness and firmness are no good with her. She's always ever so much calmer and firmer than I could ever be . . .'

I didn't know how to answer this, except to say that a mother is a dear thing; and that both my parents are dead. He gave me a queer look, then, and returned to his reading.

Was I dismissed? I stood for a moment, wondering, and then turned sharply on my heels, without waiting to hear.

It is not me who is familiar, I was thinking, but quite the other way round. *He* is easy with me in that way of men who have lived their whole life with servants: we're invisible to them most of the time, except when they need us. I picked up the breakfast things and left the room, asking stiffly if I could do anything more for him (to which he muttered something I didn't choose to hear). I left without bidding him good morning.

~

This morning I have received something vile and unwelcome. Seven pages of damn plain speaking from the eldest Olivier girl, Big Sister Margery. Any fond memories I have of the afore-mentioned with her brown mane seductively awry, romping on the grass at Penshurst camp, kicking up her skirts and holding Noel in a headlock worthy of any man dissolved at once. How mistaken I was about her.

Margery Olivier, I've decided, cannot possibly be made of the same flesh and blood as Noel – she must be a witch, sent by the Ranee to torture me. The letter was brought by Nellie, cheerily oblivious to its contents, plopping it down with my breakfast milk and apple, and as the door closed behind her, the letter cast a dark shadow – like a long, pointed finger – in my sunny bedroom.

I (not as an individual, but as a Young Man) am now, it seems, to be entirely shut out of Noel's existence. It's Margery's New Educational Scheme. Love, for a woman, she says, destroys everything else. It fills her whole life, stops her developing intellectually, absorbs her. 'You'll see what I mean if you look at a woman who married young,' she grimly adds. 'No woman should marry before twenty-six or -seven.' (That's ten more years of waiting, then! An ugly, dry decade!) 'Do be sensible,' Margery pleads. 'She is so young – you are so young . . .' All about my 'wild writing' and how I must 'look ahead' and a thousand things.

On reading it, I leap from bed and call Nellie back. 'Nell, Nell – come here!'

'What is it? Ooh, I forgot the honey!'

'No, not that, child. I need your opinion on something.'

I wind the bed sheets round my torso – conscious of the girl's blushes – and close the bedroom door behind me. Waving the letter as if Nellie had read the entire blazing sermon, I start at once: 'Do you think Love destroys a woman? Finishes her off?'

'I'm not sure what you mean—'

'Margery Olivier has a bloody theory. No woman should marry before twenty-six or -seven – marriage, or rather love, ends a girl's life, stifling her, finishing off her intellectual development, her – education, or— Oh, I'm not sure I understand at all.'

'Well.' The maid pauses, and I realise, with a furious stab, that she is seriously contemplating this theory.

'The logical outcome,' I interject quickly, 'is that one must only marry the quite poor, unimportant people who don't matter being spoiled, and leave the splendid ones untouched!'

'Yes, I see. But I think there might well be a grain of truth in the idea that— You see, when I think of my dear mother, or my sisters, well, of course we read many penny books where love and marriage bring us the greatest happiness, and the popular songs say the same thing, but then when we take the temperature of our own hearts, or look at the lives of those girls around us—'

'Surely, Nell, for *every* human being, male or female, love *is* the greatest thing? Don't, *please*, tell me you're going to agree with Margery. We must thunder against such mediocrity! Make a protest against idiocy and wickedness – not show a calm Christian spirit! Such a view is all reasonableness and cowardice and calmness – and how *evil* it is to let things slide and not snatch at opportunities!'

Staring at Nellie, her violet eyes fixed anxiously on my face,

I'm aware suddenly that I may be shouting, and that she appears to be a little unnerved. I let my hands swing to my sides and compose myself. The truth is, I feel mistrustful of myself, and full of fear and despair. A shadow of my old fears, the thoughts I have at sharing Dick's . . . instability, comes back to me. It's the tone of Margery's letter. 'Wait! Wait! She's so reasonable about you now. Let her remain so,' Margery says. *That* is painful. Is Noel Olivier reasonable about me? To have it rubbed in so. Oh, of course, I am delighted. Should I wave a hat with pallid enthusiasm, and say in a high voice: Hurray, hurray! Just what she should be – reasonable about me! Excellent, excellent!

'I'm sorry, Nellie.' I collapse on to the bed. 'I find it hard to be reasonable. It's not an emotion I admire, to be exact. It's like fondness. Throw your fond in a pond! Give me love, I say, or nothing!'

The girl's expression is unreadable. She has a practised, clever way of glancing at the door, which tells me in no uncertain terms that she is thinking of her duties, without appearing rude, or making any reference to them.

'Of course, of course. You must attend to your – your bees, is it? I see that you agree in some hideous way with Margery's diagnosis. What part of your marvellous intellectual development you believe is arrested by falling in love I can't quite imagine. I can take the wider view . . .'

There then flits over her face something that, for want of a better word, I might describe as anger. It certainly amuses me to see it and how she struggles not to show it. It makes me like her more fervently. I struggle in exactly the same way in conversations with Mother!

('I prefer Miss Ka Cox,' the Ranee says, at Rugby, rightly noting that the serious Ka has wrists very thick and an unusual downturned expression in her mouth, and rather poor posture, and is therefore unlikely to seduce me. 'I can't understand what you see in these Oliviers. They are pretty, I suppose, but not at all clever; they're shocking flirts and their manners are disgraceful.' *Mother, why do you insist on answering your own questions so elegantly?* What does she imagine the Olivier girls will do, left to their own devices? Kiss the rural milkman and eat bread without butter? But, then, if I should put in a good word for Gwen, I know how she will immediately swing the other way utterly, and say, 'I can't understand at all what you see in Miss Darwin. She's not pretty, or attractive. On the whole I prefer the Oliviers; at least they are good-looking.'

Mother's skill has always been in her colossal, enormous *steadfastness of purpose*. Didn't she once say that that was the quality she prized most in a woman? I'm sure she wrote it in some Christmas book. That in a man it would be moral fortitude or some such. Perhaps I should tell Mother about James. That would really give her Cause to be Anxious about Rupert's Friends. Poor James. If only I could tear out the heart of Noel with my teeth, and replace it with the heart of the bespectacled James Strachey, who – thank God – is not *reasonable* in the least about me.)

I finish my milk and dismiss Nellie with – I hope – a kindly nod. (Can a nod be kindly?) Her little flare-up will soon pass. The lucky girl has no idea what bliss it is to receive post only once a week, as she does. That bloody letter has ruined my day.

~

And then just when I think I have grown used to his habits, something happens that is so unexpected, so unlooked-for, that I no longer know if I'm coming or going, or which way is up.

It was only yesterday that I said to Kittie I knew his habits better than a mother. Bathing every evening, breakfast on the lawn or in his bedroom, young men and women always calling up to the window or throwing a pebble to wake him; and a pencil and a book in his hand, and somehow, it appears, he manages to be a scholar too. He mostly takes breakfast in his room. As he has sworn off meat, he breakfasts on coddled eggs, hot milk, some chopped apple or pear and a cup of tea with honey.

His room, when I enter it at seven o'clock, has that smell I know so well from old days with my brothers and Father. The warm salty smell of a man sleeping. It must be the loss of Father that makes the smell bring a lurch in my heart.

I am careful always to be brisk in my tone and not to sound sleepy myself, or anything at all that isn't fitting. Wide awake and alert, that's me. I open the curtains, my back to the bed, give him time to bestir himself. I have learned the trick to opening the window in this room now: a brutal push upwards. This admits noises from outside. Birdsong, horses clopping past, sometimes a visitor calling up to him, and the ring of a bicycle bell.

When Mr Brooke stirs, there are always more books, letters and papers next to his pillow, which tumble to the floor. Many's the time I've discovered inky-stained pillows. (I was wrong to abandon the pillow shams: they make a good disguise for the limits of the laundry soap.) Then he will prop himself up on one elbow and begin sipping at the milk (not coffee any longer, he's decided to swear off that, too) and say daft things, things like: 'Women are bloody, Nell. I pray you remain a child and never become one.'

After my blurting out my opinion on Miss Darwin, I've taught myself to pause, count to ten, hold my tongue. Does he seriously think of me as a child? He has a way of addressing grown women as 'child' – I have heard him do it more than once. Perhaps he doesn't mean to include me in the sweep of the insult; maybe he thinks I'm not human?

He loves his honey. Spoonful after spoonful into the milk. He balances the pot on the saucer of the cup, dripping sticky strands all over his mattress. And so today, this morning, I'm not completely surprised when he makes his request. Mightn't I take him out with me, show him the hives?

'Well, see, I don't know if I ought.'

'You are going out to inspect them?'

'Yes. Mr Neeve says there will be showers tomorrow so today is best—'

'Splendid!' He springs from the bed with alarming speed.

'If you come with me you must wear the veil and gloves, sir, as the bees are not – they don't rightly know you. They are more likely to sting a stranger.'

He finds the thought funny. He wonders why he should wear a veil when the maid 'goes naked'. I ignore this and tell him that the bees know me well and wouldn't dream of stinging me. 'Bluster!' he says, laughing, reaching for his razor and the bowl of hot water I've brought . . . 'And do drop this "sir" business, Nell, there's a girl. Call me Rupert, or Chawner, if you prefer – now, there's a name to conjure with. What was Mother thinking, eh?'

And so, later in the morning, he joins me and that's when it happens. We're in the ramshackle gardens of the Old Vicarage next door, him dressed in the white veil that belonged to Father, over a hat he has borrowed from Mr Neeve: *Rupert*, it seems, doesn't possess one. He is also wearing shoes for once, but no socks. I tie the gloves for him at the wrists so the bees can't creep inside them. I have to lift his hands in mine to do this, and he doesn't raise his eyes so that I see his eyelashes resting on his cheeks and notice that they are as long as the legs on a raft spider.

His student friend comes to laugh at him: the dark, beaky Frenchman staying at the Old Vicarage, Jacques. This friend stands close to Rupert and murmurs something odd, something like 'Is this your lady under ze lamp-post?' with his strange accent and plum-coloured voice, but as I can't understand, and since they speak as if I'm invisible, I continue with the pretence that I'm deaf too.

The garden stretches down to the mill stream, where the big chestnuts trail their branches in the water, and Mr Neeve has a full number of modern hives, the square-box sort with frames, placed to face the morning sun and encourage the bees to begin their work early. It makes me sorry to see these modern hives – they have so little beauty compared to the straw skeps that Father always used and that the eel man Sam makes for us, with their pointed tops and fat bellies, the shape of giant acorn cups.

And not just the hives but the garden, too, is the sort that Father would have despaired of: wild, with such an unkempt, dense thicket of trees and bushes at the bottom. There is a strange Gothic ruin there that Rupert laughs at and says is not Gothic at all, but a sham. I love the sunny part of the garden where the bees live, the part of the Old Vicarage that borders on to the apple and quince trees of the orchard, but at the bottom end near the river the air is damp and suffocating, and the huge trees smothered in ivy make me think of Sleeping Beauty, and shudder.

Mr Raverat doesn't want to stay, he says he is 'very much afraid' of being stung, and I haven't another veil and gloves so he says he has a breakfast meeting at King's, and will see Rupert later, at the railway station in Cambridge, for aren't they catching the same train? The eleven-thirty? He strides back towards the house, wishing us luck.

'He was awfully impressed, wasn't he?' Rupert says childishly, when he's gone.

I shrug.

'I mean, about the not-wearing-a-veil part. He likes a spirited girl, does Raverat. Got a soft spot for Ka Cox, as a matter of fact.'

And so we are left alone, in the sticky morning heat, while I stuff the smoker with wood shavings and Rupert watches me light it. And then leans forward and whispers, sucking the fabric of his veil into his mouth as he does, 'I think you're a rotten girl, Nellie Golightly. Perhaps you actually want to be stung.'

This remark is so surprising that I drop the smoker and blush furiously.

We both dive to pick it up. Now there is a sense around us of something very troubling indeed. The bees are so sensitive, they will pick it up at once. How can I tell him? Bees know our feelings before we know them ourselves. They know the heat, the cool, every flavour of human emotion. Father taught me that. 'Stand your ground, girl. You keep calm, keep a steady hand,' he taught me. None could handle them like me. Father! Where are you now when I need you? The bees hum round us like a gathering storm. And Rupert is in danger of sending them wild with his flirtation – yes, there's no other word for it. At last I see that this is what he has been doing, that this is what his teasing amounts to.

'It makes the bees out of humour when you do that,' I suddenly say, and watch his face behind the white material, watch his big blue eyes widen naughtily and then his slow smile, starting first with the downward turn of his mouth, then lifting upwards slightly, his breath drawing in the veil. That handsome mouth with its pouty bottom lip. I'm done for. I've only made matters a million times worse.

I call upon all my strength, all my good, sensible nature, and load the smoker afresh, then light it with a trembling hand. Rupert is standing very close to me. I move ever so slightly away, to where I can no longer smell the shaving cream and Wrights Coal Tar Soap smell of him, and concentrate on pointing the smoker towards the hives, and at once the bees start to gather their store of honey together and make ready to leave, with one or two doing their bee dance, signalling to the others. When the smell of burning wood fills our nostrils and the soft brown cloud of bees has drifted off, their noise rolling and peaking as they pass us, like a wave cresting, I pull out some of the frames, and show Rupert with trembling hands how to scrape off the remaining bees, the ones clinging to the frames, gently, using a wand of feathers.

'Not so hard – Rupert. We only mean to scatter them, not kill them.'

It is the first time I've said his name. I know without looking up that the word has drawn him like a hook and that he is staring straight at me. I can tell from the way the bees huddle in the corner of their frames like gathering moss, deep and brown and heaving, that some power from him is transmitting itself to me, to the very air around us. Even the sweetest creature on this earth can be dangerous, Father used to say, if you make it buzz too hard. Father, Father – you were never here to teach me. What do I do now?

The bees always know best, Father would say.

I put out a shaking hand to the frames and point up a fat bulge in the honeycomb.

I try to steady my voice: 'Look, here is one threatening to become a queen. We must nip that in the bud right away . . . There can only ever be one queen.' I show him how to do it, and he is shocked, he says, to see me so heartless.

He wants to know if there is 'a royal line', and I explain there is no such thing, that the egg used to create a queen is the same as the one used to create an ordinary worker. 'Fascinating . . .' he says softly.

'The queen controls the temper of the hive. A gentle queen means a gentle hive. These are good bees, but more . . . a little more unsettled . . . than my own hives at home.'

He has become silent at last, still and concentrated. The danger, the noise of the humming, the sense of being surrounded and threatened, has calmed him. He is listening to them at last, I think. He likes the work, to see the honey in its fresh form, so brown and treacly, sealed with the waxy capping, and the threads of yellow liquid shining through like sunlight.

He stands, arms folded and watching, while I load the wheelbarrow with the wooden frames, bulging with the weight of honey. But still he will not drop his look, his eyes so bold, lying softly on my skin, on my bare arms and hands, like something with a tickling, stealthy creep. Perhaps it's this: perhaps it's that when I work with Mr Neeve, he's full of commands and has never allowed this drowsy bee-humming silence to take hold of us like this; whatever it is, my eyes are suddenly glazed with tears and the ghost of Father appears in front of me, while I step quietly to one side, to watch.

A young man in Father's clothes, wearing Father's borrowed veil and gloves, is standing in an old, rambling garden, and staring hotly at me. Father steps to one side and disappears. Bees purr between us. The young man steps forward and lifts his white veil, moving his face towards mine. He pulls me towards him. The movement is forceful, not gentle. He angles his head, like a bird. Using his hand, he tilts my chin up to his mouth and moves towards me. The bees sizzle around us, like a pan of fat on the stove. I close my eyes at once. I feel the hardness of Rupert's teeth with my tongue. I open my mouth a little, not knowing what else to do. Flakes of sunlight flutter like confetti on my eyelids.

And that is it. He kisses me in the Old Vicarage garden and I disappear for a moment. Then I return, alert to the anger all around me. The bees. A bee heading straight for Rupert. Bees are quick to smell opportunity. 'You should never lift your veil!' I say nervously. 'Be still now. No, don't move – don't run! They will chase you in a bee-line, straight as an arrow!'

Now he is mine to rescue. I tell him to stay calm. He wants to put the veil back, but it is too late (much too late, I think). One bee is on his chin, edging up towards his mouth. The terror in his eyes is quite real. I see by the wildness in his look that he wants to flap and scream and run about but puts his trust in me, like a small boy, like one of my brothers. It is this, finally, that is my undoing. I could have held off, I reckon, if it weren't for this. His teasing, his naughtiness, his insults, his demands, his flirting. Even the sight of him naked as the day he was born. I could resist them all, but not that one small thing. A glimpse of the boy.

'I say!' Rupert shouts, and slaps at his mouth. The bee strikes.

With this one gesture, thousands of bees await instruction, trembling around us like an electric storm. I talk softly to them. The bees are hot and not persuaded. Haven't I been a good girl? Haven't *I* treated them well? What's one little accident between friends? I listen intently, and sniff at the air, which smells of smoke, and hear Rupert holding his breath.

Then the note in the air drops, just one notch, and that is our sign. Quickly I fasten Rupert's veil at his neck, and he, gasping and laughing quietly, allows himself to be led back to the house.

'My word!' he crows, the moment we are in the safety of the scullery at the Orchard, with his veil off. 'My word! What a thing! Who would have thought it? The bees – do your bidding.'

I pick the sting out of the spot at the corner of his mouth with my nails, dab honey on the sore place and bid him under my breath to be quiet. He should thank his lucky stars that it was just the one bee, I say, that took it into its head to misbehave. His lip is a little swollen, but that's to be expected.

This tickles him, making him hoot a little. 'Just the one! Yes, indeed, thank the Lord, eh, Nell, that it was just one outrageously naughty bee that – transgressed!'

I don't know what he finds so funny. My fondness for him of a minute ago melts. Why does he never take things seriously? Well, I'm not one of his Cambridge girls who only knows her books and bicycles; he needn't think he can take liberties with me! The bees showed him that. Nell Golightly might be just a maid from Prickwillow, but she can face facts and she won't be anybody's fool.

I thought that would put an end to it, cap it tight, the feelings, I really did. But that night, just as I am undressing for bed, Kittie already snoring in her place by the wall, the oddest memory strikes me and my heart cracks open again like a walnut shell. Father, at the front step, in the morning, polishing my boots before school. He has one hand inside the little boot and the ground is all frost and ice, and he is rubbing with the cloth and the tiny speck of polish, shining the leather until he can see his face, his old, tired face reflected in it. He did this every morning. He never wanted me to go to school. He didn't think I'd amount to anything. But this was his one austere service, year on year. Offered to me wordlessly, and accepted without thanks.

I remember it now, as the yeasty heat of Kittie in the bed rises up to me. I remember Father's tongue peeping at the corner of his mouth, the flecks of black polish on his hand, his concentration. 'Father – where are you?' I want to ask. I picture him from the dream I had of him, the night he died, the dream of him leaving me, getting up from his chair. Looking straight at me.

Father – I want to tell you something. I remember what you did and I want to say thank you. Maybe it wasn't much, by some people's standards, but I want to tell you something, something I never thought I would. It was enough. I know how to do it. How to love.

~

I have been thinking this morning of Denham. He has gone now. The sheets are a frightful mess, and I have no idea how to get them clean. I hear a cock crowing, over and over, but Nellie isn't up yet and I've no more clean water. So I sit on the bed with my knees drawn up to my chest, and think of him, and smile to myself.

He was lustful, immoral, affectionate and delightful . . . But I was never in the slightest degree in love with him. I was glad to get him to come and stay with me at the Orchard. I came back late that Saturday night. Nothing was formulated in my mind. I found him asleep in front of the fire, at one forty-five. I took him up to his bed – he was very like a child when he was sleepy – and lay down on it. We hugged, and my fingers wandered a little. His skin was always very smooth. I had, I remember, a vast erection. He dropped off to sleep in my arms. I stole away to my own room and lay in bed thinking – my head full of tiredness and my mouth of the taste of tea and whales, as usual.

I decided, almost quite consciously, I *would* put the thing through next night. You see, I didn't at all know how he would take it. But I wanted to have some fun and still more to see what it was *like*, and to do away with the shame (as I was taught it was) of being a virgin. At length, I thought, I shall know something of all that James and Norton and Maynard and Lytton know and hold over me.

Of course, I *said* nothing. Next evening, we talked long in front of the sitting-room fire. My head was on his knees, after a bit. We discussed Sodomy. He said he, finally, thought it was wrong . . . We got undressed there, as it was warm. Flesh is exciting, in firelight. You must remember that *openly* we were nothing to each other – less, even, than in 1906. About what one is with Bunny (who so resembles Denham). Oh, quite distant!

Again we went up to his room. He got into bed. I sat on it and talked. Then I lay on it. Then we put the light out and talked in the dark. I complained of the cold, and so got under the eiderdown. My brain was, I remember, almost all through, absolutely calm and indifferent, observing progress and mapping out the next step. Of course, I had planned the general scheme beforehand.

I was still cold. He wasn't. 'Of course not, you're in bed!'

'Well, then, you get right in, too.'

I made him ask me – oh! without difficulty! I got right in. Our arms went round each other. An adventure! I kept thinking: And was horribly detached.

We stirred and pressed. The tides seemed to wax . . . At the right moment I, as planned, said, 'Come into my room, it's better there . . .' I suppose he knew what I meant. Anyhow he followed me. In that larger bed it was cold; we clung together. Intentions became plain; but still nothing was said. I broke away a second, as the dance began, to slip my pyjamas. His was the woman's part throughout. I had to make him take his off – do it for him. Then it was purely body to body – my first, you know!

I was still a little frightened of his, at any too-sudden step, bolting; and he, I suppose, was shy. We kissed very little, as far as I can remember, face to face. And I only rarely handled his penis. Mine he touched once with his fingers, and that made me shiver so much I think he was frightened. But, with alternate stirrings, and still pressures, we mounted. My right hand got hold of the left half of his bottom, clutched it, and pressed his body into me. The smell of sweat began to be noticeable. At length we took to rolling to and fro over each other, in the excitement. Quite calm things, I remember, were passing through my brain: 'The Elizabethan joke "The Dance of the Sheets" has, then, something in it.' 'I hope his erection is all right' . . . and so on. I thought of him entirely in the third person. At length the waves grew more terrific: my control of the situation was over; I treated him with the utmost violence, to which he more quietly, but incessantly, responded. Half under him and half over, I came off. I think he came off at the same time, but of that I have never been sure. A silent moment, and then he slipped away to his room, carrying his pyjamas. We wished each other 'Good night'. It was between four and five in the morning.

I lit a candle after he had gone. There was a dreadful mess on the bed. I wiped it as clean as I could and left the place exposed to the air, to dry. I sat on the lowest part of the bed, a blanket round me, and stared at the wall, and thought. I thought of innumerable things, that this was all; that the boasted jump from virginity to Knowledge seemed a very tiny affair, after all; that I hoped Denham, for whom I felt great tenderness, was sleeping. My thoughts went backward and forward, I unexcitedly reviewed my whole life, and indeed the whole universe. I was tired, and rather pleased with myself, and a little bleak . . . We had said scarcely anything to each other. I felt sad at the thought he was perhaps hurt and angry, and wouldn't ever want to see me again.

And so I have Begun, and at last have 'copulated' with someone, and how surprising that it should be Denham Russell-Smith (but how much easier to find a willing *boy* than a willing girl and to feel a curious private tie with Denham himself). Here I am now – it is greyly daylight and I'm left with the chief worry of the sheets. Oh, the horrors of life with servants: how much they know about the life of the body that we'd rather keep from everyone, even ourselves. The contents of the chamber pot, the state of the sheets and our underwear, and a dozen other indignities I dread to consider. Well, I've done my best and scrubbed and scrubbed, but let us hope that for once the dear dark Nellie slept peacefully throughout, and comes to an entirely innocent conclusion . . . if such a thing is at all possible.

Two

January 1910

'It is not a question of either getting to Utopia in the year 2,000 or not. There'll be so much good then, and so much evil . . . The whole machinery of life, and the minds of every class and kind of man, change beyond recognition every generation. I don't know that "Progress" is certain. All I know is that change is. These solid, solemn, provincials, and old maids, and business men, and all the immovable system of things I see around me will vanish like smoke. All this present overwhelming reality will be as dead and odd and fantastic as crinolines or "a dish of tay". Something will be in its place, inevitably. And what that something will be, depends on me.'

Rupert Brooke, letter to Ben Keeling

Rupert's father is ill. He has gone to his mother's home to be with her and there he has been for days now. I can't quite picture the home he describes because it seems his mother lives in the school, the same one in Rugby that he went to, and no school I have ever been inside could be a place where anyone could live. It is a school full of 'charming boys', Rupert says. A charming boy was staying with him in October last year, a boy from his old school called Denham Russell-Smith.

I have heard of such things. That is, I didn't know that I knew but that night, coming late and tired to bed, after staying up to finish the washing-up and put away all the plates, I saw candlelight flickering under the door, heard the bed squeaking in Rupert's room. An unmistakable sound, and a giggle too. I stopped dead on the landing – I remember asking myself, Was there a girl with him earlier in the day? I was surprised to find myself trembling and a hot, fierce, stabbing feeling shooting through my body. It was a relief at first when I thought, No, only that young man, the smiling, jug-eared, bouncing sort of man, the one who had been at school with Rupert and turned up unexpectedly. He was like a friendly Labrador, bouncing and cheery, and Rupert said casually that Denham was an old friend and going to be staying in the Orchard and would I mind awfully making up a bed in the little box-room that was not often used?

I had done this gladly, so why, then, were the two of them now in Rupert's room, and why were the bed-springs squeaking like that, in such an unmistakable, rhythmic way?

So I stood there, trembling, fixed to the floor like a blob of wax, and I tried to move away and I tried not to listen, because it made my heart twist so, and then as the grunts and squeaks rose, my hands flew to my ears and I suddenly managed to wrench myself away and ran to my room and flung myself face first into my pillow and sobbed and sobbed, a choking, stifling kind of sob, because Kittie was sleeping her log-like sleep beside me and if she woke she would ask unbearable questions.

In the morning Rupert wasn't there for his breakfast, and neither was the boy Denham. He had already left, taking his bicycle with him. I knocked on Rupert's bedroom door, but there was no reply, so I went in. The sheets had been stripped and heaped on the floor. My first thought was to glance behind me at the open door, and when I was sure that no one was there, I closed it. It was a grim, cold girl who glanced at their bloodied stains, not the wretched, wild-hearted girl of last night. On waking I had gathered up my old self and tried to steel myself, so here I was: facing those hard facts yet again. Such a silly effort Rupert had made to scrub them. My shock on seeing those sheets sprang my body hot first, then cold. It was one thing to hear sounds, and wonder and imagine. Another to see such stark evidence. I sat on his stripped bed and, once again, tears fell.

I tried to say to myself, Nellie, so it is. Give up your silly day-dreams and admit that not only is he not for you he's not for *any girl*.

I don't think I persuaded myself. The way he kissed me out there among the bees, the way he looked at me as if he knew me, really saw me and knew me, Nell, the girl I am, kept floating back to my mind; and then I felt such a rising pain that I almost ran to the garden in fear of vomiting. How could it be so? What made a man – do something like that? My poor education in such matters and my lack of anyone to ask meant that all day I went about my duties in a state of punishing bewilderment. Mrs Stevenson asking more than once, and not with a smile, if I was sleep-walking. The only thing I was grateful for was that

Rupert was nowhere to be seen. I did not have to bump into him, nor face him, until I'd laundered the sheets and left them to flap in the weak autumnal sunlight while I placed clean ones on his bed and a whole day had passed.

There was no mistaking the gratitude and embarrassment in Rupert's eyes when he did finally pass me and I could not see how it could ever be easy between us again. First there was the problem of the kiss. And then the worse one of my knowledge of his shame and him knowing that I knew. What could be said? I felt dreadfully sorry for him; sorry for his sickness, too – how much shame and misery it must bring him I could hardly fathom. Truth be told, I struggled to accept that such a *tendency* exists, and I didn't want to know any more about it than had already been forced into my thoughts.

That was months ago, now, we've had a whole general election and the government nearly voted out, then in again, since then.

I took to my work and did it with such vigour that Mrs Stevenson made me chief among the girls, and rewarded me with an extra shilling a week. And then in January, Rupert's father, a master at his old school, was sick, and so he's gone to Rugby to be with him, and I won't see him for weeks on end, and I've vowed to put him out of my mind. His kiss – I told myself it must have been some sort of experiment. Perhaps he'd never kissed a girl before. But then, confusingly, he always spoke as if he felt great affection for Noel Olivier ... Hadn't he ever kissed her? Was it all a sham? Maybe he wanted to know if kissing me would, if it wouldn't – what's the word? – disgust him too much? (And did it disgust him, I wonder, for how could I tell? The feel of his mouth, and the hardness of his teeth, and the warmth and the feel of his little tongue are vivid with me just the same.)

There was only Kittie to talk to about my discovery, and I didn't dare. She did ask me several times, in a leading sort of way, why was I so pale, and was I pining after somebody? But for all her chatter and sweetness, I didn't know if I could trust her. And this morning, waking up at six, I find my doubts are founded. Because something dreadful has happened. Kittie has gone.

The place where her hot snuffling shape usually is is flat, with the blue counterpane smoothed over it. Now first I think, Well, fancy that! Kittie up first, and maybe making up the fire in the kitchen . . . So I tiptoe downstairs, pulling on an old sweater over my uniform, looking forward to the warmth. But, no, she's not in the kitchen, nor nowhere to be found. And when I run back to our room, I discover that her things are all gone – the little brown bag she arrived with, the skirts, the blouses, the combs and pins for her hair, the tiny bottle of Mischief she so loved. Only her uniform remains: when I peep under the bed, there it is, stuffed in a dusty corner.

Mrs Stevenson is speechless with fury when I tell her. She only paid us last night, and Kittie must have taken her wages and left in the early hours of this morning, while we all slept.

'But where can she have gone?' Lottie asks, casting her eyes on the larder, where the tins and bottles have been taken from the shelves in readiness for 'a thorough set-to with the mop and scrubbing brush', which now she will have to do alone.

'Oh, there's no doubt where the silly girl has gone. Wasn't she always talking about it? Wasn't she always poring over the paper and listening to those silly speeches? What did she say yesterday? She was reading the paper about Lady Constance Lytton disguising herself as a seamstress to prove that working women were treated differently by gaolers—'

'I don't understand . . .' wails Lottie, stupidly.

'She must have caught the train from Cambridge to London,' I say. Understanding is dawning on me, too. 'She has gone to offer her services to the Suffragists.'

'And for what, for what?' Mrs Stevenson keeps repeating, gazing in despair at the unwashed pots and pans and the piles of tins removed from the larder and stacked on the kitchen floor. 'So she can end up in prison, and starving herself, so that women might – what? Might put a cross on a piece of paper that makes not a hap'orth of difference to any of our lives . . . or behave in vile ways and ruin the girl's chances of ever finding a husband!'

Mrs Stevenson's angry words ring round the kitchen. Lottie bursts into tears. 'Poor Kittie!' she says. I glance sharply at her. Why is her voice full of such doom-mongering horror? Kittie's not dead.

'Well, no point standing around, Lottie. Let's get started on the larder. Fetch me a bucket of water,' I say brusquely, hoping to starch her up some. In truth, I'm angry too. I suddenly remember Kittie's look as she was reading the paper yesterday morning, the hot way she insisted 'See, Nellie – you're wrong. The Suffragists *do* care that there should be no distinction between us and them. Look at Lady Constance Lytton! Disguising herself as Jane Wharton to show that prison guards treated her roughly when they thought she was a poor working girl—' and pressing her finger down on the paper to show me the article. I didn't trouble to read it. I told her to get on with her task. Now I wish I'd read the look in her eyes a little better, seen what she was about.

Rupert said once to Miss Darwin that something that never ceased to amaze him was the respect women had for men, even hopeless men, as if the men had the same power over them that they are said to have over horses or, indeed, as if women see men as bigger than they truly are. That was a day in summer, and as he was saying it, Kittie was bringing over the dish of strawberries. I know she heard him, and I noticed how her hands trembled as she placed the bowl in front of him. Because – this is the ridiculous bit – for all her hot talk, Kittie was sweet on him, and definitely thought of him in exactly that way. For sure, that's the real problem between men and women. That we don't see one another in the proper way – that women do reflect men back at twice their natural size.

Well, there's nothing for it but to get on. Lottie sets to at last with the bucket and mop, and I light the stove in the kitchen, ready for the first batch of scones. The linoleum is icy beneath my feet so I make haste to get the coals burning – taking care not to smudge the stove's gleaming surfaces, after Kittie and I spent most of last night black-leading it, at Mrs Stevenson's request. Poor Kittie, I think with a stab, seeing the black-leading. All that horrible work for nothing.

Then I put my shoes on and run over to the Old Vicarage gardens to check the bees before breakfast. There is a crusty frost underfoot and the trees in the orchard are stripped and ghostly in the green morning. Once Mr Pudsey Dawson makes me squeal by appearing from behind one of them in the early-morning fog exactly like a green ghost. The bees are fine, with enough candy to last the rest of winter. The mouse guards are safe too, with no signs of interference.

Mrs Stevenson out of the room, I snatch a cup of tea and a piece of bread, put an extra log on the fire and pull my pen and paper from my apron pocket to write Betty and the littlies a note to include with my wages. Outside I hear the sound of rain dripping from bare branches on to fallen leaves, like twigs snapping. 'I hope the littlest are all attending Sunday school,' I write. 'I hope you are remembering to feed the bees over the winter.' Outside, the sky hangs low like a sodden woollen blanket. 'I hope you have remembered to put the mouse guard on so that mice can't steal the stocks.'

I know that Betty took some ten pounds of honey to Ely market, and still has beeswax candles and soap to sell, but this can't possibly sustain the whole family until the late-spring months when there will be new honey at last. So I get to thinking about Sam, the eel man, who is mentioned frequently in Betty's letters. Sam has made himself very useful to our family for many a long year now. Having no boy of his own he takes Edmund with him on the punt and two Sundays ago they came back with a whole brace of swans. I know that Betty cooks for him, and helps with the eel-hives in return for whatever Sam might be able to drop into the pot from his time on Cowbit Wash: fish, wildfowl, eels. I have not been able to visit as often as I intended: this winter has been a harsh one, with often impassable roads, so I begin wondering, reading between the lines, if Sam has moved in with them, but as I'm not there to take care of things, I don't see it as my right to ask. Stanley and Edmund need a profession, and handling a punt-gun is good learning for a boy. Still, I can't help but wish they spent more time in school.

A picture of Stanley then, with his blond curls and his rosy, skinny little naked body being bathed in front of the fire, brings a catch to my throat. I remember how he uttered not a word when he saw Betty and me trundle Father in like that, his body sprawled across the wheelbarrow, the only way we could think to move him, and how he edged closer to Father, reaching out a little finger to touch his arm once, and then burst into tears.

This is a troubling memory because it brings back queer details of the hours after Father's death. How while he lay on the kitchen table, dressed in his best clothes, now so thin and empty and cold, just like a basket of ribs, with nothing inside it, I searched frantically among his things. How few things he had! But I was all haste and mayhem, turning up handkerchiefs, balls of string, beeswax candles, socks, muslin circles for jars, a lock of Mother's hair. What was I searching for? I worked with a sense that Father was behind me, listening and watching, and I wheeled round in terror when I heard a tread in the kitchen, relieved to find it was only Betty, weeping deliriously into her apron.

Suddenly, sitting down with a plonk in Mrs Stevenson's dining room, I feel certain at last that I know what I sought. I realise I was looking for a message: a note from Father. A card, a line, a letter, a gift that would tell me. Explain. What he thought of me, why he had brought me into this world. What his life – forty-two years of it – was *for*.

Foolish, I know. I hardly ever saw Father write a word, and know that his skills with pen and paper were slight. Thinking this over, I sit in the dining room, staring out at the frosted lawn where Rupert usually sits among the roses, fiddling nervously with the lace doilies, my mind tick-ticking over it, querulous and unsettled. My eye falls on a leaflet that Rupert has left on the table, and I begin unthinkingly to read the lines staring up at me: 'Is Poverty always the Price of Idleness? Why a Man might be Poor through no Fault of his own . . .'

I wonder, then, if this is my message, at last. Rupert's leaflet about Mr and Mrs Webb and the Poor Law reform. How bitterly I've regretted not being born into a home of books and schooling, a home where my Brains would be treasured, where I would not hear every day that I should 'keep my strange ideas to myself' or that I was 'too clever by half'. Before I came to the Orchard and met Rupert, I could barely imagine how such a home might be. And yet a young woman like Gwen Darwin is evidence that some households might welcome even a girl's wit and cleverness and not punish her for it.

I pick up the leaflet, and read on. It describes a society for the Prevention of Destitution, where workers can be ensured of 'steady progress in health and happiness, honesty and kindliness, culture and scientific knowledge, and the spirit of adventure'. I can't stop myself thinking sourly of how Mr and Mrs Webb, and Rupert too, know precious little about such things! I suppose the author meant to raise our spirits with that sentence but suddenly, for me, the writing wavers. My eyes flood with tears as it looms up in front of me: Ely Union Workhouse, the place they call the Spike. Sam has said that the old ways, the ways on the water, wildfowling and eeling, can't go on for ever, now the land in the Fens is more successfully drained. He says a new pump engine is coming that will do the job it took ten men to do, and then the battle to keep the water back might well be won. And with the water would go the wildfowl, the geese and eels and pike that feed us all. Since it would take only one outbreak of disease to kill a hive and ruin a honey crop for a year, we are perilously close to ending up there, in the Spike, if things turn bad. I've never known why the villagers call it the Spike, but to me it's the exact same shape as one of our skeps, and so I picture it swarming inside, abuzz with the heaving, gathering brown mass of three hundred and sixty creatures who will never see daylight again.

I let another hot tear spill. Why dwell on all this sadness, this misery now? Is it the knowledge that Rupert, too, is attending at his father's bedside? And then I chide myself – why do my thoughts always turn to Rupert? You can be sure, Nell Golightly, that he is not thinking of you! With an effort, I think of poor foolish Kittie, giving up such a good position and a home and food in her belly for a future so undecided and all for a cause that everyone knows is doomed to failure. Then it strikes me like an arrow from Heaven. Betty. I should suggest Betty for the under-maid's job! After all, Lily will be fifteen in October; easily old enough to take over from her, and the boys will still have their mothering and cooking and cleaning when it's needed. If Betty were to work here that would be ten shillings more to live off, and one less person to feed, with Betty's food and keep all paid for.

When Mrs Stevenson at last comes downstairs and I mention Betty to her, she says at once it's a splendid idea and I'm to fetch my sister right away. She says she will 'hold the fort' in the tea gardens, murmuring that when Cambridge realises 'our dear shoeless Mr Brooke' is away in Rugby, the visitors will surely be halved. With that she scoops the Poor Law reform leaflets from the tables, stuffing them into the fire. 'Chop-chop!' she tells me, clapping her hands behind my head.

Rupert will be angry when he discovers her crime; those leaflets are sincerely meant by him, I'm sure of it.

~

January 1910, School Field Rugby

My dear James,

My father has been ill and unable to see for a week. Today, secretly, he has gone with my mother to a 'specialist' in London. At this hour, (12) precisely, the interview begins. It is supposed the specialist will say he has a clot on the brain. Then he will go mad by degrees and die. Meanwhile we shall all live together in a hut on no money a year, which is all there is. Alfred is sombre, because he thinks he won't be allowed to continue a brilliant political career at Cambridge. It is pitiful to see Father groping about, or sitting for four hours in gloom. And it is more painful to see Mother, who is in agony. But I am not fond of them. But I rather nervously await the afternoon, with their return. Will it be neuralgia, after all? Or really a clot? Or blindness? What will one do with an old, blind man, who is not interested in anything at all, on £600 a year? Shall I make a good preparatory-school master? Will it throw me back to the old, orthodox ways of pederasty?

What does one do in a household of fools and a Tragedy? And why is Pain so terrible, more terrible than ever when you see it in others?

But breathe no word. If it's kept dark, the school goes on paying us.

(Later).

Eh! Well I've had a bad time with Mother; and she's wild, praying for his death and so on. The London doctors are vague and ignorant, but not cheering. It *is* a form of Neuralgia, they say. That we may have another term's profits from the House, we're going to beg the new Housemaster to let us stay on. We'll be thrown out at Easter, all right. *Now*, we're to get a youth to take a form, and Mother and I will run the House. From now until April. So I don't go to Cambridge this term. I shall, as a matter of fact, go across for various week-ends (cheap ticket 6/6 return) to get books, etc.

All the details are too horrible – smell, and so forth – and I've not seen people dying before . . .

Rupert

And now I'm ill myself with a fever and a temperature of 102, and blackly angry at all and sundry (especially James, who writes of his love for me at the most inopportune moments). I long to talk to Nellie, to Nellie! To bury my face in her neck and breasts and blubber all the ridiculous, hideous, shameful, childish nonsense that I have been feeling these last few days. The rage that Father was never the man I wanted him to be; the shame of longing for it to be otherwise. Do other fellows get better luck? Would they find it amusing to have a father with the nickname 'Tooler'?

But then – what daydream, what fantasy is that? Nellie has no feeling for me, and would tell me to 'buck up', just as the Ranee would, and I would be shamed once more. I've tested her . . . that impulsive kiss I ventured . . . The response was calm, and unequivocal. (Oh, I want to bury myself up to the neck in a cellar full of dirt every time I remember it! What on earth possessed me? The bees, no doubt, cast some sort of spell on me . . . Nell will think me a perfect example of my class: a precise cliché in every way . . . I positively *groan* with embarrassment whenever I remember it.) She is as solid and good as a bar of white soap and nothing I press upon her can soil her or lather her. Our conversations, the occasions when I felt certain that something, oh, very close to a *real* exchange took place between us, well, of course all that feeling has stalled in the face of the tragic reality: I am vile, full of lust, and a slave to inconstancy. Nell, being the opposite of all those things, knows it better than anyone.

At least my wretched virginity is cast off. I should be more relieved or, even, delighted. I should be dancing a jig on the tin roof of the Orchard tea pavilion where the graceful Nell stands with her fellow maids, awaiting my every whim. But part of the problem is, who to tell? It was, thankfully, Nellie, not one of the others, who silently took away the sheets and delivered them back to me in snowy pristineness, as if the whole incident had never happened.

A few days later Denham and I cycled past one another near the Backs, and for a filthy moment I feared he would cut me. Then his hand flew up in an insouciant wave, and I thought, All is forgiven, and if he turns up at the Orchard again, I'm in for another go. He always was such a charming, lustful boy.

But then a weariness descends, for I have discovered that the career of the Sodomite is not for me. Practice and experience have not in the slightest erased my love for Noel, or quelled my lust for Nellie (or should 'love' and 'lust' be reversed?). I have resolved that Sodomy can only ever be for me a hobby, not a full-time occupation. I've discovered I'm no true Sodomite, at least not in the way of James and Lytton. Perhaps only one quarter, and the other three quarters shared equally between Noel, Nellie and Ka Cox.

Ka now. Why did I picture her just then? Turning up at the Orchard on her bicycle, doing something complicated with her skirt and boots to allow her to cycle . . . She would surely be a safer wager. That bear-like plodding and devotion to the socialist cause. (Isn't that Virginia's nickname for her – something to do with a bear?) That earnestness. So, for a happy moment, I picture Ka at Fabian meetings, in her secretary role, with her head bent over the accounts and her dark green beads glinting like bubbles of river-water at her throat. Jacques has admitted he finds her attractive – if only I could say the same! She does have a certain, well, *dash* in how she dresses: the peasant scarves wound round her head actually suit her, whereas on the other girls they look contrived, striving rather for effect. Her pince-nez make me think of her in the same way as Dudley – as rather kind and hapless. And she is certainly warm, and clever, with a marvellous listening ear. (A sort of cushion or soft-floor quality.) In addition to all that, she is a wealthy orphan too, so not nearly as well protected as Noel Olivier. Oh, yes, she is a friendly girl and highly obtainable, too . . . but the heart, sadly, does not work like that, and I cannot muster mine to beat quicker for the Ka Coxes of this world.

Last night I dreamed I was in love again with the One before the Last. (I'm writing a poem that begins with those lines.) Charles Lascelles, to be precise. Being here at School Field inevitably conjures up Charles for me – that day when he asked for a photograph of me! Would that it had been him, not Denham, I had seduced at the Orchard . . . or even Denham's brother, Hugh, but of course with Denham you could say there had been that long period of foreplay. We had hugged and kissed and strained, Denham and I, on and off for years – ever since that quiet evening I rubbed him, in the dark, speechlessly, in the smaller of the two dorms. But in the summer holidays of 1906 and 1907 he had often taken me out to the hammock, after dinner, to lie entwined there. He had vaguely hoped, I fancy . . . But I lay always thinking of Charles.

Denham was, though, to my taste, attractive. So honestly and friendlily lascivious. Charm, not beauty, was his fate. So it was Denham, and not Charles, whom I had, just as it seems it is destined to be Ka, and not Noel or Nell, whom I might have. I have seen the way Ka looks at me. I endeavour not to notice.

Sometimes I wonder why that schoolgirl Noel Olivier is so appealing to me. She has none of the attributes of Ka. To name three faults, she is infuriating, stubborn, ignorant. Her sister Bryn is surely the exquisite beauty and a practised flirt, too. Even Margery, maddening though she is, is lovelier. Noel is a mere child. A horrible child whom I can't seem to win over.

Little wonder that my mood is bleak. Here, death cowers in every room – inside cupboards and coiled in drawers, ready to spring.

At breakfast, the servants bring toast and tea with a shuffling gait, so unlike the lively step of Nell, and even the cups and plates smell of sickness, and remind me of long days spent in the hospital dorm, my eyes stuck and plugged with streaming conjunctivitis, so that all my attention congeals there and my eyes are the only part of my body that feel alive. Is that what Father feels now? Is he suffering, in that simple, physical way, pain and discomfort in the head and eyes, or is it something far worse? Does he in fact understand that he is facing down death – and what is it like to grapple with that particular foe?

There was that moment when I first arrived, standing in the hall still clutching my small leather bag as if there were a question over whether I might stay or not, and when we all talked of other things. Alfred and Mother and the servants – we talked of the trains and the weather and the new telephone and why I hadn't first called to say I was arriving (I hadn't the penny for the telephone at the station). Mother took me upstairs and into the room, which – never exactly a spring-like room – now was drowned in a dark, winter green light, with the curtains tightly closed. Of course thoughts of Dick hovered all around me and the terrible aching fear welled up again: that it was hereditary, this tendency to melancholy and blackness and a frail mind and worse: that even without his illness Father had always had it, and Dick too, and mightn't I be the next to go exactly the same way?

Mother sat down beside the little table with its Mer-Syren pills for Indigestion, Biliousness and Nervous Depression and I kept looking at Father, with his paper-fine skin and his eyes open but dull, then back at Mother, not knowing what to say. And nobody dared to say the things they thought, and there were words floating in the air and in the brain and in the middle of the conversation and one suddenly saw them and felt unable to speak.

Then last night the Ranee broke down with me. I have seen her weep so few times in my life that my palms sprang with sweat, and I was immediately again a child of six years old. I watched, as her bowed head shook in her hands, like a bouncing silver melon and I wondered in horrified fascination whether it might in fact drop right off and she lift only the stub of her neck to me, rather than that wild, beseeching face.

She prayed, she said, he could die quickly.

This bald statement flitted ominously in the air between us like a bat, and then she stood up. Her shaking ceased and I saw at once that she was recovering, that she was becoming again the formidable Matron, Housemistress, School Mother she had always been – and I felt a little calmer for clearly no action from me was required. I had neither embraced her nor even moved towards her, and the powerful revulsion I felt, wondering if I was called upon to do either, subsided like a wave, as she moved away from me and composed herself, dabbing at her eyes.

'Oh, my darling Rupie, thank Heaven for you!' she ejected, suddenly, as if I had risen to the occasion. My shame was absolute.

We went next door to the green Nubolic room, and sat by the bedside with the old man croaking between us. Once he opened his eyes and seemed to focus, but not on me, on something just behind me, over my shoulder. (It was ever thus. Did he ever truly see me, I wonder, see the Rupertness of me, rather than the obedient, dreary boy he longed for?)

An ugly thought came back to me then. How at fourteen, I once heard a boy say out loud what I knew had long been rumoured: that Tooler (Father) was so horse-whipped that

Mother sent him out to pick up manure for the garden in the middle of the night. I thrashed the offender, of course. Yet what I remembered was that even as I did it I wished it was Father I was pummelling. Why could he not stand up to her, just the once, and set an example for all of us?

My head began to pound with the force of these thoughts and their unsuitability for thinking so close to a death-bed. If only I could subdue them in some way! I tried offering Father a glass of water from the jug beside the bed but he made no sound, and Mother frowned and shook her head, as if to say, 'He is too far gone for that.' The smell in the room was becoming stifling – no longer just Watson's Nubolic Soap but an odd, sickening combination of that and . . . a smell like pond-weed, powerful, rotted, slippery and foul.

I stood up, as if to leave, but Mother put her hand on mine and I pretended to be adjusting the curtain, drawing the gap in the centre so that no slit of light could fall on his face, rendering the skin any greener than it already appeared. When would that foul gurgling sound in his chest and lungs cease? When would the miasma, the disgusting smell surrounding us, lift? Mother took hold of his limp hand, picking it up as if it were a dead leaf and clutching it in hers.

What on earth could he be thinking now? Did he know? After all, he was always such a pessimistic man, prone to brooding, and not much to fall back on in the way of thoughts. He had never recovered from Dick's death, and a picture of Dick now, sloppy, not quite upright, a glass of whisky in his hand, inserted itself between the bed and me, impossible to shake.

I paced the room, sat down and then stood up again, my desire to do something, *anything*, being quite overwhelming. Couldn't I, despite being such an absolute and unimaginative dolt, even with my enormous ineptitude, could not I find some way to help him, help ease the passage, say one word or phrase to help? What is the point of being a Bloody Poet if words abandon you at essential moments? Is not a word *something*, better than nothing, to offer a dying man? 'When the white flame in us is gone, and we that lost the world's delight . . .' Oh, but it's all helpless, useless.

'Father—' I said.

And there was a moment, a glint, where the word 'Goodbye' welled up and all the words stoppered up in me rose to my throat and I longed to speak something true, anything true, just the once, before it was too late.

'Father – I'm here – do you see me?'

But Father closed his eyes again. I did not have a sense, not have much of a sense, that he saw or understood anything at all. And the room drew in around us, dark and green and foul. I thought of Nellie, and something she had described about her own father slipping away in the meadow near the river, sliding out of life like something natural and good, with his bees humming round him and his hands smelling of honey, and meanwhile Mother and I continue to sit in silence, breathing in that fetid, frightening smell.

'Oh, my dearest—' Mother said, and flung herself at Father's chest.

I had my wish – the strange gurgling sound stopped, at last.

Later, much later, when the doctor had left, and the servants retired, and Mother's sobbing in the other room finally ceased to shake the house, I sat wearily on the edge of my bed, pulling at my socks and thinking. I've always felt so especially unlike and separate from both my parents – in good and bad qualities alike. It has been a constant mystery to me – and to others, too, no doubt! – how such parents managed to spawn me.

The irony is that at this moment, despite this dizzying *un*likeness, despite being the one boy in the school (along with James, I suppose) whom the masters always accused of looking like a girl, with my too-long hair and bandy legs – Father has achieved exactly what he always longed for: I shall be forced to step into his shoes and become a Schoolmaster, at least for one term.

At this thought I'm obliged to fling myself backwards on to the bed like a felled log. If one of the servants wasn't still creeping about sniffling I swear I'd throw back my head and howl like a wolf. Oh, and I'm so sad and fierce and miserable not to be in my garden and little house in Grantchester this term! I love being there so much – more than any other place I've ever lived in. I'd thought of being there when the spring was coming, every day this winter, and dreamed of seeing all the brown and green things. And I always hate being at home.

I snuff the candle and pull off my shirt, slipping beneath the cold, stiff sheets and lying on my back in horrible mimicry of a corpse. My solace will be the boys, I tell myself. They all love me. They are not very ugly. They vary from four to seven feet in height. They are a good age – fourteen to nineteen. (It is between nineteen and twenty-four that people are insufferable.) They look rather fresh and jolly too. But, oh!, the mask-like faces that come before me. I am 'master' and therefore a moral machine. They will not believe I exist. Also, I am shy.

However, they all remember I used to play for the school at violent games and they will respect me accordingly.

Father's death is what others call A Blessing: it put an end to his gurgling and choking, his face twisted out of recognition, and the hours of vigil required of us. There is paperwork and the funeral to arrange and Mother to hold up. It is exactly like the days after Dick's death, but worse. I feel sure that the unspoken – the unacknowledged fact of weakness or Brain Fever or Madness: something terrible and horrible and too dreadful to contemplate within me, too, will soon manifest, like an ugly blister that suddenly reveals how badly a shoe chafed and for how long it was ignored.

My fever has receded but I am weary beyond belief.

James assures me by letter that his penis and balls are (in the words of Mr Scott-Coward) at my disposal. Astonishing, the levels to which these Cambridge men will go to avoid acknowledging anything that matters. My father has died and Mother is in agony; Alfred's career uncertain and I'm suddenly to be a Schoolmaster (I hope for only a term but maybe for longer; perhaps I shall have to give up all hope of being a poet). Still James expects me to go on with the witticisms and the posturing. (I'm certainly making a game attempt with my usual immensely egotistic nature, but can hardly be expected to excel just now.)

I had several hours of respite yesterday: I travelled by train to Grantchester and called in at the Orchard – if I'm to stay a while in Rugby I need my books and papers. The route from Cambridge was full of cyclists hurtling through muddy puddles with their robes flowing, and Grantchester was immediately peace and raindrops and spiders busying in diamond-encrusted webs in soon-to-be-dusted rooms. I called ostensibly to pick up a few books, intending dinner in the Union in the evening with James. I had tickets for *Richard the Second* by the Marlowe Society.

In truth, I hoped to see Nellie. I felt certain that, in my present simmering mood, one brush with those flaming violet eyes and that vastly sympathetic bosom would bring all to the surface, allowing it to boil over and pour forth.

Sensibly, the marvellous child was absent. Visiting her family, Mrs Stevenson said, in some strangely named village in the Fens. I indulged myself with another brief picture of Nellie there with other buxom maids, picking celery or – what do they do in Fen country? – carrying eels in nets or milk in churns or some such glorious thing, hair shining in the golden sun, tumbling in black folds down her bare shoulders, her elegant throat freckling like a speckled egg. No rude reality (it's winter drizzle, with frost and bare twigs, no sun or eggs to be seen) interfered: the picture was a pretty one.

A telegram arrived then, which cut short my visit – Memorial for Father arranged for tomorrow: come back at once. And so here I am, in my old room in School Field, with the curtains with their swinging red parrots and their smell of cooked cabbage, and Podge stoical and podgy in the bed next door, and Father in the Chapel of Rest at last, while we prepare some sentimental nonsense of a life devoted to God and the School to be read out at the service tomorrow morning.

Will I be allowed to say that I believe God a fool and Father a bigger one? There are things – pieces of folly, or bad taste, or wanton cruelty – in the Christian, middle-class way of burying the dead that make me ill. My avowed rejection of immortality as a theory or a reality has to be all swallowed up again in speaking some nonsense about Father at peace with angels, just as we did for Dick. Preparing the valedictory lines has been the worst task of my life so far, and not, as Mother imagines, because of the sorrowfulness of losing Father that it evokes. No. The pain is caused by being forced to write and speak lines I believe to be false and unworthy! My sickness has come back with a vengeance, and in some sinister way I welcome it – as (and here I confuse even myself) with the sickness comes such intense awareness of every ache and twinge and stab in my limbs and head and neck and eyes and throat: in short, with sickness comes the strong feeling that I, at least, am alive. Which is something.

I'm sweating in a dreadful fever. I've subsisted on milk and the pieces I could surreptitiously bite out of my thermometer. At times I want to kill Podge and then I remember in a state of forgiveness that to be the favourite child (after dear departed Dick) is probably, in point of fact, a curse. Far better to be in my shoes – the replacement girl, the reincarnated babe that Mother lost! Allows me my yellow hair and my squashy nature.

Tomorrow the fifty-three boys arrive, inky babes all of them;

they are young and direct and animal. It will become my charming task to freeze their narrowing views. At least until April.

~

So I'm in full feather by the time I leave my duties at the Orchard and beg a lift from the butcher's boy, who is taking the horse van from Grantchester to Ely market. It will be but an hour's walk at the other side. I sing all the way.

In the end the boy takes me right to Prickwillow because, he says, he's never seen the Fens and 'Well! This is a funny bit of England!' I suspect he has other reasons but I give him no cause to hope, keeping my eyes straight and my shawl clutched round my chest.

The frost gives way to snow once we get past Streatham. The pretty lanes and curving hedges soon begin to flatten out into the iced white fields, so plain and flat they might be cut-up pieces of paper, the black lines being the droves and the silver the strips of water. At first the plainness is a shock to me – I realise I've quickly forgotten it – and I feel only shame, seeing my old home through the eyes of the butcher's boy, as a drab, treeless, man-made landscape, poor cousin indeed to the historic countryside of Grantchester, with its tall church spires and charming rose gardens and grand old elm trees. But as the horse takes us deeper into Fen country and the huge white sky starts to spread its arms over us, and at the first sight of a Fen skater flashing past, blue as a kingfisher, on the ice at Soham Mere, my heart lifts and my old pride floods back. We stop to watch the skaters for a while, drinking the tea from the flask that Mrs Stevenson sent with us, with the butcher's boy exclaiming over the low, clumsy Fen style ('Designed for speed, not grace,' I say) and asking me why we call the skates patines in this part of the world. (The answer is I don't know.) We stay a while, fascinated by the speed of the figures whisking past, listening to the familiar chafe of skates on ice, and the fine crusts of ice upturned by them, which look to me just like the scrapings of beeswax that we take off with the knife. Our ears and noses are singing from the cold; and we place halfpenny bets on the various boys we see racing, until he tries to pull me to him and kiss me, and I have to pretend that Betty expects me at a particular hour.

The kiss is damp and childish, and a poor specimen, compared to Rupert's.

'What's your name?' I squeal, from under the damp wool and worsted of him.

'Tommy,' he says proudly.

'Well, Tommy, you can put me off here after the three bridges and the three level crossings. The place down by the river and the shock-head willows.'

He falls silent then, hearing the sharpness in my voice. But the silly boy cannot be silent for long: 'Look at those toy-like trees, and the whole place flat as a pancake!' he says, and then, 'Tit-willer, what a funny name for a village!' I have to tell him again that it's *Prickwillow*, named for the custom of pricking the osier willows into the soil – that the whole place used to be nothing but osier willows – and he jumps down off the van as we arrive at the house, and Betty runs out into the garden, her face beaming with surprise at the sight of me.

'Any chance of giving a boy a glass of beer for his trouble?' Tommy says, to which Betty looks disapproving and replies, 'But didn't you know we're Primitive Methodists? Lily and me are just off to the church now and you're more than welcome to join us if you like . . .'

Well, that sure mops the smile from his face and, with a few coins shoved in his hand, he jumps back in the driver's seat, shaking the horse into such speed that the van's in danger of toppling. He calls over his shoulder that he'll be back at three o'clock to fetch us to Grantchester and not to be late!

Betty smiles at his haste. She doesn't mention that Sam keeps a good stock of ale in back and that our going to church has always been more through habit and schooling than conviction.

Then at last I can hug my brothers and sisters, smother myself with the rough kisses of the boys and the damp cheeks of Lily and Betty and Olive. The children look thin and they smell of sarsaparilla – a powerful stench that lets me know Betty has done a good job, dosing them up to prevent the nits and doing it on Saturday night too, as I taught her, so that it can be washed out on Sunday night and the children don't go to school on Monday morning smelling of Rankin's ointment. I look them all over carefully and it's not all cause for celebration.

'Betty, have you been giving them the caster oil?' I ask. Stanley in particular looks frail and a mite green around the gills. Lily is the opposite – a touch swollen in the cheeks and belly – but in a way that's not healthy either.

I can see Betty resents my asking but her reply is friendly enough: 'Yes, and the jar with black treacle and powdered sulphur too, and poppyhead tea for the littlies . . .'

'Not the poppyhead tea! No one gives their children that in Grantchester! They'll think us backward. It turns children sleepy and stupid. Don't give them it, Betty, you hear? No matter what Mrs Gotobed says . . .'

At this Betty turns sulky. 'All right, all right, but it's fine for you, sleeping in that warm house and your own room too. It's me here with the little ones wailing and crying about Daddy and always hungry for food and Edmund out at all hours on a sledge on Cowbit Wash when he should be chopping wood for me. It's the only way I can get a night's sleep sometimes.'

'But Edmund is working, surely, with Sam? Isn't he setting the decoy? Doesn't he bring home waterfowl?'

'Yes, yes, of course he does, but I can't rely on it, and there's still nights when we go to bed hungry . . .'

So here is the perfect moment to tell her about the live-in

position. But somehow I can feel a silence taking hold of my throat and a wish to prolong the happy mood, knowing how the others will protest if I take Betty away from them.

'Show me the skeps – have you put the mouse guard on for the winter? I have to tell you what I've learned from Mr Neeve. His methods are so modern – he doesn't kill off most of the swarm to remove the honey, he uses removable frames and keeps nearly an entire swarm. He'd be willing to sell us some of those frames so that I can teach you that way to do things, too.'

Betty sets her mouth in a disbelieving line. 'Well, Father's honey always was the best in the Fens . . . the Runhams told me the other week that they might take two dozen pots this year, as a sample. I thought you'd be pleased.'

'I *am* pleased. You are doing a fine job. Now, come, show your sister the bees, and then we'll go to church . . . And then I've some news and a proposition for you . . . We'll need the whole family to say yes, mind, and I know the littlies will want persuading . . .'

On the way back, Tommy makes no such move again. At Stuntney Fen we pass an enormous bird of prey squatting at the side of the road, like a hunched old man. It takes off at our approach and I see the vole dangling from its clutches, and the leather strap tied to its foot, too. So it's not free at all, as I imagined, for a moment, watching it enviously. No – I see the bird make for the gloved arm of its master, a black figure in the distance, the falconer. The sky over the Fens is gathering red, Ely Cathedral sitting atop. The bird rests on the falconer's arm the way a flame sits on a candle. *Does he ever think of me?* I have no need to ask myself who I mean.

~

This morning I fell out of love with the schoolgirl Noel Olivier, with a resounding crash, probably loud enough for the Ranee to hear it in the drawing room. I'm not quite sure how it happened, but only that a blank space descended where my previous affections lived and I contrived to write a whole sonnet on the subject of not loving her at all. I suspect it is absence that has made the heart grow colder; absence and the presence of fifty-three distracting young colts.

> I said I splendidly loved you; it's not true.
> Such long swift tides stir not a land-locked sea . . .

I felt the best I have felt since the funeral. I rose from my bed lively and invigorated.

This morning I caned a boy for the first time. I had no consciously sexual sensations. Occasionally I determine to make a great attempt to pierce their living souls by some flaming, natural, heartfelt remark. So I summon one. Then he trots into my study, a sullen meekness. I can only say, in a mechanical voice, 'Jones, mi, I hear your Latin grammar was not sufficiently prepared. Please do me fifty lines.'

It's really that I'm in a false position; and when I try to stretch out a jolly hand to any one of them, the shades of a thousand schoolmasters rise between us and form a black wall of fog and we miss each other in the dark. I manage my bluff Christian tone, which is wholly pedagogic. Every night at nine twenty I take prayers – a few verses of a psalm and one or two short heartfelt ones. I nearly had to prepare the lads for Confirmation but, rather pusillanimously, I wriggled out of that. But a certain incisive credulity in my voice when I mention the word 'God' is, I hope, slowly dropping the poison of the truth into their young souls.

Actually, the caning was distressing. The boy – Everett-Clegg, a yellow-haired (is that significant? James would surely think it was) sullen chap – had broken his furniture to small pieces with a coal-hammer. I could hardly let that pass. 'Come into my study at once!'

The boy's eyes were fierce but everything about his face shimmered. He was angry: he wanted to fight, stand firm, like a bull. He was red and frightened. I bade him in a tremulous voice to bend over.

A smell of something hot and familiar began to emanate from him, as he lifted up his jacket, as requested, and rested his hands on his knees. That sickening smell gave me pause. The clock behind me – Father's clock – ticked stridently. The room seemed unbearably small, warm and chalky, and I feared for an instant that I could not breathe. I saw the boy raise his eyes, the pupils rolling towards his eyelashes and I knew what he was doing. He mocked me. He saw my weakness, my hesitation. It would have spread among the other fifty-two young bullocks like a disease, in an instant. So I raised the cane and held my breath and played the part, the part of Housemaster, the five hundred years of history, the pale men who slide wearily around these halls: my father's son.

I raised and lowered the cane six times, and I did not wince as the wood fell with smart raps on reddening, then bloodying flesh. When the boy straightened up, one hand pulling at his pants, the other brushing a tear from his silent, glowering face, I had to turn my own away, making a pretence of putting the cane back in its hallowed place. 'Go to your room, Everett-Clegg, and do not let me see you in here again!'

I wanted to cry after him, 'I'm sorry! Can't you see we each must play a part, always play a part, that those powerful tides, oceans of years – no matter how courageously I struggle, they are too powerful for me? Can you not see that it isn't possible for me to ask why you broke the furniture in your room, if you are unhappy, if you are being buggered by a bigger, stinkier boy, any more than I could—'

Any more than I could declare my love for the parlour-maid.

I found my legs were shaking as I sat down in Father's chair. There was his cap on the desk behind me, his pipe, his pen, his ink bottle, his leather-bound Bible. The ghost of the figure we conjured up as boys, James and I, John Rump, the terrible bowler-hatted, umbrellaed, briefcased shell of a man, hovered over me. Everett-Clegg closed the door behind him with an insolently loud clap, and I put my head in my hands and, for the first time since Father's death, I wept.

~

So Betty takes up her place in Kittie's bed, wearing Kittie's uniform, which only needs an inch taking from the hem of the skirt and the apron to fit her, and at Easter Rupert returns from his mother's home in Rugby, looking as pale as butter and as flat and lifeless, too.

'I suppose you know that my father died, Nellie.'

'Yes.'

'And you may have heard that we were forced to leave the family home, and are living in Reduced Circumstances . . .'

'I know nothing of that . . .'

'Good.'

Here, some of the old spark flickers in his eyes. I am in his room, bringing him his breakfast and the morning letters.

'Because it's ridiculous. We are better described as living in Genteel Poverty. That is to say we just fail to live with any comfort on what would support ten working men and their families in luxury.'

I pause for a second, and then realise with relief that he is back to his old teasing.

'I have been reprieved! My career as a Schoolmaster has been interrupted by the willingness of Mother to rent a detached house in Bilton Road and give up her reign as Housemistress . . . in which case I no longer need to pretend to be Housemaster . . . Hurrah!'

I don't really understand this, but I see that he is happy and some of our old ease is between us again, and so I smile, and his face cracks into a laugh and he flings back the covers and jumps naked to the window.

I am used to this now, although I have warned Betty to allow me to be the one to bring the breakfast things in the morning. Rupert will often give me a naughty grin and pretend to cover up what he calls his 'tent pole'. I have become accustomed to this behaviour by reminding myself that he was raised by a nanny and is used to servants knowing every inch of him. He means nothing by it and I must not for one moment think otherwise.

With his face to the window he grabs a sheet from the bed and begins winding it round himself, bandage-like. When he has assured himself that this morning there are no friends about to call up to him, he proceeds to the basin to shave.

'I'll fetch your hot water . . .'

'Nellie, stay awhile! I've something to show you. '

He hops back towards the bed, looking like an Egyptian, with his long straight body in the short linen skirt.

'You remember I went to Switzerland last December? I got sick out there. Very sick. My tongue turned a bright orange and I fainted at the Louvre on our return through Paris. It was green honey that did it — can you credit it? The very elixir, the same marvellous tonic, that cured the bee-sting made me violently sick!'

I don't know what to say to this — if I should apologise, perhaps. 'The honey here is always pure, sir. Always safe to eat, I hope—'

'I know, I know that. (Do call me Rupert, child, for God's sake.) No, that's not what I'm concerned about. I wrote a poem. I want to show you the poem.'

He leaps across the room to his bed and rummages in the piles of books on the floor next to it for a piece of paper, which he then shoves at me. 'There, there! "A Channel Passage". Read it, Nellie, would you?'

His face surprises me. The paleness and flatness is gone and now his cheeks are pink and his hair sticking up where he has pushed twitchy fingers through it and he is all animation and excitement. I glance nervously at the door, mindful of the kettle I left on the stove downstairs.

I unfold the paper and read, standing up. My heart beats loudly inside my own skull, and a goblin wheels around in there too, shouting: 'Ninny! Idiot! Now you will be found out! You will not know one word to say! What could a girl like you possibly understand about a poem by a great poet?' The lines leap in front of me like horses galloping and refuse to make sense, so that I only glance up once and then turn back to the paper, silently reading and waiting for Rupert to speak.

'There! It's a sonnet, Nellie – you know what a sonnet is? Admittedly it might be the first sonnet in the English language that deals with the matter of – the question of – vomit but, well, it's a fine sonnet just the same!'

'Vomit?'

He snatches the paper from me.

'"The damned ship lurched and slithered. Quiet and quick, my cold gorge rose . . ." You see, you see, it's a *metaphor*. A metaphor for love as a physical sickness . . . "Do I forget you? Retchings twist and tie me; old meat, good meals, brown gobbets up I throw . . ." Nausea, retching, do you see, as a way to express the sickness of the soul? Sickness! Is sickness not a fit subject for poetry? It appears not! Are any of the true, the everyday, the real events of a man's experience a fit subject for poetry? No, apparently! Mr Eddie Marsh prefers poetry that he can read while lunching, so he does! The editor of the *Nation*, a certain Mr Nevinson,' (he says this name with a great sneer, and a look seeking agreement, as if I should know the man), 'would prefer it if this poem, which I *had* named "A Shakespearean Love Sonnet" – ha! before I changed it – would prefer if it were not included. He would like to publish some poems of mine, but not this one as he thought it generally "too strong". Ha! Too strong!'

This rant is delivered at such a pace that, thankfully, no reply from me is needed.

'Too strong, Nellie.' He backs towards the bed and the puff seems to go out of him. When he raises his eyes to mine I note again how they are not grey or bluish-white but of living blue, really living blue, like the sky that streams in through the window.

'Does the poem shock you, Nellie?'

'No . . .'

'Sickness has been a part of your life, too, hasn't it? It has been a lifelong companion to mine. Dick's pneumonia, Father's neuralgia, and me – if it's not ophthalmia (the "pink eye", Nellie), it's sweating in a fever or shivering in a cold . . . Oh, yes, it might be said to be a trifle adolescent, oh, yes, it's rather laid on so, I can see that – "The sobs and slobber of a last year's woe" – yes, yes, it's ugly – but – but— Oh, is it my fate to be permitted to write only what is beautiful and useless and never what is true?'

At this he sits down and sinks low on the bed, with his head in his hands. The curve of his naked shoulders and the nape of his neck present themselves to me. I try to remain business-like, and remember my duties, but it is such a long time since I saw that neck. How pale it looks, with its down of soft fair hair. How strong and how tender. My hand trembles a little and I push it into the pocket of my apron, lest it betray me by sneaking out to touch him.

At last I draw courage, and venture my opinion: 'I think it a – an *excellent* poem, honestly I do. "Heartache or tortured liver"! Yes, very fine lines.'

There is a silence, a pause, when Rupert seems to wrestle with something. His hands are still covering his face and the sound that slips through his fingers is so strange that I think for a moment he is choking back a sob. But then another escapes, and another, and he drops his hands and falls sideways on to the bed, and I realise at once that he is rolling and shrieking with laughter.

'Yes! The parlour-maid says the best lines are: "heartache or tortured liver"! Or perhaps that should be "heartache or chopped liver"! Nellie, you are a marvel! Oh, thank you, darling Nellie. I should have taken you that day in the orchard, shouldn't I, while I had my chance? You didn't get married while I was away, now, child, did you?'

'What? No – I—'

A pause. He seems to note my look of startled horror and sobers up. Another long pause.

'Will that be all then? *Sir?*'

'Yes, yes, I'm sorry, Nellie – don't be cross . . . I had hoped to explain . . .'

I close the door firmly behind me. As the wood slams into the frame, I can still hear him laughing, that horrible skittish, girlish laugh that makes him sound quite mad. I am shaking. I long to open the door again, go back in, beg his forgiveness, hear his explanation, but I daren't.

Mrs Stevenson's voice on the stairs drags me to my duties. 'Nell! Did you leave this kettle on the stove? It's almost boiled dry, so it has! You'll burn us all in our beds, you will, one of these days, my girl.'

As I am hastening downstairs, Rupert's words are running through my head, and a savage fury flares in me again: 'I should have taken you that day in the orchard . . .' How dare he? The assumption! The cheek of the man! The baldly stated, *to my face*, idea that he could have me any time he wanted, regardless of what my thoughts might be on the matter.

My face is hot, I know, and red, as I rush to cover my hand with a teacloth and retrieve the kettle. But the face that greets me in its shining surface has a surprised, wild look. I'm startled to see that it is not anger at all reflected there, but something else entirely.

~

I have been to the newspaper's offices in London to have it out with Nevinson. Fat lot of good it did me. The miscreant has no idea that it's the alteration of the little words that makes the difference between Poetry and Piddle. I had the impression from Nevinson's startled gaze that I was being . . . loud, and ruddy, and possibly ludicrously beautiful too. Or just ludicrous. He said, of course, that if he were the sole editor himself he'd let them stand. It was all nonsense.

I ranted a little to Eddie Marsh later, who smoked in silence and took me out to see *Trelawny of the 'Wells'* and then on to Lady Ottoline's salon. We stood near the window, slightly apart from the others, engrossed in our conversation.

'I don't claim great merit for "A Channel Passage", dear Eddie,' I began, *sotto voce*, 'but the point of it was (or should have been) *serious*'. There are common or sordid things – situations or details – that may suddenly bring all tragedy, or at least the brutality of actual emotions, to you.'

Eddie repeated his preference for poetry that he could read at meals. I ran my fingers through my hair, controlling a desire to punch him. He pretended not to notice and drew long and hard on his cigarette, darting little glances at me until his monocle popped, and fell on to his cheek, where he cupped a hand to catch it.

'Look, Eddie – Shakespeare's not unsympathetic, is he?' I hissed, in exasperation. 'I mean, "My mistress' eyes are nothing like the sun." What's that if not an attempt to do away with sentimental and idealistic imagery? Couldn't we compare love to something besides roses for once?'

We were both surprised to notice that I was shaking.

We travelled back to Eddie's rooms in the Gray's Inn Road by motor-car, belonging to some government friend of Eddie's – a conciliatory gesture, which I refused to be impressed by. There was a tense silence as we entered his rooms and I sniffed in that bachelor smell of cigarette smoke, books and damp wool. Eddie's rooms always make me think of Lowes Dickinson's room at King's: too many books and pictures for too small a space. Eddie strode to the window to wave good night to the chauffeur. Then he turned to the claret left for us on a tray by his bed-maker, Mrs Elgy, and poured us both a tiny glass. As usual Mrs Elgy had also left a cold supper of ham, cheese and bread, but I shook my head, feeling childish, when Eddie offered me some.

'My dear—' began Eddie.

His expression was so plaintive that I couldn't bear it. 'Oh, for God's sake, Eddie, pass me that claret. Must my glass be the perfect size for a visiting maiden aunt?'

'Mrs Elgy . . .' he began, by way of explanation.

I threw myself into his armchair, swinging one of my legs over the side in a hopeless effort to inject some energy into the room. Eddie glanced at the fire beside me and I know he was wondering whether he would appear too servile if he now knelt at it and made it up.

'What a strange evening!' I said, in conciliatory mood at last. 'Full of Ottoline's admirers and would-be lovers. Was that Henry Lamb?'

Eddie, clearly relieved by my changed mood, nodded at once, and poured me another glass of claret, filling it to the brim, where the red liquid skin trembled dangerously in the miniature glass. 'The fellow in the queer suit?' he asked.

'Oh, I thought it rather marvellous. Quite the most interesting thing about him – did you see it had tails, shaped at the hips? And the rather jaunty red handkerchief round his neck? I might adopt that myself – he looked far more elegant and fashionable than any of the men in faultless evening dress.'

'Oh, Rupert, no, you looked by far the most – dapper!'

Eddie's look of serious alarm was so laughable I spluttered on my claret. I put my hand to my tieless collar and opened the second button on my shirt. Fun to watch Eddie's eye behind his eye monocle, see him struggle with himself not to glance there, at my bare throat.

'I'm teasing, old man. Ka made me this shirt – rather nice, isn't it? I think blue's my colour.'

'Ka?'

'You know Ka . . . Katharine Cox. Newnham girl. Fabian secretary. Bad posture and serious thoughts. A fine seamstress, though. She's mad for me.'

'Ah . . .'

The words 'Aren't we all?' hovered around him like the words in a thought balloon, and I had to stifle another laugh.

The thawing of my mood seemed to give Eddie false confidence, and after a slug of claret, he suddenly ventured, 'You know, dear, it would be a great shame to feel you have to be ugly in your poetry in order to somehow compensate for your . . . erm . . . personal beauty . . .'

Immediately, I felt my ire rise again. '*Ugliness!* That's just the thing. What you call *ugly* I call realism. Oh, not the realism of those critics who believe that true literary realism is a fearless reproduction of what real living men say when there is a clergyman in the room!' I snapped. I felt a little prickle of joy at the hurt look on Eddie's face. It was the kind of remark I'd so often wanted to make with the Ranee, or even Father, but had never dared. It's always gratifying how much liberty Eddie's admiration permits me.

And with that I downed my glass and picked up the *English Review*.

There was a pause while the cogs in Eddie's brain clicked audibly, as he searched desperately for a new way to mollify me. He swept some books from a chair and perched himself on it, as close to me as he dared. 'Oh, yes, Rupert, I saw your article on *Richard the Second*. Marvellous stuff . . .'

I silently munched bread and Stilton, not feeling inclined to let him off the hook *that* readily. More cogs whirring. Eddie sat tense and alert, like a listening terrier. Then, at last, inspiration: 'You know, dear boy, I have been thinking. I'm out at the Admiralty so often – why don't you use this place as your London *pied-à-terre*? It's splendidly convenient and Mrs Elgy is very fond of you . . . and I could leave you a key . . .'

Oh, joy! Such genius! I pretended to be considering his offer. My mind immediately danced ahead with the possible freedoms this might bestow . . . Of course I will have to endure Mrs Elgy calling me 'Duck' and 'Me-duck' so often I'm tempted to quack. And that annoying habit she has of wanting to detain me with chat about the 'carry-on' of that wicked Adelaide Knight (of whom I know nothing), married – can you believe it, Mr Rupert, sir? – to a *negro* man (and care less). But Mrs Elgy aside, the spare room has a large and comfortable bed, an enervating view over Holborn rooftops, some impressive paintings and artworks.

So I leaped from my armchair and took Eddie's hands and thanked him, and drank another brimming glass of claret, and stumbled off to bed in a vastly improved mood.

It's not hard to guess why the Ranee dislikes Mr Marsh so much. She would be vastly reassured if she knew of the indomitable Mrs Elgy, with her witchy laugh and constant monologue. The Ranee doesn't even know, of course, that Eddie's a member of the Apostles, but she isn't wrong in her general suspicions. It's only that she's wrong in her estimation of Eddie's courage. Except for one extraordinary occasion after the Cambridge production of *Eumenides* at the ADC, when I was standing around in my heraldic little skirt – an occasion never again mentioned – and Eddie was horribly sloshed and crept up behind me and goosed me with his long, refined fingers; apart from that, there is no indication *at all* of what she suspects. Eddie is a model of decorum. Sober, Eddie is an exemplary companion.

I lay in the tight little bed, and contemplated his offer. At last – a place to bring my conquests! Admittedly, there haven't *been* any yet (if Denham is not to be counted, and he isn't) but, well, *I have begun – and now I give my sensual race the rein*! Ha! Thank you, Eddie, dear boy.

Whatever your motives might be.

~

There are two things I had forgot about my sister Betty. One is how vain she is about her looks. Falling dead-beat into bed each night, I'm forced to wait while she curls each strand of hair round a strip of rag before I can snuff out the candle. Mornings are delayed while she unties them again, fixing her hair in the tiny mirror we've propped against our only shelf. Since our hair must be pinned up and *most* of it is hidden beneath caps all day, I can't fathom the trouble she takes. How did she get this way, in the middle of the Fens, where there is no one to see her but the geese over the fields?

The second is that she is a worrier, in a way that I am not, nor never have been. Taking care of five youngsters from the age of eleven, I never had indulgence, and that has served me well. But for Betty, all must be talked through in the tiniest detail before anything can be done. She is very worried about her duties at the Orchard. She is terrified of some of Mrs Stevenson's new-fangled objects, like the Faithfull washer, with its dangerous figure-of-eight movement that takes flight on the kitchen floor when you rock it. I keep trying to explain that it's simply a mimicry of the sort of thing we'd do if we were scrubbing the linen in a dolly-tub, to which she wails, 'Well, then, why can't we wash the clothes in the river Granta, as we would at home?'

The May Day celebrations that Rupert and his friends demand nearly finish her off: strawberries and honey and cream and tea on the lawn for about a half-dozen of them (and every time she fetches something Betty forgets the tray, or the request of a spoon, or some brown sugar, or some plum jam, and has to run back in again, doubling the work she does). Being in service, I realise, is something I took to right away; but, then, I had always been the one keeping house, and bossing the others. Betty had some small freedoms to roll a hoop or skip with the others. And she had never been good with skinning a rabbit or baking an eel pie.

I keep trying to teach her that a good maid must listen at all times to what is being said, in case a request is buried in it. 'Oh, yes, and more tea would be good . . .' But at the same time she must never, on any account, *appear* to be listening. When the men shout strange quotes to one another, or if she accidentally comes across a joke about 'Higher' and 'Lower' Sodomy, her face must be blank. I remind her of Mrs Stevenson's warning to me that she will not keep girls who take too much notice of the goings-on of the Varsity men. When they talk of Apostles and Embryos and the Carbonari Society, Betty finds the blank eyes easy; the difficulty is if someone suddenly says, 'I thought I asked for a knife half an hour ago, what?'

She is afraid of Rupert, for his way of addressing her directly and quite suddenly, having learned her name and that she is my sister. He calls her 'Young Bet', or 'Wild Bet' and he always says this with a smile, and a glance at the dark beaky Frenchman (whose name I now know is Mr Raverat), as if to share some private joke. I've troubled to tell Betty the names of the ones I recognise: the lady with the brown hair in a long plait and the large behind and the pince-nez, with the rounded shoulders and a sort of thick mouth, is Miss Katharine Cox (the others call her Ka). She is a little greedy, and always asks for more cream. Miss Gwen Darwin is very kind, but likes to do things herself: just put the pot beside her and let her pour, and fetch her own spoon. The other lady is her cousin, Mrs Frances Cornford, a poet, very sweet on Rupert; she will always sound a little sharp in her requests, but don't be frightened, she simply has a loud voice. The man with the pressed-down hair across his bald head, whom Rupert calls 'Dudders', is Mr Dudley Ward to us: a very gentle man indeed, who will preface any request with 'I say, I don't suppose I might trouble you for the . . .' but it must be remembered that he likes a slice of lemon, not milk, with his tea and is always dropping something under the table, which, being short-sighted, he can never find. The only other person I recognise is the handsome one, Mr Geoffrey Keynes, who tends to drift off in his requests, and you must stand awhile and wait for him to finish his 'Oh – I say – might I – um . . .'

Today they are in high spirits. I have the feeling that Mr Keynes is sweet on Miss Ka Cox (my instincts are rarely wrong). He is part of some silly game, which they think is a May Day ritual; it involves planting a mandrake root and putting a sprig of blossom around it and calling it the Vegetation God. Mr Keynes finds a baby slug in a cowslip and carries it on his palm towards this mandrake root and the others sing a rhyme: 'Geoffrey who behaved so Odd; Geoffrey who put slugs in God.'

Then the heavens open and a great bucket of rain is sloshed at us. Betty, Lottie and I scurry to carry cups and plates into the kitchen and to fetch umbrellas and overcoats for our guests, but they wave them away, laughing like lunatics, throwing back their heads, and sticking out their tongues to catch the drops.

It's a wet and frantic task to fold the tables and chairs and take them in from the lawn to stack in the shed near the two-holer to keep dry. Cyril, Mr Neeve's boy from the Old Vicarage came to help us, and Mr Neeve too. The guests have gone off for a swim in the rain at Byron's Pool. Mrs Stevenson reminds us that they will soon be back, wanting scones and sandwiches, so charges Betty with stoking up the oven and kneading the dough.

'All that foolish May Day kerfuffle,' Betty mumbles, once Mrs Stevenson is out of earshot. 'And us missing May-ladying, the best day of the year . . .'

She misses Prickwillow far more than I do. I miss the littlies, yes, but the minute I arrived here I was compensated for that loss by all the new company: Rupert, Miss Darwin, Mr Ward and Mr Neeve, and all the constant visitors, and the comings and goings of the postmaster on his red bicycle, delivering another letter from London.

I try to pacify her by saying that I always forbade her and Lily to go May-ladying door to door, in any case, as in my view it's just as bad as begging, and she snapped back, 'And why shouldn't we beg? Sixpence a comb isn't going to last long when there's another mouth to feed!'

Another mouth to feed? The phrase makes no sense. My thoughts skitter wildly, thinking of Father returning from the grave, or Mother, walking back into our lives with her old babe in her arms, Ernestine, the last child, the sister who finished her off and was buried with her in that dark spot, where no flowers grow. What on earth can Betty mean?

She breaks down then. She has to tell me between tasks, between flouring the wooden board and the rolling-pin, between cutting out the scone shapes and between Mrs Stevenson's entering the kitchen and going out again, and Lottie's flapping ears. Her skin grows red and her shoulders shake and the words tumble out heavily, falling to the table like broken teeth.

Finally, the penny drops. I can't believe I hadn't seen it with my own eyes, that it had to be the simpleton Betty who saw it before me. I sink down in the scullery chair with my head in my hands. 'What's to be done, what's to be done?'

'He says he'll marry her,' Betty says, sniffing. Then, with feeling: 'You shouldn't have left us all alone if you didn't want this to happen!'

'Oh, my fault, is it, for trying to find a way to send money home? And why couldn't Edmund see the bastard off – why couldn't Edmund look after her?'

'Sam was always there! You know what he's like. You know what he was like with all of us. He loved Lily the best and he says he's always wanted to marry her . . .'

'Always wanted to! How long has it been going on? Didn't you try to stop it, if you knew? She's only fifteen! Does she want to marry him? He's – what? Thirty-five, at least! And so . . .'

A shudder runs through me as I picture Eel Sam, with his brown cap and his stubbly beard, with the long punt-gun across his knees, or sitting outside the house mending one of his eel-baskets. And always wearing wet galoshes, and with flecks of water-reed clinging to his trousers, and the whole muddy watery smell around him. And my lovely Lily, fresh and pink. Surely Lily didn't think it was right to let Sam have his way? Couldn't she have asked Mr Edwards to help her? But even as I think this, I know how foolish the idea is. To speak of such things to another man, to a church minister! And Lily with her wide eyes, her soft heart – how would she have fended off a man who could carry a punt-gun, a brace of swans, and put an eel-basket on his back and still stride through the water as if it were air?

I had had hopes for Lily. She shares my Brains in a way that Betty doesn't. The wicked thought passed through me: better that it would have been Betty, not Lily, who was lost. 'And did she not try Mrs Gotobed, and gin, and jumping?'

Now Betty's chin juts up smartly, and the eyes she raises to mine are horrified. 'Nellie! How can you say such a thing? No, she did not, and I'm glad that she didn't think of such a — wicked, murderous thing!'

I remember with a sick feeling then how strange Lily looked when I saw her last, how unhealthily swollen in cheeks and belly, and I curse myself for not seeing what was in front of my eyes. 'How far gone is she?'

'Six months. She's due at the end of summer.'

The kitchen is hot with shame. The smell of rising dough nearly suffocates us. Betty tells me that they'll be married in church next week, just a two-minute affair with the minister, Mr Edwards, doing the blessing; and Lily begged her to tell me, and she's thankful now she's got it off her chest, but I'm not to blame her. And Lily's life isn't over, Betty says, why speak as if it is? Why, it's simply the most natural thing in the world! Perhaps the best thing that could have happened. Sam will be a proper father to them now, and we can all breathe easy. And the Spike won't loom in the same scary way that it has since Father passed.

Breathe easy? While Sam's brats slither into our kitchen like a bucket of brown eels and my darling Lily is lost for ever into a life like Mother's, a life of Fen Blows, or under that foul green fog that hangs over the river, choking the life from everything? And it's all my fault because I left them, and despite my Brains and Good Sense, my facing of Hard Facts, I didn't foresee it.

We work in silence after that, and as there is so much to do, we can appear industrious to each other and yet be deep in our own thoughts. 'Lily's life isn't over,' Betty said. And: 'Perhaps it's the best thing that could have happened.' If only I could share her estimation of marriage and motherhood for Lily.

I thump the dough on to the table: it is gratifying to have a pliant substance to shake and throw around just now. My mind runs on, remembering the day Rupert opened the letter from Margery Olivier, and his fury at what he read there, the way he railed at me, at no one in particular: 'I'm informed, yes, that's the word, I'm *informed* by an estimable source, that marriage is the death of the intellectual girl, kills her off, or something, kills all development. When a woman falls in love, *apparently*, she does it so much more completely and finally than a man. (Strange, then, isn't it, that all the great poets and lovers of time have been male?)'

At the time I'd greeted his outburst in silence, confused. I thought his interests lay in another direction, quite away from girls altogether. But then I realised all men must marry, whatever their hearts desire. And all men must appear to be interested in the question, if they do not wish to reveal themselves to others in their true persuasion. That girl, Noel Olivier, with the long brown hair parted in the middle, whose serious, maybe angry, maybe – what? – sullen eyes stare at me every morning from a photograph in a silver frame on Rupert's mantelpiece. What a marvel that a girl might dare to be a doctor! I thought about what this Margery had said and whether she was just a moonstruck lunatic, as Rupert claimed. *Marriage, or rather love, ends a girl's life, finishing off her intellectual development, her education.* How angry he was when he repeated Margery's theory. How – cruel when he said so sarcastically that he wondered which part of *my* marvellous intellectual development I was afraid of losing by falling in love.

And yet. Marriage is so much the topic. I hear them talk of it all the time. Even the lady with the hooded eyes, the one who always holds her head at a cocked angle, like a little bird – what is her name? She frightens me. She always seems to be staring at something just out of sight, but then she will glance up and make the others laugh with a witty remark, or something sharp and cruel – Miss Stephen, isn't it? Even she speaks of little else. One time, when I was bringing the scones, she and Miss Cox were together and whispering . . . 'Poor thing! Well, he's not a bad man, I suppose . . .' Miss Stephen said, with not the least amount of sympathy in her voice. 'I hear her father asked her what she should do if she didn't marry. The answer, of course, is nothing: "We were educated for marriage, and that is all . . ."'

'Does she care for him?' asked Miss Cox.

'No, not in the least . . . but it's whether she can bear another year under her parents' roof . . .'

Well, that's fine for Miss Stephen and Miss Cox. Lily is already mistress of our little house in Prickwillow, and marrying Sam will just mean more of the same, for ever more. Kittie used to say that the Suffragists believe marriage is a solemn duty, the best possible way for 'women to raise humankind from the degradation to which men have brought it'. What she means is that men have filthy lusts and are for ever infecting their wives with all sorts of wicked diseases from the fallen women they visit – that was Kittie's main topic, when she was here, and half the ladies she went to London with, too.

But while weighing all this, and sweeping and dusting, and now in the kitchen making scones, another part of me seems to have been considering it quietly, like a little imp in a basement room working by candlelight while the rest of the house sleeps. And, to my astonishment, this imp comes up with a judgement quite different from my own, and it is this: the imp agrees with Margery. In some low-down never-explored place in my own heart, I realise that my despair for Lily is not because Sam is a bad man or a poor man. If she was marrying the minister, Mr Edwards, I would feel the same way. No matter how kind the man, how decent, how well-meaning, whenever I picture it, my lovely Lily married and with children clinging to her apron, a terrible picture comes to me, and a choking feeling. I glance out of the kitchen window and I see the bull-terrier, Mr Pudsey Dawson, with his nasty intent face in the wet grass, snuffling for frogs. And as a frog, a poor, sprightly, free little fellow with raised eyes and spread-fingered arms hopping foolishly towards Mr Pudsey's gaping mouth, I can see only my little Lily, green and free and wide-eyed too, now disappearing down a long black throat.

So, I have survived my stint as Schoolmaster and overseen Mother's move to the rented house, and also 'the putting an end to' of the poor old kitchen cat, Tibby, who, at sixteen, was considered too old to accommodate the change. (And the Housemaster who is to replace me, Bradby, would never keep her.) I have surely done my bit as Eldest Surviving Son, and when I think of her (the cat, I mean) she merges in my mind rather and I wonder, Did *her* face turn grey and impossible, as Father's did? Such relief that my career as Schoolmaster was cut short by Mother's sudden repudiation of her home and willingness to consider a life of reduced circumstance. Does she actually believe I might have a future as a poet after all? Or was it simply that she could not bear for a moment longer the gloomy face that greeted her every morning and the morose kickings of the table during meals?

I believe Mother fears for my *sanity* sometimes, fearing I will take to drink and crumble, like Dick, and it is this that most affected her decision.

I tried not to allow the Ranee to see the joy that possessed me the moment I knew I would soon be back in Grantchester, in my old rooms at the Orchard. And here I am – in time to spend May Day breakfasting among the apple blossom with my swarms of friends, the ones Virginia Stephen calls the 'dew dabblers'. The only frustration is that I have still not managed to manoeuvre a meeting between myself and that beguiling nymph Noel Olivier. I endeavoured to see her on a train *en route* to Birmingham but the dratted child could not bestir herself to tell me the right train. I have invited her to Grantchester countless times. I've teased and tantalised her with names of other women I spend my time with – Gwen (I know she is not in the least threatened by Gwen), Gwen's cousin Frances (ineffective now Frances has gone and married, but she might find Frances's poetry-writing a threat, with a bit of luck), Ka Cox, Virginia Stephen . . . Nothing seems to ruffle the sentimental schoolgirl Noel, however, and certainly not enough to bring her away from school and on to a train.

My dulled and deadened heart, sinking to the bottom of the river like a moss-furred stone during my term as Housemaster, has rather unfortunately bounced up since arriving back here, swinging again on its elastic before landing slap-bang at the feet of Noel once more. There is something so choking, so suffocating, about being adored. The oxygen of indifference is what I need: it surely makes my heart pump healthily. I am a Poet, so I must be the one *doing* the loving. The Great Lover, that's me, not the beloved. The beloved is despicable. That's the role of a girl.

After the rain and the swim, I come across Nellie in the kitchen, sitting alone with her head in her hands. I glance around to make sure no one can see us through the window to the lawn, then kneel at her feet and ask what might be wrong. She raises a hot face, smeared with flour. 'My sister is just about to be married. She is fifteen. It's something of a shock to me.'

'Wild Bet is to be married? So suddenly?'

'No, not Betty. I've another sister. Two, in fact. This is the middle one, Lily.'

'I see. Well, I should offer my congratulations, but I see from your face that they are not merited. Is the fellow a – what? – a drunk? A fool?'

'No, sir, not either of those. Just – old.'

'Ah, old.'

My knees creak as I sit at her feet and ponder her dear, worried face and the way her hand keeps flying to her cheek, as if to wipe at something that does not appear there. 'Ah . . . How old is he? Twenty-five? Thirty? Thirty-five! Horrible. I can't agree more.'

She smiles then.

'But must she marry the old fellow? Can't she refuse him?'

Nellie blushes then, and hastens to get up and check the oven. With her back to me she mutters miserably, 'It's him or the Spike, if you listen to Betty. I didn't think things were that bad. I've been sending money home! I can take care of them all, I said . . .'

'The Spike? The Workhouse, you mean? We wish to abolish it, Nellie, and provide properly for the aged, the sick, the children, the unemployed. Did you see the leaflets I left here? About the break-up of the Poor Law?'

'Mrs Stevenson burned them on the fire!' she says, turning round to face me, and wailing slightly. I see that her eyes glitter with tears and, feeling disadvantaged from my position on the floor, clamber to my feet to offer her my handkerchief. She sniffs into it, apologising and sobbing in equal measure.

'Things aren't getting any better in our time and our country, no matter how much we preach socialism and clean hearts at them,' I say. She snuffles quietly.

'Dudley and I plan a campaign. I, writing poetry and reading books and living here all day, feel rather doubtful and ignorant about 'The World' – about England and men, and what they're like. So I thought a trip deep into the English psyche was in order! Well, to Poole Harbour and other village greens in the south-west of England, to be more accurate. We intend to hire a horse, and take our tents, and preach by day and night in support of Poor Law reform. What do you think, Nell? Think we can do it?'

Now she looks up, surprised. She crumples the handkerchief into a ball and seems to wonder whether to hand it back to me. Thankfully she decides against this and stuffs it into her apron pocket. 'Why – yes, I – I suppose so— You and Mr Ward? In a caravan?'

'We shall need a Primus stove, plates, spoons, cocoa, salt –

any chance of you sneaking us a few things, for our supplies? I mean, not if it would get you in trouble, but it's proving rather expensive, what with the cost of the caravan I'm renting from Hugh and Steuart Wilson of King's.'

'Yes,' she says, smiling at last. 'Of course I can.'

'Marvellous! And, Nell, I've never actually, you know, minded a horse before – do you think one ought to feed it once or twice a day on such a trip? It's called Guy, apparently. The horse, I mean.'

'Oh, I'm sure once will do fine, if it's a good feed.'

'Splendid! Well, let's hope Women's Suffrage doesn't hijack our more important campaign ... and, yes, a tin of sardines for our "whales" would be splendid. Do you really think you could spare them?'

She runs about the kitchen then, seemingly cheered to be given a purpose – and I feel a queer stab of pride that I'm the fellow who lifted her mood. Her sleeves are rolled up so that I see the finely haired skin on her bare arms and, seeing her thus, I am reminded once again of that day among the bees and her magnificent command of the creatures. Of course, such a memory of last summer, of the moment when I took her in my arms and the sunny taste of her mouth in mine, leads immediately into the unwanted, ugly memory of other things. Of her in the garden pegging up newly laundered wet sheets. I watched her from my window, knowing that she, and she alone, knew about Denham, knew all about me, every last thing ...

'I – well, thank you, Nell. I – I suppose Ka Cox could get some of these things just as easily. Ka's a practical girl, you know, and an orphan like yourself, so used to taking charge of things—'

Nell had disappeared into the pantry, and appears suddenly, as I say this, bearing two jars of honey, and such a stricken look that I long at once to bite back the words, although not quite understanding which of them has offended her so. Is it the mention of her being an orphan? Well, that was tactless, yes, but it is the truth, none the less, and Nell has never seemed to me to shirk simple facts. Could it, perhaps, have my been implication that Ka might do just as well as she, when Nell is trying so hard to accommodate me?

'Oh, of course,' Nell says, glancing down at the jars in her hands, now seeming uncertain whether to offer the honey or not.

'I wouldn't want to get you into trouble with Mrs Stevenson, Nell,' I suggest, appeasingly.

Now she says hotly, 'The honey is my own to give. From my family in Prickwillow, you know. Actually, these are two very special jars: the fields near our house with their poppies make a – quite special flavour, very different from Mr Neeve's orchard honey.'

'I—' Naturally here I wish to apologise, but feel tongue-tied and then annoyed that this girl always seems to fluster me, render me foolish and clumsy and, in some queer fashion, hideously exposed. (My remarkable wit does rather desert me where Nell Golightly is concerned!) It is the matter of Denham, and the kiss, too, but more than that: it is some dreadful sense that she holds my secrets in her apron pocket along with my handkerchief. I'm delivered bound into her hands.

'I should pack some books,' I mutter stiffly, preparing to retreat to my room. 'You know, decide what I'm taking. Marlowe, Donne, the Webbs' report, that kind of thing. Yes, I need, we need, special information about the counties we're passing through to help us plan our campaign – must go. Um, thanks awfully for the honey.'

I hold out my hands and, without a word, she places the two jars in them.

Poole High Street, close to the Free Library. Principal speaker Mr Brooke. Questions invited. In support of proposals for Poor Law Reform. Sponsored by the NCPD.

I am unable to remain still in my room. I sit on my bed, pile up a few books in a desultory fashion, and leap up again. I put my face to the floorboards, breathing in dust and mouse droppings, and listen.

Yes. Nell is still in the kitchen, clattering about with the pots. Can I find some excuse to venture back downstairs, and repair the damage of my clumsy remark about Ka and, more importantly, somehow smooth over the discomfort of what has transpired between us and can never be alluded to?

I peer over the balcony in time to see Mrs Stevenson leave the kitchen. Then I return downstairs, where Nell seems happily back to her customary good spirits and Mrs Stevenson does not return. I show her one of our leaflets, which she admires. I show her some of my notes, too, and she murmurs that the Spike is indeed worse than any prison, with mothers separated from children, and husbands from wives, and hard labour all day long. 'At least in prison you might one day be released!' she says. 'In the Spike no one ever seems to come out who goes in.'

I contemplate this awful thought for a moment. 'I'm a little nervous. You know, the British Working Man can be rather – alarming to one like me!'

She laughs.

'I'm preparing my various responses, just in case.'

I leap on to a kitchen chair in my bare feet and, in a voice that mimics Sidney Webb's meaningful tones, announce: 'You may fear for the moral character of the poor, yes, if these laws came to pass. Will the fibre of the working man become weak if he has recourse to the state directly he is out of a job? It is all very well, my dear young woman, to be so concerned, so *incensed* about the moral character of the poor *individual*, but what about the moral fibre of a nation as a whole and its responsibility to its citizens in need? What of that, eh, my girl?'

She laughs again.

'After all,' I continue, dropping the mimicry in my tone and aiming for sincerity, 'why make a distinction between times of adversity and times of trouble or danger from others? If we are in danger from other people we have no difficulty in throwing ourselves at the mercy of the state in the shape of the local policeman or law courts. This carries no shame or social stigma! Why should it be otherwise in times of financial trouble? This "loss of independence" does not weaken the character. It leaves men free to use their energies more profitably!'

She claps and smiles one of her deep, bosomy smiles and I feel immensely pleased, and immensely relieved and, yes, it almost does feel easy between us again. I jump down from my soapbox. 'Marvellous! Thank you, Nell. Oh, yes, I'm quite prepared now for whatever Assaults on Reason these working folk are going to throw at us – not to mention the eggs!'

She gives a little shriek then, and disappears to the pantry again, returning with a box of eggs. 'Take these too. I've asked. I'll bring extra from home when I visit and Mrs Stevenson says it's fine.'

'Oh, Nell, you are too kind. I'm not sure young Dudders knows how to boil an egg, but we can teach him, eh?'

'You're funny,' she says.

I stare into her glorious violet eyes and I know that I was not wrong in my estimation of her intelligence. 'I'm sorry about your sister, Nell,' I say, and in an instant we are both serious again. 'Marrying an old man is a horrible fate.'

'Yes.'

Whenever I let slip the mask for a moment, Nellie never fails to respond. It is not in what she says – Tradition and Centuries are difficult to undo – but in her glances. That is where the truth between us resides. At least, sometimes I believe this. But then the glorious violet eyes of Nell Golightly could persuade a man of anything.

Now she covers her hands with a teacloth and takes the tray

of scones from the oven. A delicious hot smell wafts around us. I hear from the voices outside on the lawn that Ka and Geoffrey and the others are returning and a private conversation cannot be continued. I'm surprised at how angry this makes me feel.

'We leave tomorrow next week for our trip, so any – provisions you might secrete before then would be gratefully received.'

'I'll do my best.'

'It's all for the Cause, of course.'

'Yes, sir,' she says. I realise from her tone and that 'sir' that the others are in earshot and Mrs Stevenson's approaching tread is on the stair, so I lean forward to whisper my next remark, and I have no idea what I'm going to say until the words are out of my mouth.

'I have one more request of you, Nellie. I will make it first thing in the morning.'

'Yes, sir. As you will.'

Her eyes widen. Violets. Darkening woods. Nature hammers out a drumbeat.

I straighten up. *Quelle surprise!* Whatever that request might be, it seems Nell has said yes!

~

Rupert says, 'Let's swim at Byron's Pool.'

'What – now? At this hour?'

'Come on, no one's up. It's a glorious morning. Come, come on, Nellie . . .'

'But my duties – I haven't finished in the kitchen.'

'It's six o'clock! The sun's barely up. Surely your sister might cover for you just this once. Tell Mrs Stevenson you have some errand – I don't know . . . Don't you have to go to the butcher's sometimes?'

I smile at this, for meat is delivered, every morning, by the butcher's boy, Tommy, long before Rupert wakes. But the idea of it, of sneaking away with Rupert, of being outdoors by the river in the earliest, freshest part of the day, rather than indoors, hot and sweaty, cleaning out the copper and blackening the stove and starching the linen for the new tenants, feels so tempting, so scandalous, that I can hardly stop my heart picketing my chest for permission. How many times have I listened bitterly to the shouts, the laughter and calls of Rupert and his friends, the thud of wood and splash in the water, remembering with longing Edmund frolicking in the river Lark, while Rupert rows back along the Cam escorting some lady in a hat or being read to by some twit in a silk tie, and I'm out by the hives, working?

'All right,' I say. 'Betty will stand in for me.'

And I grab the smoker and some quicklime so that I might inspect the bees on the way back and make-believe I have been checking that no surplus queen cells have been forming in the brood chamber. Rupert goes on ahead, carrying the butterfly net, and some rolled-up towels so that we won't be seen walking together. The Stevensons are still asleep. Betty is just stirring and I tell her that I will be gone an hour and she's to make out I'm busy with the bees, if anyone asks. She looks startled but is too sleepy to ask more.

My heart raps at my ribcage for fear, for naughtiness, swift and stubborn as the spotted woodpecker at the tree. The sky is clean, the day shiny as a newborn, and a light wind is brushing my cheek as I trip along behind Rupert, watching his figure in the distance as he leaves the garden and joins the lane; his blue shirt, his long, loose-limbed gait. I haven't run away like this since I was in the schoolhouse and that was a day that the Reverend himself came to find me.

I venture this thought to Rupert when I catch up with him. Thick white dust is shifting under his sand-shoes. He seems dismayed to discover my family are regular churchgoers.

'But how else could a girl like me get an education?' I ask, and he stares at me for a moment, and nods. We cross the bridge in front of Grantchester Mill and walk through a meadow, which is still sopping with dew.

'I must give you *Principia Ethica* and more poems by Swinburne. I shall soon corrupt you.'

I set my mouth then, knowing he is laughing at me. We are now in sight of the the dam with its grey sluice gates and the deep, waiting water. The smell of mint and mud swells around us. He sits at the edge of the water, at the place where the river widens into a pool and cow-parsley grows on the banks in huge white clumps. He seems to be waiting for me to join him. I'm shy at first, but seeing him look up expectantly and brush his fringe from his eyes, I sit myself down beside him. Not too close.

'What do you think of Ka Cox, Nellie?'

This is not what I expected. I put down the smoker on the grass.

Miss Cox. Yesterday, coming back late with the Frenchman, Mr Raverat, she startled me in the kitchen, where I had my back to the lawn and the french windows and was drying crockery with the teacloth. Her sudden appearance made me jump and I dropped a cup. To my surprise she bent with me to pick up the pieces and, handing them to me, said, 'Oh, I'm so sorry! I startled you. How silly of me.' Mr Raverat stood awkwardly while she gathered more of the pieces and placed them in my outstretched palm. 'I really *am* terribly sorry,' she said, and opened her mouth to say more. I imagined she was about to offer to pay, but to my astonishment she said, 'Where does Mrs Stevenson keep the pan and brush? Let me sweep up the rest.'

'Oh, no, ma'am,' I said hastily, and Mr Raverat put his arm on hers and murmured something in French to her. He swept her out of the kitchen and on to the lawn.

'She is very . . . *kind*,' I say now cautiously.

Rupert has rolled on to his stomach, holding the butterfly net in the green eddies of the water so that the back of his head is towards me. 'Kind . . . Hmmm. How observant you are!' He sits up and pokes me with a little twig, and laughs.

I blush, wondering if my interest in Miss Cox betrays me. But he seems not to notice.

'Kind, though. Is that enough? Is kindness what a man wants . . . after all? Not especially pretty . . . She's sweet on Jacques, of course,'

'Oh. For myself I thought your friend Mr Keynes rather fond of her,' I answer.

Rupert seems surprised. 'Geoffrey? Surely not? But, then, that's the surprise with Ka. Other chaps do seem rather to find her – attractive. It's a mystery to me. Jacques is perfectly smitten.'

To my surprise, now that she is being so dismissed, I feel obliged to defend Miss Cox. 'Well, there's plenty to be said for kindness, after all. For warmth and a generous nature . . . more than, you know, looks alone . . .'

'Perhaps. Or perhaps it's that some men wish to be mothered. And some of us would run a thousand miles before taking up that particular offer!'

Knowing this to be a reference to *his* mother, I now feel the need to defend her, too. 'I don't see that maternal affection is so . . . dreadful . . .'

'No. Quite. Perhaps not for those who don't have it. I'm sorry I mentioned it yesterday, Nell, you being an orphan like Ka. It was horribly tactless of me, but I only meant that Ka not having parents means she's not chaperoned the way Noel Olivier is, she's rather more free . . . but, then, you working people are always free. You have no idea how – how stultifying it is to be a nice upper-class girl like Noel Olivier!'

He is chewing on a strand of dewy grass and spits it out angrily.

'I HATE THE UPPER CLASSES!'

This he says with such a shout that I glance over to the

riverbank, fearing someone might appear there and discover us. I am sitting with my skirts tucked round my knees, watching a ladybird travel carefully down a blade of grass, the grass arching with her weight; bending, but never breaking. 'I'm not sure we have such freedoms.'

The ladybird's wings spread like a shell cracking open and she takes off.

'No, forgive me, Nellie. I suppose not. It's only that – it's just that. I once saw a working girl. Not a prostitute, you know, just a girl with her lad, under a lamp-light, on Trinity Street. And she was kissing him, and I saw her face shining in that yellow light, and her eyes were open and in that glimpse— I can never get that glimpse, that expression, out of my mind.'

I shoot a shy glance at him. We are close enough for me to see the blond hairs on his upper lip. Something has peeled back. His face is so naked that I glance hastily away again.

We do not acknowledge what I have seen. He shifts, props himself up on one elbow and pats the dandelions in the grass beside him.

'Lie here beside me, Nellie. Can you swim? What time is it?' (He glances at his watch.) 'The water will be icy so early in the day before the sun has properly warmed it, but I am certain you are a splendid swimmer! Tell me I'm right?'

He is pulling off his sand-shoes. Now the woodpecker in my chest starts its knocking again. I could not have believed he meant it when he first suggested swimming this morning, but here he is, stripping off his blue flannel shirt so that his bare chest, sun-browned with its light fur of golden hair, is suddenly in front of me, and nowhere to hide my face.

'Be brave, Nellie. No one ever comes here. Only his ghostly lordship practising his stroke.'

I don't understand, and my face betrays it.

'Byron, Nellie. The poet. Safely dead these ninety years.'

When I still say nothing, he lowers his voice to a whisper:

'Take off your dress. You must have done it once – swum naked as a child?'

I have, of course, only last summer. But that was a river filled with noisy children, with Stanley and Edmund and Lily and Olive, and splashing and mud-drenched limbs, a river in which I had been a child myself. A summer when I still had a father.

Slowly, without looking at him, I begin unbuttoning my boots. My hands are sticky with sweat and the clamouring in my heart is so loud that it seems to bounce from tree to tree. Since I'm not properly dressed, there is only my nightdress, with a coat thrown over it, and my drawers. I take off the coat, and shiver in the flimsy cotton-lawn. I don't like him watching me, and tell him so. He pretends to look away, shielding his eyes, then peeping from under his hands. This makes me laugh.

'You're very beautiful, Nell,' he says softly.

As fast as I can, I pull the nightdress over my head, taking an enormous deep breath. Then the drawers are flung high, so that they catch on a branch behind me. My whole body sizzles, as if the trees might catch fire.

I run to the water's edge and dive, and Rupert shouts, and the green water rears up to smack me with a cold, a startling, a gloriously shocking slug.

～

So we are on the road, in a cart, to be exact. We left Winchester this morning. A cat – a tabby stray, we've named it Pat the Cat – has accompanied us, which gives Dudders something to stroke (he is missing Anne-Marie, his new love). Dudders sits up front on the box while I keep Guy stocked up with his nosebag and whistle happily, all the while composing more Poor Law speeches, planning the meeting with Noel and her delightful sister Bryn and thinking, beneath it all, of Nellie Golightly. Remembering her leaping into the river – such a lightning jolt of joy stiffening my entire body as I watched her. What a swimmer! What a girl! Such thrilling transgression in even sitting by the water and talking to her. But it's impossible. How could one ever continue a dalliance with the maid when one is watched over at every turn by kindly friends, like James and Lytton and Eddie, with an interest in assuring one remains a committed Sodomite? Which I clearly never was – only an adventurer. Easier to have such an adventure with a boy from one's own class than with Nell.

Too much thinking about it makes me sigh, and I cannot share it with Dudley. I know his feelings on Inversion and Sodomy. And for all his fine talk and good intentions, he is even more afraid of the lower classes than I am.

Last night two local fellows pelted us with stones and we had to wake up the damned horse and move on. We have not yet addressed one meeting but we have a plan that if such stone-throwing happens again we will simply display the poster, look wise and scatter pamphlets.

There was a frightful scene with the Stevensons the morning we left. Something about going barefoot – villagers have talked. The apple-cheeked old lady was quite unsentimental about it and the apples looked hard and crisp and even, suddenly, not cosy at all. She even brought refined Mr Neeve to make the point more *refinedly*. It was most embarrassing. I had to stand at the bottom of the stairs like a naughty schoolboy and was horribly reminded of the Ranee on one of her rants and did not like the craven small-boy stance I could not help taking up. I caught a glimpse of Nellie, hovering at the top of the stairs, her hand to her cheek in that mannerism she has, and I wondered. Had a villager in fact seen me at Byron's Pool with Nellie? Was that what Mrs Stevenson was alluding to?

Not that anything happened, of course, except for swimming and nakedness. Oh, and a kiss. One more small kiss. However, this was no ordinary nakedness. Oh, my word, no. It truly was the most extraordinary nakedness. That's the problem. Nellie's naked loveliness is something even the naiads at the water's edge have never before seen the like of. With her upturned girl's breasts like the bellies of little sparrows – well, it was quite enough to signal to the whole village that Lust herself was in the garden.

I caught a fish. A tiddler. (*A minnow! A minnow! I have him by the nose!*) He turned over fitfully and we saw the flash of his gold stripe and Nellie crouched beside me, shivering, asking if I would put him back since he was so tiny. I was reluctant – it had taken a good ten minutes of standing in the water with the disturbed mud billowing round my legs like smoke, carefully hovering behind him (so as not to make a shadow), hands cupped, to accomplish my goal, but I did as she bade, and the lucky fellow flipped over on one side and limped off to his cool, curving world. My thoughts had not been entirely on the fish, and my concentration, with Nellie standing so close beside me, her water-drenched body slim and green in the watery light like the shoot of a young tree, giving off her salty intimate river smell, was stiffening me so violently that I had to plunge quickly into the cold river to disguise it.

The child acted as if she had not noticed, just as she did that time in the garden. I do not know how to corrupt her. I do not *want* to corrupt her. Or only a little. And then I should regret it horribly. It seems, for all my posturing, I am not in the cast of Henry Lamb or Augustus John. I am shy. I like her rather too much. I did kiss her, damp and trembling in the boat-shed, and then I rubbed her hair with a towel, but she was by then in a fit of terror and kept wailing that she was late for breakfast duties. It was not the moment for a seduction scene. I found I was trembling myself, and couldn't quite explain it.

I did regret my ill-judged remark in the bedroom that I should have 'taken' her that day by the beehives. How ferociously she glared at me! I almost ducked.

No, she's hardly a girl to mess with, this Nell Golightly. Far too fierce and resolute for that.

So we arrive, and tie up the horse, in the spot we identified the night before, nailing a poster to a tree, announcing our intention to deliver an Important Speech at 10 a.m. prompt. The audience, eagerly gathered for our performance (one old gent), is filling a pipe in great anticipation. I inspect my watch: ten precisely. But surely Guy needs a feed, I decide, and Dudley agrees. And after that Dudley finds that posters must be added beneath the one advertising our speech, and a wooden soapbox carried from the caravan and leaflets spread upon the grass. The old gent coughs impatiently.

Dudley decides that Pat the Cat needs feeding, also, and offers her the last in our tin of sardines.

I stand on the box. Our audience swells to two as a delivery boy joins the old gent.

I clear my throat. 'Between two and three million are destitute in Britain! If the whole population were under the command of one sane man, the first thing he would do would be to feed those millions so that they could contribute towards the production of wealth!'

'Aye,' says the old gent, to my surprise. The delivery boy stares, bottom lip dropping open, placing his basket against his bicycle, and waits for more. Dudley, having finished feeding Pat, hovers behind me, studiously cleaning his pince-nez.

'The Poor Law has remained untouched for more than eighty years! The system of the Workhouse is an abomination in a civilised society such as ours! Lumping the poor, the sick, the aged and the crippled together and blaming them equally for their ills is outmoded and – and – why, it is *ridiculous*!'

Ha – my strongest sentiments yet. There does not appear to be much disagreement, however. The old gent puffs at his pipe and the boy draws on a non-existent beard with his fingers. Which makes it rather a task to summon up the necessary passion.

Where is the argument I'd been anticipating? Where the philosophical objections – the great debate about the fibre of the working man being weakened if he has recourse to the state the moment he breaks his leg? Where is the concern about the moral character of the poor if we offer them greater aid in times of hardship?

After a few more rousing phrases, the old gent claps his hands together noisily and the boy with the bicycle begins to wheel it away.

'Thank you, gentlemen!' I shout, stepping down from my box. 'Thank you for your concern, your outrage – nay, your *devotion* to the cause of reforming the Poor Law. Do, please, take a leaflet.'

The old man and the young one shuffle away without a word. The leaflets remain on the grass.

'The average British Working Man is a rather lacklustre fellow, wouldn't you say, Dudders?'

We chuckle as we set up camp on the village green and, at top speed, make a small fire and fill a pan with water from the village tap to prepare a late breakfast of boiled eggs. Dudley has, in fact, become rather skilled at these. But it's only a matter of time before the kindly village policeman arrives to shoo us along.

Only twelve more days of this and as many places. The tour is not a success. It is hard to say which of us is the most ill at ease with the folk whose lives we hope to ameliorate. I am the better speaker. Dudley is the better egg-boiler. That is all.

We cannot admit this to each other. We wriggle into our sleeping-bags at night with cheering remarks, such as 'Well, that's another five fellows who know more than they did a day ago!' and stirring discussions about Progress and other Marvellous Things. I know that Dudley falls asleep thinking of his German love, Anne-Marie. And that we are both counting the days until the camp at Buckler's Hard (ha!) with Noel and other girls, where I will be free as the wind, and Dudley as a monsoon. There I might even accomplish a further sighting of Noel's water-nymph self so that I might make a fair and accurate comparison with my exquisite, my tender new shoot Nellie.

One night I dream of my days at Rugby before Dick died. I was lying out under a full moon. It was of two people – Charles Sayle and Kenny Cott (the latter in his eighteenth year, perhaps, or even younger) and . . . Charles got at it with Kenny by pretending he'd lost a Penwiper, and making out Kenny ('naughty boy!') had taken it, and searching his pockets – his trouser pockets – for it. Kenny accepted it, giggling. Excitement rose, and finally they left the room together. There were other details. I expect it all happened, really, some time.

In between our fine speeches (mine infinitely better than those of poor old Dudders, who stumbles, and drops his glasses, whereas I merely blush, which makes me appear passionate), I compose – mentally – my September talk to the New Bilton Adult School about Shakespeare. 'This glutton, drunkard, poacher, agnostic, adulterer and Sodomite was England's greatest poet.' I like telling the story of Shakespeare's love affairs. It shocks the Puritans, who want it hushed up. And it shocks the pro-Sodomites, who want to continue in a hazy pinkish belief that all great men were Sodomites . . .

The truth is that some great men are Sodomites *and* womanisers. Perhaps when my career as a womaniser has begun in earnest, that will be the category to which I belong.

The truth is, sex is fundamentally filthy.

How glorious that my darling girls know better than to give in to my base desires and prefer to let the river cool my ardour.

Or cool me harder, as the naughty James would say.

~

When Rupert returns from his lecture tour and his camping trip he must stay at the Old Vicarage, Mrs Stevenson says. She won't have him in the house a moment longer.

I don't dare to protest. I feel a broad misery as she says it that I struggle to disguise with sweeping. I have heard – Mrs Stevenson has heard – that the lecture tour was not all Rupert hoped for and he is compensating by staying longer with his friends at camp. 'Silly boy,' is all she says on that matter. She has much to say about his other misdemeanours.

Mrs Stevenson says it is the final straw. His bare feet, his friends, his strange hours and stranger requests – it's all been too much. What is the final straw? I want to ask, but she doesn't say. I tremble. Is it possible someone saw us at Byron's Pool? On our way back we stopped in the little boat-shed to dry ourselves with the towels that Rupert had brought, and he showed me the saucy drawings on the walls and kissed me and I flared hot and then cold and felt swamped with confusion, and then he pushed me lightly and said that we should leave separately so that no one would see us. I ran, after I left him, my body aching with hurt but my blood singing from the cold water; in my mind scuttled all the things I didn't dare ask him. I ran back to my room, praying that Mrs Stevenson would believe my story about washing my hair.

Now she says, 'There's been a mix-up with his room,' as if that would answer matters. Mrs Stevenson rolls her eyes to the ceiling and wipes her hands firmly on her apron in a look that says, 'We're well rid of him.'

And so, suddenly, his room is filled with another man, a tall, stooped man, who does not admit me when he is bathing or shaving. It's for the best. It's surely for the best. If only I believed it was for the best! That day at Byron's Pool, our conversations, the way he looked at me – his kiss: what sense can I make of it all? I know I wasn't mistaken about the boy Denham in his room. I know that whatever sport he makes of me, it can only ever be that – cruelty and sport.

But he doesn't seem cruel when he smiles, or when he kisses me, or when the early-morning light grazes the blades of his shoulders.

I put my face in my hands, remembering, and chide myself for such deep, deep foolishness, and hide myself in the pantry to weep. A scuffle outside tells me that Lottie is in the scullery so I wipe my face on my apron and rearrange my hair.

'He's back! He's staying at the Old Vicarage!'

'Who? Who on earth do you mean, Lottie?'

'Why, Rupert, of course. And – imagine! He proposed while he was away! To that schoolgirl one, the one with the plaits. Noel Olivier.'

I sit down on the pantry floor.

'Nell? Nell, what is it? Are you sick?'

'It's nothing. I'm fine. I just – I—' I feel the touch of cool jars behind my neck. Nausea rising up to my throat and subsiding.

'Nell, Nell, let me fetch Ma—'

'No!' I say fiercely. 'I'm fine – I'll be fine. Leave me alone, Lottie, there's a good girl. I'll be fine in five minutes.'

She backs away. I see from her face, her glances at the kitchen door, that she wants to tell someone and that she won't be able to keep quiet so, with an effort, I pull myself together, compose my face and stand up. 'It's that time of the month is all. Let me get some air in the garden for five minutes. Go fetch me a glass of water, Lotts, there's a girl.'

Glad of the errand, she finally leaves me. I step out into the garden and breathe hungrily. My stomach wrenches and I taste bile in my mouth.

I will go to the Old Vicarage to inspect the bees, I decide. See for myself.

~

I have moved out from the delightful Orchard and my Arcadian adventure there with the bee-keeper's daughter is over, perhaps for ever. I shall no longer sniff the lilac in bloom beneath my little room as I wake and pump ship to the sound of Little Nell sweeping the stairs, that mouthwatering rump swaying from side to side. Or, rather, I have moved next door to the Old Vicarage. The maid has accepted my kiss with a warm mouth. I was afraid to go further, and my heterosexual virginity remains filthily intact.

The Neeves – Henry and Florence and their son, Cyril, who models himself on me – are more tolerant of my bare feet and thousands of visitors. For this tolerance I will forfeit Mrs Stevenson's apple pies and all-round superior cooking. And, in fact, I will escape the shame that Mrs Stevenson's lecture produced, and I could never thereafter shake off on bumping into her in the scullery or on the lawn.

There *is* the compensation of the Old Vicarage garden: the cement sundial in the shape of a lectern, the ghosts of vicars past, the proximity to the riverbank and a creepy, ramshackle lushness, which, I believe, will be conducive to poetry. Or to merry-making.

Nellie and her subtle, discreet ministering will be the greatest loss. It is difficult to admit to myself *how* great a loss. I am puzzled by my own tendency to dwell on the matter and the melancholy thoughts it has produced. She is only next door, I remind myself. But it is only when I have concocted A Plan for redeeming the situation that my mood lifts, and I cannot wait to convey it to Nell.

Here is the girl herself, suddenly, striding towards me with great purpose.

'Nell! Nell – where are you going so fast? Slow down, I have something to ask you.'

'I was coming to see you, in fact, sir – I mean, Rupert. I – had heard you were back.'

'Yes, and here I am. My new home. You heard, I suppose, that Mrs Stevenson was not entirely happy with my shenanigans.'

Nell looks as if she is about to say something, but her eyes suddenly widen and I realise that someone has stepped outside to the garden and must be standing behind me.

Dear Noel. Noel is staying here.

Clumsily, I grasp at once for my plan, trying to speak as if this is what we had been discussing. 'So, Miss Golightly, if you would be so kind as to continue to do my washing, bed linen, that sort of thing . . . I don't feel able to further burden Florence – Mrs Neeve, kind as she is . . .' And, I whisper this part, 'I have a horror of the multitudinous creeping creatures that live in the Old Vicarage – no amount of Keating's insect powder will vanquish them.'

'Huh?'

'And would an extra two shillings a week be sufficient? Would you make sure Mrs Stevenson is happy with that – with using her hot water and such? You can pick it up when you come to the Old Vicarage to tend your bees . . .'

Nell's face is a picture. It seems to glow with anger, or self-righteousness, or something. Noel is striding towards us, her boyish frame bounding across the grass. There is no time to say anything more, and I'm rather startled when Nell makes a furious turn on her heel and stalks off.

'Three shillings, if you prefer!' I call after her. 'I appreciate the marvellous way you have with the Jay's woollen underwear!' She hurries towards the hives. I am well aware that my laundry request is not the true source of her annoyance.

～

I hear Rupert's voice first, reciting his lines from the play to a fat and snuffling Mr Pudsey Dawson in the garden. On seeing me he calls out, and I stride over. Something about the washing. I cannot really take in what he is saying. Because there, behind him, is the girl. The one from the silver photo-frame. How can I ask him now?

And so I murmur some assent to his request, and the sum of money registers with me in some distant part of my brain, and even his little joke registers: that he appreciates the way I never allow his Jay's woollen underwear to shrink. My fists curl and uncurl under my apron; and I walk towards the hives, and set myself to work. The bees will know at once how upset I am. So I take several long, deep breaths and push my hands down into my pockets, and though tears prickle under my eyelids, I don't allow them to spill over. After a moment, I have control of myself once more.

I'm lifting out the honey frames, filling Mr Neeve's old wheelbarrow with them, and suddenly become aware of someone watching me. At first I think Rupert has returned. I refuse to turn my head.

Then I realise it is her, the girl. She stands at some distance, no doubt frightened by the humming of the bees swelling around us, like the sound when a bottle of fizzy lemonade is opened. Perhaps she is impressed – like Rupert and Mr Raverat – that I wear no veil (although I am wearing Father's gloves, my arms and wrists being covered in red welts from various oven burns). I brush the creeping bees clinging to my skirt with my stick of tied feathers, trying to see as much as I can of this girl without turning my head. From the corner of my eye I see that she – Noel – is wearing an olive green headscarf over plaits, in a funny sort of knotted style, and I feel, rather than see, that she is staring at me in the same way that I would like to examine her. I am forced to continue as if unaware of her.

So, he has proposed to you, has he?

She has hair the colour of a mule's. Face somewhat square. Overall: something serious, intent. Very quiet. Her frame like that of a boy. Bosoms – none to speak of. Oh, yes, for a man who likes boys, she fits the bill all right, I think bitterly, then chide myself. Within the range of persons he is *allowed* to fall in love with, this Noel Olivier, much too firm and steely for his mother, would certainly be a reasonable choice.

She continues to stare, and again the thought of a mule comes to me. It's like being stared at by a stubborn grey donkey. She moves then, and I gloomily trundle the frames back to the kitchen at the Orchard, where Betty and Lottie help with the spinning, with Lottie 'testing' the honey every five minutes. This is a mixed-flower crop, with a different flavour from the dense sweetness of the high-summer crop. The kitchen soon rolls with the sound of the spinner as the girls take it in turns with the handle, and I hold the jars under the tap to catch the amber bulb of liquid, and try with all my might to put Noel Olivier out of my mind.

And that's when it happens again. Father. The kitchen is crammed with the syrupy smell of deep purple heather, and I am thinking of that girl, Noel Olivier, staring so fiercely at me; and of Rupert, naked in Byron's Pool; and I'm not thinking of Father but only watching the honey, green and flecked as pond-water, pouring from the tap, when things suddenly stop, and I'm not there at all, but outside the window, looking in at the scene, at the rattling spinner on the table with the frames revolving in it and the noise and the sweat on the girls' arms and faces, at the white-muslin circles laid out next to the empty jars; and I feel certain that Father is beside me, white as smoke in his ghostly form, thin and fading, but this time, unlike the last, he is tugging at my arm, he is trying to speak.

The next minute things go on again as normal and I know then there is bad news in Prickwillow. When the last honey jar is sealed, I take off my apron and beg leave of Mrs Stevenson to go home at once.

It's late afternoon by the time Tommy fetches me to Prickwillow and by then my stomach has turned to stone with the worry, with the knowledge that something is not right. It must be Lily, of course. Here I have been, stupidly dwelling on Rupert and the daft comings and goings of his heart, and my poor dear Lily's time is drawing near. There's nothing ghostly or magical, really, about my feelings; plain common sense would tell you that a girl of fifteen with her firstborn is never going to have a bed of roses.

Tommy turns the horse for Ely after he has dropped me at the drove, allowing me to walk the last fifteen minutes alone. He can tell from my mood not to try it on with me, so he tells me that after he has delivered the meat he can call back for me at five, but I shake my head – I want at least to stay the night.

I find Lily in the front room where someone, Sam maybe, has rigged up a space, with a curtain attached to the wall by two screws, and Lily lying on her side. Mrs Gotobed is with her, her fat rear greeting me from behind the curtain, and the others are outside, in the meadows down to the river, where she has sent them to catch rabbits and stay out of the way.

When I pull back the curtain the smell that only a woman knows reaches me. Mrs Gotobed is muttering her prayers – 'I pray thee Lord her soul to keep' – as she tries to sweep Lily's damp hair from her forehead. For one horrible, breath-stopping moment, I think my sister is dead. Then Mrs Gotobed turns to me with her strange, flattened face, and says, without looking up, 'She's small, Nellie. The baby's aside, and feet first too. Fetch me that brandy and tell the littlies not to come back till they've at least two rabbits apiece.'

I pass Sam outside on my way to fetch the brandy, kept hidden at the water's edge under a large stone so that he won't drink it. He sees me and lifts one eyebrow but carries on with his smoking and stripping the willow for an eel-grigg he is making, asking me mildly as I pass where his tea is, so I put the kettle on and set to making him some and taking it out to him, since there's not much else I can do to help.

Lily's damp hair is spread out like a giant golden spider on the pillow. Her head is as red as a bright poppy, so much redder than her pale swollen body in the sticky nightdress. She is not looking at me, but staring down at the pillow. I am filled with a longing to call her, to bring her back to me, but I know from the look in her eyes that she is fixed on the pain and on the urging inside her, tearing at her like a hook twisting inside the gut of a fish. She has no way to see that I need her, that I feel such fearful failure.

How did it get to this, when my little sister is going the same way as Mother? How could I have made such a choice . . . to go to the Orchard, to want so much to hobnob with the Varsity types, to better myself, to indulge in ridiculous flirtations with Rupert? And all for what? So that my family could fend for themselves, merely survive, take in the first ragamuffin man who needles his way inside them? I'm sorry, Lily, I'm sorry, sorry, Lily, I'm sorry, Father, I see now how I have failed you, failed all of you.

And then I fall to praying too, praying in a way that I haven't since Mother died. Please, God, please save Lily. I will do anything, I promise. I will give up my foolishness, give up Rupert, yes, I will, I really will, I will give up whatever you ask of me. Only please save my darling, innocent Lily whom I love more than myself, who has only ever been good and true, Lord, and your servant.

Mrs Gotobed says it's been twelve hours already and no crowning, barely even a peek of the baby's head. Lily's hips are not childbearing hips, and she is foolish and weak and malnourished and more besides. She won't take the brandy-soaked rag that Mrs Gotobed holds out to her, panting between her waves of pain that she hasn't forgotten Temperance, and why should we?

We carry on like that all through the hot afternoon and the sultry evening, while the littlies trickle in one by one and sit on the other side of the curtain, playing Whist and pausing in their soft chatter every time one of Lily's screams pierces the curtain.

In the evening I hear Sam go down to the river to take the boat out and set the eel-traps. He returns, poking his head under the curtain, and gets shooed away, and we hear Olive crying and saying she is hungry and I leave Lily for a moment to skin the rabbits and set up a stew on the stove that they can have with bread before they go to bed. So then the house is filled with the strange smells of onions and cooking meat, and blood and salty water, and my stomach groans with hunger but I could no more eat than fly. I offer Mrs Gotobed some and she comes outside the curtain to take a bowl, and the clock ticks and Mrs G sits with a half-finished rug that Lily had been making across her knees, and Lily sleeps for a while.

Then suddenly an owl hoots and Lily stirs and gives her own, animal-sounding howl. I leap to the curtain to see her sitting up, her face contorted like the screwed-up shapes of a walnut shell. 'Lily, Lily dear – push now, push!' I say, feeling, without knowing how, that the baby is really coming at last, that maybe my prayers have been answered.

She kneels up with her nightdress raised and uttering one long howl like the sound of the sky wrenching in two. The house waits in silence. And then the dark wet plop of the child finally slithers on to the bed with such a dull, damp thud that I know at once my prayers may have been answered, but at a terrible price. Only Lily is saved. The blue-green rope of bloodied cord is wrapped right round the baby's neck – something Mrs Gotobed suspected and had her arm nearly up to Lily's neck trying to put right, but couldn't. The mess plops all over the bed just exactly like the dead lost flesh of the skinned rabbits, and Mrs Gotobed is beside me at once, cutting Lily's cord with a practised slice, and encouraging her to deliver the afterbirth with one last great push.

We wrap the tiny wet red thing in a torn sheet and take her outside before Lily can see her. I can't think where to lay this bundle, and it's dark, so I give her to Sam with one angry thrust and decide that he must do as he sees fit. He is smoking his pipe and accepts the damp bundle, and he gives only a muffled cry, like the yelp of a dog when its tail is nipped.

You might wonder how I behaved so badly but I'm blind with rage by now and thinking only of my sister, and what she has been through. All that labouring, all that labouring, a lifetime tied to Sam, and all for nothing, I think.

As I come back into the sitting room Lily sits up, thrusts back the curtain and staring directly at me, asks, 'Did I pull the child through? Did the Lord help me manage it?'

I tell her He did not.

We eat by candlelight, and the children sigh and make up their beds once again in that loamy green room, soaked with the smell of death and babies and the feeling of some barrier passed through and not yet travelled home from. Olive's tearful face shines up at me from her pillow. 'Lily won't die, will she, like Mother?' she asks. I assure her that she won't.

'We should have called for a doctor!' I say just once, and bitterly, as Mrs Gotobed is pulling her shawl from a nail near the door and turning wearily to leave. She makes no reply, instead merely returns to the bed to stroke Lily's head and whisper to her. I hear the muttered name 'Emily', which must have been Lily's chosen name for the girl. It was cruel of me to mention the doctor, I know, because it was Sam had forbidden him, saying the man was a drunkard anyway, and Sam didn't have money to 'throw around'. In any case, what was good enough for our own departed mother should be good enough for Lily.

Mrs Gotobed leaves with a great huff, her enormous bulk immediately emptying the room. Sam finally comes inside. I hear him breathing, I hear the thud of heavy leather on the rug as he takes off each boot, then another breath as he blows out the candle, and a creak, and then a long, slow, rolling fart, as he climbs into bed on the other side of the curtain from his now dry-eyed, wide-awake wife.

> *Yet, you had fancied, God could never*
> *Have bidden a child turn from the spring and the sunlight,*
> *And shut him in that lonely shell, to drop for ever*
> *Into the emptiness and silence, into the night . . .*

I found those few lines in Rupert's study. A poem in his black inky scrawl called 'The Vision of the Archangels'. I don't know if it is a good poem or a frightful one. All is stuff and nonsense with him, all jokes and games and silliness. But then suddenly the words, phrases, lines I'd found so surprising at the time come to find me:

> *God's little pitiful Body lying, worn and thin,*
> *And curled up like some crumpled, lonely, flower-petal . . .*

Yes, that was exactly how she had seemed, Emily, when I thrust her at Sam. A scrunched-up, unfurled flower-bud. How could Rupert know of such things? Of the sorrows of women? Then I remember that he had a sister, who died as a baby of one year old, a year before he was born. He told me of her once, as if she was of no consequence. But, then, he speaks of everything that way. His poetry puts another slant on things.

Such a foolish blond boy with nothing to concern him but learning his lines for some play with his friends. And yet, try as I might to be angry with Rupert, it is his lines that come to me, lying in the cot amidst my snoring family, Rupert's words that comfort me. He is angry with God, and so am I. Rupert's true heart beats only on paper.

Three

January 1911

'My subconscious is angry with every dreary young woman I meet if she doesn't fall in love with me: & my consciousness is furious with her if she does.'

Rupert Brooke

I asked Noel Olivier to marry me. It wasn't a success.

I declared myself. I don't remember my exact words, only the shy expression on her face and the fact that the solid Noel suddenly cracked open and – admitted she loved me too! I wanted to rush back at once to the others (we were at Summer Camp at Buckler's Hard) and bellow the news from the treetops, but she put a hand on my arm and stopped me. And there, frozen, we have remained ever since.

I can only assume that she regretted immediately her frankness, but I can't believe there is no truth in the declaration itself. Why *did* she say it if she did not feel it? Did her witch of a sister Margery persuade her to recant? She writes mysteriously that 'what happened at Camp will not affect her' (whatever *that* might mean!) and her photo sits again on the new mantel in the Old Vicarage, her face brown and inscrutable. She agreed to play Envy (oh, wicked tease) in *Faustus*, along with the lovely Bryn, who played, of course, Helen of Troy. She did permit me the odd occasion where my feet tickled hers under the Old Vicarage table a day or two ago when she stayed here – and she smiled at me above her grey pinafore – but that was all.

Two and a half years I have laboured like this. If it weren't for Margery's absurd position about intellectual women and marriage, and Noel's hopelessness at defying her . . . but that's not the only reason. Noel does not trust me. She thinks I am – what was her word? She thinks I am in love with being in love rather than with her.

Am I capable of loving one person for more than one day? Is everyone capable of this, or is it denied to some of us?

Gwen and Jacques announced their wedding plans yesterday, which doesn't help. I kept having a strange flash of the square-headed woman who cuts wood (Gwen) with the beaky botanist (Jacques) doing something disgusting in a train carriage. Of course they would probably never do any such thing but that did not stop the mental picture plaguing me.

Now that Noel has returned to Bedales I write her ridiculous letters full of hot feeling and beastliness. (It does show one up, this business of being in love.)

I have grown closer to Ka, who offers some solace. Ka is squashy and has a good listening ear. With her I do not feel quite so ashamed and out of control – especially in the regions of (a) jealousy and (b) mistrust. (I want so much to be splendid.)

The thing is. Nell.

That moment in the boat-shed.

How exquisite it was to roughly towel her dark hair, to see it damp and curling down her neck like fronds of seaweed. To help her slip her arms into her coat, smelling the water-mint that clung to her skin. The memory of her, the way her hot wrist shivered in mine, her burning, bending head as she bent to button up her boots; my throat was dry, like a man starving. I practically had to push her out of the door. I leaned back against the cold wood of the shed and wanted to weep. What is it that so inhibits my career as a lover? What on earth prevented me catching hold of her once more, pulling her back and making the kiss longer, and harder?

I might wish to name it Honour and Goodness. Or is it Pride, and Caring What Others Think? Or, more likely, simple Fear of Mother? Or All-round Hopelessness? Well. I closed the door behind her and, ha!, later I wrote a poem about it. I thought myself fine and clever to have resisted. Oh, my cleverness! My poor, grubby cleverness. Because the truth is, I worship her. I do not *want* her defiled. These days I can't even allow myself to imagine her pale silky limbs when I'm pumping ship for even *that* would sully her. That holy far-off serene splendour would all be *spoiled* if she returned my desire.

My conqueror's blood was suddenly cool as a deep river.

So, with that miserable realisation, the Obelisk – as James and I call Henry Lamb's active member (or, rather, in my case, the Sad Little Cock) – withered despairingly and a sonnet was written. I called it 'Success'.

I longed afresh for a clean, rushing splash in the river.

My plan, my escape route, is to travel. Away from the Ranee and Eddie and the confusions of Noel Olivier and her rejections of me, the temptations of the bursting cream-puff of a maid or young boys who are in love with me, to a place that is manly and swimming in beer, where I can finish my essay undisturbed. I've decided on Munich.

❧

Betty saw me talking to Rupert. That day in the garden when his *betrothed* was there. We are lying in our bed in our little room, the blue counterpane pulled up to our chins.

'What were you talking about?' she asks.

'Nothing – his laundry, if you must know. Why do you ask?'

'Was it only that? You seemed – you looked— I thought you looked upset.'

'Upset? Of course not! Why should I be upset?'

'I know you have been sad,' she says, after a pause, 'and not just about Lily and the baby. I— Nell. Why do you never confide in me?'

'Why should I?'

She begins sniffing then, and calls me a 'hard-hearted Hannah', and says I'm 'not much of a sister at all'.

I lie in the darkness beside her, a desire to confess welling and subsiding in me in waves. 'Oh, Betty, please don't press me. It will only make it worse!'

'So there is something? Something else, I mean. I knew it! You *are* in love with him. Or has he – you know— Is it that he has tried it on with you?'

'Oh, he's kissed me, yes . . .'

'He kissed you?'

Betty's excitement crackles beside me. In a minute, she will be asking for details and chattering with girlish fever – I must tell her at once before she makes matters worse. 'But, Betty . . . Don't go on so. It's not that simple. I don't know how to tell you – I don't know if you will understand.'

I take a breath before saying it.

'Rupert is – he— He doesn't like girls.'

'What?'

'He is— Oh, Betty! You must have heard of such a thing.'

'I don't understand.'

'You must have heard of men who – of some men who – of, you know, men like Mr Eddie Marsh . . .'

'Eddie Marsh? Government secretaries, you mean?'

'Oh, for God's sake, Betty. You know! Boys who like other boys. Ah – don't make me say any more, *please.*'

Such a long pause then in the beating darkness. I can hear Betty breathing. I can feel her shock somehow, so great that it is like a vibration, through the satin coverlet between us. I feel her body stiffen, and her long silence. I can almost hear her thoughts violently leaping.

'Are you sure?' she asks eventually, in a tiny child's voice, aghast.

I say yes. I do not want to explain about Denham and the sheets, so I just say to rest assured that her big sister knows what she's talking about. After a pause I remind her to tell no one. Especially not Lottie. Men can go in prison for it, and women never do it, but for the men who go in for it, it is probably a sight more common than we could guess, especially among men who get sent away to school, who spend so much time in each other's pockets, and where doing such things with ladies from their own set is so restricted.

'That's true, but it's easy for them to take liberties with us!' Betty answers, after a moment, recovering her voice.

So then I say again, wearily, that I don't know, and I don't want to say any more, because look at what has just happened to our poor dear Lily, and isn't it best not to go on with talk of love for a man you can never have, a man who doesn't love women in any case? The only thing you could have from such a man is trouble.

'What a filthy thing.' That's all she says for a long while.

I lie there listening to the call of the tawny owl, soft and familiar, and thinking of Lily.

My words seem to have satisfied Betty, and believing that the end of it, I allow sleep to press its fingers into me. Then there pipes a small voice, still bright awake: 'But how can you be so *sure*, Nellie? Is it something to do with that strange Eddie Marsh, or the other one with the pince-nez and way of creeping up on you like a black cat? What is his name – Mr Strachey? Mr James Strachey? Is it because of those two? You can't imagine Rupert is in love with either of them . . . pansies?'

She has heard the word 'pansy', then, and now understands it.

'No, of course not!'

'Well, then. If he doesn't – if he isn't drawn to girls, I don't understand! Why is he getting married? And why did he kiss you? It makes no sense . . . and I have even seen Rupert look at that plain Miss Ka Cox in a sweet way, if you want my honest opinion . . .'

'Oh, go to sleep, Betty, for God's sake, and keep your honest opinion to yourself.'

I feel little better for my unburdening. In fact, telling Betty has only made it more real, and seem more hopeless. But I mean to keep my vow to God. I promised to give up Rupert, or mooning after him, and didn't I say that when I made up my mind to something I'm stuck to it, like honey cappings?

~

I'm here at last in Germany, where I intend to stay, probably for ever. Or at least for three days. From there I shall wander south and east and no one will hear of me more, save the mariners who ply among the Cyclades, who will bring back strange tales of a bald, red-bearded man sitting on the rocks in the sun, naked, chanting wicked little Latin poems. Actually, it will more likely be three months. Here is a good place to (a) write my Webster essay, (b) improve my German, and (c) be free of Mother and all the conflicting feelings about Noel and Ka and Nell.

I have put Nell out of my head. It was difficult, involving a knife, a chisel and a clamp. Ka Cox and I had a small spat in a bookshop before I left London for Munich, and I hurt her, and for that I feel bloody. She wanted to buy me a book and I acted as if I couldn't care less, and Ka felt slighted and snubbed and sniffy and a million other things beginning with *s*, and the truth is, I did feel bad. I suddenly waved my arm in the bookshop at thirty books, but by then it was too late. Ka's sweetness, her reliability – I saw in a flash that even they might one day be snatched from me. My cushion, my sofa, my safe place to park my weary backside! I considered fleetingly pressing my mouth to hers, knowing that such behaviour would seal her in my thrall for ever, but even I hadn't the heart to do it. And in any case, I am, of course, deluding myself. If my kisses are so powerful, why hasn't the lovely Nellie Golightly succumbed?

Of course, I didn't venture a full and thorough test. I cut the experiment short – and now I am wailing and gnashing my teeth and wondering why the devil did I? Why do I lack the necessary detachment with that girl, the little voice that simply says: 'An adventure!'

Thank Heaven, then, that Nellie has the marvellous talent of forgetting, a few moments afterwards, and never mentioning the indiscretion again. She took the same attitude towards my glorious steaming erection that time when she saw it in the garden. (I've tried waving it at her timidly a few times since.) She acts always as if I – it – were nothing at all, so I must assume that this is indeed true. Difficult, then, that I remember the experience of kissing Nellie rather differently. Difficult that even here in this ridiculous *pension* (like something out of a Forster novel, with ladies ludicrous and serious, dropping words of wisdom at breakfast like pats of butter . . . thank God for Frau Ewald, the portrait painter), I remember most vividly the warm, living shape of Nell, how it felt to hold her (it felt hot and good and ordinary, the way it feels when Laddie, the Old Vicarage dog, sleeps at the bottom of the bed), and her startled expression when I pulled away from her. Difficult, too, that it is Nellie I wish to confide in now about the young Dutch sculptress I met yesterday in the alley, during the Carnival, the Bacchus-Fest.

Right now I'm lying in my room in the Pension Bellevue in Munich where the blanket is emaciated and grey and the smell of smoke rising up through the floorboards makes me lonely and excited at once, and am wondering whether to seek her out again. The Dutch sculptress. Elisabeth, I mean. Elisabeth van Rysselberghe.

The trouble is, she smells of lemons and sawdust and the alcohol used to clean paintbrushes. She has a tiny chin, and a certain roundness of form that puts me in mind of Lord Rosebery, and eyes big as golf balls, and her mother is an artist with free ideas. There was a terrifying moment when anything might have happened and almost did – we had been roaming among the gay young in the street and even dancing and talking, yes, talking and talking, and the night wore on. Confetti sprinkled our hair and everyone was in costume of a riotous kind – myself in Greek dress, which meant a great deal of freedom and rather less of modesty. We moved to Luitpold café together to drink beer and black coffee and then more beer, and I was so surprised to find myself unchaperoned with a young woman that even had she been ugly (which she wasn't) my thoughts would have turned to Taking Advantage, or Making the Most of an Ideal Opportunity, in a good Christian sense.

So then we kissed and, in poor German, I suggested taking a room at the hotel next door and, to my enormous astonishment and no small amount of fear, Elisabeth acquiesced. We kissed all the way up the stairs (full of fat, simple Germans and dreadful Jews) and the kisses were feverish but more than a little repulsive to me because I began to realise how fervently she desired them and, as of old, such expectation kills off feeling in me. Immodest though it is to say it, knowing myself so desired is familiar enough, and every lover seeks the unique, the exceptional. And, furthermore, the taste of beer in another's mouth is not especially nice.

We stumbled to the bed in the corner, and Elisabeth sat down and patted the counterpane, with its glut of apricot roses and disorderly green leaves, and I moved in to kiss her again. In fact, the kissing was helpful in dulling my brain, being damp and excessive and not enjoyable. But I kept on with it in order to put all thoughts aside. Then Elisabeth was munching on my fingers, my head in her lap. However, just as she was tugging at the buttons on her dress and giving me my first glimpse of a large flat saucer of nipple I felt myself fizzle like a cork going out of a bottle and knew it to be quite, quite hopeless. (That breast put me in mind of pink babies and of the Ranee.)

Elisabeth's enthusiasm was filthy. Her watery, protruding eyes swam in front of me and I suddenly realised from the catches in her breathing and the faint sweat that gleamed on her forehead and upper lip that she was in the sort of state that I had naïvely believed only young men ever reached. There was a Crisis at hand. Our kissing and my meaningless caresses had brought her to it. The caresses were the work of an amateur; I aimed anywhere I could reach; twice I thought I had a breast and discovered it a pocket handkerchief; once I thought I'd traversed the top of her thigh but couldn't break away to check if I was inside or outside her stocking. I had been prodding her (through my Greek robe) with a baton that was now limp and extinguished and she, poor sculptress, had every right to expect me to – to put it colloquially – 'go on'.

It was five in the morning. A beetle crawled along the floorboard and some bed springs squeaked mournfully next door as I pulled away from her politely and told her how much I respected her and understood the delicacy of a woman's situation and of having an unimpeachable reputation, and how much I admired her, etc., etc. Her mouth opened and closed like Mr Pudsey Dawson's when eating a frog. Her golf-ball eyes swelled larger than ever, but she was too much a lady to protest. It was like extricating oneself from an octopus. My shirt button caught on her brooch and we had to untangle it with our faces horribly close so that I smelled the white-spirit again and glimpsed the pores at the side of her nose and vacillated wildly between thinking, Oh, for goodness' sake, have done with it, and Hang it all, the girl is repulsive! No wonder the obelisk refuses to stand up!

I wandered home down Ludwigstrasse and thought about Isben and composed a letter in my head to Dudley. (*Dudeln*, I plan to tell him, is a verb meaning to play the bagpipes.) But now I have escaped the Dutch sculptress, and am alone in my room. The Algerian dancing master next door is, for once, silent. My feet, infinitely disconnected from the rest of my body (sticking out from the covers as I'm too tall for this cot), tell me it is freezing again. I fondle only a cup of hot milk and my Webster essay and a pile of Elizabethan and German books that I may never read. Suddenly I am immensely regretful. Elisabeth, I realise, was uniquely *willing*. She is the first.

I will write to James and ask his advice. French letters, pessaries and such. After all, I must practise, if I'm not to remain an unconverted Sodomite for ever. I can hardly practise on Noel or Ka, and the maid is far too clever. Plus, I like her. The maid, that is. She has short nails and normal-sized eyes and her body when you hold her doesn't yield but maintains its own shape, slender and well formed, like the trunk of a good tree.

I must stop thinking of Nellie Golightly and write my letter of enquiry to James, and stop flogging the pillow with my umbrella.

As a footnote, I have sampled and sought out German culture. It has changed all my political views. Everyone is right! Germans are arming ferociously. I am now wildly in favour of nineteen new dreadnoughts. German culture must never, never prevail. The Germans are nice and well meaning and they try; but they are SOFT. Oh! They ARE soft. The only good things (outside music, perhaps) are the writings of Jews who live in Vienna.

James replies by return of post with a long list of advice. I read it sitting in the Café Bauer drinking hot milk and reading yesterday's copy of *The Times*. I hide the letter under the Sports Section as it is full of crude drawings but I can't hide my smiles. I laugh so much at one point that I spill my milk and another cup must be brought. I am planning a long round of social engagements – Fifth Symphony, Wagner, Debussy, Valkyries. But plans to Complete the Task with Elisabeth loom large.

So. The gist of it is. Preventatives are of three kinds: letters, pessaries and syringes. Letters are condemned on all accounts for you get hardly any pleasure from them and they are most likely to be torn in the excitement of the moment. (This information from James's brother Oliver who is an adept.)

Pessaries. Sound like very unpleasant things. James draws me a picture of Rendle's Wife's Friend, obtainable at all chemists in cardboard boxes as shown. It's made of quinine and oil and you shove it up the lady's cunt before you start, he says. It makes a filthy soapy mess that comes out over everything. In general, it's efficient.

Syringe. James draws terrible pictures of these too. Used to clean out the lady's insides. The enema is far the most popular instrument, apparently, but has to be used after you've emitted and James stresses that everything must be cleaned really thoroughly, everything (meaning Elisabeth's insides, presumably), with quinine. This immediately presents a picture so awful, so foul, that all stiff parts of me wither in horror.

No method is certain. James added that the best time to attempt it is as nearly as possible halfway between 'the monthlies'. If you do it just before a 'monthly' you're most likely to have a baby. To do it during a 'monthly' is too incredibly disgusting. And Henry Lamb uses the withdrawal method, which requires an iron nerve. Hmmm. Not surprisingly, James tells me to spare myself the whole filthy business and come to bed with him instead. But I'm resolved to approach Elisabeth again and talk to her this very evening. This state of ignorance and inexperience cannot be allowed to persist! I know it is only the Bloomsberries who copulate and we Neo-Pagans (Virginia Stephen's name for us) simply walk together in woods talking about poetry and Nature, but personally speaking, I wish to expand my knowledge of the world and in particular my experience of emitting into something warm and accommodating. (Always assuming Elisabeth possesses such a place.)

I finish my hot milk, and slip James's valuable reading matter under my sleeve. I pen him a reply, marvelling at the equally fascinating subject of his brother Lytton, at twenty-three, having the mumps, to which I reply with a description of my own experience at sixteen. Not so much the pain as the Disgrace, and the madness. At first they just swell and swell till they're tight and shiny and cracking, two monstrous red balloons. Then, all of a sudden, they go hard – hard as a rock. You lie and stare at the mountain under the bedclothes, and you pretend it's your knees. The doctor strips you and eyes them till you have an erection, then thinks you're a bad lot. You cannot pump ship and your semen turns green. It lasts for months. I suppose the fatal cases are when they grow too far and explode.

When I've finished this brilliant epistle I leave at once in search of a chemist. The pessaries sound messy but the easiest to persuade Elisabeth to use, so I go in search of them. And book myself a hotel, since the *pension* would be an impossible venue for the seduction. I perk up just thinking of it all, and my homesickness for the Orchard Tea Gardens and its inhabitants, and honey-scented flowery English girls generally, begins to fade away in lovely anticipation of my sweaty Dutch sculptress and her hot and salty delights.

(By the way, I have discovered she is Belgian, rather than Dutch, but I cannot see that it makes the slightest difference.)

(Later) The Hotel Berchielli.

Elisabeth arrives looking flushed and nervous and I announce at once that I have something important to discuss. She perches on a pink-cushioned chair at some distance from the bed and I stand leaning one knee nonchalantly against the counterpane. This starts to be so uncomfortable that the knee begins to tremble and my words come out a little staccato so I straighten up and then begin to feel I am towering over her, idly wishing that she would stop looking up at me with those bulbous eyes and let down her pinned hair so that I might find her attractive again.

I outline the methods for avoiding pregnancy and show her the options: a box of Rendle's Wife's Friends or the syringe. (The Jew who sold them to me could hardly keep the smirk from his face.) I am red in the face by now and unable to meet her eyes. I have not felt this bad since practising my let-us-support-working-class-artists speech on Augustus John and cannot silence the little voice in my head wailing, *Stop, stop!* throughout. But some devil makes me persist in outlining the ways in which a little preparation is infinitely preferable to a state of heated intoxication such as almost overcame us a week ago. Then I pause and the room shudders and Elisabeth emits a piercing sob.

'How could you?' She staggers to her feet and I think for one moment she is going to slap me.

I step back and fall on to the bed. Elisabeth stands over me, glaring. (I haven't seen a face so alarming since the Ranee last slippered me.) My courage utterly fails as I see how badly I have understood the whole affair and my heart starts a drumbeat of terror as Elisabeth makes clear how wrong, how very wrong, I have been in my assessment of her, in her saliva-specked, broken English. How could I be so cruel, so evil, make such assumptions – the outburst goes on and on. I see instantly my enormous error. (I feel disadvantaged by my prone position, made even more foolish by a tassel from a cushion tickling my face.) Elisabeth is a woman who wanted to feel that if she gave herself to me she did so in a dream, a stupor, like Tess of the d'Urbervilles. That she was hypnotised, hoodwinked. In short: that I made her. When I protest breathlessly – swiping the tasselled cushion dramatically aside – that I had assumed we were both interested in the same thing and had only looked at practical, sensible ways to achieve our goal, she says suddenly: 'And are you then going to marry me as you so – *desire* me, as you say?'

'Good God, *no!*' Perhaps not the most advised reply but it leaps out before I can silence it.

Then she hurls herself sobbing on to the bed, giving the loudest of animal-like shrieks. 'Oh, Heavens above, I am – you have – I cannot believe you said that to me!'

'Ssh, Elisabeth, others will hear!' I'm afraid the bellboy will skate across the icy blue lake of carpet outside our room with his supercilious air and arrest me for a rapist. What is interesting, in a passing kind of way, is that in her damsel-in-distress pose her hair has come loose and is now tumbling round her face in tendrils and if it weren't for the fact that her extreme response has made her repugnant to me, she might once again be attractive. (If that isn't a contradictory and nonsensical statement, which I fear it is.)

I make one last attempt to rescue things. 'Elisabeth. I'm so sorry. I've misunderstood – I'm an awful snake – forgive me – I thought it something we *both* desired. I misunderstood— Forgive me, Elisabeth, I thought you were – a *Modern*. I thought we agreed on these things. Forgive me— Here, take my handkerchief, ssh, darling, please . . .'

At length she allows herself to be calmed a little, and I stop feeling like a desperate character from *Ann Veronica*. What I do feel is bloody angry. Surely it's not honest to want to be raped? Why must everything be so difficult and deceitful? I know I have rather muffed the thing but I do feel resentful that my frankness has been met with such nineteenth-century histrionics.

I'm sick of Munich and quite frightened of Elisabeth. She's given me a cold in the head and I'm not sure she isn't mad. I should return home at once.

~

I have heard Rupert is coming home. I have more to worry about here. Lily is not well – she is with child again, so soon after her loss that she is naturally thin and struggling – and Betty has gone this week to Prickwillow to take care of her. Kittie has returned, full of her Suffragette talk and London ways and not in the least shamed of her actions, or grateful to Mrs Stevenson for giving her back her position.

When Mrs S is out of earshot Kittie can't wait to tell Lottie all about the last few months, and how she met Miss Emily Wilding Davison, the one they call Guy Fawkes in Petticoats, and how it was absolutely true, she did indeed conceal herself under the Houses of Parliament for forty-six hours. 'We'd stocked her up with meat lozenges, you know, and lime juice to keep her going and she spent Sunday night there.'

'And all for what?' I say. 'I remember hearing Mr Dudley Ward talking about it – a cleaner found her before she had her chance to leap out and frighten Mr Asquith with her protest, anyway, so what was the point?'

'The point is—' Kittie starts, but on Mrs Stevenson suddenly appearing in the garden, where we are, she falls silent, only soon she can't keep it up, and begins singing the dreadful 'March of the Women' under her breath – 'Cry with the wind for the dawn is breaking ... March, march, swing you along ...' I have a horrid picture of eager women barging forward, with overmuch action from the rump. The type that describes itself as Awf'ly Fit. The Miss Ka Cox type, for instance.

It's washday and we've dragged the tub and the Faithfull washer out into the garden to make the most of the spring sunshine. Of course, Kittie being Kittie, she has her opinions on my doing Rupert's washing. It was Mr Neeve who told me he was coming back and sheepishly handed me a bundle of Rupert's things that had lain in the laundry basket these last three months. And the bed linen that they might make his room ready. Mr Neeve hands the bundle to me with a thrust, as if he can't wait to be rid of it. Taking in lodgers was not his idea.

'And Rupert pays you, then – you don't just do it as a kindness?' asks Kittie, when Mr Neeve has strode off towards the Old Vicarage garden.

'Of course he pays me! And he says I do it better than Mrs Neeve.'

Lottie goes inside and comes out again, struggling to carry

the tub with the shirts that have been soaking in lye. She plonks it on the grass with a heavy splash. 'It's cos Mrs Neeve boils wool and flings the rest in the Granta. Her place is riddled with lice and mice and more besides!' Lottie has a horror of anything small that creeps, and will never go in the apple loft here at the Orchard for that reason.

'Oh, don't be silly, Lottie. What's a few fieldmice when you can live as a Poet wants to, with friends to stay and – and reading aloud from books at midnight?' I say. I feel very loyal to the Neeves and can't stand Mrs Neeve's housekeeping skills to be compared to Mrs Stevenson's in this way.

'Ooh, hark at you,' says Kittie, mockingly. 'Living as a Poet wants to? What on earth can that mean? Our Nellie's smitten, isn't she?' She pulls some woollen underwear out of the tub and watches it stretch its long legs into the water. 'Are these his?' she whispers to Lottie, and the pair of them cackle like old hens while I seize the leggings and stuff them back into the water.

Kittie laughs. 'I mean, who's paying for him to swan around, that's what I'd like to know? I thought he had to work as a schoolmaster . . .'

'That was only to help his mother. So they could stay in their old house. His mother agreed to move.' Of course, this information betrays some of my conversations with Rupert and Kittie looks surprised. Surprised, but unrelenting.

'Three months in Germany doing what? This lot love the Germans, don't they? Mr Ward is smitten with a German girl, I heard . . . And, ooh, Lottie, did you hear that our French froggie Mr Raverat proposed to Miss Ka Cox? You know who Miss Cox is, don't you, the one who stoops so badly she looks as if she's nursing a child?'

'Oh, you're years behind,' Lottie says importantly. 'Miss Cox turned Mr Raverat down! She's sweet on our Rupert . . . and Mr Raverat has married the artist one, the one at the Slade, Miss Darwin, you remember her? Gwen Raverat, she is now. Although, for a while, there was a suggestion . . . Well, listen to this . . .'

She whispers something then, and Kittie snatches her ear away as if on fire.

'He didn't! Mr Raverat openly proposed Miss Cox as a mistress? And what did Miss Darwin have to say?'

'She seemed to think it a good idea. It was Miss Cox who said no to the arrangement, and only, it seems, because she didn't love Mr Raverat, not because she thought it wrong to be a mistress! They're like those gypsies who stayed in Grantchester Meadows, no more morals than honey bees . . .'

'Bees have morals! They're loyal. They're devoted to their queen and they work so hard! There's no shame in service . . . Bees live only to serve!'

I'm plunging the dolly-peg into the tub of linen with a fierce push as I say this, making it splash all around us. My misery at Rupert's sudden departure to Germany has dulled as the weeks have gone by, but the careless comments of Lottie and Kittie make it surface, like the mucky water swirling back up despite all my pushing and pressing down.

I try to steady my voice. 'Well. Despite everything I've taught you it's clear you have no love for the bees as I have,' I mutter . . . I'm surprised that the girls have fallen silent. So I glance up and it is Kittie's face that tells me he's arrived – the way her eyes widen suddenly and her cheeks turn scarlet. I wheel round, and there he is in his cream flannels, a blaze of sunlight, his eyes the colour of the brightest morning glory.

'Ah, to find the prettiest maids in England washing up a storm in a garden full of blossom and – what's this? Extolling the virtues of service, too! Am I in Heaven? Or merely dreaming?'

Did he hear me defend him? Lord, how long was he standing there?

'Mr Brooke, sir—'

'Nellie Golightly. Lovely to see you again. Good morning to you all! Nell – a word, my dear.'

His hand is on my arm and I know the others are watching. He flashes each a smile but speaks quietly to me, steering me away from the garden and towards the kitchen at the Orchard, then towards the bottom of the stairs leading to his old room. Here he pauses. I am fiercely conscious of his hand, brushing the bare skin of my arm.

'I left some things here. A small diary – buff-coloured? Some papers, part of my Webster essay, which I must finish this year to be considered for the Fellowship. And . . . the other matter is . . . letters, I wonder if any letters have arrived here from a very strange lady? You would notice the stamp, Belgian, and the return address – a Miss van Rysselberghe? I've never seen her handwriting but no doubt it has all the distinguishing features of a madwoman's . . .'

'I can look for you, sir—'

'*Sir?* Nellie! Have you forgotten me so soon?' In a pretend whisper, he says, 'Did our swim mean nothing to you?'

When he teases I have no idea how to respond. After a second's pause I become as serious as he is flippant, and try to explain. 'Sorry. It is hard for me to call you – Rupert. Surely you don't want me to – not when there are – when Kittie and Lottie are about? I haven't found any of your things. But I shall certainly check for you. There's a new gentleman in there now, so it will have to be later.'

'I know. Dratted fellow. Sleeping in my friendly sheets! Why does nothing ever stay the same?'

I have no reply to this. My sleeves, I notice for the first time, are becoming unrolled and, being wet from the washing, are dripping on to the red-tiled floor. I stare down at them and then up again at Rupert's enquiring face. A little thought goes through me that he looks tired, that his brows are lighter than ever, his hair a little longer. As if he could read my thoughts he suddenly runs a hand up through his parting, letting his hair fall between his fingers. Then he nods, as if I had spoken, pursing his mouth and looking closely at me. A tiny petal of blossom that had been caught in his hair floats to the floor. I think for a moment he wants to say something more but he merely swipes at the white petal with his foot as if it were a cigarette to extinguish, and strides out of the kitchen.

It is only when he has left that I notice how vividly I remember his smell, the smell of him, and how I have missed it. It's a clean green river smell, the smell of warm flannel and Wrights Coal Tar Soap, and the smell of my childhood, my brothers playing in the river, or stripping bark to make a pipe: something fresh mixing with something older, something male and a little sour, too. The smell reminds me of the other things he left here in his room at the Orchard that I didn't tell him about: a half-empty tin of Cherry Blossom boot polish, one black leather-bound notebook, some strands of sandy-gold hair wound round a masculine kind of no-handled comb, one old dark green woollen sock, the melting lather on his razor.

I'm weak suddenly, with his remembered smell, and sink down a while on the kitchen chair, my face in my hands. He might just as well be in another country.

When I rejoin Kittie and Lottie they've stopped staring after Rupert and are eagerly discussing the Great Procession of Suffragists planned for next month, which Kittie says she intends to sneak away to and join.

'Why did you come back, then, if you're still keen to be in the thick of it with your Suffragist friends?' I ask her, surprising myself with the spite in my voice.

'To educate you, my dear!' she says, flipping a bubble of soapsuds at my ear with the wooden dolly-peg. 'The Lord knows, someone must!'

I know this can't be true. And when she says it her eyes slip away, as if there is something she doesn't want me to see. Lottie doesn't notice – the girl is a simpleton. So he is back, I'm thinking, and sweet torture must begin once more.

The worst has happened. A letter from Elisabeth. Clever Nellie intercepted it. (Of course Mademoiselle van Rysselberghe believes me to be still living at the Orchard, and has guessed at my address – she must have heard me mention it.) On the pretext of checking on her hives, Nellie comes over to deliver it to me in the Old Vicarage garden. I open it in front of her, read it, turn green and then pale and then green again, smoke pouring out of my ears. And then I calm down and stuff it into my pocket.

Elisabeth's purple prose dances wildly round my brain. *I know not what I will do but ending my life appeals to me as the only true course* . . . My God! She's madder than I thought. I give a huge, drawn-out sigh, and turn to Nell with my hands in my pockets. 'Do all women want to be raped, Nell?'

Of course the sentence shocks her, but it is interesting, watching her stiffen, rally, recover, and then determine to meet my eyes. She has spark, that girl! Oh, yes, she is – magnificent! Whenever she is here I find myself searching for conversational gambits to detain her. This one is a corker.

'I don't believe so, sir. Rupert. No.'

'That is . . .' I take a step towards her, and she takes a tiny step back '. . . do they wish to act chaste, and pass the blame for all lustful feelings on to us?'

Here Nellie permits herself a smile, a very small smile, with only the corners of her eyes crinkling to show she means it. Sometimes she has a way of looking at me as if I were a very silly child. A naughty way of looking at me, indeed.

'Well, it certainly would be – would be hard for a girl to act anything *other* than chaste . . .' she says uncertainly.

'I imagine you can guess that my Flemish acquaintance –

Flemish? Belgian, I think – is rather . . . What can I say? . . . taken with me, and has an understanding of our relations that I did not intend.'

Nellie, tactful girl, says nothing, but I am filled with a desire to confide in her, in any case. 'Ah . . . I have been foolish, Nell.'

'You have?'

She stands a little way from the hives. I know she does this because the bees recognise her, and will agitate if they smell her presence. I have a notebook on my knee and my poem, 'Lust', in front of me.

'Let me read you a few lines of this – did I tell you that the Ranee is paying Frank Sidgwick nine pounds to publish my poetry? I'm having the devil of a job putting my collection together but, well, I know that this one is going to make Eddie spitting mad and Sidgwick too, no doubt! Not decent . . . I actually mention a person's "remembered smell". But people do smell, don't they?'

She looks startled, as if I read her mind, but nods and lifts her eyebrows, and I carry on. I stand up, cough, sweep a low bow with one arm and pretend not to be serious. Then I read from my notebook:

> Love wakens love! I felt your hot wrist shiver
> And suddenly the mad victory I planned
> Flashed real, in your burning bending head . . .
> My conqueror's blood was cool as a deep river
> In shadow; and my heart beneath your hand
> Quieter than a dead man on a bed.

When I finish, I have the oddest sensation. I do not want to raise my eyes from the page. The line 'my heart beneath your hand' suddenly suggests something else entirely that had lain limp beneath Elisabeth's hand. Might Nell guess this? Oh, Lord, why did I try this out on her? What devil makes me long for the maid's approval so?

But she is smiling. I finally meet her eyes and cease blushing, and the girl is smiling, properly, her deliriously desirable mouth a little open. She nods, saying eagerly, 'I like it very much. I – I don't see why it isn't a fit subject for poetry. After what you said last time, I've been thinking. About what is a fit subject and what might not be. And I decided – it came to me – that all feelings should be equal. The good ones and the – the ones we are ashamed of.'

'Ah, Nell – my only true convert! Would that everyone was as broad-minded as you! So my "Channel Passage" poem worked on you, did it, to loosen up your thoughts on the matter? And you don't feel certain that my first collection should be entitled *A Flowery Book of Flowery Florets* by a Mr Flowery Brooke?'

She laughs and then nods again, now looking a little doubtful, as if wanting to be serious again. But I suddenly long to tease her, for the sincerity of a moment ago is such that I'm quite drained. (I find such self-revelation can only be done comfortably in the most minuscule of packages.) Why is it that I want to unpeel another layer when I'm with Nell? There's such loveliness and wisdom in her. And she has *feeling*, real feeling, without ever being sentimental or squashy. Unfortunately, as I am standing beside her, contemplating this admirable aspect of her nature, one who is not immune to squashiness appears in the Old Vicarage dining room and I see she is about to stride out towards us.

Ka Cox is staying here. Sleeping in a little bed across the corridor from me, in the Neeves' side of the Old Vicarage. Following the direction of my eyes Nell turns silently back to the bees. I feel a stab of sorriness, but there is no chance to say more. I return to my deckchair and sit down in it, picking up my Webster essay, which nicely covers the letter I was writing to Noel Olivier.

I've such a passion to see you again, and talk, having kissed you. We've denied ourselves so much . . . We deserve something

... Oh, Noel, remember Grantchester! I want to sit and talk and talk and talk, and see you, in every light and mood and position ... my dearest dear ... I love you. Rupert.

My God, sometimes I write well. Better than almost anybody in England!

As I'm writing, and dwelling on all this, Ka wanders over towards the hives. Without looking up I hear the humming bees intensify – a warning sound, like the waves of the sea gathering towards a storm. 'I say, Ka, don't go too close!'

'Oh, I saw the maid there just now,' Ka replies. 'She brushed them away with her hands ...'

'That's the maid, though. She has a way with them. She's a bee-keeper's daughter. I wouldn't risk it.'

Ka looks a trifle piqued at being told not to do something, but seems to take my advice and strides towards me. With her hair wrapped in some sort of emerald green scarf and those rather loose, full skirts she wears, I do see it, just for a moment. What Jacques means when he describes her as looking like one of the peasants in Augustus John's paintings. But, then, Jacques is in love with her.

'How's it coming along?' she says, in that deep, hot voice she has.

She means the Webster essay, I suppose. Or perhaps my poems. I cast around for a line to try on her to persuade her that this is indeed what I'm writing, meanwhile closing the notebook (Noel's letter inside it), and standing up to stretch, hoping the sight of my manly torso elongating in miraculous fashion might temporarily distract her.

A timely shriek from the Old Vicarage rescues me. It's a shriek so piercing and frightened that we both run at once towards the sound – coming from the kitchen. Billows of black smoke greet us and the sight of Mrs Neeve in a panic, face smeared with soot, shrieking, 'Help, help!', smoke everywhere in black clouds – the beam in the kitchen is on fire. It is difficult to get at, being in part the chimneypiece, but I dash for a bucket and Ka runs to the garden tap to fill it, while I flap at the beam with a rug, meaning to smother it, but succeeding only in fanning the flames.

Tommy – the butcher's boy – has dashed for the Brigade, borrowing someone's motorbike. Good, practical, bear-like Ka attacks the beam, sloshing water at it and then running to the mill stream at the bottom of the garden again to fill another bucket, until with a foul, sizzling smell the flames start to die down and the kitchen is full of maids from next door (Nellie silent and – could it be? – amused) and Mrs Stevenson saying, 'Oh, these old houses!' and Florence Neeve answering her, 'There can be no doubt we were all Lying in Danger last night!' (She means that the chimney beam has been smouldering all night long, which is patently not true.) And all the time Ka and Nellie appraising one another in that way women have and Tommy arriving back to announce, with glorious cheer, 'The Brigade is on its way!'

I don't like the way he looks at Nell, that young man.

I feel, of course, faintly ridiculous and undoubtedly irrelevant. (There is something particularly galling about the British Working Man that makes one feel this way when one is attempting to do something male and heroic around the ladies.) Tommy wears no shirt, and one cannot help observing that his chest is golden and glazed like a good apple pie. And that he and Nell giggle together and she seems to be very well acquainted with him.

Infuriating. I am still smarting from my recent brush with Tommy's equivalent in Dorset – men who made no mystery of their contempt for Dudley and me, whatever our intentions. My eyes keep returning to Nell. How well does she know this fellow?

My nose is covered with smuts, my shirt is blackened and hanging out from my trousers, and my besocked feet are grey and soaking wet. I catch sight of Mrs Neeve glancing at me and nudging her son, Cyril, and with a dignified sniff, I decide I can be most useful by returning outside to my writing.

As I go I hear Mrs Neeve say firmly, 'Ooh. That was a Danger Closely Avoided.'

Sheepishly, I pick up the notebook from the grass and sit back down in the deckchair. And there suddenly is Nellie, hurrying, scurrying, with blackened beams and detritus to a bonfire near the sundial.

'I trust you weren't hurt, child?' I ask her, leaping up and offering to help.

'I'm fine, thank you.'

She doesn't look at me but wipes at her sooty hands with dock leaves and tries to rub the soot from her dress. I move to help her, taking my handkerchief from my pocket, but from the corner of my eye once again I see Ka approaching – God, does the woman have clairvoyant powers? – with her unmistakable swinging stride.

'Ehm – when you've a moment, Nellie, would you be so kind as to bring us some apple cider? We'll take it in the Orchard gardens rather than here, if you prefer.'

'Yes, Mr Brooke,' Nellie says simply, and if she feels offended, there is no sign of it.

Ka, recovered from her exertions, comes to join me under the apple trees, selecting a tree furthest from the house and pulling out a deckchair after thoughtfully doing the same for me. Absently I brush some of the white crust of bird droppings from the wooden frame with my handkerchief.

'She's pretty, isn't she?' Ka says.

'Who?'

'The maid, of course. Nellie. The one you said was a bee-keeper's daughter.'

'Is she? I hadn't noticed.'

Ka plumps herself down in the deckchair, leaning her head

back and stretching her legs beneath her skirt, while I search for something to change the subject.

'You didn't turn up to Gwen and Jacques' supper party, Ka. I was relying on you. *More* of our circle joining up and abandoning us single folk . . . Didn't we pledge never to do it? Married people make me sick. They suddenly have secrets – it's like being a child outside one's parents' bedroom!'

Her face tells me that I have departed the frying-pan and plunged into the fire.

Hurriedly I carry on, 'Ah, well, they will be safely on their honeymoon by now . . . Virginia Stephen is coming to stay here next week. How do you rate my chances at getting Virginia to swim naked in Byron's Pool?'

To my horror, a large tear rolls down Ka's face and she succumbs to a gulp and then a full-blown sob. She lifts her pince-nez to wipe at it with her fingers but another soon follows and she can only close her eyes and cover her face with her hands.

'Ka, Ka – what have I said? I'm sorry, what is it? Don't you like Virginia? But you know she and I are practically cousins, have been friends since childhood . . .'

Ka shakes her head, giving me to understand that this is not the source of her pain at all. I feel for my handkerchief again as Nellie arrives, puts the tall glasses of cider in front of us with a napkin for each, and turns soundlessly away. I know she has seen Ka's tears. I wonder at the light she will cast them in, but there is nothing I can do about it. When Nell is out of earshot I leap from my chair and hurry to Ka's side.

Ka shoots one glance at the bird-stained handkerchief and, with a wet laugh, pushes it away. 'No,' she says, sniffing. 'No, not Virginia, nothing about that . . .'

'What then, dear Ka? It's surely not Jacques and Gwen . . . I can't understand it! You turned Jacques down . . .'

'Yes, yes, I know. I'm foolish and – and it makes no sense! But when you mentioned their honeymoon, and I thought of them in Churchfield House, in Lulworth – the very place he proposed to me! – it was only then that I minded . . . not the marriage, no, not that. But more – well, what you said about feeling excluded. That's the part that hurts. Being excluded from a friendship with both of them. And then Jacques' suggestion to me, his marvellous *solution* . . . You heard, I suppose?'

I *am* listening, I swear I am. But there is something else going through my mind, as Ka leans forward, the large green baubles round her neck glinting in the sun and tinkling like a mountain goat's bells . . . I see the deep place between her breasts, and the tear-streaked cheek suddenly appears downy and young. And my attention is diverted by a wood-pigeon cooing away incessantly in one of the trees and the departing figure of Nell disappearing between them; so that I miss a little of what she is saying . . .

'Ah, yes, I did hear something,' I say diplomatically. In fact, Jacques discussed it with me at length and I'd advised him to have a punt on the taking-up-Ka-as-a-mistress idea. Wasn't surprised to find dear Ka appalled, but three months ago I didn't know Ka as well as I do now. Actually, I am impressed that she's made of stronger stuff at least than the dreadful mad witch Elisabeth. 'Yes,' I say, 'that was pretty low of him. Anyone can see you're not that sort. What a – snake!'

Ka falls silent. The wood-pigeon finally seems to invade her consciousness too, like a child insistently tooting a paper whistle. The tears have dried; she even gives a hollow laugh. 'Illogical . . . isn't it, that when we feel we can have something at the snap of our fingers we don't want it, but when obstacles are put in our way . . . ? Funny creatures, human beings, aren't we?' she says, to which I agree, heartily glad to return to cheerier mode. I am not used to Ka being anything other than Ka – jolly Ka, making sandwiches for picnics and diligently carrying buckets to put out fires.

'Do you think it's safe to venture back to the Old Vicarage without fear of being burned in our beds?' I ask, standing up.

She says she thinks it is. But later, in my bed that night, I marvel at my own silliness in the Old Vicarage kitchen, grabbing Florence Neeve's best Indian rug. I picture myself rolling the thing up and flapping demoniacally towards the fire on the chimneypiece. The rug was heavy and didn't roll easily, the underside rough and reeking of floor-polish and dog-hair. Laddie cowered in the corner, watching me warily, as if I was a madman. As I flapped, more and more flakes of beam and black wood swooped down and showered me like angry bats. Ka and Nellie watched too; the other maids hovered somewhere around the edges. I felt Ka's eyes on me, and I felt Nell's attention slip away, turn towards that boy Tommy. It was a horrible moment, when I realised that I seemed to have snared one at the same point that I let another go free: like an eel-catcher opening the trap inexpertly and seeing his prize slip away down the river.

Not that Nell is an eel, of course. She is a bright country girl and a maid-of-all-work, I chide myself, trying to reel in my maddening thoughts. But she *is* a prize, and any man, even perhaps the dreaded Tommy, can surely see that.

~

Lily's health is picking up, and Betty has gone to visit her, sending word that she is carrying well, and plumper. My own visit is due Sunday, but learning this news from Betty last night is like a stone lifting from my heart; I attack my chores with vim and vigour, even bursting into song sometimes. I realise from my own gladness that I had feared (without knowing it) for Lily's life. I resolve to stick firmly to my pact, to give up all thoughts of Rupert, and feel reassured that God will reward me by taking care of my family.

My heart is lighter than it has been in a while.

Tommy offers to take me, come Sunday. He brings me a small

packet, pink and sodden, and shyly pushes it over the tabletop to me on a morning when Mrs Stevenson is not at home. I peel off the paper to find two beautiful lamb chops. 'For you,' he says. 'For your family in Prickwillow.' Tommy has freckles and a direct brown stare, and there is no mistaking his kindness. He has not tried to kiss me again but he is watchful and, I suspect, patient.

So for now the only irritation is sharing a room with Kittie, who loves her secrets and is always gossiping: 'Do you think he'll marry her? Which one will he marry, do you think? The prettiest of all is Miss Olivier, not the young one, you know, but the older one, Miss Brynhild – the one with the big hats and the lovely cheekbones. She's the one I'd pick, if I were a man.'

I consider for a moment passing on to her the same information about the tastes of Mr Rupert Brooke that I passed on to Betty. That would surely hush her. Rupert himself told me, laughing, of an occasion in Munich where he mistakenly called a gentleman by the familiar 'you' (in German there must be a more proper, formal way to address a gentleman you don't know) and the same man's hand leaped to his trouser buttons and he was practically on top of Rupert in an instant! Rupert laughs about this, and I smile as I bring him a clean pile of bed linen, and pretend not to be shocked. It is simply understood now, by Rupert and me, that the whole world is in love with Rupert, men and women, and he in love with no one. Oh, yes, he has a fancy to be in love with Miss Noel Olivier, a wish to believe himself in love with her. But, if you ask me, that's a desire born of frustration, and part of his disguise. He acts like such a Gay Dog, such a Jack-among-the-maids (in his case *truly* among the maids!) only to hide his true persuasion.

Tonight, Kittie and I are no sooner lying side by side under the blue satin counterpane than she starts on her campaign: 'Why would a brainy girl like you, Nell, *not* think it better for women to have the Vote? Don't you believe we're as good as any man, any day?'

I wonder about this. Father made me feel so strongly that I wasn't as good as my brothers. Since Kittie asks such a searching question and we're alone in the darkness I rummage around for an honest answer. 'I think I do. It's not that that makes me doubt. It's – well – some of the speeches I've seen in the newspaper. Miss Pankhurst and those others. They talk of men as if they were savage beasts, every one of them wanting to steal us for the white-slave trade. And it's our job to raise them from their filthy needs, their diseases, that sort of thing.'

When Kittie says nothing, and I gather from her breathing that she is still listening to me, I grow bolder, and carry on: 'And then I examine myself and I think – I don't want to do that. To be as good as a man, yes. But not to – to take care of his soul. Not to be an angel without – without a body of my own . . .'

The pillow next to me moves suddenly and Kittie sits up. 'Why, Nellie, are you saying you have impure thoughts?'

'No, of course not!' I struggle to change the subject. 'But . . . I'm not so sure your precious Votes for Women Bill will achieve anything much for girls like us – we wouldn't even have the Vote anyways. It's only for married ladies.'

'And won't you be a married lady one day? And able to vote then?'

This startles us both, with a gasp from me, and then a funny little silence.

'I can't imagine it,' I finally say.

'Well, isn't that just like you? You can only imagine your life as it is, wedded to the Orchard, scrubbing and sweeping and running errands from noon till dusk . . .'

It's true. Her words alarm me, because what Kittie calls drudgery is freedom to me. My little room – the first bedroom I've not shared with five others; the kindly way Mrs Stevenson lets us eat the broken scones for breakfast, warm and crumbling with butter; the new-pin order of the kitchen; the shouts and capers of Rupert next door, with his constant stream of visitors turning up on bicycles, arms always heaped with books; the snatches of their conversation, the lines from poetry and plays; the ladies in their lovely hats demanding strawberries brought to them at the riverside at their punts; Mr Neeve carefully removing the frames, and the swarm, brown and gold and shimmering in his hands like a field of old fen sedge with the wind rippling through it. How could I give this up and go back to a life like Lily's, never to see a soul all day besides Mrs Gotobed and wailing little ones? And since it's not marriage but *work* that has widened my world, why should marriage hold any charms for me? The others tease me about Tommy, but *marriage* . . . doesn't enter my thoughts. Even Betty has started mooning over the boy who works at the mill, a boy named Jack, who delivers flour to us; a boy with squinty eyes that make me think of a mole, although he is cheerful enough, I suppose, and not a bad sort, and kind.

While I'm lying on my back beside her, thinking this, Kittie then takes it into her head that she needs cocoa. She sits up again. It's past midnight, we'll be up again at six, but she wants us to sneak downstairs and make ourselves some.

'You'll get us both sacked!' I whisper, but I'm giggling too, because for all her sauciness, and her want of good sense in the kitchen, I *am* used to the company of sisters and things are always more gay when Kittie is here.

We take a candle and carry it trembling down the stairs, not wanting to risk the sound of the light switch, which, nine times out of ten, fails to work anyway.

Kittie finds the Bournville powder and rations us a careful spoonful each so that Mrs Stevenson won't notice. I help her by washing the spoon and setting it back on the dresser. A mouse flickers past in front of us, making us shriek and cover our mouths. Luckily the fire is not yet out and with a little raking and a small cup of coal, can be made to crackle into life, so that we can set the pan of milk and water atop it.

We then sit at the kitchen table, smiling at each other, the candle flame between us, ducking its head every few minutes, dancing to some unseen draught. Kittie's eyes are bright, and though I yawn and slump in my chair, she is so wide awake that I begin to wonder.

'Why did you come back from London, Kittie? What happened there?' I ask her this when my back is to her, hearing the milk and water rise to the bubble and taking it off the heat to pour into the waiting cups.

Her face in the firelight is only two big eyes, like a cat's at night. I can't read her expression but see from the glitter in them that she is blinking back tears. 'You heard, I suppose? Mother was so ashamed. She told me not to tell a soul but Grantchester is such a place . . . I knew we couldn't keep it quiet.'

Now, it would be honest of me to say that I haven't heard, that I don't know what she is talking about, but my curiosity is so piqued that I keep mum, thinking this the best way to find out. I put the cup of cocoa in front of her with a soft thud.

'It was horrible, Nell. Worse than you could ever imagine. Several times constables and plainclothes men passed their arms round me from the back and clutched hold of my breasts in as public a manner as possible and men in the crowd did it too! My poor chest was black and blue with bruises by the time I got to my cell. And they tried to lift my skirt and called me names you couldn't dream of hearing . . .

Poor Kittie is sobbing now, ever so muffled, so no one might hear. I feel the wretched way I always do when someone cries; I slide the cup of cocoa across the table towards her and am glad when she pauses to sip.

'So many people . . . I was – terrified. I thought I would never get out! And although I got word to Mother she never would visit me there . . .'

Now I understand about Kittie's absence and sudden arrival back. How sorely we resented it, Lottie and I, the curt way Mrs Stevenson reintroduced her: 'You know our Kittie, girls, and you know how to make room for her.' And after that it was all chop-chop and change about and Betty and Lottie packing up their things: Lottie and Betty to take Rupert's old room while the new tenant is in London and Kittie temporarily reinstalled with me. Mrs Stevenson must have known everything.

'The worst of it was, Nell, there were other women I knew in there, oh, yes, some of our lot, but they didn't talk to me! They were in separate cells with copies of the *Home Beautiful* in them – can you believe that? I'm not lying, Nell, I saw them carrying those very magazines! It's because Lady Constance complained, and nearly died after *her* prison sentence, but it made no difference to *our* treatment. And those ladies could call on the Governor whenever they wanted and visit the library or the chaplain . . . Oh, I thought, it's fine for them, for when they get out they have homes to go to and husbands to forgive them, but what about me? I thought I'd never get a position again, or the prison guards might just think I was a common girl of the streets and never let me out!'

'But then why must you go on another march next week? Weren't you talking only this morning about the procession from the Embankment and the white horse that must be found and . . . Why, surely it's a terrible risk, Kittie, you might get arrested again!'

Whatever her reply might be, I am none the wiser as a sudden noise outside makes us jump out of our skins and snuff the candle. We sit frozen at opposite sides of the table, the smell of hot wax sharp between us, listening. All at once I feel the hard wooden chair under my backside, through the cotton of my nightdress, and taste the cocoa on my tongue, and notice my fingers smoothing the grain of the table, my feet shuffling beneath it, dusty and dry.

Is it a fox? Someone is outside in the garden.

I'm the bravest, and tiptoe to the french windows to look. Of course I see nothing but glassy black, and when I press my face to the pane, only moonlit lawn and grey rosebushes, poised and still.

'It's over there, by the two-holer!' Kittie whispers, her hand on the key, opening the door to get a better look. She's right: I can make out a figure in the moonlight. A barn owl, silver as a ghost, flies suddenly past it and the figure ducks and lets out a shout.

'I know who that is,' I whisper.

Then I hear his voice, and a pebble rattles the glass: 'Nell! Nellie Golightly – is that you?'

I twirl round to Kittie, and her look in the semi-dark tells me what mine must be: alarmed, excited, surprised. 'It's – Mr Brooke, Kittie. He must need something. I can deal with this. Quick, wash the cups and leave them on the dresser – and go back to bed!'

Then she gives me a different look entirely. I can just make out the set of her fat bottom lip and the saucy narrowing of her eyes, the direction her thoughts are taking, but before she can speak I say, quickly and fiercely, the wickedest thing I've ever said: 'Kittie. I will keep your secret. I promise to keep it – to tell no one about your time in prison. I can keep a secret sometimes, if I really try. And if I feel sure that *you would do the same for me.*'

She is holding the snuffed candle. Her eyes widen, and I know at once she has grasped my meaning. She turns on her heel without another word and her nightdress swishes the stairs as she heads towards our bedroom.

My hand is trembling, too, as I struggle to open the french window. I'm thinking how well I know his shape, how I can recognise him from the shoulders, which are straight, like coat-hangers, and the loose way his arms hang, the set of his head, the wave of hair sticking up at the crown. I am thinking that despite all I tell myself of his persuasion there is a part of me that beats still, that is not in the least quieted. Just seeing him makes me know my efforts have been hopeless.

I expect him to be smiling, to giggle and grab my hands, but instead his eyes are glassy and he looks round me, as if there is a ghost behind me. 'What is it? What is it?' I say, and his mood affects mine: I feel my fists clench, expecting danger.

'I – I— Come swim with me, Nell.'

'What – now? It's past midnight. You'll lose me my position!'

Looking out into the garden I see that, for once, no dog has followed Rupert from the Old Vicarage, and the lawn is still and black and empty. I peer out at him. He hangs back a little from the house, nervously surveying the windows above him. In the moonlight he is pale as the barn owl in his flapping shirt and white flannel trousers. I realise as I'm doing it that I'm studying Rupert to try and understand what it is about him that is so unfamiliar. He steps forward suddenly, reaching out a hand and dragging me towards him.

'Come on, Nell, you won't lose your position. If you do, I'll find you another, I promise. Mother always needs a maid. Hang it, who doesn't? I want – I need a swim, and I— You know I hate to swim alone.'

His words are beseeching and his look is angry rather than playful. I'm not afraid of him – I believe a girl knows instinctively which men she should be afraid of – but naturally I hesitate, the request being such a strange one.

'Do come, Nell. I'm all alone . . . Virginia's gone . . . I can't work – I need to talk!'

So I fetch a coat – Mr Stevenson's coat – from a hook on the door to the scullery and once again throw it over my nightdress, and step out on to the springy grass in my bare feet. My heart launches itself at my ribcage like a cat in a basket, with the vivid memory of last time, the hot sense of a person standing beside me, knee-deep in a brown river, naked as God made him, the sun melting his back to honey, and trying to catch a fish.

The roses are grey and closed for the night. The night air smells of Rupert to me, and nothing else, and I slip into step behind him, and follow him across the lawn and down the lane. Walking two steps behind him, trying to follow the pale figure of him as a light and a guide, I almost have to run to keep up with him: over the bridge in front of Grantchester Mill and across the meadow until we reach the dam, with the sound of water tipping into the black below.

Here we stop, breathing heavily, and staring into the deep, blank water, and I acknowledge to myself the one hard fact that, despite my nature, it has taken me so long to face. There is no request Rupert could make of me that I would refuse. Whatever the pledge between me and God, this is the truth. I almost gasp aloud. What foolishness has stopped me knowing this until now? And why, thinking it, do I once again have a small dread sad picture of Father, keeling over in the meadow all snowy white in his veil and suddenly old and finished?

What would Father say if he was here now and I could ask him about Rupert? Nothing, is the likely answer. I can only imagine his look of surprise and confusion if I raised such a thing. Father's world was . . . ordered, where even bees who have chosen to swarm in a cluster in a high tree can be coaxed down into the skep by his soft voice and a little smoke, without even the need of a gentle shake of the branch. But Father's skill was only with bees. He had nothing to teach me about men, nothing to pass on beyond his limited, silent life, sitting on our front step, smoking his pipe and cleaning his uncapping knife.

Who on this earth might I ask the strangest question a girl ever formed in her head? When a man favours other men, can he ever have the needle of his compass changed, ever find it pointing towards a girl?

Could it ever point towards me?

I'm shamed now by my wicked behaviour with Kittie – pressing her like that, nearly blackmailing her with her secret. At the same time, I pray bitterly that she keeps her word and says nothing, or I'm sunk.

Rupert leans over, peering into the water, and says, 'A man I knew once wanted to know what it felt like to shoot the rapids, and he did it here, and that wooden thing under the water is all full of little nails or something so that when he came out again he was all covered with longitudinal scratches. It was rather pretty, like some sort of pattern, and it didn't hurt him very much!'

He doesn't seem quite himself and this remark only confirms me in my worries. Surely such a dive would wound or sting powerfully? I steal a glance sideways at him and a funny thought pops into my head. His ghostly profile in darkness is like the head on a coin – a noble head. The minute this thought is formed, I snuff it. It is the thought of a romantic girl who has lost her best skill – to look at things squarely! And because I cannot trust myself just at this minute to do that, I stare instead at the river's surface, homely as the back of a grater: black and full of little dimples.

Rupert bends to take off his boots. Again, a part of me is admiring his toes in the moonlight, those long, elegant toes I saw the first time I met him – what is wrong with me? Why do I keep veering from my purpose like this? I'm here to help him, surely, unburden himself, or whatever it is he longs for, not to admire his fine toes!

He makes a show of squinting in the silvery light, searching for fallen chestnuts among the leaves at the water's edge. I don't believe in this playful mood one jot. There is something glittery and brittle about him that isn't cheerful in the least. I'm not so far gone that I flatter myself he wants especially to talk to me: I know already that Rupert has a fear of being left alone. My true feeling is that he has times when to talk to the cows in the field would be better than nothing.

Suddenly he is turning his face towards me; squinting at me in the same searching way. It's hard to hold his gaze, but I do.

'We played a game, Nell. Do you see that paper boat there – that little flash of white on the bank? There's a prize being offered for the best poem, and some friends of mine were trying to guess who might win it. We made a paper boat for each person we knew had gone in. Drinkwater, Masefield, Abercrombie – they all went off so merrily. That's me – there – on the bank. Stranded helplessly, stuck like a sorry fool in those branches.'

He says this with such bitterness, with such a catch in his voice, that I know at once I have tapped the source of his misery.

'Oh, I'm sure your poetry will – will swim off as merrily as you might hope . . .' I say, hoping to be reassuring.

He greets this with a harsh laugh. 'You think so? I wish I was so sure. Can you imagine, Nell—' He turns to me so suddenly to say this that I slip a little in the soft mud and he has to shoot out a hand to help me. The coat over my shoulders slips a little and I feel his hand on my bare shoulder, and notice it there, and wish I hadn't. 'People have no idea at all. You people have no idea,' he says.

'No idea of what?'

'How painful it is! How embarrassing! How ridiculous. One imagines the glow of pride when an author sees his own name in print. It doesn't occur to anyone – why should it? – that the author might feel something else entirely. Something inexplicably ridiculous. A fraud. An idiot – to see one's own ambition and limitations writ large.'

He links his arm in mine, rearranging the draped coat so that it covers me more thoroughly. Then, hiding his tenderness with a gruff push, he steers us away from the sluice gates and towards a part of the river where we swam last time. The light is enough to see by, but the ground beneath our bare feet is full of peril – the spikes of the horse-chestnut shells, acorns, twigs, and every few seconds one or the other of us stops to squeal in pain or brush a barb from our soles.

'I *can* imagine that!' I say boldly. 'To have the world read your innermost thoughts, committed to paper ... I – well, I do understand it would make a body feel ... shy.'

'Shy. Yes. You've met Mother? No, of course, she's never been to the Orchard, nor the Old Vicarage. Well, then, dear Nellie, imagine a woman – a rather beautiful woman, actually – tall and grand and of the same severe disposition as, say, Mrs Stevenson, with none of Mrs Stevenson's apple-roundness. There you have my mother: the Ranee. And now picture the same woman reading the poetry of her beloved son, one Mr Rupert Brooke! Her eyes flickering over a word like "Lust" and her fierce mouth hardening at lines like "her remembered smell" – the worst kind of disgust would fill her mind!' He puts his head in his hands and groans. A white cow at the other side of the river skitters in fright at the sound.

'Well . . .' I venture, and stop. One minute I'm standing next to Rupert in a wood, by a river, late at night, the next I'm somewhere else – I don't know where – watching. A chill passes over me and I observe only two figures talking: one tall, troubled; the other wearing a coat over her shoulders and looking up to the man with a shining face.

It lasts only a moment, then I'm back at the river, back in my body, with my heart hammering and the scent of river garlic floating round me, and I'm talking. I'm trying so hard to be helpful, to respond to the request made of me. Help me, he says.

'Why write, then? No one is making you—'

This comment makes him angry.

'No, it's true. Ha! My own hopeless vanity and – compulsion, which catches me in its snare. I can neither stop, go back, nor go on.'

'Well, then,' I say, 'it *is* a brave thing, to – expose yourself so. I'm sure all of us have . . . secrets . . . parts of ourselves we labour not to show others. I can't imagine my father, for instance, understanding for one moment why I would risk my position to stand at night with you looking into a black river. That would be a part of myself I would not want to show to him.'

'Oh, Nell, how sweet you are. Such a small risk, compared with mine.'

I am silent, pondering this.

'Whereas I,' he goes on, 'risk exposure to the whole world! And then there is the further, ghastly, conflict of knowing that, even as I suffer them, these fears are ridiculous, too, and how much I despise myself for them, and how I am unable to confess to anyone but you. Can you imagine Abercrombie or Drinkwater or just about anyone else caring – for God's sake – what one's *mother* thinks?'

At this he gives another sulky laugh. 'And if it were only Mother that might be bearable. But the next minute I imagine the thoughts of certain Rugby masters on reading it, or my godfather, or my aunts or – Mrs Stevenson, or God knows who, really. But each time, at each looming person, another doubt presents itself, another opportunity to be mocked, judged and disliked. Each for a different line, or poem, or reason. I've had one devil of a fight with Sidgwick and I don't suppose it's over yet. Is his objection to including "Lust" only that it's bad poetry or that it's shocking as morals? Technically it's not much, I admit – any fool can write a technically good sonnet! No, that's not his real objection, although he disguises it as such. If he takes it out of the collection, the whole thing is reduced to unimportant prettiness. No one offended, Mother least of all, but nothing achieved either!'

I pull my coat round me, feeling the chill at last. An owl just above us gives a soft, soothing call. 'Shall we go back?' I say, at last.

He catches me up and kisses me, another of those dark, impulsive kisses that make my body tighten, as if he were pulling taut a string from my drawers to my neck. 'So you do like me, Nell,' he suddenly murmurs, 'just a little?'

We break apart for my answer, tears springing to my eyes. 'Of course I do! Of course!'

And he kisses me again. My body is still, like the black water gathering in the pool below us, but I'm almost choked by the power of it.

He breaks away to try to look at me in the darkness, then wraps his arms round me in a deep hug so that I breathe in the smell of him, the grass and Coal Tar Soap, the woodsmoke from his room, and shavings from a pencil, and the texture – the flannel shirt, the softness of his hair, the prickle of his mouth where his stubble rubs me like sandpaper. He doesn't *mean* anything by it, I try to tell myself, with one last feeble gasp of reasoning, but the feeling is of something else entirely. Something hot and close and true.

'You've no idea,' he mumbles, 'the things I feel. I am without a skin, permeable, terrified . . . I think I must be a – filthy person. I have such foul thoughts and I can't sleep, and yet I'm *so unutterably* tired, and I lie down and my thoughts race and I feel a cloud in my head that won't go away . . .'

'Ssh, now, of course you're not *filthy*! You're just tired, and you've been working too hard and, well, anyone would be a little nervous about their first book of poetry . . .'

The direction of his mumblings now is more alarming than it was a moment ago. I have to admit to myself that, despite all my good sense, I am surely at sea. My response to his kiss – Lord, my conviction that he meant it – seems wrong suddenly. The strong feeling I have, flooding from him in the darkness, is like the feeling I have sometimes standing near the bees. A swell in the air, something massing: a warning. He does not seem to be talking to me at all, but to the night. There is something very wrong indeed with Rupert.

Father would say it's no more than he deserves. If he knew, if he knew what Rupert had done with that young man in his room at the Orchard, he would see it as God's punishment, his sickness coming to taunt him. Maybe that's what Rupert believes too. Is that the 'filthy' thing he's thinking of?

'I'm a mean thing, full of smallness and jealousies and dirt,' Rupert murmurs.

I put my arm firmly in his, and steer him back towards the meadow and the lane.

When we reach his rooms at the Old Vicarage, I discover that his part of the stairs has a little wicket gate (for his bedroom was once a nursery). He steps over this without pausing but I hesitate. 'Yes, Nell, the ghosts of Victorian children pluck at our sleeves here, don't they?' he whispers, but I shake my head. It's clear he's asking me to go with him, to help him, so I step over the barrier too, and carry on past the glass door with the beautiful flowery designs on the yellow panes and into his bedroom. I close the door as softly as I can manage, and sit heavily on the bed beside him. It's a bigger room than his old one at the Orchard, but it smells the same: of warm paper from books, the smoke from a recent fire, and of him, of course.

'Stay here with me, Nellie,' he whispers.

I light the candle beside his bed with an ember from the fire in the grate. His flickering face looms in front of me and, to my horror, I see that his cheeks are wet, that big tears slide down his face. I take a corner of his sheet and dab at them, and he smiles at me, and in an instant his mood has changed and he nods and mutters quickly, as if I had refused him, 'No, I'm sorry. You're right. Of course it's a big thing to risk your position. An enormous thing! I'm being selfish and silly. I shall get us both into trouble – lose my lodgings again! Thank you, child. You're a very sweet girl.'

And so I find myself on the wrong side of his bedroom door, and wondering how in God's name it always happens: that whatever my heart desires, my mouth fails to utter it.

∾

Virginia was here at the Old Vicarage. She stayed a week in the room that Ka stayed in, and we played at being interested in one another, and we mostly sat in the garden and wrote. She is writing a novel called *Melymbrosia*. I tell her I do not care much for the title. She asks me laughingly if the blank spaces left in my sonnets are to be filled later with 'oh, God's'? She is different, alone. Not the Virginia of our childhood. Quieter, for one thing. And the pallor of headache is always upon her.

I did persuade her to swim with me one warm night. She was terribly thrilled with her own daring, and one couldn't help considering throughout that it was merely an experience with which to regale Vanessa, or perhaps Lytton, not a real experience at all. I saw her glance slyly at me once, and as the moon was full I saw her ghostly limbs. They left me rather limp, and made me miss the plumper charms of dear Nell.

Virginia undressed is a rather vulnerable creature; I much prefer her clothed. The moment her dress was on she recovered her wits and said, laughing, 'Ah, so your legs are not bandy at all as Lytton claims!'

I chased her back to the Old Vicarage, to sit and dry our hair in front of the fire.

One morning that week we were at work under the shade of the chestnuts, and I was reading a newspaper and exclaiming about the national rail strike. 'Don't you feel we live in extraordinarily violent times? Women picketing Parliament and throwing stones at shop windows almost daily, unrest, strikes, upheaval at every turn . . . and yet when Dudley and I try to engage the Working Man in debate about his own predicament . . .'

As I said this Nellie appeared at the other end of the garden in my line of vision and, seeing me with Virginia, turned on her tail smartly and left. I knew that Virginia's beady eye didn't miss this, and I wondered what she might have read into it.

'Oh, I heard about your little tour. Must have been terribly disappointing for you. Yes . . . your interest in the wretched lives of the lower classes is legendary, dear,' she said mildly, without looking up from her notebook. 'No need to waste time on persuading me of its veracity.'

This was laced with sarcasm, of course.

Nell's retreating figure was dark in the dazzling whiteness of the day; like a drop of ink on a page.

'Virginia – what's the brightest thing in Nature?' I asked, pretending to be considering.

'Sunlight on a leaf,' she provided, without looking up.

Cloud-like we lean and stare as bright leaves stare.

I tried not to stare after Nell, but when I closed my eyes her figure appeared on the inside of my eyelid, like a shadow puppet on a canvas screen.

The week after Virginia left, I sought Nell out. I don't know what I planned. A full declaration, perhaps? An assault on her person? But I hadn't allowed for the return of my most fearful thoughts and feelings, and by the time I'd gathered my strength, the occasion was lost. No man wants a woman to succumb to him out of pity.

I have the book in front of me. The proofs that is. *Poems, 1911.* There is still time for corrections and I intend to ask – who? Ka? James? Yes, only those two. James has Judgement. Is it true then, as I told Nell, that an author feels no glow, only shame on seeing his name in print? In my case, this morning, tearing it out of the envelope I felt – yes, I think it was indeed the hot glow of shame.

I had dreamed of Nijinsky again, and the dream clung to my skin, like dew. He was dancing the part of the golden slave in *Scheherazade* and I was – I think I was the shoe-maker. Yes, that was it. I sat in the bowels of the theatre sewing, surrounded by wooden shoe-horns, making little shoes for that perfect man's feet, and then helping him into them, encasing his wondrous heel with my hands, nestling it with reverence, as if it were an egg. But he said, in this strong Russian accent, 'No, for I dance the part barefoot, of course!' And I felt such shame, powerful shame, for such a simple error, for getting everything so awfully, catastrophically wrong.

I woke up with a pounding erection, of course.

Noel has rejected my offer of the Dedication in the book, so that page remains glaringly vacant. My humiliation is absolute.

I quickly thrust the pages into an envelope to Ka. Ka I trust. Ka is not unkind and there is still time for her to make some corrections to such things as italics and capitals although as for the rest— My heart beats a tattoo every time I look at it. I have half a thought to fling it on the fire and shoot myself.

Later, in the same dream, the one I was recalling, I was given the task of helping Nijinsky into his bejewelled codpiece, and as I was rising to this task, studying the beautifully sewn construction with great attentiveness, Dudley rushed into the room and began shouting at me!

I wake to find him downstairs. Dudders, that is. He has been shouting up to my window. Mrs Neeve had sent the maid in to take the chill out of the room by making up a fire, and to see if I was awake but I pretended not to be. Autumn is over. No more stumbling by the water with Nellie; the bitter weather is here and with it my bitter mood, quite confirmed.

Dreary, blasted, filthy development. Dudley's getting married.

They're dropping like flies. First Frances, then Gwen, now Dudley. He speaks of his betrothed with such touching embarrassment that I *almost* feel glad for him – he told me a few weeks ago on Hampstead Heath, saying, 'She only weighs six stone eleven, can you imagine it?' as if this was some sort of recommendation. Anne-Marie. A German. A German with the physique of a tiny child. During the telling, a cat attached itself to Dudley's legs, and I remembered the other cat, Pat, on our Poor Law Caravan Trip and that, and youth, seemed a small number of centuries ago. Dudley and Anne-Marie I saw as two little mice about to be eaten. Not a happy thought.

My dream of *Scheherazade* was rather detailed. (Small wonder, since I must have seen it now at Covent Garden at least a dozen times.) But interesting that I had cast the concubine Zobeide dancing in some of the scenes and, well, who would be the obvious person to cast? Elisabeth? A concubine who can raise an ankle to her ear and causes our marvellous Nijinsky to prostrate himself? Noel? But there I've given up. She has a fairly serene future in front of her and I have decided I must go away. Somewhere far. Germany again, if I can manage to avoid Elisabeth.

It was Nell. I've just remembered. In the dream. Darling Nell had the part of the saucy concubine. With her plummeting black hair and her snake hips, her defiant little chin, her extraordinarily supple white limbs, dancing with surprising skill for one so untutored. Very surprising indeed.

Of course, my shame really swells when I turn to the poem, 'Lust'. Sidgwick has changed the title to 'Libido' and this foolish compromise leaps out at me. I feel the despair of one who has caved in like a collapsed pudding. I've behaved like Ophelia and turned 'thought and affliction, passion, hell itself . . . to favour and to prettiness'.

And then the ghost of Denham comes to stand behind me, with his remembered smell, and looks over my shoulder, and laughs aloud. Surely I am the subject of your poem? he asks.

He flings my notebook at me, with the scribbled lines of 'Lust' jiggling and dancing amid the drawing of the young sleeping figure, and it's true: it looks exactly like him, his head turned away from me, the line 'the image of your kin' being his brother Hugh, of course, nothing at all like Elisabeth. Who on earth have I been trying to dupe?

I feel so awfully lonely. And sorry that I'm so filthy. I have written Noel a package of vile letters, accusing her of everything from flirting with Other Poets (Békássy) to driving me to suicide. I believe the last line of the last letter was: 'I love you more than anyone ever will – damn you!'

Even I know this is not the lexicon of a lover.

But I put on a jolly face, shove the rest of the proofs under the bed and join Dudley – waiting for me by the sundial like a man condemned – for a breakfast of tea and a slice of apple cake, placed invitingly on a frosted tray on the table. We step on to the iced lawn, which cracks beneath our shoes. We pull blankets round ourselves and pretend it's summer: I even manage a cheery smile when the conversation turns again to Anne-Marie and Dudley's Plans. (Plans with a capital P is what engaged people have, the rest of us are only half human, of course, and our plans don't matter.)

This is all very well and I am just about managing it, and half listening, when Dudley suddenly delivers a glancing blow: 'And Lamb. Yes, I imagine she would become his mistress at a pinch.'

Who would become Henry Lamb's mistress? Noel? My mind does some sort of piercing dive, somersault and back-flip until I remember – he was talking about Ka. Lovely, firm-rumped, predictable Ka . . . Ka become a mistress of anyone, least of all that greasy painter Lamb? But Ka said no to Jacques. Ka is – incorruptible. Dudley must be mistaken . . . A presentiment of alarm shivers through my body.

'Lamb? The disgusting snake? Isn't he— I thought he was

fully engaged in pilfering Augustus John's mistress – what's her name? Not Dora, the one before that.'

'No, no, that's old news, Brookie. Where the devil have you been?'

Where, indeed? I pull the blanket more tightly round myself. I must have been far away, and I am having trouble returning.

I'm thinking of Nellie and my Nijinsky dream again. And how once, when I was a very, very small child, the Ranee told me of a dream *she* had had. 'About your poor dead sister,' she said. 'What do you think that means, darling?' she'd asked, in such a wistful, intimate, caressing voice, as if she'd forgotten for a moment precisely who I was, and actually believed I could help her.

'Why, do dreams *mean* something?' I piped, in my shattering, six-year-old way. She looked startled then, and retreated.

'I've made a date with Noel,' I announce to Dudley, standing up, flinging the blanket to the chair. 'December the fifteenth. We'll see the Cezanne-Gauguin exhibition and talk.' I wave my arms around to emphasise this breakthrough. (And to warm up.) 'I find I can think of nothing else.' (A fat lie, of course, but tactful Dudley keeps mum about how much my forthcoming book of poetry preoccupies me.) 'I have to resolve things with her once and for all because the tangle is spoiling my health. And, more to the point, interfering with my Webster essay. And, in any case, I must see these marvellously pornographic South Sea maidens that are causing such a Tear in the Fabric of British Morality, eh, Dudders?'

Dudley springs from the chair at my feet to give me what he imagines is a reassuring pat. 'Bravo, bravo! That's the spirit.' I nearly choke up breakfast.

We both sit down, and Dudley pours tea, trembling a little in the cold. After listening to the sound of the amber liquid tinkling into blue-rimmed porcelain, Dudley says cautiously, rather quietly, shivering before pushing his pince-nez up his nose first, 'I wonder, though . . . Is that wise, old chap?'

'What – immersing myself in the unnatural colours and gaudy nakedness of Gauguin's South Seas?'

'No, of course not. I meant Noel. You know that pressing her in the past has only ever strengthened her resolve . . .'

Ha! Such expertise now, such superior skill in love-making, my friend might have been married twenty years, not merely become betrothed a week ago. I stare at the top of his pate with a swell of loathing. 'Well, you may be right, but I find I *want* to push. To discover when, indeed, the Surrey and St John's Wood upper-middle classes will permit that she and I walk together. Do you know I saw a letter from Noel in the hand of that damned poet Ferenc Békássy. Did you know that Noel and he were acquainted?'

'No. A letter, though. Might have been two lines at most! What's to say there was anything to fret about?'

'What's to say there wasn't? I mean— I'm sorry, old man. I'm – I'm tired. I haven't been sleeping. I find that I can't. Every time I close my eyes some fresh horror emerges.'

'Fresh horror?' Dudley sounds anxious.

'Oh, nothing, really. Just, you know, a few small worries about my poems coming out, I suppose. And then I'm so tired, and the not sleeping is exhausting. Grantchester used always to afford me that. Sleep, I mean, even when London or Rugby didn't. Such a shame it no longer works.'

The white sky bulges between the trees like a hanging wet sheet. I sip my tea and stare at the spot where the Madonna lilies bloomed in summer. 'So glad they're dead now, aren't you? I find them rather ugly. Too much.' The light that falls on their dead clump is bleak, as if spilled hopelessly. (What is it waiting for? What am I waiting for? Mild Deaths gathering winds, frightened and dumb.)

'What?' Dudley says, bewildered. 'Oh, the lilies . . .'

'Did you know a young woman, a young artist, called Phyllis saw me on a train and has tracked me down? She was sketching me. Very pretty she is. She persuaded her aunt to write me a letter. It's all very amusing.'

'The lengths the New Woman will go to!'

We snicker at this and Dudley is eager to believe my black mood has passed. It is freezing cold out here in the garden. Some large plops of rain drip on us, flooding the dregs left in our cups, so we make a dash for the dining room. Dudley smiles – ah! the scaly cheerfulness of the engaged person! – and passes some comment about Florence Neeve's new antique, a gigantic white vase of marble with a single flower in it. I stamp my feet and shake the raindrops from my hair, then dart off to a side issue – my impending trip away – hoping to forget that I'm a desperate worm, or a fly crawling on the score of the Fifth Symphony.

Mrs Neeve brings a fresh pot of tea. She sets it next to her grand antique with a flourish, and Dudley laughs, as if we are schoolboys again, smirking in the dorm, and all is right with the world.

So. I arrive at Lulworth, at Wool station, shortly after four. I spent the entire train journey worrying that it was too horrible of me to send my poems to unsuspecting individuals who have never done harm to a soul. Bill and Eva Hubback. Sybil Pye. Eddie, of course. I suppose they might burn them, should they wish to. In any case, one hopes that they never refer to it again. Apart from Eddie, who, bless him, has written a fine letter, which reminds me of why, contrary to the feelings of some notable others, I persist in our friendship.

I have been sleepless these last four nights. My Webster essay is done but at what cost? I am in a stupid state, and the hopeless, helpless conversations with Noel roll round and round my head like a bag of marbles on a ship's floor, all against a backdrop of Gauguin's colours, colours so strange that I cannot begin to describe the troubling emotions they raised. Looking at them, trying not to listen to Noel's sensibleness, I thought, These forms are like something created in a stage of the earth's dark history when things were not irrevocably fixed to their forms. It is curious that the befrilled spires of King's College Chapel have never inspired in me the same shock and awe. (Clearly, I have a Pagan soul. These days, I only ever look upon the spires and wonder why they are all wearing baker's hats.) Oh, Gauguin's work is not shocking or scandalous in the way that critics suggest. Contemplation of the Tahitian School will not make maiden aunts turn primitive and drop their drawers, or young men take up cannibalism and ravish their neighbour, more's the pity. But there is something – something unsettling – in the work that calls to me.

I asked Noel if she agreed with the *Daily Express* that the show was pornographic, and the three figures of brown women in *Maternité* repulsively ugly and no better than drawings on a privy wall.

'No, of course not,' she said, in that considered Noel sort of way. So then I quoted Byron's *The Island*, the bit about the young hearts of the mutineers ending up languishing in some sunny isle, half uncivilised, preferring the cave of 'some soft savage to the uncertain wave' and, to my surprise, it made her angry.

'But isn't that just like you? You want to go so far from the common view – that we have made some progress over savagery and barbarism – that you take up the opposite position with equal zeal. That everything the natives do is perfect, and superior, and *noble*.'

'Well, he is certainly a perfect specimen . . .' I pointed out, pressing my face close to a fine example of noble savagery in a loincloth. 'What fun to knock about like that, naked under the sun and having your feet nibbled by fish in lagoons all day . . .'

'I'm sure it would only seem that way to a drifter, to a foreigner, to Gauguin, for instance. In fact, I'm very sure that South Sea island people have their privations, Rupert, like everyone else!' she retorted angrily.

And that was when she said it, there in the Grafton Gallery, just as another livid Tahitian breast loomed into view, words of soft kindness that slid like a knife under my skin: 'I'm afraid we must give it up. Until you love less or I love more.' Then I knew I must leave England. I glanced around the gallery, as if expecting a surge of people to come forward and clap me on the back: 'See, old man? She doesn't want you. Your work is no good. Your poems are shoddy. In short, you are an embarrassment. Slip quietly off to some foreign shore, there's a good lad, or do as your brother did and slip away entirely.'

Noel found me, head in my hands, under the rosewood carving of a Polynesian girl with flowers in her hair. She took pity on me and held out her hand, but she did not take back what she had said. 'You know Eddie loves my *Poems*,' I told her. She seemed startled. 'Oh, yes,' I continued, 'he is the only one who has troubled to write to me about it. I know you all hate him, I know what you all say about my friendship with him – don't bother to deny it! But only Eddie has taken the trouble to say that I have "brought back into English poetry the rapturous beautiful grotesque of the seventeenth century" – thank God for Eddie, wouldn't you say?'

'Let's have some tea,' Noel suggested, to which I wittily countered, 'Yes.'

She was right, though, to refuse to be impressed by Eddie's review. For, after all, there was more in his letter. Of the 'smell' line he still managed to say: 'There are some things too disgusting to write about, especially in one's own language.'

And yet people do smell, don't they?

I did not dare mention this to Noel, but I *do* remember asking Nellie this. I remember that she started – as if I'd interrupted a private thought she'd been having about that very subject – and then smiled, and I sniffed the air close to her and answered inwardly: honey. Violets. Beeswax candles and polish. Then: fish. Eels – I don't know why; perhaps she had been handling them that morning. Then: hair – earth, blackness, salty, girlish sweetness with a nip of something sour. And a whole host of other things that had no name, but did indeed have a fragrance.

Christ, four hundred poems are written every year that end 'The wondrous fragrance of your hair' and nobody objects. And, for God's sake, why am I thinking about Nell?

I have telegraphed to Lytton to send a driver to take me to Churchfield House. The sea air is grey and snippy with wailing seagulls and I find myself strangely unwilling to stay with the others at Cove Cottage. Who is to be there? Ka, of course. James arrives Monday. They will all know of my book. They will all know that 'Lust' has been renamed 'Libido' and is not a good poem.

The driver duly arrives and in the carriage I get my first sight of a prowling grey sea, and a hundred army volunteers in white tents, like a strange spore of mushrooms on the hills above me. I wonder if they have read my *Poems*. I wonder if even now, within those white tepees, there they all are, a hundred young men, tittering at my literary ambitions and foolishness.

I have the strongest feeling of foreboding. Something beyond my worst fears is about to happen. I don't know what it is but I know I'm right because I'm almost there. I'm approaching it with every rattle of this coach's wheel. The sea slides beside me, just within my vision, like a strip of grey slime, persistent and unfriendly. And I think I know what it might be, but what I cannot tell is whether it is coming from inside my head or outside. Whatever it is, it is here at last. The construction, the Rupert Brooke, cannot hold me any longer. I am surely a Lulworth lobster, dropped into a pot, about to be boiled to death.

Lytton announces, standing on the flagstones in the doorway of Churchfield House, that Ka has begged 'a word' with me. Will I take a walk with her tomorrow along the clifftops?

'I'd forgotten you'd grown that ridiculous beard,' I say, noticing it afresh.

'And I don't know if – if James mentioned it but Henry is here. I just took them over to Lulworth Cove Inn.'

'Henry?'

'Henry Lamb, of course.'

Lytton's simpering is insufferable. He practically drools as he says it.

And so the name seeps into my pores like arsenic. Ah. This is what I have been anticipating. This, then, is the blow, the bomb, the reason to feel such inexplicable dreary terror.

'Will Ka bring a lobster pot on her walk?' I ask, but Lytton only stares at me with an expression concerned and uncomprehending.

'Come inside, old fellow,' he says gently. 'You are drenched through with rain.'

'Oh, is it raining?' I murmur, as I begin to unravel myself from my sweater. A Christmas present from the Ranee. I'm surprised to find that Lytton's right: the wool is soaked through, now smelling of damp old sheep and other Christmases when I was a boy. Ha! It smells of my remembered smell. I cannot dislodge the line from my head.

Lytton is still staring at me, in the most ridiculous, lugubrious fashion. 'You look terrible, my dear chap. Are you sick? It's so awfully mild, though, isn't it, despite this confounded drizzle? Some of us thought we'd bathe in the sea . . . see the New Year in. We've arranged to meet at the cove.'

'Yes. I'm sick. Off to bed. Count me out. Don't worry about me! Oh, no. I have my Pride to keep me company.'

I stomp up the stairs towards the top bedroom, grinding the name of Henry Lamb underfoot with each step.

It's morning and Ka appears. She is wearing a peacock-blue scarf and heavy boots. She has never looked lovelier. The wind whips hair in front of her face and wraps her legs with her skirt and I remember seeing her naked once, posing in nothing but her pince-nez for the camera (who was it took the photograph, I wonder now) and how, despite the beauty of her sculpted white body, she looked like a woman destined always to be matronly before her years, as if someone had stuck the wrong head on the charming young figure.

We set off on our walk. Behind her the divinely beautiful sea, the creamy white cliffs, the sky a Giotto blue . . .

But too soon the words coming out of her are disgusting, filthy, foul. Unbearable foul sickening disgusting blinding nightmare – is she truly saying she loves him? Loves the vile Lamb? Wants to marry him? Would do *anything* for him? Including, by implication, spreading her legs?

I must be mishearing. It's this sickness, this head-cold. Inside my head is so much sheep's wool.

She is intent on dirtying everything, everything I felt for her. Our boots marching together across the downs. I watch the imprints as they magically appear behind us, side by side in the frost. After Noel's rejection, I believed dear Ka was safe! Believed her pure!

My head pounds with a thousand bees hammering to escape. Death and Hell! Ka's doing the most evil thing in the world. She says she is willing to be his mistress, allow that soiled snake to sneak between her legs, degrade her, everything . . . The filthiest image of all for the fouling comes into my head: and that is what Ka is willing to do.

'Rupert – please,' she says. 'You're exaggerating horribly. One can't choose who to love.'

Seagulls are screaming overhead; the bees inside me clamour to get out; the sea rises up in a great green tide, ready to throw itself at us. Ka moves towards me. Her face comes into view with her fat mouth and her stupid fat chin – something of Elisabeth van Rysselberghe about her – and her gross neck, with its folds of white flesh.

'Why are women such *whores*, Katharine Cox? That's it, isn't it? You simply long for the *artist* Henry Lamb to drive supremely home and you'd open your legs, whimper and smirk and submit, accept his mastery, and you believe I am a bugger like the rest of them and not up to the task—'

'Rupert! I can't believe you would say such things! No! No, that's not it. I had no idea you had feelings for me – you never said. I understood that you loved Noel . . .'

'I did love Noel. I do! That sweet child is everything you are not. Noel is fine and true and pure and clean and—'

So she crumbles down on the Purbeck Hills and puts her head in her hands – Pah! A bid for sympathy, nothing more – and she keeps muttering, 'Rupert, darling, you are being cruel, cruel – I had no idea, no idea . . .'

Women have such twilight shadowy souls, like a cat behind a hedge. What can one do? And, what's more, they offer themselves endlessly, pathetically. How dreadful that the whole world's a cunt for one.

'So, you won't marry *me*, then? You prefer that greasy, slimy, blisteringly foul Henry Lamb with his giant Obelisk—'

'Marry you? Are you serious? I— But you never asked me! How could I know it was in your mind? And why now, when it should only be a marriage of pity?'

'Ha! It's no, then! Is it my *Poems*? Do you find them so vile, so laughable, so beastly and unnatural that you must refuse my proposal for fear of befouling yourself by connecting with my name?'

'No, no, that's not it. Rupert, you seem so – unwell, I'm frightened for you. I had no idea that my – my confession about Henry Lamb would bring you to this. We have always been honest with one another . . .' she is standing up now, attempts one hand on my shoulder, her scarf unravelling and flicking between us in the wind '. . . and I have always understood how much you loved Noel . . . Couldn't you be a little happy for me?'

'Happy? Happy for you? When you want to sully your life by mingling it with these detestable buggers? Lytton, James, the fucking Blooms*buries*, the lot of them. Jews and buggers! I wash my bloody hands of you.'

This feels good. At last – saying what I feel. I stride off, away from her, and she is a only a bright blue dot, tiny as a forget-me-not, on the green hills. It's as bracing as a dip in the Granta. Oh, if only the cloud in my head would lift, I could taste the real pleasure of this, of finally, finally, uttering exactly what I long to. Goddamn buggers the lot of them.

God burn roast castrate bugger and tear the bowels out of every last one of them.

I'm on the train, then, and Lytton and Ka and James somewhere else, and Lamb too, and only Gwen and Jacques in the seats opposite, glancing at me all the time in that frightened, pathetic way they both have, as if they want to offer me bromide and tea, or strap my arms to my chest. In between these kindly injunctions I sleep. In sleep Lytton appears to tell me how he orchestrated the whole thing: *You needed taking down a peg, Brooke old man.* 'Of course I invited the creature (Lamb) to Lulworth and left the others to go out on walks with him so that the whole disgusting, unbearable, sickening nightmare could happen right under your nose. I knew you were a virgin after all. What splendid sport!'

I open my eyes and meet Gwen's anxious gaze. 'I loathe Lytton!' I tell her.

Gwen and Jacques start in alarm, and Gwen reaches for her flask, enquiring if I'd like brandy. 'You're crying, dear,' she says very softly, as she leans towards me and, ridiculously, fetches my own handkerchief from my pocket and dabs at my face as if I were a child.

The brandy burns my throat and makes me cough and we roll through tunnels, and in the black window beside me my own face appears, striped with white lines and fields and rabbits running through it. 'Where are we going? Where is Ka?'

'She – she left, Rupert. She was very upset. I think you – perhaps you were a little cruel to her.'

'Was I? Where are we going?'

'We've made an appointment for you with Dr Craig in London. We'll take you there. And we've telegraphed your mother. She says you're to come to Cannes with her at once.'

'Does she indeed? And is Ka coming with me? I've asked her to marry me, you know.'

'Yes, we do know,' Gwen says, with a quick glance at the carriage door as if someone might open it. She says nothing more but dabs at my cheeks again, which are surprisingly wet.

'Are we to be married then, Ka and me? Is it agreed?'

'No, dear.' And Jacques begins telling me in great detail about this man, this Dr Craig, and how renowned he is, how he has helped others – why, Virginia Stephen, he thinks, has been to see him.

Mentally, then, I compose a letter to Virginia. 'Let me implore you not to have, as I've been having, a nervous breakdown. It's *too* unpleasant.'

'Poor Virginia,' I say out loud. 'What tormented and crucified figures we literary people are!'

This at least raises a smile from Jacques. 'I've heard Dr Craig is excellent,' he assures me.

I tell them both about an incident at Holy Trinity in Rugby three Sundays ago. In the afternoon there is first a choral service, then a children's service, then a service for Men Only. Two fourteen-year-old choirboys arranged a plan during the choral service. At the end they skipped round and watched the children enter. They picked out the one whose looks pleased them best, a youth of ten. They waited in seclusion till the end of the children's service. Then they pounced on their victim as he came out, took him each by a hand and led him to the vestry. There, while the service for

Men Only proceeded, they removed the lower parts of his clothing and buggered him, turn by turn. His protestations were drowned by the organ pealing out whatever hymns are most suitable for men only. Subsequently they let him go.

'He has been in bed ever since with a rupture,' I announce.

Gwen materialises again in front of me with the handkerchief. Now I see that for some reason it is *she* who is crying.

'Hush, dear . . .' I tell her fondly, and the train slices through the pink of the neat little English hills on their perfect drawing-room scale; just like the blade in a bacon-slicer.

~

Rupert is sick. He's not here. After New Year he was taken off to somewhere in France by his mother, but everyone at the Orchard is talking about it, and Kittie tells me with great excitement that she heard Mr Ward talking to Mr Raverat about it, and she gathers that Rupert had a nervous breakdown and began cussing and wandering the clifftops of Dorset like a madman – as she says this, she's glancing sideways at me all the time, as if she expects me to slap her – and had to be taken to the famous Dr Craig for his stuffing treatment.

We're in the kitchen with the wax kettle on the stove. I wonder hopelessly how to hide the trembling in my hands as I hold the kettle; the shaking in my shoulders as I turn my back on them, reaching for the candle moulds. I knew something was very wrong that night out by Byron's Pool. Should I have done something? Stayed with him in his room, despite his telling me to go? Have I failed him once again, despite all my best intentions? What, what on earth could I have done?

'They all break down in the end,' Kittie says cheerfully. 'Writers, I mean. This doctor makes them drink milk and stout and stop writing. Stopping writing is the only cure.'

'Oh, don't be ridiculous!' I reply, so fiercely that three moulds topple over. I'm trying to teach Kittie and Lottie how to make candles. Lottie, being a diligent girl, is applying herself to the task; Kittie's tongue keeps up steady work of another kind.

'Stopping writing – oh, and drinking the blood of bullocks or something – is the only cure,' Kittie repeats, undeterred, 'but *Love* is the cause. I heard he asked Miss Cox to marry him and she turned him down! But why would our handsome Mr Brooke choose Miss Bespectacled Cox with the fat behind when he could have Miss Olivier or, well, anyone at all?'

'Here – put the muslin over the spout,' I tell her, a warning in my voice. 'The wax is melted enough – can't you see it there floating on top of the water? – so now we can tip it into the moulds. Here, Lottie, get the first cast ready. We need both of us to lift the kettle – it's heavy.'

'And there was another young woman came asking for him the other day. Did you see her, Lotts?' Kittie is not in the least put off. She slaps her hand over mine on the handle of the kettle, but carries on, 'Miss Phyllis Gardner. Came on a bicycle. Long red hair. Shameless, she was. She showed me a sketch she'd made of him and asked me, "Do you know this gentleman?"'

This gives me a stab of fury to almost take my breath away. 'Hold the kettle, will you? I can't do it on my own – put your back into it, Kittie!'

Another young woman, asking after him. Another young artist with modern ideas who thinks he belongs to her.

'And were it a good likeness?' Lottie wants to know.

'The sketch? Not bad at all. Easy to see it was our Mr Brooke. Had his nose, you know, fine and straight but with a sort of little snub at the end. He's made another conquest, no doubt, but I told her he was away "convalescing". I thought that was the best word for it.'

'Oh, where in God's name can Betty be?' I burst out, my voice ringing in the kitchen. She was sent on an errand an hour ago to fetch the meat from Tommy, who has been flat on his back with a broken ankle and unable to make deliveries. As if in answer to my lament, Betty appears at the kitchen door, just as the three of us are struggling to lift the kettle and direct the spout towards the moulds. She hurries to help by steadying the candle casts so that the wax pours in the right place and does not end up all over Mrs Stevenson's table. I notice some hot, honey-coloured blobs dripping on her hands and marvel that she makes no response, nor snatches her hand away. I soon learn why: her mind is entirely elsewhere.

'I've an announcement to make,' she says, glancing up shyly at Kittie, but avoiding, I think, my eyes. 'Me and Jack. You know Jack? The boy who works at the Mill? Jack and me. He asked me – he asked me— Oh, Nell, do say you'll look well on it. He wants us to get married!'

The kettle is nearly dropped as the girls crowd round Betty to kiss her and shriek with excitement. The room is full of commotion and it falls to me – as ever – to remember that Mrs Stevenson is only in the apple loft on the floor above and can hear every word.

'Ssh, ssh now, girls, the wax is hardening – this is not the moment to neglect the task completely!' I cry.

'Oh, do say you think it a grand idea, Nell – *please*,' begs Betty.

I pull her towards me and kiss her cheek. I feel her pounding heart under her apron and regret my selfishness, my own foolish woes. But the wax is cooling and will form badly if we don't attend to it now. 'Of course I do!' I say. 'That's fine, fine news. Father would have been very proud of you. Now help me, won't you?, or the candles will be spoiled and we'll have to start all over again.'

Her hair smells of the silky hot beeswax, the melting flavour of our childhood, and I believe my instinct for guessing at Father's feelings might, on this one occasion, be true. Jack is the good, steady sort and his family is kind, even if they are not Methodists and do have some funny *traditions*. Yes, of course I'm glad for her, for she will stay in Grantchester now and be part of another family, with a new mother and a father and even new brothers and sisters. Perhaps my prayers – the bargain I struck – are being answered after all? To live in Grantchester, near the millstream? That's surely a life, a life for a girl with Betty's inclinations and dreamy, well-meaning nature?

It's only in bed that night that I'm able to let my mind run on and think of what Kittie says about Rupert. Could it really be that easy to go quite mad like that – and for what? Because Ka Cox turned him down. This seems an easy explanation, but not a true one, because what I saw in him that night by Byron's Pool was already glittering in his eyes, and I know he hadn't asked her to marry him then. How do people *break down*? And do they mend again? Can this stuffing cure really work? I realise I know nothing about madness, if that's what it is. I don't understand at all, and it frightens me. The mood I felt crackling in him that night, the look in his eyes, did it seem like madness to me?

I think back to that time in his room, going over and over how he appeared. One moment his face was lit up with some of its old naughtiness; the next he was serious, and somehow frail. But there was that moment when his words were mumbled and the edges of him seemed to be blurring, softening. He did not seem to know that his face was shining wet, that he was crying. As if the very boundaries of him, of his face and his body and being, were melting. Yes, that's it. Rupert was melting, like a candle, down to a liquid nothing. Thinking this, I'm oddly comforted. For after all, after today, didn't we see how the wax hardens again and takes up fresh shapes? Maybe that is what the London doctor will bring. Maybe, God willing, that is what will happen to darling Rupert.

~

Ka is like having black beetles in the house. I put down carbolic powder. That did not work. The Ranee took me to Cannes to cure me of my madness and I wrote to Ka, over and over, and arranged for her to meet me in Munich. That did!

Meeting with Ka in Munich was achieved after much wrangling and conniving, for Mother had to be deceived at all costs. By then I was desperate. I wrote and wrote. I pleaded, I begged her. Give up Lamb, I said. In Cannes the Ranee was at her most magnificent and frightening. I *was* afraid, truly afraid, of Mother's strong, womanly powers, no doubt about it. Such awful scenes, with Mother always restless for facts, always suspicious, with a nose for . . . what? The word I wanted there, the one I paused over, was 'erotic'. Yet it's true. Mother has an extraordinary skill for sniffing out my every erotic thought. No wonder I felt so invaded, so trespassed upon!

Once I managed to convey to Mother that I *hated* her, hated Cannes, the sea, and I reduced her to a crumble, and it wasn't good at all. A Pyrrhic victory. It's beastly hurting people, especially the Ranee, who looks to me for so much now that Father and Dick have both gone. Thankfully she put it down to my sickness and telegraphed Dr Craig, who repeated the advice: no writing, more stuffing. I put on a stone, became as fat as a baby. Of course, it was the Ranee's money I needed. How to get to Munich without it? I told her I was meeting Dudley and she caved in, finally, and was generous, too, and I felt worse than ever.

So, *enfin*, there were those nights in Munich with Ka, and *that* put an end to all desire. I had Ka at last, and that did the trick, like a colossal dose of bromide. I realised in the first glow of tumescence that it was a terrible mistake. I didn't pause –

that would have been impolite – I ploughed on, gave up my prolonged chastity to plunge into the abyss of Ka's body and show her a little more than the Apollo-golden-haired version of me, show her the true horribleness of my nature. I thought of Denham only briefly, how lustful he was, how immoral, how affectionate and delightful, and wondered whether I could, after all, put the thing through with a woman. But the image of Denham, the one touch of his that made me shiver so much I was frightened ... I used that to blank out Ka's anxious expression, and her little, tough, brave '*Oh*' as I entered her. Afterwards she said she was willing to give up Lamb and marry me. My misery was complete.

I sat up all night, sweating in a fever. (Perhaps it was the word 'marry'.) I could not tell if it was sickness of the body or mind or soul but it felt like all three. There was a dark little cave in one part of my brain, and I knew that inside it there was someone or something that I wanted badly, so badly, but couldn't quite see or reach. A feeling so infuriating and frustrating that I wanted to tear my hair and scream.

Kind Ka sat beside me, concerned, warm, hoping to infect me with her calm, but it was no good. I told her strange things that night, cracked open the contents of my vile brain and spilled them before her, trying to find this one good patch, this little nugget. But it remained out of reach.

The idea that I was *recovered* from my breakdown began to fly from her understanding. As the morning light crept through the green gloom of the room I remembered only Father's death and the futility of it all, green and foul and reeking of disappointment. Nothing will come of nothing – and nothing, worse than nothing, is who I am.

She told me she pictured our children: a son, she said, and sobbed. She lay naked as she said this, her hair spread on the pillow, pince-nez on the lace doily on the table beside her, along with the hotel-room key – the number was twenty-six, I remember

– and the unwritten postcards of Munich and the emerald green beads that Ka always wears. Her goodness made me feel worse. We had tried the irrigator and the syringe that I had ventured with Elisabeth with more success. It made an awful mess. But I hoped it had worked. I was sad that Ka had not seemed to enjoy the experience much, and I remember writing to her, later, when we thought she might be pregnant, to try to establish what, in any case, a woman should expect:

The important thing, I want to be quite clear about, is, about women 'coming off'. What it means, objectively – What happens. And also, what you feel when it happens. Have you (I'd like to hear when there's infinite leisure) analysed, with the help of that second night, the interior feelings you were yet dim about the first night (at Starnberg)?

Oh, yes, there was a second night, despite everything, more than one – a second honeymoon, in fact, a month later. I did, in some dim place of pride in my man's soul, believe that I came a little nearer to achieving it, this *rapture* that women, too, are supposed to experience. I saw perhaps a small sign of it in Ka.

Perhaps not. Undoubtedly I am as useless a Lover as I am everything else. A Fabian, a Socialist, a Poet, a Son. The Ranee plainly accused me of the latter, writing in a letter: 'Why are you so unsatisfactory? Is it my fault?' And this because I begged her to give me the money to travel for a year, to escape. Ka says she will give it to me, she has her inheritance, but I don't want her money, that is too cruel. I want to go to America and to the South Seas. The Ranee is against it. She thinks my scholarly efforts should come first, but that was before we heard the results of the Fellowship. Oh, yes, my marvellous Webster essay that I risked my health for rather failed to perform. Fellowship went to some other chap. Seems a long way away now, and of tiny importance.

The only good thing is a poem I managed to write in Munich. 'A Sentimental Exile'. I cabled the editor of the King's magazine from the Café des Westerns: 'A Masterpiece is on its way.' Of course I instantly regretted that, when it was only in fact a silly, quickly written thing that might amuse.

And yet, as I arrive back in Grantchester, in a cab from Cambridge station, 'Just now the lilac is in bloom, All before my little room' echoes in my head as I glance up at the Orchard from my banished position as ex-tenant, then turn sorrowfully towards the gravelled approach of the Old Vicarage instead. Who was I thinking of when I wrote those lines? It wasn't Florence Neeve.

('Hypersensitive and introspective,' the good Dr Craig said I was.)

There are sounds of laughter, and people arriving on the road behind me, and I turn quickly and see that the servants are arriving back from somewhere, all dressed in their church clothes, with hats on and flower buttonholes. Could it be? Yes, it is! Nell. In fact, the two Golightly sisters: Betty and Nell, glorious Nell coming into view in a blush pink dress, with rice confetti on her shoulders. Rice. Confetti. Flowers. Church clothes.

Nell wearing church clothes, with petals caught in her dark hair.

I find my stomach lurching to my boots and cannot speak, but only stand staring at her, like an imbecile, trying to take in the information.

Quite horribly the lines from my poem float tauntingly back to me:

> Unkempt about those hedges blows
> An English unofficial rose . . .

A lump rises in my throat, as my English unofficial rose stops in her tracks, one arm linked in her sister's, and we appraise one another. I watch Nell's expression – shock, also, I think registers there, and then she struggles to compose herself.

'Nell! And Betty! Not at work today, girls?' Does my voice sound strained, high-pitched? I fear it does.

'No – it's—We're just back from a wedding celebration, sir.' This is Betty, beaming and blushing. Yes. There it is. There can be no mistaking it. A wedding celebration. Nell's eyes are fixed on the gravel and she is unable to meet mine. I remember suddenly the way she dabbed at my mouth once, after I'd been stung, and the touch of her finger, sticky with honey, at the corner of my mouth. Such a combination of pain and sweetness. It was nothing, I see now, compared to this.

I manage to force out the next question: 'I see. And who is the lucky groom? Someone I know?'

'It's Jack, sir,' Betty says, turning to her sister and blushing again. 'You know, the boy who works at the Mill and brings the flour for the bread in the mornings . . .'

'Ah, Jack.' A very long pause. We all stare horribly.

'Well, I'm not really in England,' I say loftily. 'It's just a – an interim between periods abroad. One gets into the state of mind for being abroad . . .'

'Yes, sir!' And the girls suddenly break into peals of inexplicable laughter, put their heads together and skitter away from me.

So. That is it, then. Horrible truth like egg in the face. Nell is married.

The two girls disappear down the lane as I stare after them. I have so rarely seen Nell without her apron and her uniform, without most of that long black hair tucked away behind an ugly cap. Their dresses, the colours, make me think of dog-roses, shades of eyelid pink, fragile against dark leaves. ('And down the borders, well I know, the poppy and the pansy blow . . .') What is the point? What is the point of this feeling? I am melting with weariness; my legs will hardly hold me.

I lean against the five-barred gate to the Old Vicarage, hooked back in the bushes, and listen for the dull beat of my heart. It feels like one of those paper boats, sailing hopelessly away from me and catching in a twig, to falter there for ever. (Oh, I know it's a trifle to lose a heart such as mine but, after all, it is the only one I've got.)

With great weariness I pick up my bags. Time to face Florence Neeve and the creepy-crawlies in my old room. Suddenly it occurs to me that I haven't bathed since November, and there is such a lot of dirt to wash off. A pale flash in the corner of my eye stops me. It is Nell, running back along the road and reaching the Old Vicarage gate.

She is out of breath, her hair falling from its pins and her dress clinging to her. Her cheeks are flushed and her forehead shines with sweat. The sister is nowhere to be seen. Nell stops at a little distance from me. 'I – I loved your poem, Rupert. We saw it, we all saw it – "Ah God! To see the branches stir, across the moon at Grantchester!"'

'You read my poem?'

'Mrs Neeve read it out to us in the kitchen at the Old Vicarage. To all of us. "And laughs the immortal river still. Under the mill, under the mill?" Or my favourite bit: "To smell the thrilling sweet and rotten, Unforgettable, unforgotten, river smell; and hear the breeze, sobbing in the little trees . . ." And she said, Mrs Neeve said, "Of course! There *is* honey still for tea."'

'Nell, you didn't memorise every word, I hope?'

She laughs, and glances back along the lane to see that her sister is waiting for her.

'Well. Who would have imagined that Mrs Neeve read the pleasant silly passages of my musings in the King's magazine? And did you find it horribly sentimental and insincere?'

'No, I—' Here her confidence crumbles, which gives me a cruel pulse of pleasure.

'Well, I'm very pleased that my little ornamental gesture has pleased you. I may have to rename it – I had no idea that the Old Vicarage would *so* approve.'

Now she is staring at the ground again, and biting her lip, and her hand flies up to her forehead to sweep at invisible locks of hair. 'Are you – well now, then? You are recovered?' she asks.

Finally, anger and disappointment swell to boiling-point and spill over. 'No, I am not well,' I answer shortly. 'I am rather fat and stupid, wouldn't you say, from looking at me?'

I am gratified to see my words have reached their target. She takes a step back and glances down the lane towards her sister. 'Well, I should go – we're having a little party, you know, at Jack's house.'

The knife twists again as she mentions the wedding. 'Yes. I see that. Acres of fun for all.'

She turns to go, then whirls round suddenly. 'I wonder what it would cost you,' she asks, quietly, her face strangely close to mine, 'to be sincere for once?'

Birds cease their piping. Nell's white face blots out the sun.

'Ah, my dear Nell. How disappointingly predictable of you. You have confused sincerity with constancy. Does it not occur to you that one might be both ludicrously flippant and hideously serious – and truly sincere in both?'

With that I turn away from her, and after a moment's hesitation, I hear her steps behind me, snapping smartly down the lane.

I spend a sad night at Florence Neeve's with legions of woodlice dizzily climbing the walls, their babies trotting in and out between their legs, until I am mad with chasing them and despair of ever sleeping or (perhaps my true fear) ever waking again.

Four

'This is Samoa, by a full moon. You're in London, in a fog. Both are very wonderful. I love you.'

Rupert Brooke, letter to Cathleen Nesbitt, November 1913

Pango-Pango
Samoa

November 1913

My Dear Phyllis,

Your letter of May or June found me wandering somewhere in
Canada. Now I'm here, in the South Pacific, for how long, I
don't know.

For nearly two years I have planned to get away like this. I
think it is a good thing. One sees more clearly. Perhaps it would
have been better, had I done it sooner.

My dear child, there are only two ways of approaching
relationships. One is only to allow love on the supposition that
it may lead to marriage – the other is – the wandering way.
And there are people made for the first way and perhaps people
made for the second. But to introduce those made for the first
to people made for the second is to invite pain and endless
trouble.

You are the first kind. That need not imply that you are
better or worse than the second kind. Only different. You are
meant for love and marriage . . . I'm a wanderer . . .

God, bugger and damn. Letters are hellish hard to write. Now
Phyllis, too, weighs on me with her dark red hair and her hurt
eyes, and I have yet another devouring woman to appease when

239

I should be making sport with the finest-made man I've ever seen: like a Greek statue come to life, strong as ten horses. (To see him strip and swim a half-flooded river is an immortal sight.)

Last night I stayed in the house of a mountain chief who has fierce yearnings after civilisation. When these grow strong he sends a runner down to the coast to buy any illustrated papers he can find. He knows no English, but he pastes his favourite pictures around the wall and muses over them. Result: I have a curious version of what is going on back home. The miners are balloted on the question: Are you in favour of a minimum wage? And nearly five hundred thousand of them reply yes. An overwhelming yes, to make the heart sing again with faith in the intelligence of the Working Man, a man whom once, many moons ago, one was interested in helping. A major coal-mining strike looks imminent. Yet wait. Didn't one once care about such things? And wasn't the date some time around September 1911, before one's poems came out, before one became officially a crackpot, and then a Georgian Poet? And when I look again, that's exactly the date of these papers. Here's the Prince of Wales with his arms around two ladies, in dresses *circa* 1911.

It's very perplexing. *These* people – Samoans and Fijians – are so much nicer and so much better-mannered than oneself. And they are – under our influence – a dying race. We gradually fill their lands with plantations and Indian coolies. The Hawaiians, up in the 'Sandwich Islands', have almost altogether gone, their arts and music with them, and their islands are a replica of America.

And they're so . . . impossible to describe. How far nearer the Kingdom of Heaven or the Garden of Eden these good naked people are than oneself or one's friends.

I seem to have shed my Fabian self, the same way I've shed my Apostle's wings, in favour of being a genuine child of nature. Fiji in moonlight is like nothing else in this life or the next. And here, where it's high up, the most fantastically shaped mountains in the world tower all around, and little silver clouds and wisps of mist run bleating up and down the hillsides like lambs looking for their mother. There's only one thing on earth as beautiful and that's Samoa by night.

Why write to Phyllis now? The distance, I suppose, makes one feel safe. When I think of Phyllis I burn with all the lust that Ka erased in me, and there's fury burning there too, for the way Phyllis denied me and misunderstood me, and twisted my every word. When I said last time I saw her 'there were ways' – thinking to be helpful, nothing less – she flew into a passion and accused me of murdering future children of ours! The girl was a terrible temptress. Stripping naked at the flimsiest opportunity, only to brush me with her long hair, then bristle if I put my hand in the place that she delicately called, playing the artist, 'the centre of the figure'. When I said I had to have her, she would suddenly come over coy and accuse me of bestiality! Her thoughts, apparently, were only ever noble. I suppose she longed to see me naked only to – what? Purify her soul? Women! How damnable they are, really, with their dishonesty and their chaste souls and the ways they like to make us rise and fall and then laugh in our faces.

I shan't finish that letter to Phyllis today. I should wait until my mood is calm.

Yesterday, in the fish-nibbling lagoons, I seem to have really been nibbled. That is, my foot has begun to hurt, and now that I look at the toes, I see that three on the right foot are swollen, and joining together in a way that is ugly and disturbing. Is it possible I have actually been bitten, or poisoned in some way?

I'm reading Robert Louis Stevenson's *South Sea Tales*. I wish I could find a little wifie, a little Uma, like his story 'The Beach of Falesa'. Or a handful of uninhibited virgins, like Gauguin. I have read avidly the accounts by Bougainville of the first landing he made in 1768 and the Venus-like women greeting sailors with 'lascivious gestures'. Yes, that's the ticket. A few lascivious gestures to show me I'm on the right track. Not a great entangled argument with someone like Phyllis (who in the end said no anyway) or a dizzying affair with a Cathleen Nesbitt.

Cathleen.

Unfortunate timing or brilliant timing, I can't decide, to meet her so soon before leaving like that.

The problem was, of course, how fresh my wounds were. And Cathleen's too, as it happens. Although she had laid hurts aside, she said, like a dress upon a chair.

Supper at Eddie's, I remember. Mrs Elgy hovering, clumsily taking plates before guests had even finished. (She wasn't used to 'entertaining', she grumbled later.) Cathleen sat in a corner, showing off her perfect nose. When I complimented her on it (later, days later) she laughed and said that mine turned up at the end and was awfully cute. My heart broke like a flower, to badly quote someone or other. Masefield, perhaps. Do flowers break? In any case, there she was in Eddie's room and I approached her with extraordinary wit by asking, 'Do you know everyone here?' I was thinking of the Violet Asquiths, the Lady Eileen Wellesleys, all those grand folk. Surely this was her circle, more than mine.

She replied, 'Only two people besides Eddie.'

And then that silly gambit she had. Of telling me she loved a poem called 'Heaven' by someone called Rupert Brooke in the *Georgian Poetry* anthology, and had I read it? I know I blushed. God, I blushed. One of those dreadful oh-so-familiar occasions when my wish to convey only nonchalance and urbane acceptance of her flattery was in complete conflict with my idiotic imbecile of a self. While I was glowing hot as an ember and wanting the floor to swallow me, what did the glamorous, perfect-nosed Cathleen do?

She laughed. And all I can remember about the rest of the conversation is that laugh. I told her I'd seen her play Perdita twice and think that I advanced the view that acting is a rum profession for a woman. To which she laughed again, annoyingly.

Cathleen – loveliest creature! Nymph divine!

These thoughts in a hot country are not cooling. I need someone easier to dream of. A memory that doesn't bring with it such a poor version of myself as Lover. Who could that be?

Ah, a throb then, when I think of her. Good, firm Nellie Golightly. Only she with her silky black hair could ever command moonlight like this, floods and floods of it, not sticky like Honolulu moonlight, not to be eaten with a spoon, but flat and abundant, such that you could slice thin golden-white shavings off it, like cheese.

It was a moonlit night, that last one. The one before I left Grantchester. It seems a hundred years ago, although it was only the summer. Bathing was what I longed for. And bathing is what I remember now, the river Granta holy and clean because Nell's naked body had been in it.

But I'm confused. It wasn't Nell, was it, who swam with me that last night? Wasn't it . . . Phyllis Gardner?

It is Nell I remember, though. Nell's smoky violet eyes smiling at me.

Do I dare to write to her? Since I did not see her that following morning, I owe her – a goodbye at least. Nell, who knows all my secrets, the men *and* the women: the secrets of the sheets. But does she ever think of me?

In January I sail for Tahiti. I begin the new year – 1914 – with a whole new island to discover. I have a strange, excited feeling about this, a feeling beyond the general thrill of boarding a ship again. I feel I'm hurtling towards something. I'm out of control, like a man in a barrel hurling himself down the Niagara Falls. Perhaps I shall dare, at last, to write Nell a letter from there.

~

I hardly saw Rupert the year before he left for his travels. Kittie said he was back in his lodgings at the Old Vicarage but, as far as I could tell, he was never there. He seemed to be ignoring all his old friends, moving with a different circle – Lady Eileen someone or other, Violet Asquith, the daughter of the Prime Minister, people like that. He was in London, or at the Russian ballet again in Covent Garden, or his mother's in Rugby. After we bumped into each other that day of Betty's wedding I saw that he was not at all recovered. Not really.

Then this young woman, the brazen artist one, Phyllis, she starts turning up. She cycles here and she asks after him and she won't take no for an answer. When I tell her he's away, or staying at Mr Marsh's again in London, she sighs as though she's sure I'm lying.

She orders lemonade and strawberries and sits in a deckchair in the orchard, takes out his book of poems and reads it under the trees, one eye on the page, one watching the path to the Old Vicarage like a hawk. She doesn't seem to believe me. I think she writes letters to him. Oh, she's modern, all right, that one. Sometimes she's sketching, and I've seen the drawing too, and it's not a bad likeness. Once, when I took her more tea, I saw her prissy black writing creeping up and down the page and felt sure I read 'Rupert'. What on earth did he see in her, I wonder, beyond the obvious?

Yes, she has long hair, the colour of Kittie's, which some might think fine (for myself, I find it rather brassy). Yes, she has big eyes and is one of those large-bosomed girls, where the buttons strain a little and the fabric gapes and she'd be better off with a decent bib to cover it.

And then there was a day at last when he *was* there, he came back, and I did something I should never have done.

Well, I'm not proud of this. And I confessed in my list of faults and talents that I'm not good at keeping secrets, and not too shamed of reading other people's letters neither. Nor following them, once in a while, when my heart urges me to and won't take no for an answer.

Phyllis had chased him to the Old Vicarage that day. I know it was that way round. She'd been following and pursuing him, Kittie says, since she first saw him on a train from London, not last November but two years ago. She'd sketched him (she is a student at the Slade like Miss Gwen – I mean Mrs Raverat) and showed everyone she met the sketch, and eventually identified Rupert as the owner of the cheekbones and the nose with its tiny upward tilt. She got herself invited to a poetry reading of his, or something like that, and got herself under his skin for, the Lord knows, Rupert is susceptible to flattery even while he despises it.

Kittie says Phyllis found Rupert the very first time by calling at the Orchard Tea Gardens. She called Kittie over, bold as brass. Did she know the house on this sketch? Did she know this man? Did she perhaps recognise . . . the profile? The thought of it makes me blaze. No shyness for Phyllis, no hiding her interest in him! No doubt she found him, too. Sitting outside under the huge drooping trees in the Old Vicarage garden reading or writing (those were the days when a Swedish student was visiting him, another doe-eyed girl, and he was translating something or other for her).

I saw Phyllis once or twice again after that, but I think she mostly met him in London, during that year, that horrible year after his breakdown, when I never knew if he would be sweet to me or cruel. At Mr Eddie Marsh's place in Gray's Inn Road. I heard them giggling once, about Eddie and his housekeeper, a woman called Mrs Elgy.

I had hardened my heart to Rupert then. It was easier to do when I didn't have to see him every day. And there was Tommy, who would bring me gifts and take me for drives in the van on my Sunday off; Tommy, who was as predictably sunny as Rupert was dark and changeable.

Then there was that day, that one day, just before Rupert left for his travels, when all my efforts to put him out of my mind came crashing around me.

It was her, that vixen Phyllis, who was my undoing.

It was summer, but straggling, heat sucking all the life out of the day. I remember she stood waiting for Rupert by the sundial, examining it, and the way it is shaped like the curling leaves of a book. I had some tasks to attend to with my bees and had followed her, watching her lean the bicycle up against the ivied porch and step boldly into the green gloom of the Old Vicarage garden. I passed her with great purpose, strode over to the hives, nodding to her and feeling myself happier once surrounded by the bees' hubbub, busying myself with checking for rogue queen cells.

I somehow knew that she was as aware of me as I of her, and pretending. The noise the bees made as I tended them – a warning, like the reminder of a restless sea – kept her away. I made gentle entreaties to them but they continued to fuss angrily at my mood. She moved from the sundial to the Wellington pine, pretending to examine it. A smell of stew wafted towards us from the kitchen as the doors opened.

And then, suddenly, on the lawn there Rupert was, dressed in white flannel trousers and a blue shirt, open at the neck. My heart lurched, and dived, and surfaced, like someone gasping for breath. It was months since I'd seen him. I'd thought I was cured.

'Let's go for a walk,' Rupert said to her, without so much as a glance at me. He didn't seem to know I was there. I knew where he meant. He could only mean along to Byron's Pool, to the floodgate that crosses the river. The same place he'd taken me. So, after a minute or two, when the garden shrank in silence, dank and dark suddenly now the bright blue of Rupert was no longer in it, I left my bees and followed them.

January 1914

So the boat arrives in a lovely, bewildering port, and there are people everywhere, just as there have been each time we docked, and excitement and an unidentifiable scent in the air, a foreign scent of smoke from the chimneys of houses, heat and some kind of frangipani flowers. The sea is a coloured soup, heaving with boats of brown-skinned merchants, naked except for their red and peacock-blue kilts, holding out baskets and shouting. Coconuts and pineapples piled high, and coconut leaves littering the water. The men carry a splendid little tool, tucked into their colourful wrapped skirts – it's shaped like a flat spoon, made of bone and with a serrated edge. One of them, standing up in a canoe nearest to our boat, demonstrates its use: for scraping the meat out of the coconut once opened.

'How much for the tool?' I call out, towards his canoe. Fellow passengers start, and turn to stare at me, but my target seems not to hear and simply stands holding up more coconuts.

We queue on the deck to leave, fanning ourselves in the sticky heat, staring out towards the rocky lump of that mysterious island Moorea, rising from its plume of mist, one huge forest of palm trees and secrecy. Someone on board was telling me that its name means 'yellow lizard', and I try hard to discover if it is because the island itself is shaped like a lizard, but the sea breeze and spots of rain whip tears into my eyes as I try to look harder.

'Look at those niggers! Whose are they?' calls an American Suffragist lady from the SS *Tahiti* as we enter the harbour.

The white population of Heaven, I think, must be very small.

And afterwards, my first step on Lafayette beach, the strange, fine black sand, dark as iron-filings, crunches under my feet. I immediately feel a desire to take off my shoes and socks, which

I succumb to, while children laugh and point and run to carry them for me, taking hold of my hands, while their older brothers hustle to act as porters, and smiling women place garlands of sweet-smelling white flowers over my head.

I long to leave the umbrellas, rope and Gladstone bags of my English life on board but, of course, nothing is that easy. There are rooms to be got, and merchants to turn down. I have introductions at least, and I must hunt up some Gauguins, although I heard – damn! – that a man had got there ahead of me and carried off some paintings on glass.

The blasted boat was nearly a week late so I've had to spend three weeks in New Zealand, a sort of mildly Fabian England, very upper-middle class and gentle, with laws in place that should make me happy: old-age pensions, access to the land, minimum wage, insurance, etc., etc. And yet it's not Paradise. All the women smoke and dress badly, and nobody drinks. There are the same troubles between unions and employers. Perhaps there'll be no peace anywhere until the rich are curbed altogether.

Among the crowd a young woman or, rather, a girl – thirteen years old, no more – is holding out a flat basket full of *tapa*, the bark made into stiff cloth, covered with a brown pattern that I saw in Samoa, too, and calling to *me*, I think.

'Pupure! Pupure!' she says, laughing, pointing to my hair, so that others in the throng turn and look and smile, too. What can it mean? Something about my fairness, perhaps? I nod and laugh, as if I understand, and lift the garland of white flowers round my neck to sniff its warm, waxy scent. (Thinking: Perhaps, like my old Rugby master, she's saying I look like a girl. Ah, shame that, even here, my golden locks cannot go ignored.)

I smile and nod, for the excitement around me seems to demand it, press coins into the hands of the children, and gaze up at the little huts that surround the beach, their roofs a mixture of corrugated tin and pandanus leaves, then glance around for Banbridge, the fellow I met on the boat, who says he knows a place we might stay. The Hotel Tiare in Papeete. He knows a merchant, too, a chap to show us how to find the best black pearls in the world, which no one, Banbridge insists, must leave the island without purchasing. These black pearls – *poe rava* – signify undying love, according to Banbridge. They are the finest of all pearls, fetching higher prices than any other variety due to the unique blackish-green tint, often tinged with yellow or rose. I must not leave Tahiti without purchasing some . . .

I play along, wondering. For whom would I purchase them? Phyllis? Cathleen Nesbitt? Ka? Noel Olivier? Lady Eileen Wellesley? Elisabeth? James or Eddie, perhaps? Undying love. The Lord knows, I have no need of that.

~

First he took her to the boat-shed at the end of the garden. There was no possibility to follow them there without being seen, so I stayed for a moment by the hives, and watched. I knew the inside of that boat-shed. Lined with little drawings of figures bathing naked as God made them. How they made Rupert laugh – he liked to point out how silly were those who disapproved of the drawings, and the antics of the bathers, the shapes their bodies made.

The two emerged from the boat-shed and I knew Mrs Stevenson would miss me from the kitchen and might take some convincing. Maybe I'd used my excuse – the bees – once too often. But I couldn't stop myself. I watched them take off towards the lane and my feet wouldn't stop. They urged me on, after them.

They were laughing. It was early evening, the sky plain, the colour of milk. I stayed a good distance behind them. Once they reached the river, I was hidden by the trees that line it. The wood-pigeon came with me, hooting his call: hollow and lonely. Every so often I paused, holding my breath after I had stepped on a twig and felt sure they must have heard me. But their thoughts were elsewhere. I heard their giggles and read his mood well enough. It was that brittle, high-pitched laughter, the kind that flickers dangerously into something else. Was he well now, or likely to tip over again? I told myself concern for his nerves was my reason for sneaking after them.

They came to a place by the river that was studded with pollard willows and a notice that trespassers would be prosecuted, and here they wanted to cross. And I knew he was asking her to bathe. I hid behind a bush, a distance from them, my boots disturbing the slippery leaves and the chicken-of-the woods and arched earthstar and, after a minute, accidentally rooting out a little frog, which hopped off in terror. I was peeping through the lacework of branches. I could see from the tilt of her head and the set of her shoulders and the tone of her voice – I couldn't hear the words – that she was afraid. My bad heart said, 'Ha! Not so bold, then, after all!' since *I* never hesitated when he asked me to swim. No, not once.

But the next minute my same bad heart hurt again because I saw that they were undressing. I shrank back behind my bush, face close to a branch heavy with huge rosehips, only peeping out as they both reappeared, naked, carrying bundles of clothes.

And then I had a strange sensation. Watching them. Him so tall and beautifully formed, just as he was that very first time I ever saw him naked, in the garden at the Orchard; she so slender and small with those big bosoms, and bigger in the hips than I'd thought, too: like a candle melted down at the bottom. I could not understand the feelings it produced in me to see them both. My body felt on fire. I didn't know whether to sob or run. Oh, I knew he came here with others. Miss Virginia Stephen, Kittie said. But I'd never witnessed it and so, in my mind, it had been *our* place and ours alone. A place to play, and swim, like children, the way I used to with my brothers in the river Lark. The place of his poem, which stupidly I had thought was somehow – how could I have thought it? – meant for me.

I watched them wade to the other side – she dropping his boots once, and screaming with the chill of the water, and the dark tones of his voice, playfully chastising her, splashing. And then hot tears sprang to my eyes and my ears drummed, as they wrestled on the bank on the other side, rolling naked and laughing and play-fighting, and I strained and strained to see how he put his hands round her throat and his face close to hers, and I wondered – I could hardly breathe as I wondered – whether he might kill her?

I swear, so clotted with grief my heart was, I almost wished he would, as that would have been easier to bear than what I was watching.

Then suddenly there was *her* voice, loud and angry, and she sitting up, and him releasing her. The afternoon turning chill and the church bell in Grantchester striking. The beginning of grey darkness melting the trees so that I could no longer really see their shapes. Then raised voices again – I heard him say, 'You are a fool!' – and a moment when she sat up quickly and grabbed her clothes, and I suddenly thought they might look over at my side of the river and see me. But, no, they stayed on the other bank – they must have decided not to go back through the water but to cross at the bridge – and their grey shapes moved away, and darkness began to fall.

You are a fool. He might have been speaking to me. Nearly four years, I've laboured like this. Persuaded myself. That it's only men who make him feel passion, that he feels nothing of *that* hot sort for a girl. All of his ranting. How he hated Sodomites, how filthy James and Lytton and Denham were – I took to be his way to convince me, convince himself, and the more he said it, the more I understood it to be deep in him, and stuck fast. When he talked of marriage, whether to Ka Cox or Noel Olivier – I always understood it to be about marriage of the necessary sort, the sort a person of his upbringing *had* to take up. I never thought – not for one minute – that he *could* feel that way towards a girl.

And when he kissed me, when he held me, when his hot mouth and his tenderest caresses, his hand in my hair, seemed to speak of something else, why then I had only fought more fiercely; fought my understanding of *everything* to persuade myself that I could not trust him, that he did it for show and that I must not for one minute believe him.

That way, I told myself, he will have no power to hurt you. Well.

How wrong can a girl be?

The pain I felt watching him with that Phyllis was unlike anything I'd ever felt before. Even Father's passing did not hurt me like that. I did not know you could feel hurt this bad inside you, and live. I wanted to scream – I thought I was dying, my breathing came so hard, my lungs hurt so much. I rolled myself into a ball, under the bushes, pushed my face into my knees and sobbed.

Still I could not blank the picture of her. That saucy girl with her red hair down, and her plump backside, turning her head into the ground. His head dipping towards hers, his hands on her skin, and even from a distance I could feel it: like heat coming off the ground, like steam. This thing. This thing he felt for her.

And then I lifted my face up, realising that they had gone, and that I was alone out there, on the other side of the river, and it was dark, and the trees were creaking.

I looked down at myself and stood up. My dress dirty, my bib fraying. My nose snotty, my face streaked: a grubby little child, a street urchin, an elf. An ignorant bee-keeper's daughter, a maid-of-all-work, with five siblings to take care of, a girl who had never read Webster, nor carried a sketch in a bag and ridden a bicycle.

A good, sensible girl, capable of facing hard facts?
Or the biggest fool a girl could ever be?

~

We reach our hotel as evening falls, having spent most of the afternoon idling along the waterfront trying to regain our land legs on the street known as the Broom, where Chinese merchants offer us Tahitian black pearls of every hue. I do feel I'm walking like a drunk with the swell of the boat still in my gait, but nothing like as bad as my buffoon of a companion, Mr Arnold Banbridge, sweating in his heavy jacket, and examining each pearl for so long that the Chinamen grow anxious and hammer at him to give it back. I soon enter the grip of the man's obsession, however – it's impossible not to, bowling along among the thousands of these glorious, luminescent little balls. Black is an inadequate word to describe the hypnotic range of shades and tones.

Our minds eventually boggle and our senses revolt; and so we progress to stalls where the curio-makers with their dusty fingers and sharp tools endeavour to sell us objects carved from mother-of-pearl, which they call here nacre. I search for the coconut tool I saw demonstrated from the SS *Tahiti*, and one of the Chinamen possesses a fine specimen, carved, he indicates with much pantomime gesturing, of volcanic rock, and called, if I'm hearing him correctly, an *anna*.

'Gin? Gin?' the Chinese merchants ask us, hoping we might have some to barter. (I'd hazard a guess that my moustachioed friend has some stashed in that jacket of his, but if he does, he's not saying. I've discovered he has an enormous repertoire of smut and is very self-consciously Kiplingesque in a way that even Kipling himself was not.)

So then we hitch a lift from a passing boy, driving a horse

and cart, who claims to know the hotel that Banbridge mentions, run by a native woman called Lovina. This rickety mode of travel is swift, only interrupted when Banbridge loudly mentions his thirst and the burnished youth stops to shin up an immense, almost perpendicular coconut palm with utter ease and grace, to pick a baby coconut. He cracks it open Tahitian style, by spearing its hairy shell on a pointed stick. Once he has released the large nut inside and shaken it to check for freshness, he whacks it firmly on the nose with a rock (the coconut always looks like a little face to me, with dark spots for eyes, nose and mouth) and splits it neatly open, offers it to us both: chock full of the best drink in the world.

(Glorious youth! Before I leave here, I'm going to learn to handle a coconut like that. I might introduce it to Rugby as a sport.)

My sense of barrelling towards something, of something imminent, of great importance, looming in front of me, has only intensified since we docked. What this is, I know not . . .

Back at the Papeete post office I picked up my mail and my heart went through a very curious performance. Letter from the Ranee – including a cheque from the *Westminster Gazette* for my 'Letters from America'. I kiss the envelope. Letter from Phyllis. Heart sinks. Letter from Cathleen – heart lifts again, soars. Letter from Lady Eileen Wellesley. Oh dear – have I accidentally garnered another convert? I laid the airmail envelopes flat inside my suitcase, atop the shirt that Ka made me and my new toy, the camera, with little desire to read them. I want only to be here, my back bumping against my case, drinking this sour, strange juice, and watching the palm trees twitch in the twilight as we pass, as though a ghost or an invisible black cat tweaks at the fronds to tease us.

Lovina – 'Mrs Lovina', Banbridge calls her – turns out to be a white woman, or perhaps a very light-skinned islander. She speaks perfect French, Tahitian too, one presumes, and not half bad English, and is informal, smiley, with a 'native' feel about her, and immensely welcoming. She wears the long dark dress the missionaries have imposed but in her case it is a relief not to see her naked. A marvellous plate of some kind of raw fish, and *poe* – crushed banana mixed with starch, wrapped in a banana leaf and baked with a vanilla bean – is devoured in what feels like seconds, by both of us, and soon the day's sensory excesses are making our eyelids droop and Banbridge and I are ensconced on our cool flat pallets, lined with white mats, listening to a cockerel outside our window.

A cock crowing? At – what? – midnight? (Am I in the Garden of Gethsemane then, not Eden after all?) Banbridge snores and bubbles like a volcano guttering.

I am trying not to think of Ka Cox or Noel Olivier, for that way madness lies.

The cockerel confuses me and I feel propelled from my bed to tiptoe downstairs to look outside and – spark awake as I suddenly am – to see if there mightn't be some kind of nightcap on offer. Excitement, the sense of something about to happen continues to prickle, just under the film of sweat on my skin. It's the same something that makes me not want to read my letters, not connect at all with that broken poet-boy back home, the one who cracked apart and made a sorry mend by mixing with a new crowd; but to travel only forwards and onwards, to meet whatever it is that I can feel tweaking at palm fronds and waiting for me here.

I'm glad to discover a bar at the front of Mrs Lovina's hotel, with gin shining on shelves and an equally shining barman. A small brown man wearing the fascinating concession to the missionaries that most adopt here: the blue-flowered *pareu*, or skirt, with a white shirt and hat, and when the hat is removed (as now), usually white flowers tucked behind each ear. To cap it all, this man has a moustache bigger even than Banbridge's. He stands, his hand twirling a teacloth inside a glass, and talking softly to a native girl beside him; a girl swathed in a dress of royal blue.

The cock crows again – wildly this time, as if demented – and this girl, this exquisite, shimmering, black-eyed girl, glances up. I'm tiptoeing down the stairs towards her, feet bare, limping inelegantly on my bad toes, wrapped like a parcel in my native-style *pareu*. Our eyes meet, and I can only think, in my startled, not-quite-awake way, that this girl, despite her brown skin – how can that be? – this girl is the living image of another girl I know: Nell Golightly, back home in Grantchester.

'*Ia ora na*,' I venture. My first attempt at Tahitian.

The girl says nothing, but the barman answers at once. 'Good evening, sir. *Bonsoir*, Monsieur Rupert. *Je m'appelle* Miri. Very good, sir. Sleep no good?'

'The confounded cockerel. I thought it was morning.' I grin to acknowledge that it's a lame excuse, and nod at once to accept the bottle of rum he smoothly produces from under the counter. From a jug he tops the rum with some kind of juice, smiling broadly and pushing the drink towards me. 'Good for sleep,' he says.

So I sit at the bar and sip the dark, honey-tasting liquid, and from nowhere and despite the hour, others appear: a native boy of five or six in a blue-flowered *pareu*, with missing teeth at the front; another young woman, slim and tall with coffee-coloured skin, broad shoulders and hair in a straight plait down her back. This woman, while taking the teacloth from the barman and shaking her head at him as if to insist she take over, offers me a convoluted explanation for the crowing cock: something like a bad god, Pae, trying to steal the island of Raiatea and how the cocks crowed a warning and woke Hero – presumably the good god; no, she says, he was the god of thieves and sailors – who rose up and rescued the isle, and now cocks crying all night long is a reminder, a warning, to those who might wish to steal the islands that they are guarded.

I can scarcely follow this story, told in the usual mix of Tahitian, French and English, because my attention is so diverted by the deepness of this woman's voice, rich and baritone. She, too, wears the missionary-style dress, dark green this time, buttoned to the neck, shapeless and long, but when she catches me looking at her, she swishes her plait over her shoulder coquettishly, and adjusts the white tiare flower behind her ear. Though her chest is straight and fallow, my eye is drawn there. She seems pleased and acknowledges me. Then, calling to the child to cease his sport – pulling faces at me – she turns her attention to him, shooing him back with her towards the kitchen.

The blasted cock crows on.

From above us we hear the rumbling of Banbridge's snores and the wooden floorboards tremble so violently the oil lamp shakes.

The barman – what did he say his name was? Miri? – is now slumped on his stool behind the bar, his eyes half closed, so I reach for the bottle and help myself to another shot of rum. I had forgotten about the other woman, the one who looks like Nell, but now she appears, slowly swishing a pandanus broom from one side to another and watching me out of the corner of her eye.

'Your foot hurting plenty? Mr Monsieur Brooke? You would like Tahitian medicine?'

'Ah, my foot. I stepped on – one assumes – something poisonous. In the coral, in Samoa, you know? I must say, it has been giving me some gip.'

She nods. She rests her broom against the polished wooden bar. 'I'm good nurse. Show me le pied, Monsieur,' she says, and gestures with her hands, making pushing movements, as the other woman did when shooing the child. Obediently, I climb down from my bar stool and head in the direction she sweeps me towards.

So I followed them back to the Old Vicarage and my tears soon dried. I saw him part from Phyllis, and I saw that it was done without friendliness, and that she took off on her bicycle and he made his way to his rooms at the Old Vicarage. And this was where I should have turned back, gone to my little bedroom at the Orchard. I dried my tears on my apron and watched as a light appeared in his window, and thought of that nursery gate to his stairs and how everyone else, Mr and Mrs Neeve, their son Cyril, the girls at the Orchard, would be sleeping, for it was dark now suddenly, but the moon was full, fat as a giant white eye.

I think I had been standing there a long time, my heart beating furiously.

I was remembering that first time, when he cheekily said, '"Down, little bounder, down!" as Edmund Gosse said to his heart . . .' and how angry I had felt towards him, how I lay in my own bed with that stricken heat flaring up in me, over and over. How exhausted I was by morning. And how it crackled again right now, under my skin, the same fury and wildness, the same desire to go find him, to give him at last 'what for', as Mother used to say: a piece of my mind.

But not anger. Not really anger, no. I was a girl then, not quite seventeen. Newly without a father. A long time ago. Almost four years since I first met Rupert and in that time I have grown up, and understood certain things. I have listened to Kittie talk about women and their purity, their pure minds, and I've turned inside to listen to my own blood and learned plenty.

So I dried my face and tidied my hair with my hands, and straightened myself up as best I could. I unbuttoned my boots and shoved them under a hedge where I'd be able to find them tomorrow. I felt my breath catch and the heat settle in me, low in my body. I knew its name, at last, and I knew it was not ugly or dirty any more than it was pure and holy, but only *true*. I tiptoed barefoot across the gravel, and through the french windows, which I knew I'd find unlocked, and stepped into the Old Vicarage. I knew where the doors to the pantries were, without being able to see them. I knew the tiles beneath my feet were red; they still held a trace of the day's warmth. Then I felt my way in darkness, my hand sweating stickily on the banister as I guided myself up the stairways and to the nursery gate that guarded Rupert's rooms. I stepped over it. I knocked boldly on the door. I knew he liked boldness. Boldness was something he found hard to resist. I went in.

I stood by his bed. I did not know whether he was asleep at first, but then he whispered: 'Well?' I sat down on the bed, and he put his arms around me, and I laid my head on his shoulder. He pressed me closer, and something in the touch of him made me suddenly afraid, and I began to tremble violently from head to foot.

'Are you frightened?' he said.

'Yes,' said I.

'You needn't be,' he said, 'I wouldn't do anything you wouldn't like.' (This very quietly.)

And that was when I had to admit it. I would like it. I would. Very much.

～

And that's how I end up here at Hotel Tiare Tahiti, in a queer back room, a small room with only a wooden pallet on the floor with white sheets on it; a kind of hovel, with a door open to a yard and this young woman beside me, swishing a huge fan in front of my face (made of the ubiquitous pandanus leaves). She has poured coconut juice over my foot, which made it sing with a flaming, shooting pain; but I understand from her utterings about 'clean, clean, *propre*!' – that this is a folk remedy, which makes sense as the coconut liquid is sterile; and so I submit, delirious and beyond defending myself.

But for two days now the foot has got worse, and a general sickness has taken me over. I'm sweating in a fever. Strange thoughts are crowding me. It is as if I've submitted at last to something I fought off for so long. Am I back in chilly Lulworth, after the débâcle with Ka on the clifftops, crying into my pillow, and hoping – in lucid interludes – that no James or Lytton will visit to witness my misery? Sickness always returns me to my childhood bed, and as I feel the soft smack of another damp cloth on my brow, I imagine I am back in the sick dorm at school and that it is the Ranee or perhaps Nell whose white hand smoothes my forehead – and then I catch sight of the brown hand of my Tahitian nurse and realise with a jolt where I am.

She brings me bowls of some yellow fruit – *nono* or *noni* or some such thing – tells me to 'eat, eat, Pupure!' – that word again, only on her tongue it sounds more like Pu-pu – but when she lifts my foot, the injured one, that only a few days ago was bearable, simply inflamed, now it is burning. A fierce flame at the end of my leg, and her touch is like knives digging under the toenail.

I long to scream in complete ingratitude: 'Get this witch doctor away from me!'

On the third day it is not her, whose name I discover, from listening to others calling to her, is Taatamata, but the other, the fruity-voiced one with the broad shoulders and the plait, who attends me. *Her* touch is kinder and she lays tiare flowers on my pillow so that when I toss and turn it is their waxy white scent snaking up my nostrils. Now *she* with the flirtatious flicking of hair is a little more like the lascivious girls I was led to expect. Her name, I discover, is Mahu. Not that anyone calls her this, only that Taatamata nods and says, 'Eh, Mahu,' in answer to my questioning glance. So I suppose it might mean something else.

That night Taatamata appears in the doorway with a bowl of, she says, *poulet fafa* – 'very good stew with plenty chicken and coconut milk' – and I sit up to take some from the spoon she offers, feeling, for the first time in a while, hunger pangs. She places a candle on the floor beside my bed and proceeds to dip the spoon in the stew and hold it to my lips, offering me sip after sip, tipping my chin with her other hand. 'Excuse me, Monsieur Rupert, you feel better?'

I can hardly speak between the fast-arriving spoonfuls. 'A little – yes.'

'Excuse me, Monsieur Rupert, you must eat plenty. *Vous êtes trop mince* – like little boy. No good. I should look at your foot?'

I stick the foot out of the sheets and she puts the bowl of stew down to examine it, lifting it gently, tutting and shaking her head. The pain shoots up the toes as she handles them; sweat springs to my brow, and drips from my arms to the sheets. She returns thoughtfully to feeding me spoonful by spoonful, until it occurs to me to mention, 'I say, I can do that myself, you know.'

Now I have offended her. She shoves the bowl towards me, slaps her arms by her sides and looks angrily at me. Suddenly nauseous, I decide my brief meal is over and lean over the low bed to place the bowl and spoon on the earthen floor.

'Monsieur Rupert must take some new medicine. Your foot is not better, *pas bien*. I think you have plenty sting from Taramea starfish. Like this, *oui*?'

She demonstrates with her hands a round shape, indicating with little movements that the offender had spikes.

'I don't remember. I didn't see. I stepped on something – I felt a sting, or what I thought of as a nibble in the water, yes. But it wasn't too painful at the time.'

She nods at this and seems relieved. 'Not *nohu*, then. Stonefish. *Nohu* is very bad! Plenty die stepping on *nohu*. Big men faint with pain.'

This Taatamata now demonstrates with an exaggerated swoon, falling all the way to the floor. I peer over at her, suddenly at the same low level as me.

'No, not this *nohu*, stonefish chap, then, I don't suppose. Just some run-of-the-mill coral or poisonous fish that I stepped on and my foot has become infected. I'm very prone to sickness, I'm afraid. Spent a lifetime in beds and sick-bays. Second nature to me.'

She gets up, brushing down her dress. Nods at me, seeming to be studying me hard. The room is lit by flickering candles. I return her stare. Tonight she looks nothing like Nell: her features are too fine, her nose straight, her cheekbones high. She might have noble blood, French perhaps. It's only something in her expression – large eyes of the darkest brown, almost black, her gaze direct and intelligent, like Nellie's.

'What's your name?' I ask her, trying to summon up some of my former Apollo-sun-god charm, although I know her name already.

'Taatamata.'

'What does it mean in Tahitian?'

'*Rien*. I don't know. What does Monsieur Rupert mean? *Popaa*?'

To my surprise, she grabs a lock of my hair, shakes it. Now I'm confused. *Popaa*, I thought, meant white man or European. But Pupure – the name the child at the harbour called out – I had thought meant pure, or perhaps pale. Which pleased me. Is it in fact another word, or the same one pronounced differently?

'*Popaa*? Pupure. Ha! That's me. Pure one. Yes, do call me that. Not Monsieur Rupert, he's – I left him back on the boat.'

And now Pupure, I tell her, wants to sleep, as the fever starts to rage again, and sweat drenches my skin and soaks the sheets, the effort of speaking becoming too much.

I think she has left. The candle is blown out and the smell of wax overcomes the strong tiare-flower smell, a sweet gardenia scent. The room crackles darkly. Outside the cockerel crows insanely and the voice of a child – the boy from the bar, Georges, can be heard; along with the occasional rumble of Banbridge opining about something or other upstairs. I believe at first that Taatamata has gone; then I hear water splashing in an *umete*, and feel the icy stroke of a cloth against my burning foot. Relief seeps up towards my calf with infinite pleasure. Perhaps I even moan a little; certainly someone does. And so it goes on: stroke after stroke, cool and sweeping, soothing and divine. She works in a marvellous, seamless way, each stroke following the last without pause; and when she refreshes the cloth she keeps one hand on my leg so that contact between us is unbroken. Soon waves of pleasure are sneaking along my calves and, inevitably, onwards and upwards. Shame floods me, and panic, lest she notice! But my sickness melts my body and my will, and darkness hides the rest.

I find myself longing for her to go on and dreading a sign that she might stop, but she doesn't. Stroking, sweeping, cooling, calming, soothing. Then I hear the droplets splashing in the *umete* as she refreshes and wrings out the cloth and starts again on the other leg. When was I last bathed by another, so gently and so expertly? Not since . . . being a little boy . . . that nurse Mother so despised . . . Dorothy . . . It's such a tender, exquisite sensation, and I let my sticky mind wander in the heat, thinking how clean I am now, cleaner than I've ever been, perhaps, here on Tahiti, with all my woes behind me in England and all my bad behaviour, my ghastly errors . . .

Munich, with Ka. The lamp wobbling on the bedside table as I bucked like an animal on top of her. And afterwards, her sudden cry: 'Oh – I'm bleeding!' Her face shamed and startled, and then horribly in pain, and me hopping about with only one pyjama leg on, fetching more of the grey, hopeless towels to staunch the flow and saying, 'I say – was I a beast, then? Is this normal? Dear Ka, I'm sorry, I— Is it all right?' And only later, only in a roundabout way when I mentioned or hinted at something of it to James, did it occur to me. Was that a miscarriage? Did we – did Ka and I – copulate so foully, so dirtily, that we *murdered our own child*?

But my mind was so deranged in those months. It was all I could do to silence the clamouring that told me generally I was dirty, a dirty little boy. I bought Ka a gift, a tactless gift of an Eric Gill statue – a square-headed Mother and Child. That was the closest we came to speaking of it. I angered Phyllis, and I – I— Lord knows what damage I did to Nell Golightly.

Now Taatamata's skilful hands are working further up my thighs. Cleansing, purifying. Now she is lifting the sheet and uncovering me like a mummy, black and hotly stiff in the darkness. Even here, when she reveals me, she does not hesitate. I think I hear her mouth widen, not in shock but into a smile. The stroking continues, on my stomach, my thighs, this time – is it my imagination? – more intense, more deliberate, determined. Heat burns every inch of me; I place my hand on my cock, I hardly know what I'm doing, I feel my nipples stiffen and my whole body rise and buck, but I'm too weak to get up off the bed or roll over, or touch her or take her, and so I merely spill myself, with a sob that I take no trouble to stifle, on to the sodden sheets. Taatamata hardly breaks stride to sponge the sheet too. Patting me tenderly on my stomach with the cloth, she leaves, tactfully closing the door to the noisy yard.

~

The next morning I can hardly look at her. She draws the curtain, takes off the straw hat she is wearing, and produces an orange, which she proceeds to peel and offer me segment by segment. I open my mouth like a child and taste the most glorious orange in the world.

'Pupure, you now feel better? No more fever?'

'Ah! How right you are – Pupure feels like a Changed Man. Perhaps I truly am Robert Louis Stevenson now – in both thinness, literary style and dissociation from England! Pah, what glory—'

She frowns at me and shoves the last piece of orange into my mouth. (An uncharitable reading of this would be that she wishes to shut me up.)

'Mama Lovina *m'a donné* these. For you.'

Letters are produced from a pocket deep in her drab dress. Who can this chap be – *Mr Rupert Brooke, c/o The Union Steamship Company Agents, Papeete, Tahiti*? Put like that, it does give one some kind of jolt. Feeling Taatamata's eyes on me I pick the envelopes up, recognise the handwriting of Eddie, Phyllis, Cathleen. A distinct smell of the theatre floats from Cathleen's letter – of greasepaint, wooden boards and yards of Irish green tulle. I resist a powerful desire to hand the letters back. No further cheques from the *Westminster Gazette* for my 'Letters from America'. And none either from the Ranee.

As I sink back to my pillow, closing my eyes, she says slyly, 'Pupure, your letters are from a sweetheart? Or wife?'

'What an extraordinary question! Where I come from a girl could be hanged for asking such a thing!'

More frowning. She folds her arms across her chest to indicate that she is patiently waiting for a decent answer.

I sigh. 'Yes. My dear – many sweethearts. Too many! But no wives.'

This satisfies her and, gathering up the orange peel, she leaves me.

So, later that day I'm well enough to join Banbridge at table, and have my delicious *mahi-mahi* ruined by his opinions on the German government of Samoa. As he speaks I am thinking that I see no reason for his existence, and several against.

'You were in Samoa, weren't you, Brooke? My view is that the English in Fiji handle things far better – we know what we're about, eh? I'm sure the niggahs would prefer it, too.'

'Oh, I don't know. The Germans seem to govern it much better than I thought they would. The first governor was a wily man and studied Fiji, then started German Samoa entirely on British lines—'

'Well, that's my point, man. They need *us* to show them how to do it. And I hear that whenever the Germans' backs are turned the Samoans cheerily forget the German they've been taught and return to speaking English.'

Taatamata, Mahu and another native girl slam plates of breadfruit on the table, and jugs of some strange drink we're assured is not alcoholic. I tentatively spear a piece of yellow-white breadfruit flesh, cut into triangular chunks, noticing Mahu smiling encouragingly – earlier today I saw her cook the fruit, skin and all, in the fire, and scoop out the flesh. It has a smoky, faintly sweet, bland taste, and dense texture, rather like plantain – not offensive at all. And I catch her eye to nod my approval.

A scarlet and turquoise parrot replaces the hysterical cockerel in accompaniment to Banbridge's diatribe. I don't know whose squawking is worst.

I cannot help myself from persisting in my defence of German rule. 'Most people in the Pacific, black *and* white, agree that the German Customs officers in Apia are incomparably more courteous than the English in Fiji.'

Banbridge practically chokes on his fish. 'But the private traders complain bitterly! Their trade is interfered with by so much regulation.'

'Well, that's partly so that they can't exploit the natives in quite the same way the British in Fiji can.'

'Look here, that's a bit rich, isn't it? Under British or American rule we'd have four times the trade in Samoa. And look at how the Germans tax them in Samoa.'

'Ah that's only in direct taxation. In indirect taxes the Fijians under us are far worse off.'

'Where do you get your facts, Brooke? A Samoan head of the family has to pay a pound a year—'

'Yes, and that represents, oh, three days' work picking and drying coconuts for copra – so they needn't kick. You know, I'd warrant a guess any time that the Samoans are richer, and far happier, than the average European.'

Here Banbridge puts his fork down and brushes angrily at imaginary mosquitoes near his face. 'Ah, now I understand you, my man. Full of admiration for the "noble savage", are we, whose life, I presume, you find infinitely preferable to ours?'

His eyes skim over the *pareu* I'm wearing as if noticing it for the first time. And, if I'm not mistaken, they slide over Taatamata too. 'Actually, Brooke, that's jogged some memory in me. Are you a Kingsman? A poet, perhaps? I think I've heard of you. Did you in fact go native in – where was it? Oh, somewhere rural in Cambridgeshire, a village . . . you know, barefoot with a bunch of cronies, eschewing meat and tobacco and that sort of thing, what?'

'What can I say? Guilty as charged, Officer.'

He pushes his *umete* away and shakes his head as Lovina leaps up to offer more breadfruit, more *mahi-mahi*. He mops at his moustache with a piece of *tapa* cloth he finds on the table. (No doubt the pattern has some spiritual significance – I will ask Taatamata later. The bloody fool thinks it's a napkin.)

'Your defence of the Germans in Samoa is a surprise, though, Brooke,' he pronounces. 'I think I'd heard you had some strange Fabian ideas, knew the Webbs, that sort of thing. I didn't have you down as pro-German.'

The parrot squawks triumphantly. Man and bird are detestable. His last remark reminds me horribly of Augustus John: 'I didn't take you for a socialist, Brooke.' Why is it that everyone in the damn mother country thinks they know who I am; what *to take me for*?

'Ah, well,' I announce, rising rather unsteadily and eyeing with longing the corridor that leads to my little bed, the room I called a day ago a 'hovel', which now appeals to me as the most entrancing luxury because it is no longer a shared bedroom with Banbridge. 'That reminds me. I've been reading the "Account of the Natives of the Tonga Islands", you know. You'll remember what King Finow said on seeing how he was described by the white man.'

Banbridge shakes his head and continues distractedly stuffing his pipe.

'"This is neither like myself nor anybody else! Where are my eyes, where is my head? Where are my legs? How can you possibly know it to be I?"'

Banbridge's face is a marvel. Even the native child Georges couldn't contort his features into *that* particular monster.

The dear fellow is no doubt at this very moment remembering he had also heard that this barefoot Georgian monstrosity, this Rupert Brooke, had, incidentally, gone quite mad.

Hardly surprising, then, that I am not charmed by Banbridge's plans to leave the Hotel Tiare and travel to Mataiea tomorrow. (The month, I discover, has changed, and is now February, although no one told me.) Mataiea is about thirty miles from Papeete, in the heart of the island, a native village with one fairly large European house in it, possessed by the chief. It's the coolest place, everyone says, and we can make an easier journey to the coast where the pearl divers are to be found.

At first I try protesting that I'm not yet well enough to travel. As I had spent the morning swimming in a lagoon with two large Tahitian boys, spearing fish, this was patently a lie.

He leans in then and I smell his dreadful stale male breath and do my best not to reel back in horror: I think I am in the sixth at Rugby again. 'Take her with you, what?' Banbridge says. 'The native girl. No one here will bat an eyelid.' He straightens up and, with a disgusting wink, says to Lovina: 'Brooke here needs a nurse for our travels. And we'll need a guide, too. Your man Miri, perhaps? Or what about the pansy? What's his name? Teura? I'm sure under that dress he's quite the muscle-man, what? Two weeks is all. Surely you can spare them.'

Lovina laughs her big laugh. To my astonishment, I realise that the 'muscle-man' Banbridge is referring to is the woman with the long braid, the one I thought was called Mahu (now sitting out on the terrace, making a basket from pandanus leaves). Of course, the minute the truth is out, the 'woman' reshapes in front of my eyes and I realise at once that her tallness, her broadness of shoulder, the deepness of her voice and the blunt flatness of her chest should have made it obvious. Not to mention – now I'm staring at them, plaiting the leaves – the size of her hands! I remember, with a curious, humiliated sensation, my pleasure at the tiare flowers she left on my pillow . . . Am I so transparent, then, even here? And Banbridge, Lovina, no doubt everyone else, appear so untroubled, so wholly unsurprised by her, *his*, hermaphrodite status. I have a stab then of an old feeling, one that Lytton and James used to provoke in me: of being naïve, inexperienced and unworldly – clumsy, foolish and *wrong*. I stomp towards my room, while Banbridge continues to make his loud arrangements. He wants to feel safe, what, in case he carries back the pearls or better still the Gauguins, and three fine young Tahitians with a pansy built like a tanker should, he says, be just the ticket.

I go in search of Taatamata. After her devoted ministrations to me, she is the only one capable of reassuring me. I've no wish to think of England, or remember my quarrel with James and Lytton, or my humiliation at the hands of that sleek operator Henry Lamb, which has somehow, just then, unbidden, managed to skip over the ramparts and enter my mind.

She is busy when I find her, cleaning fish for supper. I don't know at first what to say, how to ask her, but when this Mahu appears and then disappears, Georges trailing behind him, I find that a nod towards him, and a few gestures make the question clear enough.

Taatamata laughs and says, 'Eh, *mahu*,' which I now understand to be the name for the males who are raised as girls in, apparently, almost every family in Tahiti.

'If Tahitian family has eight children, one be *mahu*,' Taatamata says.

And – with a few crude gestures I get to the nub of the matter – not all of them are inverts either, although the fact that many are seems to surprise nobody. Well. It seems the missionaries weren't able to halt in Tahiti all things they found abominable, after all.

Later that afternoon we step down to the beach to help the day's gathering of clams, and when she is intent, bent over, her hair curtaining her face, I suddenly ask her what I really want to know. 'Taata, do you think a person has only one true self? You know, underneath it all . . .'

'One true self?'

'Yes, yes, you know – *un vrai* . . .' Stupidly, I can't remember the French for 'self'. I shrug, point to my chest, hoping to suggest this might be where my 'true self' resides.

'*Non*,' comes the reply, swiftly, once she understands the question. She straightens, rubbing the small of her back. 'Many selves,' Taatamata says. She sweeps an arm round the beach. 'Plenty selves like – *pahua*.'

Pahua. Clams. I stare at the thousands and thousands of shells lining the beach inscrutably, as far as the eye can see. She said it with complete conviction.

~

Afterwards, lying in his bed, Rupert whispers, 'But, Nell, I thought you were married now, a mill worker's wife, or whatever?' and I realise he believes I married Jack.

That gives me some peace, for I understand at last some of his coldness. 'Tommy has asked me,' I confess. I haven't told a soul this.

'Tommy? The marvellous British Working Man?'

A long pause, and he offers me a cigarette, and then, to my surprise, takes one from the case on his bedside table himself. I've never seen him smoke before. I thought he didn't smoke. I shake my head, trying to make my thoughts settle.

'Do you think there are some people who are not made for marriage, Nell?'

'Yes,' I answer, without hesitating.

He props himself up on one elbow, making the cigarette glow in the darkness as he draws on it. I'm dizzy with the smell of him, the salty nearness, the liquid feeling of my own hot nakedness flowing in the sheets beside him and that great huge kick sizzling along my stomach like a seam of fire whenever a memory of what we just did surfaces. I can barely think straight to answer him.

'Not a feminist, I hope, child? Never be a feminist or – God forbid – a marcher, or a Sapphist. Be a woman.'

And there it is again, my anger with him, for his annoying habit of spoiling everything, of always thinking he knows best. Maybe that's why I don't answer honestly when he whispers plaintively, 'Will you say yes to the spotty Tommy?'

I laugh, and simply murmur, 'That depends.'

On what, I never said. Perhaps I hoped he would understand. But of course, nothing between us could ever be simple, or spoken aloud, and he did not understand at all. I might as well have been from a South Seas island myself for all the likelihood of Rupert understanding me.

Rupert dashed the cigarette in the saucer by his bed, turned over and was soon asleep. I crept out of his room and retraced my steps. I knew with absolute certainty that what we had just done was an end to it, not a beginning, and I lay awake all night, in my own little bed back at the Orchard, thinking about it, reliving every last caress.

Rupert left the next day and travelled by train to Portsmouth, to sail, and that was the last time I saw him that year. We never spoke of it again.

~

Poetry comes creeping back. My traveller's letters to the *Westminster Gazette* are one thing: they pay the bills. But poetry! Such joy to wake to the sight through my open door of a strange bird pecking in the yard, a bird the size of an English thrush but with a black crest atop its head and a vermilion splash under its rump.

I thought that poetry was done with me. I thought I had decided to be a playwright, albeit a wretched one. Then last night, at the lagoon with Taatamata, I wrote – *surely* – my best poem ever. Eddie has been begging me to send more verse and I have been reluctant to oblige. I'm far too old for Romance and my soul is seared! It's horribly true, as Edmund Gosse wrote, that one only finds in the South Seas what one brings here. And what did I bring? A longing to return to childhood, not the real childhood, rather to the childhood that never was, but exists only as a sentimental constructed memory; a place where time is not, and supper takes place at breakfast time, and breakfast in the afternoon, and life consists of expeditions by moonlight and diving naked into waterfalls and racing over white sands beneath feathery brooding palm trees.

A childhood before the Ranee banned the nurse, before being cast out of the Garden. *This* side of Paradise.

With Taatamata. For when she lifted a hand to stroke my face, and said again, 'Pupure,' in that way, and looked at me with those black eyes, as big as olives, and took off her hat and laid it on the sand, stepping into the small, wobbling boat, it was an invitation, like no other, and not simply because I wanted it to be.

Taatamata told me many things that night. She told me – it was no small shock – that the child Georges was her son; his father had been a French soldier who sailed two days later and whom she never saw again. She told me she'd seen twenty-eight summers, she thought, making her two years older than me. 'Mama Lovina', it transpires, is her aunt, and Taatamata is now an orphan, having been the daughter of a chief, an important man, distant cousin of the great Queen Pomare herself. (As she says this I think of the first night I saw her, and how I considered her features 'noble', attributing them to a French heritage and never once considering the aristocracy of her own native line.) As she speaks – in her queer French with many gestures and acting out – I remember her friendly hands on me, and the way she patted my stomach during my sickness and my wondering if it wasn't a feverish dream.

The foam on the waves of black water is pearlescent, lapping beneath us, as we lie in a wooden canoe, as far from England as it's possible to be, under stars one cannot even recognise and doubts very much are real. I lift myself gently on top of her, and bury my face in the salty-sea scent of her neck, loosen the shining black oil of her hair around me, and I hazard, with one hand, the buttons at the neck of her dress. She nods for me to remove it, smiling at me in the darkness in a flash of white, and as there can be no mistaking her meaning, it would be – ha! – ungentlemanly of me to refuse. Nell. I think of Nell again, and her courage, in coming to me in that way, and how I wasn't really well, not well enough to appreciate her.

Taatamata rolls up her dress and, placing it like a pillow under her head, lays herself down with unmistakable felicity, and when I murmur her name she smiles and shakes her head and says something I take to mean 'Sweetheart'; and so I grow bold at last, after what feels like a courtship of twenty-six years, my entire life leading to this.

Taatamata, with great patience and skill, shows me the error of my ways in the past, laughing and kissing my hair and taking my hand and guiding it here and there, as if it were a darting fish, catching hold of my fingers and prodding them at hot wet crevices, and holding my head, calling me Pupure, and pressing my mouth down at her breast, her stomach and her neck, guiding me the way a skilled boatman slides his boat through water; and when clumsily, trying to shift position in the canoe, I smash one elbow on the inside of the wood and cry out, she takes it only as a sign of coming off and tightens the grip in her thighs with such mastery, lifting her legs high up over my shoulders. Then the boat rocks so hard it threatens to spill us into the black sea. No man could doubt her meaning, or the loving offer she just bestowed: to deliver oneself to her, whole and unpeeled, every last drop.

~

Tiare Tahiti

Mamua, when our laughter ends,
And hearts and bodies, brown as white,
Are dust about the doors of friends,
Or scent a-blowing down the night,
Then, oh! then, the wise agree,
Comes our immortality . . .

Taü here, Mamua,
Crown the hair, and come away!
Hear the calling of the moon,
And the whispering scents that stray
About the idle warm lagoon . . .
Well this side of Paradise! . . .
There's little comfort in the wise.

Papeete, February 1914

Does Taatamata believe in an afterlife? In Paradise here on earth or . . . somewhere else? I ask her, rightly or wrongly understanding this word of hers, *Taü*, to mean the same thing; to mean Heaven.

We are lying in the canoe and she is – such awful lack of dignity! – smoking a pipe, the way so many of the native women here do, stuffing it with tobacco from the pocket of her dress. It makes me smile, the combination of pipe and white flowers in her hair – dreadfully the most fashionable way to adorn oneself in Tahiti. (Taatamata is puzzled when she discovers that poor ugly European women don't dress their hair in this way – how can man desire such woman? she asks, astonished.)

Lights glimmer from the huts on the beach and the warm sea breeze flecks water on to my salted skin, dry as the skin of a fish. *I have been so great a lover . . . oh, tra la la . . .* Who can I tell? Shall I write to Dudley, or James – Eddie perhaps? Jacques? Gwen? Is Gwen the same girl I once told with such certainty that two people can never kiss and *see* each other at the same time? Tell them all I have it at last: the secret of the Universe . . .

A stray thought enters my head: Gauguin's comment that in Europe you fall in love with a woman, and eventually end up having sexual relations with her. In Tahiti you first have physical relations, after which you proceed to fall just as deeply in love. Yes. And what is the secret of this, the reason for it? It's because Taatamata has a child already, a boy so clearly loved and accepted by her aunt, Lovina, and evidently Taatamata has no anxiety about accidentally falling pregnant. If bastardy were tolerated – if illegitimacy was not the greatest stain a child could endure, unmarried pregnancy the foulest blow to a girl's repper – how might things alter in England?

Taatamata's answer to my question about immortality is convoluted. It involves a lagoon, water so deep that only the best divers venture into it; and according to Taatamata, once you make that dive, and reach that mysterious place, if you survive you will never be the same again; you will come up transformed.

Such nonsense . . . *wash your mind of foolishness* . . . Hour after hour we have floated here in the blossom-hung darkness. I stroke her silky black hair and soon she is closing her eyes and purring and, with unmistakable gestures, snuggling against me again and touching my skin, smoothing her palm over the hairs on my chest, murmuring, 'Pupure, little sweetheart, so pale . . .' She seems to find it perverse when I try to kiss her, preferring instead to rub her face against mine, and bend her nose against my skin. Under her touch my skin grows more sensitive to light and night air and the feel of water and wood and sea breeze. Desire flares up again and this time she surprises me by sitting upon me in the most extraordinary way.

That alone is life, I say to myself. All else is death.

That night, the first spent in Mataiea, I dream of Father, who turns into Dick. We are in the dorm at Rugby. Father and Dick are interchangeable; I only know that it's my brother by the glass of whisky in his hand. They are standing over me now; we're in the sick-bay and I'm half blind with the pink-eye, and feverish. A cockerel is crowing. Someone – Teura, the *mahu* girl-boy – is tending me, pounding some mother-of-pearl into a paste in a jolly little bowl, then laying it gently on my eyes with his big, city-gent hands. Am I dead? No, only suffering with conjunctivitis.

Father and Dick are smoking and nodding. 'He should have been a girl,' Father says. 'It would have compensated Ruth so.' (It seems the Ranee had a name once, before she was Mother.) So then I stare down at my body and it is changing: I am now a small brown-skinned girl, crowned with flowers; I'm gambolling round the bedroom. I have a name, a new name, but I don't know what it is – a girl with blonde hair and dark skin, but ancient eyes and refined cheekbones, like Taatamata. At last everyone is happy. Father tweaks my cheek and calls me Pupure.

My eyes open and the pink crust on my lids crumbles: I see properly at last – a vast lagoon of the most limpid blue. *Swimmers into cleanness leaping.* Now the lovely nymph Nell is standing there, under a mountain, dipping a basin into the pool and trickling it over her hands, just like my dear nursie used to do. Nell touches my mouth, the corner of my mouth: I have been stung by a bee. Her fingers taste of Grantchester honey from the apple orchard. *Bathtime!* She calls, *Taü here! Sweetheart.* And I wake up.

My little hut is cool, and there are leaves on the floor, walls made of leaves, leaves woven into the roof above my head, a white canopy draped like a tepee above our bed to keep out the mosquitoes. And suddenly it's damned cold, an icy breeze, and a blond ghost is here, still hovering from the dream; someone young, and naked, slipping between those draped veils. Is it a boy? A young man? Is it Denham? Denham died. Back in the summer of July 1912, in the midst of the worst times, the times when my mind seemed to slip its moorings. He died of – of what? A short illness. I wrote a brief letter of condolence to his father. I could not be truthful. That is all.

Denham seems to have been, in the end, a pretty affectation I had no desire to repeat. As the figure turns to face me, though, I see it isn't Denham at all. It's a boy, much younger, a small, stubborn, serious boy, pudding-bowl hair and eyes the colour of the brightest parrotfish, and he's staring at me. Just for a moment. If I sit up, he will be gone.

We drank the strong narcotic last night, arriving late in our new hotel, and no doubt that explains my dreams and the waking hallucination, but reason doesn't make the boy run away. He hangs in the folds of the mosquito drape, shyly staring at me, as if I am the most extraordinary, the most unexpected thing. At last I know who he is and why I feel such a stab of love for him, and such loss; enough to cross the Pacific ocean, the furthest seas. 'Did you keep faith with me?' he asks.

'In my fashion,' is all I can grunt in reply.

'As you see,' he says, 'unwanted or not, I'm still here.'

'*Eh*,' I murmur, and the ghost vanishes. I'm awfully fluent in Tahitian these days. *Eh*, I believe, is the Tahitian word for yes.

Banbridge has not given up his quest for the most lucrative pearl. That's why we're here in Mataiea, apart from the fact that it's cooler, and therefore bearable. Today we go out with the divers to a secret location (Banbridge says so many of the pearling beds have been ravaged already by rapacious rascals – he does not include himself in this category – that we must search further afield).

En route to Mataiea Banbridge kept up his travelogue with relentless zeal. A cart – the sort used for transporting bananas – and two mangy donkeys provided our car, and it was so bumpy, and so full of hot air, that most of the time I preferred to walk beside Miri and Teipo. Only when my toes began to smart, with a remnant of my old infection, did I permit myself to get back in the cart and sit with the girls (I continue to think of Teura as a girl, no matter what), little Georges and Banbridge.

The house where Paul Gauguin lived is pointed out at Punaauia. I challenge Banbridge on this – it could hardly have been Gaugin's only home at Punaauia, for I've heard that the house he lived in was burned, after he left, by natives who feared the 'spirit' of the paintings and carvings. We make a short stop here, in search of Gauguin's son Emile, the mighty fisherman who still lives in the neighbourhood, along with his mother, the model for the painting *Nevermore*. Both are absent.

'All paintings gone or burned. *C'est fini!*' the barman Miri says, as we climb back into the cart, his moustache twitching with satisfaction. But *tupapau*, Miri insists, can be seen at the windows of the house. *Tupapau* walk in the shadows of the forest.

'Spirits of dead people. Gauguin's ghost,' Taatamata helpfully translates.

Hard to mistake the pleasure these people take in thwarting our desires, or of proving us wrong. Gauguin's paintings – carried off or destroyed. Pearls – best ones robbed by divers and merchants from every nation. It reminds me of an argument, of sorts, between Taatamata and myself when I told her of the Samoan princess I'd heard of who, after a Samoan dinner party at Apia, led her guests – the officers of an English gunboat – to the town flagstaff and, before anyone could stop her, leaped on to the pole and raced up the sixty feet of it. She thereupon seized the German flag, tore it to pieces, brought it down and danced on it.

I told Taatamata this tale after my discussion with Banbridge about the curious fact of Samoans preferring us British to Germans, despite the fairness of the German government. It was meant to illustrate the same thing. But, to my astonishment, Taatamata didn't see it that way. 'Samoan princess not a good diver,' she suddenly said. 'Good climber, *eh*, but not a good diver, like me. I dive *très bien* – better than Samoan princess.'

This made me laugh. 'Surely the point is, my dear sweetheart, not simply the extravagance of the feat, and how good a climber she was, but her purpose. To demonstrate that she would prefer to be ruled by the British, despite everything, and that Samoans are therefore wholly irrational.'

Taatamata narrowed her eyes and folded her arms across the ugly missionary dress. 'Samoans prefer Samoan rule. Not German flag. *But I dive better than princess.*'

There is no budging her. So I am not in the least surprised when, on arriving at our destination – a lagoon of turquoise cream, buttery and silky-smooth, with glittering jewel-like strips at the centre – and after being shown to the canoes, Taatamata insists on coming with us, hoping to impress me, I believe, with her superior diving. It may be a secret location, but not to everyone, and is obviously a fruitful spot, as our boat joins several others, full of ropes and gleaming brown bodies. Most wear the strange wooden goggles with glass eyepieces that Miri now hands to me and Taatamata. She refuses them, suspicious.

Little Georges starts up a cry and clings to her skirts but Teura soothes him and he seems to accept her as a perfectly good substitute, as she peels an orange and sits beside him on the beach to watch. Banbridge, still sweating in his city clothes, wants to come out on the boats with us, but of course has no intention of getting wet.

The sea is so transparent that even wading out to the boat, carrying the ropes, I see the yellow trumpet fish hovering there, as if mindful of how ridiculous they look, with their black button eyes and silly noses. Taatamata has stripped to a *pareu,* her small perfect breasts bare to the sun, in readiness for her dive. Apparently before the Church got here this was the custom; Gauguin did not exaggerate, only found girls who had not yet discovered the fig-leaf injunction. (With her hair loosened down her back and a stray garland of flowers still dangling there, I can hardly look at her for fear of losing my head and throwing her down at once on the sand.)

'First our divers will go down the rope,' Miri says, to show me how it's done.

The boat is anchored and the rope lowered into the sea with its heavy lead attached, plopping with a small splash, and the first boy flies off the boat like an arrow, diving after it. A second follows, this time sliding slowly into the clear water with his *tete,* his shell basket. These are slim boats, big enough for two people at most, their hulls full of long ropes, so we are anchored close together (the better to cover the entire sea-bed), about half a dozen canoes, all of us craning over the side to await breathlessly the boy's reappearance. Taatamata stretches up and shields her eyes against the sun. Long minutes pass. A tern flies overhead. Then, splashing, laughing, both boys appear, the one triumphantly holding up a handful of oysters, the other his basket, with a scattering of shells. Miri explains that they hold on to the rope and skip out on to the sea-bed somewhat like a parachutist using his free hand to alter the direction of his descent until carried to a promising patch of reef. *Tete* seems also to be the word for the boy, not just the basket, so I wonder if it translates as 'helper', but Banbridge has no interest in this point. His eyes graze hungrily the basket of oysters and he slaps me on the back. 'You next, old boy!'

But he's too late – Taatamata has already dived, smart as a fish, over the side of the boat, arcing into the water. I see from the way the rope tugs that she must be pulling it out sideways. I slip into the water beside her, cursing for forgetting my spear-gun – I can never quite dispel my fear of sharks, no matter how often the natives describe them as 'friendly' – and marvelling, as ever, at the sudden shift in time and space that occurs as soon as one enters the water. Time itself re-forming to reveal a busy little world of darting, iridescent fish, electric blue or sooty black; tiny striped clown-fish; leopard fish; one about a foot long and shaped like a bullet; or the ones with the serrated, blackened frill on their backs; or the translucent ones that flutter like pieces of paper.

Through the glass of goggles, about twenty feet down, I quickly spy Taatamata, her black hair gesticulating like arms. The goggles are a novelty for me and not a comfortable one: disconcertingly they give Taatamata the appearance of an exotic fish too, one caught in a tank. She dives deeper, working her way down by grasping the rope, then makes excited movements, in a graceful underwater ballet, as she reaches the sea-bed lined with sea slugs, like a carpet of sandy turds, and spies a terrific booty of oysters. I am so excited I almost let out my breath but as neither of us remembered the basket, I swiftly gather as many as I can, eyes now stinging behind the goggles and the same hissing sound of the hive of the sea in my ears. I accept the shells she pushes into my arms and thrust myself to the surface, blood now clamouring in my ears.

There are cheers as I scramble, panting, into the boat, tumbling the sharp shells in my arms beneath me.

I look round for Taatamata to compliment her on her work, but the surface of the water is unbroken, and she is not in the boat.

The tautness of our rope shows she must still be holding on. I lie on my stomach to peer over but see nothing. I stare wildly round at the other boats. I shout – but most canoes are empty or too far off, their divers busy pulling up baskets, preoccupied. Banbridge has his back to me and is avidly watching the other side of the lagoon for the return of his boy. I tug on the rope. I feel the weight of something. Something dark and tangled wraps round it – Taatamata's hair? But no, it's only seaweed.

My heart has started to press at the cage of my chest, and although my lungs are burning, I dive again, flinging the wooden goggles on to the boat. The canoe tips and sways, threatening to throw my small hoard into the sea.

I work my hands down the rope, to push myself deeper, and can still feel its tautness. Despite the pure turquoise blue, I see nothing except the silver barracuda, so fine they barely look real, like silk ribbons. How long can a person stay down like that? How long can she hold her breath? *Taravana*, Miri said, is the greatest danger to divers: a mental disorder caused by lack of oxygen to the brain. 'Divers look like drunk,' he told me cheerfully. Where is Taatamata?

And then, as my lungs feel ready to split, and I can hold out no longer, I spy her. Another ten feet down, calmly gathering shells. She waves to me with her one free hand; the other still holds the rope, which billows out like a giant question mark – it must be fifty feet long. My ears suffer a sharp, stabbing pain and though I want with all my might to reach her, to go further, down deeper, something stronger is pushing at me, forcing me up, up to the surface.

As I rupture the water I feel as if a long bird-like scream rends the air but it is only the sound inside my ears and perhaps a voice in my head crying, 'Taatamata!' I glance quickly towards the beach where the little figure of Georges is innocently chasing turtles, oblivious to the danger his mother is in.

I start pulling on the rope, hoping to haul her up that way, and Miri sees what I am doing, dives towards my boat and comes to my aid. My bowels seem to be tearing away from my body, my arms wrenched from my shoulders. And as we pull together, the head of Taatamata suddenly breaches the surface, shining black hair splaying out like a bejewelled starfish, and – I hold my breath – at last she gasps, splutters, frantic for air, but alive.

Miri and I lift her naked self into the boat, her body almost slipping from our arms, and she releases a great bundle of oysters knotted in her *pareu* on to the floor of the boat. 'I am good diver,' she says, at last, when words stumble back to her. 'I dive like princess.'

I have vomited quietly over the side of the boat.

Taatamata gives me a sly look, remembering, no doubt, the terror that blazed in my eyes as she surfaced, knowing at last the devilish handle she has on me.

I want to weep and wail for, of course, it hurts, it *hurts*, damn it – but I take the wicked, magnificent, triumphant girl in my arms and cradle her and squeeze her lavishly, not caring at the looks from Banbridge or the others. She takes this as her just deserts, absorbs the petting luxuriantly, wallowing back in the boat, truly like a princess. She is not smiling.

So this is when I decide that my soujourn in the South Seas is over. I have learned my lesson, and I understand it. Of course, I do not tell Taatamata then and there. There is the celebration on the beach to go through, when the oysters are cleaned and ransacked with knives, their shells prised open and their fruit revealed.

Banbridge stands with his arms folded behind his back, in the stance of a hungry heron, watching for fish. Excitement crackles in the air as the divers go through their task of sorting the shells: no doubt Banbridge is convinced he will find the huge *poe rava* he has long dreamed of, worth several thousand dollars. The men sit at their boats, using the oar to rest the shells on as they prise them open with their knives. The shells are then lined up neatly, each man according to the haul of his own boat, to display the nacre linings. When a pearl is found men crowd round, examining each for flaws, ridges in the lustre, and colour identification. Someone has produced a makeshift scale for weighing the mother-of-pearl; the beach is full of traders and excited villagers. The scent of smoking fish and a child's drumbeat tell me they are warming up for a celebration.

As the findings are sorted, the divers mutter a kind of chant to categorise their finds: '*rava*' (greenish-black), '*motea*' (silver-grey) and '*uouo*' (white). Finally the bunch of shells from our boat is reached and Taatamata and I cluster round to see the results of our catch. It seems that only one oyster in several thousand contains a pearl, most of practically no value. But as the haul that Taatamata brought up is worked over, she turns confidently to me and announces, 'Taatamata plenty lucky. Always find *poe rava*,' and, sure enough, one appears, a glistening dark eye in its satin lining. Banbridge grabs it at once, holds it to his eyeglass, then sniffs in derision: merely the size of a pea, and with a visible fine ridge round the middle, a flaw. He tells me at once, in his supercilious way, that it's worthless – 'Here, have it,' he says, thrusting it back at Taatamata. Now wearing her ugly blue dress again, she slips it into a pocket, smiling at me.

The day is growing dark, and torches are fetched. The faces of the fishermen, growing tired of their task, are now lit up by these flaring lights against tropical stars, like a Rembrandt picture with lights on the immediate faces and the rest in inky darkness; and here, some dancers appear, six girls and six men from the village, naked to the waist, and glistening with coconut-palm oil. They begin dancing to a sound of high nasal wailing and hand-clapping. Despite everything, despite my resolution to leave, I feel my blood thrill once more.

The dance is so much more marvellous and curious than I can ever describe. The women face each other mostly, making very slight rhythmic motions with their hands, feet and thighs. And as the crisis approaches, the movement grows slighter and, in proportion, more exciting. Which is queer. But reveals the dancers' greater skill, because, yes, this smallness and intensity works in the way that lavish, frantic gestures at this moment would not.

(I cannot stop myself considering in the darkness how it is that Taatamata knows a thousand little things I could not imagine an English girl knowing, and how her preference for the position 'originale' during love-making (that is, *not* the missionary) means her own pleasure is guaranteed, and like Gauguin – for I know he wrote this – I feel there is something so much more exciting about gaining pleasure from someone who knows how to receive it.)

I eat my fish, with its black, smoky taste, and say nothing to Taatamata, who sits beside me with Georges sleeping against her chest. After half an hour, the dancers vanish as suddenly as they appeared.

When Taatamata reaches for my hand, and drops something in it, I know at once that it is the pearl. Europe slides from me, terrifyingly.

I have already stayed almost two months longer than I intended. I know how the peacock-blue lustre of that pearl will burn a hole in my pocket, but tomorrow I intend to read my letters from England and see if they can't exert a pull. Perhaps Cathleen – ah, Cathleen Nesbitt: eminently suitable, eminently charming, beautiful and accomplished, can Cathleen call me back? Should I marry Cathleen, if I marry at all?

It's true we hardly know one another. Four months is not a

long courtship. But dear Cathleen has Suffered in Love, as I have. She told me about some fellow in the theatre, a married man, who took to drink, and I saw at once her capacity to suffer, and shuddered. But, after all, he did not seduce her. He took her to his rooms; she refused him. Phyllis Gardner all over again. It's hopeless. Cathleen would not contemplate a liaison without marriage. She would not accept . . . that part of me. Separate rooms, pure white sheets, and sitting on her bed, talking to her in the fresh morning, as if she were an Irish elf (which she is, of course): a green child of twelve years old. That is what I picture when I think of Cathleen. Ironically, for all that: despite her purity, her job as an actress means Mother would disapprove.

Marriage. It's that word – the thought of it – that chills me, as ever. I feel older than I was. Mightn't I, perhaps, have a life like Eddie's – the life of a confirmed bachelor, with so many gay young friends? If only I could hire a boat and spend five years cruising around these parts. But five years would be too long. One could never then go back to bowler hats and the Strand and the *Daily Mail* and tea-parties . . .

I suppose I have some shadowy remembrance of a place called England. I suppose I shall see it again soon.

❧

March 1914

My Dear Nell
Dear sweet Nell
Dearest Child,

(How to begin this letter, is, as you see, causing me no small difficulty. I wonder if you have ever expected to receive a letter from me?)

I write to you from a distant place – a place steamy and green and teeming with the wildest flowers in the most vivid colours – a glowing scarlet hibiscus your bees would love! – a place called Mataiea, deep in the heart of the island of Tahiti. I am planning to come home and might – imagine it – perhaps be in Grantchester by June. (I must spend time with Mother at Rugby first to compensate her for my immense wanderings.) I wonder if you could be so kind as to enquire as to whether my room might be free at the Old Vicarage by asking Mrs Neeve? I would write to her myself, but I wanted to include a poem I wrote while here in Mataiea and thought you might appreciate it more than that lady.

The poem is called 'The Great Lover'. It's rather a lark. It starts off full of idle boasting ('I have been so great a lover: filled my days/So proudly with the splendour of Love's praise' . . . that sort of thing) but ends in a kind of paean to ordinary things – white plates and cups, ringed with blue lines; the fragrance of live hair, shining and free (I was thinking of a Tahitian girl I know); the comfortable smell of friendly fingers, the rough male kiss of blankets; the cool kindliness of sheets – one can see the idea, I'm sure. All the lovable things of this world – including the people we love – that we shall have to leave, because we can't take them with us, and there isn't a next. A dull idea, I'm sure, and a very ordinary one, and perhaps it is not a good poem at all and I shall be mocked for it . . . but still . . .

On second thoughts, the poem is hardly splendid. In fact, I've decided, ha!, belatedly, it's true – I'm not much of a poet. I wrote a play a while back that I'd like to see put on in Cambridge. About a man who goes a-wandering, and returns, and decides to play a trick on the family and forestall the announcement of his happy return by pretending at first to be someone else, a rich stranger. Well, the family believe him all too well, and the mother and daughter end up beating him to death with an axe for his money. The moral? Well, a sensible girl like you, Nell, might say it is never a good idea to try and dupe a mother. Or perhaps never to go a-wandering. I'd say the opposite. How evil is the mother – whose loyalty is first to her daughter – who cannot recognise and *see* her own true son. I know you would never be such a mother. You would love your son no matter who he was. It's based on a true story . . .

I have been wandering a great deal, and that has its charms. The sort of thing I searched for in Grantchester, the things Virginia Stephen mocked me for, paganism and honey and fruit and goodness and such: I *have* found it here and now I have it inside me, and might – with some luck – even be able to bring it home and write about it. What I'd like most would be to write a novel, about the girl I mentioned, the Tahitian one. Her queer mind quite intrigues me. (Sometimes, my dear, she reminds me a little of you.)

I once wrote to Ben Keeling that there were only three things in life: to read poetry, to write poetry but, best of all, to *live* poetry. I feel I have done that now, at least a little.

Do feel free to burn it. The poem, I mean, should you so wish. Such a simple idea, really. That once one loves, is perhaps taught to love, loves well, I mean, one loves everyone and every*thing*. The domestic. The stuff of life . . . I can't imagine why it took me twenty-six (nearly twenty-seven) years to come to *that* discovery. (You, of course, learned this lesson early. I thank you for your setting me on the road to recovery, Nell.)

Quite properly, I seem to have given up writing with any enthusiasm. While in the South Seas I found I had stopped thinking, and that was a Good Thing! My senses instead became more authoritative, more demanding, and I trusted them a little more. I do a little work, as I knock about. (I await a cheque from Mother for my fare home.) But it seems, somehow, more amusing just to live.

I also include a pearl, for safe-keeping. I'd like you to have it. It's not valuable, apparently, but it does have a rather jolly lustre and an unusual colour, and . . . well, I hope you like it. I wish you all the luck in the world and hope to see you in Grantchester some day soon.

Your Rupert

I have a letter from Rupert. My first and only letter. And to come on such a day – 1 April 1914 – April Fool's Day! The day my son, my own little boy, is born. I can't stop weeping. Betty says, 'This must be what they mean when they talk of waters breaking!' and Tommy watches anxiously as I kiss the baby's head, over and over, and cry some more. But he doesn't ask to see the letter, nor what its contents are. Tommy is such a good man, and such a tactful one. He says nothing. He sees that I open the piece of tissue in the envelope and roll out the shiny pea-sized pearl and hold it to the light and admire its strange colour, one minute black, the next a gorgeous peacock-blue, then clutch at it. All the while the baby is sleeping hot as a fresh bun in my arms with his tiny, tiny nose with the turned-up tip just like the tip of a pencil, and then I sob some more, and Betty says I'm exhausted, and all women get the blues like this during their confinement, and Tommy's to leave now, and let me sleep.

She sits on the bed beside me and we unfold the poem included in the letter and read it together. 'The Great Lover'. Then I fold it up again.

'Is it for you?' she says. 'Did he write it for you, do you think?' Then she asks, in a different tone, 'Will you tell Tommy?' I shake my head so hard that the baby opens one milk-encrusted, dark blue eye, and stares quizzically at me.

'And what of— Will you tell Rupert, if he ever comes back to Grantchester?'

Again I shake my head. 'Don't be daft . . . Tommy will be a

good father, he won't ask questions. He's never suspected a thing between me and Rupert. Never even saw us together. Why, he's not said a word about the name I'm wanting . . .'

'Oh, Nell! Don't tell me—'

'Yes. And before you say anything, let me remind you: I'm your Big Sister and I know best. In any case, the dates are so close. Who could ever say? I can't be sure myself.'

Betty gives me a big grin, and stares hard at the baby. She murmurs, 'Funny little chap,' and strokes the baby's toes. Rupert Christopher Sanderson's toes. They open briefly, like an anemone being prodded, then curl up again.

~

Taatamata comes to the boat to see me off. She has been crying, but not in the way the Ranee cries, with weeping and demonstrable sniffing and handkerchief-dabbing, and glancing over it at me to see if I'm yet quite crumbled. In Taatamata's case, her face is impassive, except for the odd rolling tear, which she brusquely wipes away.

She brought me gifts this morning. As we're now back at Lovina's hotel in Papeete, she is dressed in her city clothes, the high-necked dress and hat, and she hovers at the door of my room, not knowing if the rules have changed again: is she allowed to enter? She is employed here at the hotel as a maid and cook and goodness knows what else, and even though Lovina is also her aunt, that does indeed change things, making her role a little like Nell's at the Orchard, friendship strangely compromised.

Wanting to dispel this idea, I nod at once to her, but still she does not rush in. She hesitates further, simply showing me, one by one, the things she has brought: a string of amber beads, some shells, some congealed strangeness in a little bottle, a knife with a nacre handle. She seems unsurprised by my leaving, as if she never for one moment believed I might stay, even when I spoke of it.

She opens the bottle to show me the oil scented with tiare flowers and indicates the foot she nursed, reminding me to take care of it. At that moment, the whisker of the tail of a yellow lizard flickers across my bedroom floor, and soon afterwards Georges appears in the doorway in pursuit of it. As the animal flashes out of sight and into some crack between the window and the wall, the boy quickly loses interest and rushes instead to his mother to be petted. Only after doing this, after immersing herself in a flurry of tender caresses, does Taatamata suddenly lift her face to mine, over his dark head, and sear me with a look of hot, fierce pain.

I rise from the bed and close the door behind them both before dressing.

'Don't forget me,' she says. Georges, meanwhile, rummaging in the pocket of her dress, finds her pipe there and, pulling it out, pretends to smoke it. This is such a funny sight that I cannot stop a guffaw, but one glance at Taatamata's face and my hand shoots to my mouth to stifle it.

Now, feeling horribly lacking in gifts, I look around for something to offer. A yellow silk tie she once admired, the one Ka bought me and the Ranee *so* hated, finding it appallingly gaudy. I press it into her hand, and close her fingers round it, and she, using it as a ribbon, ties it round her straw hat, cocks her head as if to ask for my opinion. *Yes, you are very beautiful indeed*. I smile admiringly at the effect, and take one last photograph of her, standing outside on the balcony, staring wistfully out towards the sea.

Back in my room again, I rummage in my case for the little coconut-scraping tool, the *anna* I bought from one of the traders, and present it to Georges. He pockets it at once, and holds out his hand for another. His mother scolds him and we both laugh.

A light tap at the door, and Lovina tells me that Miri will carry my baggage down to the harbour.

That is my signal to take Taatamata in my arms at last – hang it all, in front of her wide-eyed son, too – and kiss her. Poetry swims at me, like shoals of fish. *But the best I've known stays here, and changes, breaks, grows old, is blown about the winds of the world, and fades from brains of living men, and dies . . . Nothing remains . . .*

That is one lucky little fellow, I think, as Taatamata bends to include Georges in our embrace, squatting on her haunches better to enable her to enclose us both in the circle of her arms. I whisper into her ear, opening my mouth against the black screen of her hair, drinking in the smell of her, the taste. She is hot, alive, beating. The child stands immobile and absorbent, as if to be drenched in love like this is customary for him, no more than his lordly due. 'Sweetheart, *mon petit* Rupert,' a weeping Taatamata says, patting my back convulsively, as we remain in our clumsy knot, the three of us, crouched by the door. I say stiffly that I will not forget her, forget this moment, no, *never* . . . and on that last word, my voice betrays me at last, fracturing slightly, sounding awfully – one has to admit – like the helpless cry of a child.

On the boat that night I looked for the Southern Cross for the last time, seeking it in vain. It must already have slipped below the horizon. It is still wheeling and shining for Taatamata, for that bastard Banbridge, for Lovina and little Georges and Miri and Teura, but for me it is set. As the vessel pulled away I watched the green shores and rocky peaks fading with hardly a pang. But when the Southern Cross left me that night I knew I'd left those lovely places, lovely people, for ever. So I wept a little, and very sensibly went to bed.

In bed I read my letters, and tried to inject a little Englishness back into my soul. Cathleen – she is the most effective remedy, being capable, *almost*, of out-perfuming the others. Sweetly fragrant Cathleen, who nevertheless knows about sorrow and the alcoholism of loved ones, and other things besides.

'Parting, it's always a little like death,' an old Frenchman, watching me, leaning over the rail, commented. He said he was going home to France for a year for his health, but he resented it bitterly. Home! His home was in Tahiti, he told me repeatedly. He's been married to a native woman these last fifteen years. No children of his own, but plenty adopted. She was so much finer than a white woman, he sighed, so lovely, so faithful, so competent, so charming and happy, and so extraordinarily intelligent.

I am not cheered.

So I lie in my bunk, clutching the letters and reading them by the light of a kerosene lamp. The black sand of Lafayette beach still clings to my body and grits the sheets, like poppy seeds. The letters cover three or four months. The accounts of England are depressing and confirm my worst fears. *Blessed are the peacemakers. For they shall have the fun of knocking a lot of bloody men on the head.*

When I have read them through, several times over, and decided that I must put a bullet in Sir Edward Carson and another in Mr Murphy for smashing the Dublin strike, I settle down to write a letter to . . . the new baby of Frances and Francis Cornford, whose name, I'm told, is Helena.

What kind of England do I travel back to? An England of houses and trams and collars? Will I be forced to endure the total prohibition of alcohol in England, which is the female idea of politics, and the establishment of Christian Science as the state religion, which is the female idea of religion? I begged baby Helena not to grow up a feminist, but to become a woman. I *hate* feminists.

Everything's just the wrong way round. I want Germany to smash Russia to fragments, and then France to break Germany. Instead of which I'm afraid Germany will badly smash France, and then be wiped out by Russia. France and England are the only countries that ought to have any power. Prussia is a devil. And Russia means the end of Europe and any decency.

I suppose the future is a Slav empire, world-wide, despotic and insane. If war comes, should one enlist? Or turn war correspondent? Or what?

My mood, my tone, has altered entirely. One might detect a complete solidifying, congealing, rather like my gift of coconut oil from Taatamata (mysteriously transformed, without the tropic's liquid heat, into something the colour of milk, lumpy and hard as stone). Whatever cool Cambridge irony the South Seas erased is slipping back with every knot of this ship. What *will* happen tomorrow? And whatever it is, won't it be dreadful?

Feeling my old voice returning, I suddenly leap from my bunk and, grabbing my coat, make my way to the deck. The sky is inky and pricked with stars; salt spray leaps into my mouth. There is the moon, full and fat, shining on Taatamata, on the island, on the hibiscus flowers that bloom orange in the full of day, purple at night, and disappear by morning. I picture Taatamata somewhere, and know that I should have stayed, but could never have stayed, and wonder if she understands. And Nell. Dear Nell too! I finally wrote Nell a letter. Both women are there, somewhere, in words. Words are things, after all. And the night is sweet as thickest honey. Tenderly, day that I have loved, I close your eyes.

I saw Rupert only once after his return to Grantchester. I wasn't working at the Orchard at that time because of the baby, and I'd moved in with Tommy at his parents', and I was full, full up with my darling baby, and the hard work of it all, and the tiredness. I had no regrets. I hadn't reckoned, in those youthful thoughts

I'd had that were so bitter towards marriage, on all the simple ways in which it would be good to be loved. To be held, to be called tender names, to see a man's face light up when I came into the room. That was my marriage to Tommy. And best of all was to share a bed, to lie with a small warm baby between us, breathing hotly. Then, finally, the summer came and I worried about my bees. I'd left Betty in charge of them and I knew she was doing her best, and so was Mr Neeve, of course, but I was their mistress now, and surely they must be missing me.

So I went to the Old Vicarage, wondering if he might be back from his travels (although Betty had reported that he hadn't been sighted in Grantchester) and there he was. He was in the garden, standing near the sundial with a couple of people I didn't recognise, although one might have been Mr Eddie Marsh – I couldn't tell, he had his back to me. Rupert was laughing. I saw that his skin was sun-browned, and he was a little thinner. He looked healthy. I was glad of that. Inside, all of me was alive: my body set up a kind of chattering, quivering feeling, but I managed to keep my head, and simply nod to him. I saw at once how hard it would be for him to acknowledge me in front of his friends. The two men were talking excitedly to him – no doubt about Germany, about politics, for that was all anyone talked about that summer – but Rupert did his best: he raised his chin and stared over their heads; he met my eyes, and held them for a second. We smiled at one another, and he nodded back, and that was it. Then he went inside, into the house.

All that he was to me was gathered into that look I cast, but I don't know if he saw it, or knew. I turned towards the hives, and directed a few puffs from the smoker I was holding towards the crown board to warn the startled bees of my arrival. I put my face a little closer to the hive, and a few bees circled round my head, making a dark looping shape of a lasso in the air. 'I'm back,' I whispered to them. 'Stop your naughtiness and set to work – here's sensible Nellie. I'm back!'

Underneath I was thinking, So that's it, Nell, be done with him. He was trouble from the start. Be glad of all you have. Your lovely son. Your lovely Tommy. And soon I was calm, and no tears threatened, as I turned my full attention to the bees. The mischievous ones flew off. I looked for the queen in the hive, reminding myself, as Father taught me, keep the sun over your shoulder and watch for her running to the darkest side. It's a curious thing that the queen is the one who will always head for darkness. Every good bee-keeper knows that.

~

To Dudley Ward (envelope marked: *If I die to be sent to Dudley Ward, etc.*) Sent from Lemnos, during the Gallipoli advance, March 1915:

My dear Dudley,

You'll already have done a few jobs for me. Here are some more. My private papers and letters I'm leaving to my mother, and when she dies, to Ka.

But I want you now – I've told my mother – to go through my letters (they're mostly together, but some scattered) and destroy all those from (a) Elisabeth van Rysselberghe. These are signed E.v.R: and in a hand-writing you'll pick out easily once you've seen it. They'll begin in the beginning of 1909 or 1910, my first visit to Munich, and be rather rare except in one or two bunches.

(b) Lady Eileen Wellesley: also in a hand-writing you'll recognise quickly and generally signed Eileen. They date from last July on. If other people, Ka for instance, agitate to have letters destroyed, why, you're the person to do it. I don't much care what goes.

Indeed why keep anything? Well, I *might* turn out to be eminent and biographiable. If so let them know the poor truths. Rather pathetic this. It's odd, being dead. I'm afraid it'll finish off the Ranee. What else is there? Eddie will be my literary executor. So you'll have to confer with him.

Be good to Ka.

Give Jacques and Gwen my love.

Try to inform Taata of my death. Mlle Taata, Hotel Tiare, Papeete, Tahiti. It might find her. Give her my love.

My style is rather like St Paul's. You'll have to give the Ranee a hand about me: because she knows so little about great parts of my life. There are figures might want books or something of mine. Noel and her sisters, Justin, Geoffrey, Hugh Russell-Smith. How could she distinguish among them? Their names make me pleasantly melancholy.

But the realization of failure makes me *unpleasantly* melancholy. Enough.

Good luck and all love to you and Anne.

Call a boy after me.

Rupert

'The Great Lover' by Rupert Brooke

I have been so great a lover: filled my days
So proudly with the splendour of Love's praise,
The pain, the calm, and the astonishment,
Desire illimitable and still content,
And all dear names men choose, to cheat despair,
For the perplexed and viewless streams that bear
Our hearts at random down the dark of life.
Now, ere the unthinking silence on that strife
Steals down, I would cheat drowsy Death so far,
My night shall be remembered for a star
That outshone all the suns of all men's days.
Shall I not crown them with immortal praise
Whom I have loved, who have given me, dared with me
High secrets, and in darkness knelt to see
The inenarrable godhead of delight?
Love is a flame; – we have beaconed the world's night.
A city: – and we have built it, these and I.
An emperor: – we have taught the world to die.
So, for their sakes I loved, ere I go hence,
And the high cause of Love's magnificence,
And to keep loyalties young, I'll write those names
Golden for ever, eagles, crying flames,
And set them as a banner, that men may know,
To dare the generations, burn, and blow
Out on the wind of Time, shining and streaming . . .
These I have loved:
White plates and cups, clean-gleaming,

Ringed with blue lines; and feathery fairy dust;
Wet roofs, beneath the lamp-light, the strong crust
Of friendly bread; and many-tasting food;
Rainbows; and the blue bitter smoke of wood;
And radiant raindrops couching in cool flowers;
And flowers themselves, that sway through sunny hours,
Dreaming of moths that drink them under the moon;
Then, the cool kindliness of sheets, that soon
Smooth away trouble; and the rough male kiss
Of blankets; grainy wood; live hair that is
Shining and free; blue-massing clouds; the keen
Unpassioned beauty of a great machine;
The benison of hot water; furs to touch;
The good smell of old clothes; and other such –
The comfortable smell of friendly fingers,
Hair's fragrance, and the musty reek that lingers
About dead leaves and last year's ferns . . .
Dear names,
And thousand others throng to me! Royal flames;
Sweet water's dimpling laugh from tap or spring;
Holes in the ground; and voices that do sing;
Voices in laughter, too; and body's pain,
Soon turned to peace; and the deep-panting train;
Firm sands; the little dulling edge of foam
That browns and dwindles as the wave goes home;
And washen stones, gay for an hour; the cold
Graveness of iron; moist black earthen mould,
Sleep; and high places; footprints in the dew;
And oaks; and brown horse-chestnuts, glossy-new;
And new-peeled sticks; and shining pools on grass; –
All these have been my loves. And these shall pass,
Whatever passes not, in the great hour,
Nor all my passion, all my prayers, have power
To hold them with me through the gate of Death.

They'll play deserter, turn with the traitor breath,
Break the high bond we made, and sell Love's trust
And sacramented covenant to the dust.
– Oh, never a doubt but, somewhere, I shall wake,
And give what's left of love again, and make
New friends, now strangers . . .
But the best I've known,
Stays here, and changes, breaks, grows old, is blown
About the winds of the world, and fades from brains
Of living men, and dies,
Nothing remains.

O dear my loves, O faithless, once again
This one last gift I give: that after men
Shall know, and later lovers, far-removed
Praise you, 'All these were lovely'; say, 'He loved.'

Mataiea, 1914

Acknowledgements

The Orchard House and garden still exist in Grantchester and host the Rupert Brooke Society. I first had the idea for this novel when visiting with another writer (Martin Goodman), and buying a postcard of the maids who worked there in Rupert Brooke's time, standing in their aprons in front of a tin-roofed pavilion. These girls were possibly the daughters of Mrs Stevenson, but one of them soon became, in my mind, Nell.

This is a novel. I have made things up. Nell and her family are made up, as are the other maids. Of course I made Rupert up, too, and he is 'my' Rupert Brooke, a figure from my imagination, fused from his poetry, his letters, his travel writing and essays, photographs, guesswork, the things I know about his life blended with my own dreams of him, and impressions.

Those wanting to know more about Rupert's life are referred to the following books and letters. Where I think the reader might be interested to know in the novel whether there is a basis in fact, I've indicated what my source might be. I've also embedded in the text many of Rupert's actual letters and phrases from his own writings, and where I could find them, first-hand accounts and recorded words of others, such as Gwen Raverat and Phyllis Gardner.

Photograph of Rupert Brooke, 1913, on p. vi reproduced by permission of the Provost and Fellows of King's College, Cambridge and of the Rupert Brooke Trust [reference RCB/Ph/202].

Preface from a letter of Rupert Brooke to Bryn Olivier, reprinted in *The Neo-Pagans: Rupert Brooke and the Ordeal of Youth* by Paul Delany, the Free Press, a division of Macmillan Inc., 1987.

Preface quote from child psychologist D. W. Winnicott.

In fact, Nell is wrong to say that Brooke's biographers, being male, did not spot the meaning in Taatamata's sentence: 'I get fat all time Sweetheart'. It was Mike Read who revealed the existence of a daughter, and information about Arlice Rapoto can be found in his *Forever England*, Mainstream Publishing Company, Edinburgh, 1997.

Extract from *The Times*, 26 April 1915, by the First Lord of the Admiralty, Winston Churchill. Reproduced with permission of Curtis Brown Ltd, London, on behalf of The Estate of Winston Churchill. Copyright © Winston S. Churchill.

The biography that Nell suggests Arlice should read is Christopher Hassall's *Rupert Brooke: A Biography*, Faber and Faber, 1964. Extracts reproduced with permission of Faber and Faber Ltd. The prose book is: *The Prose of Rupert Brooke*, edited with an introduction by Christopher Hassall, Sidgwick and Jackson, 1956. Brooke's lecture, 'Democracy and the Arts', in which he put forward an argument for endowing the artist at public expense, was enormously radical at the time. Thirty years later a body was instituted to do just that; it became the Arts Council of Britain.

The Royal Literary Fund also benefited from the estate of Rupert Brooke. I have been financially supported at different times by the RLF and I'm immensely thankful.

Nell's account of how the letter from Taatamata was lost in the *Empress of Ireland* is true. The letter, dated 2 May 1914, reads:

My dear Love darling

I just wrote you some lines to let you know about Tahiti to day we have plainty people Argentin Espagniole, and we all very busy for four days. We have good times all girls in Papeete have good times whit Argentin boys. I think they might go away to day to Honolulu Lovina are give a ball last night for them. Beg ball. They 2 o'clock this morning . . .

I wish you here that night I get fat all time Sweetheart you know I alway thinking about you that time when you left me I been sorry for long time. We have good time when you was here I always remember about you forget me all ready Oh! mon cher bien aimee je l'aimerai toujours. I send my kiss to you darling. Mille kiss. Taatamata.

anything you wouldn't like."' are verbatim from Phyllis Gardner's account in her memoir of Brooke, *A True History*, written in 1918.

John Frayn Turner, *The Life and Selected Works of Rupert Brooke*, Breese Books, 1922, contains the version of the obituary from *The Times* that includes the missing phrase: 'ruled by high undoubting purpose'.

Mary Archer, *Rupert Brooke and the Old Vicarage, Grantchester*, Silent Books, Cambridge, 1989.

John Lehmann, *Rupert Brooke*, Weidenfeld & Nicolson, 1980.

Collected Poems of Rupert Brooke, with a Memoir by Eddie Marsh, Sidgwick and Jackson, 1926.

Gwen Raverat, *Period Piece: The Cambridge Childhood of Darwin's Granddaughter*, Faber and Faber, 1952. Nell's ability to slide outside her own consciousness and see herself is taken from Gwen Raverat's description of the same. Also, descriptions of naked boys swimming in the river on page 37 are hers, and the conversations with Rupert, such as the one about the seventeen-year-old girl painting her face, on page 44. According to Raverat, this conversation took place in 1912. Reproduced by permission of Faber and Faber Ltd.

Page 28, Letter beginning: 'I am in the country in Arcadia; a rustic . . .' is to Noel Olivier, reprinted in *Song of Love: The Letters of Rupert Brooke and Noel Olivier 1909–1915*, edited by Pippa Harris, Bloomsbury, London, 1991. Letters of Rupert Brooke © Estate of the late Rupert Brooke.

Page 48, The sonnet 'Oh! Death Will Find Me', written for Noel Olivier, can be found in the *Collected Poems*.

Frances Spalding, *Gwen Raverat: Friends, Family and Affections: A Biography*, Harvill Press, London, 2001, was useful for details of the relationship between Gwen Raverat and Rupert, details of Jacques Raverat, Jane Harrison, and Francis and Frances Cornford.

Michael Holroyd, *Augustus John: The New Biography*, Vintage, 1977, describes Augustus John and party visiting the Orchard. Nell's description of the artist on page 46 is taken from Edward Thomas's: 'exactly like a pirate: standing over six feet high, wearing the strangest jersey and check suit, and with a long red beard, just like the beard of Rumpelstiltskin', reported in Holroyd's book on page 282. Rupert's letters to Noel (in *Song of Love*) contain further details. It is here that Rupert repeats the 'two wives' rumour. Dorelia was in fact not a wife, and not mother to all the children either. Four were the sons of Augustus John's wife Ida who had died in 1907. David would have been the eldest boy.

The Diaries of Beatrice Webb, edited by Norman Mackenzie and Jeanne Mackenzie, abridged by Lynn Knight, with a preface by Hermione Lee, Virago Press, 2000, contains details of H. G. Wells's affair with Amber Reeves, and Beatrice's opinion of Rupert Brooke and his friends.

Page 75, Remarks of Rupert's beginning: 'Parents . . .' are taken from an unpublished, novelised account by Gwen Raverat of conversations between herself, Rupert and others, reported in Hassall's *Rupert Brooke: A Biography*. Reproduced by permission of Faber and Faber Ltd.

Rupert's description of the encounter with Denham Russell-Smith on page 88 starting, 'He was lustful, immoral, affectionate and delightful . . .' and ending, 'and wouldn't ever want to see me again' is in Rupert Brooke's own words, verbatim, from his own unabridged account in a letter to James Strachey, written in 1912. Copyright © The Trustees of Rupert Brooke. The letter is reproduced in Nigel Jones's *Rupert Brooke: Life, Death & Myth*, Richard Cohen Books, 1999.

Page 102, Letter beginning: 'January 1910. My dear James . . .' is from a letter by Rupert Brooke, although with exclusions and more than one letter merged together, so not verbatim. Copyright © The Trustees of Rupert Brooke. Included in the collection: *Friends and Apostles: The Correspondence of Rupert Brooke and James Strachey*, edited by Keith Hale, Yale University Press, 1998.

Page 153, Rupert's description of a dream, 'I was lying out under a full moon . . . I expect it all happened, really, some time' is in Rupert's own words, from an abridged letter to James Strachey, included in Hale's *Friends and Apostles*. Copyright © The Trustees of Rupert Brooke.

Page 222, 'How dreadful that the whole world's a cunt for one': from a letter to James Strachey, *ibid*.

Hermione Lee, *Virginia Woolf*, Chatto and Windus, 1996, for descriptions of encounters between Rupert Brooke and Virginia Woolf (née Stephen), alongside descriptions of the same occasion by Christopher Hassall.

Michael Holroyd, *Lytton Strachey: The New Biography*, Vintage, 1995, for an account of the relationship between Lytton Strachey and Brooke, and Brooke's breakdown at Lulworth. John Lehmann's *Rupert Brooke: His Life and His Legend*, Weidenfeld & Nicolson, 1980, gives a good account of his breakdown.

Page 225, Rupert's description to Gwen and Jacques of the incident at Holy Trinity in Rugby is in Rupert's words from an account in a letter to Virginia Woolf, written to her after her nervous breakdown.

Page 231, Letter beginning: 'The important thing, I want to be quite clear about, is, about women "coming off",' are Rupert Brooke's own words, from a letter to James Strachey. Copyright © The Trustees of Rupert Brooke.

Page 239, Letter beginning: 'Pango-Pango, Samoa, November 1913', is from Rupert to Phyllis Gardner, included in the collection that her sister gave to the British Library.

Page 247, 'Look at those niggers! Whose are they?' This and other descriptions, and Rupert's thoughts on Samoa and Fiji, are from Rupert Brooke, *Letters from America*, with a preface by Henry James, Echo Library, reprinted 2006.

Page 289, 'Quite properly, I seem to have given up writing with any enthusiasm. While in the South Seas I found I had stopped thinking, and that was a Good Thing! My senses instead became more authoritative, more demanding, and I trusted them a little more. I do a little work, as I knock about' are the words of Rupert Brooke, in a letter to Phyllis Gardner.

Page 295, 'Words are things, after all.' Brooke's words, as recounted by Reginald Pole in a fictionalised narrative, included in Michael Hastings' *The Handsomest Young Man in England, Rupert Brooke*, Michael Joseph, 1967. Supplementary accounts of this time in Rupert's life are in Maurice Browne's *Recollections of Rupert Brooke*, Alexander Greene, 1927. (Thank you, Geraldine, for the gift of a first edition.)

Page 295, 'Tenderly, day that I have loved, I close your eyes' is a line from a poem 'Day That I Have Loved', written 1905–1908, published in *Poems, 1911*, Sidgwick and Jackson.

Page 296, Letter beginning: 'My dear Dudley' is copyright © The Trustees of Rupert Brooke.

Cathleen Nesbitt, *A Little Love and Good Company*, Faber and Faber, 1975. Letters between Brooke and Nesbitt went on sale at Sotheby's in 2007 but were not bought.

I am grateful to the Arts Council of England for a generous grant in support of research for this novel. I'm thankful, too, to Mike Read for meeting with me to share his knowledge of Brooke; also Robin Callan, owner of the Orchard, Grantchester, for allowing me access to Rupert's old bedroom, to the Orchard and gardens and to Rupert's diary, and for many hours of wonderful conversations about Rupert Brooke; also Andrew Motion, for his initial enthusiasm for the idea, and to him and Jon Stallworthy, the Trustees of Rupert Brooke, for their support and encouragement. Dr Mary Archer kindly showed me around the Old Vicarage in Grantchester, where she now lives, and was generous with her time and considerable knowledge of Brooke and his life; Lorna Beckett was helpful on questions regarding Phyllis Gardner; I'm also thankful to Karen Smith and all at the Rupert Brooke Society, based at the Orchard in Grantchester, and to Patricia McQuire, the archivist at King's College, Cambridge. The warmest possible thanks must also go to my editor Carole Welch and my agent Caroline Dawnay; to John Lewis for expertise on beekeeping; to Ruth Tross, Hazel Orme, and all at Sceptre; also to writer friends Louise, Kathryn, Caz and Sally for helpful conversations; and to my beloved Meredith, the greatest lover of all.

P.S.

Insights,
Interviews
& More...

First Words

About the author

Timothy Allen

I CAN'T REMEMBER the first book I ever read, but I can remember the first words: *ice cream*. My sister taught me to read before I went to school. What I remember, and think has influenced me most in my writing, was the physical pleasure a particular word could suggest, the powerful feelings reading it aroused. I wonder now if it was a kind of synesthesia, but I suppose it was also logical. The words *ice cream* are particularly delicious—to say, to read, to write, to think about.

I wanted to be a writer from the age of nine, but I would never have told my parents. That would have been showing off, something that was ferociously crushed in our family. Being gifted at something, or excelling, was drawing attention to yourself and greeted with palpable contempt. Perhaps this is a British thing, or to do with the surprise my parents felt—disliking as they did the discussion of feminism or politics or religion or literature or philosophy or, well, anything at all really—on producing a child who wanted to discuss these things, who went around *expressing herself* all over the place. I still feel a trace of shame about being a novelist, not least because I enjoy it so much. How did I become a writer, in such a family? I have a stubborn streak.

It's really all I've ever done. I've never had another "proper" job. I had a ten-year apprenticeship after graduation where I lived in squats and subsidized housing in London, writing poetry, winning a few prizes, having a child, being very poor, and becoming dispirited. Then suddenly, in my early thirties, I ended a relationship, studied for an MFA in creative writing, bought my first house, and published my first novel. I met my husband six months later.

By the time I started this, my sixth novel, I had quite a few friends who were writers; a couple of them were renowned biographers. I read a lot of biography, and I've always been fascinated with it as a form. So I felt some trepidation on beginning *The Great Lover.* I challenged myself with the questions about Rupert Brooke that my fictional character Nell is asked in the book: What did his living voice sound like? What did he smell like? How did it feel to wrap one's arms around him? And lastly, Was he a good man?

These are subjective, emotive, relative questions that it seems to me that fiction—especially fiction written in the first person, which never claims to be objective but only human—is well placed to answer. In *Orlando,* Virginia Woolf writes, "A biography is considered complete if it merely accounts for six or seven selves, whereas a person may well have as many as a thousand." That idea went into *The Great Lover,* spoken by Taatamata, who claims we have as many selves as there are clams on a beach.

"Do you change facts, if they don't suit the ▶

❝ How did I become a writer, in such a family? I have a stubborn streak. ❞

First Words *(continued)*

plot?" I was asked, at a book event, on a panel discussion. The other novelist on the panel, writing her own family's story, agreed at once that she did, if it might improve the storyline. Briefly I felt like a fraud. Surely hers, I thought, is the proper reply for a novelist. Isn't it our job to fictionalize, to make things up? But then I understood my own compulsion better. For me, it's not making up, entirely, but a belief in fiction or the logic of imagination as a means of discovery.

I think of it as applying fiction to facts like a poultice, to draw something out. . . . My novels based on true stories probably evolved because of the decade of psychoanalysis I underwent in my twenties, and my beginnings as a poet. I wanted psychological truths, not representational social realism.

I like to explore characters through their dreams, or rather the dreams I make up for them. Anaïs Nin, in her essay on the poetic novel, says: "What the psychoanalysts stress, the relation between dream and our conscious acts, is what poets already know. The poets walk this bridge with ease, from conscious to unconscious, physical reality to psychological reality."

When I have a "fact" about a character I'm writing about, I want to investigate it the way a therapist might. Tell me about your mother, I might ask Rupert Brooke. Tell me about this fact that she lost a child, a one-year-old daughter, before you were born. Then I will go over this detail: the accounts, the references by other biographers, the letters, possible references in his poetry, the phrases Brooke used to describe this one small "fact." It's as if I have my client (Brooke) on the couch and can get him to tell me something over and over until the truth—or, I admit, what feels like the truth to me—emerges, in certain words, the perfect words, which briefly feel not to be mine but coming directly from somewhere else. ❧

> ❝ When I have a 'fact' about a character I'm writing about, I want to investigate it the way a therapist might. ❞

The First Tiny Throb
How a Novel Begins

IT WAS SEVERAL SUMMERS AGO. A sultry day in Grantchester, Cambridge, England. I fancied iced lemonade in the lovely Orchard café, where you take your drink and sit in a deck chair under branches drooping with apples and daydream.

I picked up a leaflet about the famous writers who had once visited the Orchard or lodged there and found a photo of the young poet Rupert Brooke. Twenty-two at the time, he was described by W. B. Yeats as "the handsomest young man in England." Did I find him handsome? He had a beautiful jawline, yes, and a broad brow, yes, and a floppy Hugh Grant quality to his fringe. But it was the gaze that hooked me. Direct. Staring down a hundred years and challenging me. Okay then. *Write about me, if you dare.*

I think I've always been a sucker for a sexy, brilliant, *impossible* man.

I didn't know much about him. I knew the poem about Grantchester, "The Old Vicarage" (which is next door to the Orchard café and now home to author Jeffrey Archer and his wife, Mary), and I knew the lines: "If I should die, think only this of me: / That there's some corner of a foreign field / That is for ever England. . . ." I'd heard that Brooke and his friends loved swimming naked in nearby Byron's Pool and that he had a trick of emerging from the icy water with a "steaming erection." His letters revealed a playful sense of humor, a subversive wit, a passion for nature, and a paranoid, jealous, and unhappy side, too.

"But wasn't he gay?" people asked whenever I mentioned Brooke's various girlfriends and his love affair with Phyllis Gardner. It seems that his relationships with women have been forgotten next to the more salacious details of his relationships with men. I read a startlingly modern-sounding account, written by Rupert, of his first sexual experience with a man, which had taken place in his little bedroom in Orchard cottage. ▶

5

The First Tiny Throb *(continued)*

Intrigued, I got myself an invitation to the Orchard cottage to be shown into that same bedroom. My heart was beating like a schoolgirl's as I took the steps to Rupert's floor of the house. Of course the furniture wasn't original, but the door, window frames, floorboards, and fireplace were. The owner of the cottage (a huge Brooke fan) went downstairs, saying mysteriously that he would fetch "something you might like to see." I was relieved to be left alone. I sat on the bed, staring at the wooden boards, and thinking, Rupert Brooke's bare sole stepped over that, a hundred years ago.

My mobile phone went off, and I jumped. "I'm in Rupert Brooke's bedroom!" I whispered.

The owner appeared with the treasured object, presenting it with a flourish. Precious documents in libraries are usually brought out with strict instructions not to touch. Here I was being handed Rupert Brooke's pocket diary from the time he lived at the Orchard, 1909. Buff-colored. Small enough to pop in his shirt pocket. *Right next to his heart.*

I held it in my palm, and wondered.

> 66 I was being handed Rupert Brooke's pocket diary from the time he lived at the Orchard, 1909. . . . I held it in my palm, and wondered. 99

This Side of Paradise

WHAT DO PEOPLE KNOW of the poet
Rupert Brooke?

That he was part of a circle that included
Virginia Woolf, John Maynard Keynes, the painter
Augustus John, and James and Lytton Strachey?
That he died young, on his way to Gallipoli,
and was thereafter taken up as a national icon,
the golden boy poet of the First World War?
Or possibly only that he wrote the lines: "If
I should die, think only this of me: / That
there's some corner of a foreign field / That
is for ever England. . . ."

That he fell deliriously in love with the
South Seas and with a young Tahitian woman,
Taatamata, is not well known. (Brooke is an
inconsistent speller, and her name is sometimes
Tata-maata, sometimes just Taata). That he
possibly had a child with her—a girl called Arlice
Rapoto, who lived until she was ninety and died
only a few years ago—is a fact that, when I tried
pursuing it in Tahiti, was greeted with surprise and
silence. It was the DJ Mike Read who first raised
this possibility in his book about Brooke, *Forever
England,* and who unearthed a photo of Arlice,
which, though grainy, does bear some resemblance
to Brooke.

In 1913, the young poet was twenty-six,
restless, and horny. He'd had a recent nervous
breakdown, brought about partly through
overwork but mainly by the rupture in his finely
wrought love life. He had been balancing two,
probably more, relationships for several years, and
now one of them—with the motherly, safe one,
the one he thought he could rely on, Katharine
Cox—has abruptly ended. So he did what
countless young men from similar backgrounds—
Rugby School, Cambridge University—have done.
He spent a year traveling by boat to North
America and the South Seas. It produced the best
writing of his life.

Plenty is known of Brooke's predecessor in ▶

This Side of Paradise *(continued)*

the French Polynesian islands, the painter Paul Gauguin, whose lonely death from syphilis happened ten years before Brooke arrived. Colonial attitudes toward the sexuality of Tahitian women—renowned for their sexy, bare-breasted dancing—did not escape Rupert Brooke. In a travel article, he mocks the mix of Puritan disapproval and slavering lust. For him, the battle between his mind and body was easily won. He writes: "The intellect soon lapses into quiescence. The body becomes more active, the senses and perceptions more lordly and acute."

Little is known of Taatamata. ("What does her name mean in Tahitian?" I ask a guide. "Nothing," he replies. "It must have been made up.") In some accounts, she worked at the hotel where Brooke stayed and was virtually a prostitute. In others, she was highborn, the daughter of a village chief or even a mythic princess, protector of the sacred turtles of Tahiti. Surviving photographs show a shy, elegant young woman staring wistfully into the distance beneath a straw hat. She wears the long unflattering dresses the missionaries introduced and stands smiling at a discreet distance from Brooke. He wrote in a letter that she was "a girl with wonderful eyes, the walk of a Goddess, & the heart of an angel, who is luckily, devoted to me. She gives her time to ministering to me, I mine to probing her queer mind. I think I shall write a book about her—only I fear I am too fond of her."

In poems written in Tahiti, Brooke's passion pulses off the page, but the affair was fleeting: he had to leave the islands after three months. Traveling there myself—following the route that he took from the sweltering capital, Papeete, to the cooler, rainier Mataiea—I find that little is known of the famous English poet the Tahitians affectionately nicknamed Pupure, meaning "fair."

It is possible to spend hours, as Brooke did, floating in warm lagoons the color of "all the buds of spring" (his words), staring at the radiant, butterfly-colored fish. The coconut palms, the

> **In poems written in Tahiti, Brooke's passion pulses off the page, but the affair was fleeting: he had to leave the islands after three months.**

dawns of pearl and gold and red, the Tahitian habit of wearing single white tiare flowers behind their ears—everything mentioned by Brooke in his poem "Tiare Tahiti" is available to anyone chasing his story here, but I find nothing more, no record of his daughter, no traces of his life. This is deeply frustrating and yet enticing.

Novelists thrive on the gaps in a story, the murky places that only imagination can illuminate. I'm guided by Brooke's own words. His love for Tahiti quickly infects me: "And after dark, the black palms against a tropic night, the smell of the wind, the tangible moonlight like a white, dry, translucent mist, the lights in the huts, the murmur and laughter of passing figures, the passionate, queer thrill of the rhythm of some hidden dance . . . That alone is life; all else is death."

That alone is life—not a bad claim for a place, a way of life, or a girl. That is where I will start. ❧

> ❝ Everything mentioned by Brooke in his poem 'Tiare Tahiti' is available to anyone chasing his story here, but I find nothing more. ❞

The Old Vicarage, Grantchester
by Rupert Brooke

Cafe des Westens, Berlin, May 1912

Just now the lilac is in bloom,
All before my little room;
And in my flower-beds, I think,
Smile the carnation and the pink;
And down the borders, well I know,
The poppy and the pansy blow . . .
Oh! there the chestnuts, summer through,
Beside the river make for you
A tunnel of green gloom, and sleep
Deeply above; and green and deep
The stream mysterious glides beneath,
Green as a dream and deep as death.
—Oh, damn! I know it! and I know
How the May fields all golden show,
And when the day is young and sweet,
Gild gloriously the bare feet
That run to bathe . . .
                    'Du lieber Gott!'

Here am I, sweating, sick, and hot,
And there the shadowed waters fresh
Lean up to embrace the naked flesh.
Temperamentvoll German Jews
Drink beer around; —and THERE the dews
Are soft beneath a morn of gold.
Here tulips bloom as they are told;
Unkempt about those hedges blows
An English unofficial rose;
And there the unregulated sun
Slopes down to rest when day is done,
And wakes a vague unpunctual star,
A slippered Hesper; and there are
Meads towards Haslingfield and Coton
Where das Betreten's not verboten.

ειθε γενοιμην . . . would I were
In Grantchester, in Grantchester! —
Some, it may be, can get in touch

With Nature there, or Earth, or such.
And clever modern men have seen
A Faun a-peeping through the green,
And felt the Classics were not dead,
To glimpse a Naiad's reedy head,
Or hear the Goat-foot piping low: . . .
But these are things I do not know.
I only know that you may lie
Day long and watch the Cambridge sky,
And, flower-lulled in sleepy grass,
Hear the cool lapse of hours pass,
Until the centuries blend and blur
In Grantchester, in Grantchester. . . .
Still in the dawnlit waters cool
His ghostly Lordship swims his pool,
And tries the strokes, essays the tricks,
Long learnt on Hellespont, or Styx.
Dan Chaucer hears his river still
Chatter beneath a phantom mill.
Tennyson notes, with studious eye,
How Cambridge waters hurry by . . .
And in that garden, black and white,
Creep whispers through the grass all night;
And spectral dance, before the dawn,
A hundred Vicars down the lawn;
Curates, long dust, will come and go
On lissom, clerical, printless toe;
And oft between the boughs is seen
The sly shade of a Rural Dean . . .
Till, at a shiver in the skies,
Vanishing with Satanic cries,
The prim ecclesiastic rout
Leaves but a startled sleeper-out,
Grey heavens, the first bird's drowsy calls,
The falling house that never falls.

God! I will pack, and take a train,
And get me to England once again!
For England's the one land, I know,
Where men with Splendid Hearts may go;
And Cambridgeshire, of all England,
The shire for Men who Understand;
And of THAT district I prefer
The lovely hamlet Grantchester.
For Cambridge people rarely smile, ▶

The Old Vicarage, Grantchester *(continued)*

Being urban, squat, and packed with guile;
And Royston men in the far South
Are black and fierce and strange of mouth;
At Over they fling oaths at one,
And worse than oaths at Trumpington,
And Ditton girls are mean and dirty,
And there's none in Harston under thirty,
And folks in Shelford and those parts
Have twisted lips and twisted hearts,
And Barton men make Cockney rhymes,
And Coton's full of nameless crimes,
And things are done you'd not believe
At Madingley on Christmas Eve.
Strong men have run for miles and miles,
When one from Cherry Hinton smiles;
Strong men have blanched, and shot their wives,
Rather than send them to St. Ives;
Strong men have cried like babes, bydam,
To hear what happened at Babraham.
But Grantchester! ah, Grantchester!
There's peace and holy quiet there,
Great clouds along pacific skies,
And men and women with straight eyes,
Lithe children lovelier than a dream,
A bosky wood, a slumbrous stream,
And little kindly winds that creep
Round twilight corners, half asleep.
In Grantchester their skins are white;
They bathe by day, they bathe by night;
The women there do all they ought;
The men observe the Rules of Thought.
They love the Good; they worship Truth;
They laugh uproariously in youth;
(And when they get to feeling old,
They up and shoot themselves, I'm told) . . .

Ah God! to see the branches stir
Across the moon at Grantchester!
To smell the thrilling-sweet and rotten
Unforgettable, unforgotten
River-smell, and hear the breeze
Sobbing in the little trees.
Say, do the elm-clumps greatly stand

Still guardians of that holy land?
The chestnuts shade, in reverend dream,
The yet unacademic stream?
Is dawn a secret shy and cold
Anadyomene, silver-gold?
And sunset still a golden sea
From Haslingfield to Madingley?
And after, ere the night is born,
Do hares come out about the corn?
Oh, is the water sweet and cool,
Gentle and brown, above the pool?
And laughs the immortal river still
Under the mill, under the mill?
Say, is there Beauty yet to find?
And Certainty? and Quiet kind?
Deep meadows yet, for to forget
The lies, and truths, and pain? . . . oh! yet
Stands the Church clock at ten to three?
And is there honey still for tea? ❧

Tiare Tahiti
by Rupert Brooke

Papeete, February 1914

Mamua, when our laughter ends,
And hearts and bodies, brown as white,
Are dust about the doors of friends,
Or scent ablowing down the night,
Then, oh! then, the wise agree,
Comes our immortality.
Mamua, there waits a land
Hard for us to understand.
Out of time, beyond the sun,
All are one in Paradise,
You and Pupure are one,
And Taü, and the ungainly wise.
There the Eternals are, and there
The Good, the Lovely, and the True,
And Types, whose earthly copies were
The foolish broken things we knew;
There is the Face, whose ghosts we are;
The real, the never-setting Star;
And the Flower, of which we love
Faint and fading shadows here;
Never a tear, but only Grief;
Dance, but not the limbs that move;
Songs in Song shall disappear;
Instead of lovers, Love shall be;
For hearts, Immutability;
And there, on the Ideal Reef,
Thunders the Everlasting Sea!

And my laughter, and my pain,
Shall home to the Eternal Brain.
And all lovely things, they say,
Meet in Loveliness again;
Miri's laugh, Teipo's feet,
And the hands of Matua,
Stars and sunlight there shall meet
Coral's hues and rainbows there,
And Teüra's braided hair;
And with the starred 'tiare's' white,
And white birds in the dark ravine,

And 'flamboyants' ablaze at night,
And jewels, and evening's after-green,
And dawns of pearl and gold and red,
Mamua, your lovelier head!
And there'll no more be one who dreams
Under the ferns, of crumbling stuff,
Eyes of illusion, mouth that seems,
All time-entangled human love.
And you'll no longer swing and sway
Divinely down the scented shade,
Where feet to Ambulation fade,
And moons are lost in endless Day.
How shall we wind these wreaths of ours,
Where there are neither heads nor flowers?
Oh, Heaven's Heaven! —but we'll be missing
The palms, and sunlight, and the south;
And there's an end, I think, of kissing,
When our mouths are one with Mouth. . . .

'Taü here', Mamua,
Crown the hair, and come away!
Hear the calling of the moon,
And the whispering scents that stray
About the idle warm lagoon.
Hasten, hand in human hand,
Down the dark, the flowered way,
Along the whiteness of the sand,
And in the water's soft caress,
Wash the mind of foolishness,
Mamua, until the day.
Spend the glittering moonlight there
Pursuing down the soundless deep
Limbs that gleam and shadowy hair,
Or floating lazy, half-asleep.
Dive and double and follow after,
Snare in flowers, and kiss, and call,
With lips that fade, and human laughter
And faces individual,
Well this side of Paradise! . . .
There's little comfort in the wise.

The Soldier
by Rupert Brooke

If I should die, think only this of me:
That there's some corner of a foreign field
That is for ever England. There shall be
In that rich earth a richer dust concealed;
A dust whom England bore, shaped, made aware,
Gave, once, her flowers to love, her ways to roam,
A body of England's, breathing English air,
Washed by the rivers, blest by suns of home.

And think, this heart, all evil shed away,
A pulse in the eternal mind, no less
Gives somewhere back the thoughts by England
　　given;
Her sights and sounds; dreams happy as her day;
And laughter, learnt of friends; and gentleness,
In hearts at peace, under an English heaven.　❧